Mary Jane picked up her daughter...

"Well, how about you go with your mama and Miss Hawthorne and the others, and make sure they get home safely. Can you do that for me?" Raine asked.

Sarah Jane thought about it for a moment.

"That's a pretty big responsibility," she said.

Mary Jane laughed and kissed her daughter's face.

"But I can do it."

"There's no time to waste, M.J. You and Sarah Jane need to get home. I'll stick around here long enough to make sure all these people get out safely," Raine told her, motioning to all the vendors who busily cleaned up their booths and were heading for the livery stables and feed store.

Why did she have to fall for a lawman?

"What about you?"

"I'll be fine," he said.

She didn't want to leave. She wanted to stay close to him, to make sure he would be all right, but she looked at her little girl and knew he was right.

"Be safe," she said, relenting to their fate.

He nodded, then took a step toward her and leaned down close for her to hear.

"And just so we're clear," he said firmly with a look that turned her insides to jelly. He bent down, so his lips were mere inches from her ear. "That kiss…*is* going to happen."

Mary Jane sucked in a breath, the flurries in her stomach blowing wildly about, and she bit her lip at the thought.

"See you soon, Mr. Redbourne." Sarah Jane squirmed out of her arms and went to Raine.

He hugged her close to him.

"Yes, you will."

Also by
KELLI ANN MORGAN

THE RANCHER
REDBOURNE SERIES BOOK ONE

THE BOUNTY HUNTER
REDBOURNE SERIES BOOK TWO

THE BLACKSMITH
REDBOURNE SERIES BOOK THREE

THE IRON HORSEMAN
REDBOURNE SERIES BOOK FOUR

THE OUTRIDER
REDBOURNE SERIES BOOK FIVE

THE WRANGLER
REDBOURNE SERIES BOOK SIX

THE LUMBERJACK
REDBOURNE SERIES BOOK SEVEN

JONAH
DEARDON MINI-SERIES BOOK ONE

LUCAS
DEARDON MINI-SERIES BOOK TWO

NOAH
DEARDON MINI-SERIES BOOK THREE

AN ANGEL IN THISTLEBERRY
DEARDON MINI-SERIES BOOK FOUR

HOLDEN'S HEART
SILVER SPRINGS SERIES BOOK ONE

LANDON'S LOVE
SILVER SPRINGS SERIES BOOK ONE

Available from INSPIRE BOOKS

REDBOURNE SERIES BOOK EIGHT
RAINE'S STORY

KELLI ANN
MORGAN

Inspire Books
A Division of Inspire Creative Services
937 West 1350 North, Clinton, Utah 84015, USA

While some of the events described and some of the characters depicted in this book may be loosely based on actual historical events and real historical figures, this book is a work of fiction. Other names, characters, places, and incidents either are the product of the author's imagination or are used factitiously, and any resemblance to actual persons, living or dead, business establishments, events, or locales is entirely coincidental. The publisher does not have any control over and does not assume any responsibility for author or third-party websites or their content.

THE LAWMAN

An Inspire Book published by arrangement with the author

First Inspire Books paperback edition December 2021

Cover Design by Kelli Ann Morgan at Inspire Creative Services

ISBN-13: 978-1-939049-60-5
ISBN-10: 1939049601

Printed in the United States of America

PRAISE FOR THE NOVELS OF AMAZON BESTSELLING AUTHOR

KELLI ANN MORGAN

"Strong characters and a compelling story make this an unforgettable trail ride…"

—*RaeAnne Thayne, NYT bestselling author* on THE RANCHER

"This story could have flowed from the pens of the masters; Max Brand, Zane Grey or Louis L'Amour. These greats have stood alone for decades upon an acme seldom reached or yet to be passed by others that have tried. Kelli Ann Morgan has done the unthinkable and written a story that is equal or better than those western-writing icons of the past."

—*Thom Swennes* on THE RANCHER

"A must-read for anyone who enjoys westerns with adventure, romance, and humor."

—*Amazon Reviewer* on THE BOUNTY HUNTER

"Entertaining...informative...delightful!!!!"

—*Suzanne L. McConnell* on THE BLACKSMITH

"I have never been so emotional in reading as I have with your books. Thank you and keep writing. I'm an 80-year-old cowboy. Again thank you."

—*Amazon Reviewer* on THE IRON HORSEMAN

"A phenomenal read a must-have for any library."

—*Francie* on THE OUTRIDER

"Excellent, well-written plot that kept me reading past bedtime!"

—*Pamela Hastings* on THE WRANGLER

" Fun entertaining and emotional."

—*Kindle Customer* on THE LUMBERJACK

ACKNOWLEDGMENTS

I am so grateful for Grant, who is my alpha reader, content editor, my grounding stone, and my true love. Thank you for all you do both personally and professionally for me! Love you, baby!

I am truly blessed with an incredible team of editors and beta readers--Rocky Palmer, Jenn Cooper, Janene Morgan, and Kathy Hathaway. Thank you for all you do in helping to make sure my books are the best they can be.

Garth, thank you for your subtle encouragement and for reminding me just how much readers love complete series'.

Noah, thank you for celebrating every bit of progress with me, even though we're apart right now while you serve the people of Tennessee, and for brightening my hard days and pushing me forward. You are truly an inspiration to me. Love you tons, kid, and I am SO proud of you!

To all of you, my readers, who have waited so patiently for Raine's *book, as I took a short, two-year hiatus from writing. You are appreciated, loved, and oh so valued. Thank you!*

REDBOURNE SERIES BOOK EIGHT

RAINE'S STORY

CHAPTER ONE

Late September, Silver Falls, Colorado 1876

Raine bolted through the streets of Silver Falls, certain the townsfolk would think him a madman with a telegram clutched in one hand while the other worked to keep his hat on his head.

He could hardly believe the news.

Rafe had done it.

When Raine finally reached the hitching post where he'd left his paint mount, he quickly yanked on the end of the lead to release the slip knot, grabbed onto the seat, and pulled himself up onto the saddle. With a firm squeeze of his knees, he turned the horse toward the Gnarled Oak Ranch and set out at a hearty pace.

Cole is not going to believe this.

As he passed the SilverHawk, his father-in-law, Clay McCallister's place, he whooped and waved at the hired hand Bert, who looked up from the calf he was trying to corral back into a pen with other weaning youngsters.

"Where ya headed in such a hurry?" the cowpoke called

after him.

Raine laughed.

"Home!" he yelled over his shoulder.

It had been several months since he and his brother Cole had left their family ranch in Stone Creek, Kansas, to pursue a killer. He'd never expected to stay as long as he had, but Cole had needed help rebuilding the Gnarled Oak and surrounding properties on the spread he'd inherited.

It was time.

He'd felt it for a while now, and this was just the push he needed to get himself back home.

As he pulled up in front of the newly renovated homestead, he slid down from his horse, tossing the reins to a stunned stable hand, and cleared the front porch stairs in two jumps, then threw open the door looking for his brother.

"Charcoal!" he called, peeking into one room after the next until he arrived at the kitchen where his baby brother sat at the table eying the meal his new bride had placed in front of him.

Cole glanced up at him but didn't say a word as he picked up the fork next to the plate.

"Abby," Raine greeted his new sister-in-law, lifting his hat and nodding at her.

It was nice to see the woman in a simple dress instead of her usual button-down and britches. He imagined his brother was partly responsible for making her feel more feminine. She hadn't had a lot of experience in the kitchen growing up and Raine found the idea that she had even attempted to cook, something admirable.

His brother raised a full fork to his mouth and took a bite. His nostrils flared as he forced a smile and nodded at his wife.

Abby laughed as she walked toward her husband. He pulled her down onto his lap, evoking a playful giggle, and wrapped his arms around her.

"Any luck finding us a Martha?" she asked as she scooped the plate off the table and escaped Cole's grasp to toss the remainder of food in the garbage pail to feed the pigs. "Nobody cooks quite like Martha."

"Except Lottie," Cole disputed.

"Her buñuelos." Raine's mouth watered at the thought.

"Her lentejas."

"Tortilla Española."

"The flan," they both chimed at the same time.

Cole licked his lips. "Are you expectin' a man to starve, woman?" he asked with feigned indignation and a wink. "A man cannot live by bread alone." He raised his day-old buttermilk biscuit off the table.

"It seems as if all the womenfolk are too busy looking after their own than to hire on here," Raine told them. "You may have to look outside of Silver Falls." He looked at his sister-in-law with a slow shake of his head, still chuckling at the playful exchange between the two. It was obvious they were in love.

"What do you have there, big brother?" Cole asked, nodding at the crumpled paper in Raine's hand before taking a bite of his biscuit.

"A telegram," Raine stated matter-of-factly with a shrug of his shoulders.

Cole raised a brow.

Raine smiled, pulled out the chair next to his brother, flipped it around, and sat backward, slapping the communique down on the table in front of him.

"There is going to be a wedding at Redbourne Ranch."

Cole's brows scrunched together as he slowly picked up the paper.

"A wedding?"

Raine could see the wheels turning in his little brother's head. Rafe had never had any trouble gaining the attention of any number of females, but for him to actually be settling down was more than surprising.

"Whose?" Cole's eyes grew wide as he looked down and read the brief message. "I don't believe it. Rafe?" He turned to

Raine, "Our Rafe? Spurned at the altar, turned his life upside down, bounty hunter brother, Rafe…is getting married?" He shook his head. "Rafe would never take Tessa back after what she did to him."

"Not Tessa, Charcoal," Raine said, stabbing at the paper with his finger. "Tayla."

"Who's Tayla?" Abby inquired. She placed a small plate of biscuits in front of Raine along with a jar of apricot preserves and a bottle of milk she'd retrieved from the icebox.

"Thanks, Abby."

"Tessa Hawthorne is the…"

"Cole," Raine said slowly, his voice laced with warning.

"Tessa Hawthorne is the…," Cole began again, "…person…who left Rafe holding his hat on his wedding day. She ran away without a word. Tayla is her little sister. Rafe blamed Tayla."

Raine nodded.

"And now he is marrying her?" Abby shook her head. "Sounds like a fascinating story to me. When are we leaving for Stone Creek?"

Someone knocked.

They all looked toward the door.

Raine pushed up off the chair. "You expecting anyone?"

"Nah." Cole stood, bent over to kiss his wife on the forehead, and strode toward the front of the house.

Raine followed.

"Sheriff," Cole said, greeting the young newcomer in town. "Is everything all right?"

"Mr. Redbourne, I'm sorry to call during suppertime, but I wanted to check in with you to see if you might be missing a very large, polled, black Angus bull."

"Not last I heard, but I do currently own three of them. Why?"

"Because as we speak, there is one making his way toward town. I'd rather he not make it that far."

Cole grabbed his hat from the rack to the side of the door, pushing past the new sheriff with both Raine and Abby on his heels.

"Cole! Abby!" Nathan, one of the new hires on the ranch, came rushing toward them from the bull shed.

"Let me guess," Cole said with a note of sarcasm as he picked up the pace toward the stable, "one of the bulls is missing."

He whistled.

It was the time of year the bull needed to be with the herd, and one that size on the street could only mean trouble as he would be unpredictable and dangerous.

Within minutes, several cowhands had joined them, and Abby had changed into her usual getup. One of the boys had a cow in tow, one a sack full of feed, and the rest, including Cole and Raine, had their lassos at the ready. He had been party to capturing a rogue bull several times over the years and it never ceased to amaze him just how powerful they were. If the riders didn't handle the animal properly, the situation could turn deadly in seconds. He glanced over at the two kids Cole had just hired and hoped they had the experience they'd claimed to have—for all their sakes.

Just a mile or so beyond her father's ranch, Abby yelled.

"Over there!" She didn't wait for the rest of them to catch up before she was off, one hand clutching the bulk of her lasso.

"Fool woman," Cole said under his breath as he headed after her.

While Abby could ride and even shoot better than half the men Raine knew, she was still a woman and would not have the strength needed to corral the bull on her own. Truth be told, none of them was strong enough to take down the bull alone. Maybe Ethan. Having been a blacksmith for so long, his younger brother was stronger than any of them.

The Gnarled Oak had seven bulls in total, but two of the Angus were new to the ranch. They'd been purchased just a week ago and had not been trained sufficiently. That made them even more dangerous.

"Abby!" Cole called out. "Don't go roping him just yet. Put some pressure on until he starts moving the direction we want him to go, then back off a little."

She hesitated, rope in hand.

"Abby."

"Cole Redbourne," she said, turning around and pulling her horse up alongside her husband's black Arabian. "I have been herding and corralling cattle since I was seven years old, my love," her smile held a hint of weathering patience. "I am capable of roping a bull."

"Oh, I know exactly how capable you are, sweetheart, but we've discussed this. We are trying something new, remember?"

Raine raised a hand to his mouth, his fingers attempting to hide the grin that had formed there.

Ah, newlyweds.

Raine coughed to cover his amused chuckle.

"That bull isn't going to get back to the ranch if you two lovebirds don't stop yakking at each other."

"All right, boys," Cole said, not taking his eyes off his wife, "driving positions."

They all moved into the same spots they would take on a cattle drive. The idea was to herd the bull back home without the use of force. It would be extremely hard to contain a fifteen-hundred-pound bull this far from the ranch without his consent.

Abby raised a brow with a smile. "We'll do it your way, but I get point."

"Wouldn't have it any other way, *my love*." Cole winked.

A familiar pang hit Raine in the gut. It had been more than ten years since Sarah had passed, but he still missed her and longed for her companionship, her touch, her love. Seeing his little brother and his bride together brought tender memories into his mind and heart.

He sat back in his saddle and watched as the others took

their positions. There was no longer a need for him in Silver Falls. He knew it. He'd known for quite some time, but now it was clear the time had come for him to get back to his life.

What life? he asked himself as he pondered returning to his deputy job in Stone Creek. He needed more. Wanted more. *But where? What?*

He took flank.

Luckily, the bull did not seem to be in a foul mood and after a few attempts at applying pressure—riding straight toward him when he acted contrary to what they wanted and taking the pressure off by backing away a few paces to give him room when he faced the direction they desired—he finally began moving north toward the Gnarled Oak.

Cole had all the help he needed.

Yep, he thought to himself, *it's time!*

CHAPTER TWO

Thistleberry, Montana 1876

Mary Jane Bennett pulled her wagon to a stop in front of the boardwalk by the stagecoach depot sign where a young woman with rosy cheeks and coifed hair sat with her feet perched atop a large traveling trunk and several smaller bags. Her elbows rested on her knees and her forehead on her clasped hands.

"Miss Judith Evans?" she asked as she jumped down from the box seat of the buckboard.

The girl looked up, her eyes wide and a small smudge of dirt now gracing her tear-stained face.

"That's me." She stood up and brushed at her skirt with a gloved hand, then swiped quickly at a rogue tear gracing her cheek. "Have you come to collect me for Mr. Spitz?"

Mary Jane picked up the collection of small bags and tossed them into the back of the wagon, but when she eyed the trunk that had been the girl's footstool, she was sure it weighed more than the both of them put together.

"Well, come on," she said, motioning to the far side of the

trunk.

Mary Jane bent down, her fingers of one hand settled into the metal handles and the other beneath the luggage, ready to pick up her end of the case.

"Surely, you don't mean to have us lift the trunk by ourselves," the girl said sheepishly. "It's heavier than you might think. It's all I have left that was my mother's."

"I'm sure it means a whole lot to you, but, yes, we are fully capable of lifting this trunk into the back of that wagon—unless, of course, you'd rather we drag it behind the rig?" She stood up and placed her gloved hands on her hips.

Judith would make the eighth displaced bride she'd seen come to this part of Montana in the last few years—each of them with hopes of a bright future with an unseen man, only to be disappointed by a failed arrangement of one sort or another. This one, however, was the first to actually be delivered directly to Thistleberry since Mary Jane herself had come nearly five years ago.

No time to think about that right now, she told herself as she bent down to grab hold of one of the leather handles on her side of the trunk.

As Judith stepped down onto the street, bending down to pick up her end, the little bell on the door of the mercantile rang and Andrew Deardon stepped outside, placing his hat on his head and carrying a single small flour sack.

"Ready?" she asked the new girl.

"Don't you think we could ask someone to help us? A man maybe?"

Mary Jane let go of her end and looked up at Andrew. A grin spread across his face, as he jumped down from the boardwalk and crossed the street to the depot. He'd obviously spotted their attempt to lift the traveling case. He set his purchase down next to the wagon's wheel—goodies and toys of all sorts spilling over the top of the sack.

"Mr. Deardon," she acknowledged with a brief nod.

His grin widened.

"Allow me," he said, walking around to the front of the trunk.

"I've got it quite under control," Mary Jane insisted, but Andrew had already heaved it up into his arms.

"I don't know why you always think you have to do everything yourself, M.J. Everyone knows that you are quite capable and don't need anyone's help, but sometimes a man just likes to do something nice for a woman. Is that all right?"

"Of course."

He walked around her to the rear of the wagon where the hinged door already sat open, his muscular arms straining against the sleeves of his shirt, then set it down and gave it a good push. With a satisfied smile, he dusted off his hands, walked back to the front of the buckboard, and picked up his flour sack filled with goodies.

"And, what's with all the formality, *Miss Bennett*?" he asked with a strong, but lighthearted emphasis on her name.

The Deardons were one of the most prominent families in Thistleberry and over the last few years, she had grown quite close to them. They were good folk, and many of the older ladies in town had advised her—more like prodded her—throughout the years to encourage courtship with any one of them.

Most of the town wanted nothing more than to see her settled down and married, but she'd already had her chance at espousal. After that horrifying experience, she'd found it difficult to let her guard down enough to trust any man sufficiently enough to allow him to get close to her on any kind of personal level.

Even a Deardon.

It wasn't just about her anymore.

"Thank you kindly, *sir*, for your unwarranted, but much appreciated help in loading her enormous trunk into the back of the buckboard."

"It was my pleasure, *ma'am*."

"Oh," she'd almost forgotten to introduce them, "Mr. Deardon," Mary Jane flashed a smile at him, "Miss Evans here is the newest addition to Happenstance Ranch. Just arrived today."

"I can see that." He nodded to the luggage now heaping in the back of the buckboard, then turned to the young woman. "Ma'am," he said with a quick raise of his hat, "it's very nice to make your acquaintance."

Judith's cheeks reddened under the attention Andrew had offered her, but her brows drew together in confusion as she looked over at Mary Jane.

"I beg your pardon, ma'am," she said quietly, "I don't mean to be rude, but I think there has been some sort of mistake. I'm supposed to be meeting a Mr. Walden Spitz today and we are to be married." She reached down into the satchel she still carried in front of her and retrieved a folded collection of letters. She held them out just in front of Mary Jane's face, a photograph of a stoic Walden Spitz in a suit and a black string tie situated just beneath the plum-colored ribbon that held the small bundle together. "See?"

Mary Jane hardly recognized the man.

"I know the name is an unfortunate one," Judith said, her eyes downcast as she returned the letters to her satchel, "but I figure it doesn't really matter if one can call it her own, isn't that right?"

"Oh, honey," Mary Jane said with as kind a smile as she could muster and a well-placed hand on the girl's arm, "there is no mistake. Mr. Spitz isn't coming. Our territory Marshal carted him off to jail last month and he's going to be there for a very long time."

Judith's mouth fell wide open.

"Jail?" Her shoulders fell, then her eyes widened as she shook her head and began to pace, talking to herself more than to anyone in particular. "But he's a deputy. Going to be sheriff in Thistleberry one day."

Andrew leaned down toward Mary Jane. "Lucy know you're coming?"

"She's the one who sent me. She would have come herself, but our new neighbor stopped in for an unexpected visit this morning and she couldn't get away."

"I've heard about him. Apparently, he's some cattle baron from Houston looking to expand up here and has been making the rounds to all the ranches here in Thistleberry looking to buy, but he doesn't act or dress like any cattlemen I have ever known. And if he has so much money, why wouldn't he be staying at the Thistledown?" he asked, pointing to Thistleberry's only hotel.

"Maybe you should ask Cornelia Wilson. She always knows everyone's business."

"Are you calling me a busybody, Miss Bennett?"

"Are you finding the need to satisfy a sweet tooth, Mr. Deardon?" Mary Jane asked, motioning to his haul and desiring a change of subject.

"Nah," he laughed, "this is just the easiest way to stay the favorite uncle." He shoved the end of a licorice whip into his mouth and winked.

Mary Jane giggled. "They're lucky to have you."

Andrew raised his hat.

"Let us know if you need any more help." He held up a hand and bowed his head as he retreated. "Not that you can't handle anything on your own, mind you, but you know where to find us."

"I do," Mary Jane conceded. "Thank you for your most gracious offer."

"Miss Evans," he said with a departing nod. "Miss Bennett."

"Mr. Deardon."

With a throaty chuckle, Andrew headed toward the telegraph office where a beautiful black Palouse with a dappled white back and rump was hitched to the post.

"Come on," she motioned for Judith to join her as she lifted herself up into the driver's seat of the wagon.

The young woman looked up at her from the street with pouted lips and wet eyes.

"Jail?"

Mary Jane understood all too well what it was like to have her dreams swept out from beneath her, her entire world turned upside down all in a day's time by a lawman gone rogue. She closed her eyes and exhaled slowly before climbing back down and walking over to Miss Evans. She placed an arm around her shoulder and pulled the frightened young girl in close as they walked around the buckboard to the other side.

"It's going to be all right, you'll see," she coaxed, as she helped the young woman up onto the seat, then walked around and climbed up beside her.

Judith wrapped her arms around herself and nodded ever so slightly.

Mary Jane placed a hand on the girl's arm.

"It's going to be all right," she said again.

Lonely, maybe, but all right.

They'd been traveling for about a quarter of an hour when Judith finally spoke again.

"What am I supposed to do, Miss Bennett?" she turned in the seat to face Mary Jane.

"Well, the way I see it, you've got two choices. You can either let this be what breaks you or what makes you stronger? It's up to you."

"I want to be strong. But I have nothing. I spent the last of my earnings on the voyage here. You told Mr. Deardon that I was the newest addition to Happenstance Ranch. What does that mean exactly? What *is* Happenstance Ranch?"

As they drove through an immense cluster of cedar and pine, there was a break in the copse of trees and Mary Jane pulled to a stop just inside the large timbers that towered over the entrance gate to the ranch. The leaves on the foliage across the property had already begun to change color, bringing in deep reds and bright oranges and yellows to accent a wide variety of greens.

Sheep, dogs, and a llama dotted the pasture as she looked over the vast fields that surrounded them and smiled. The west paddock bustled with activity as it appeared that Mona, one of the five ranch hands currently at Happenstance, had just turned the ram out into the first band of ewes.

"This," she said, picking up the reins and starting through the gate, "is Happenstance."

Judith looked around, her face contorted slightly as she watched the animals.

"They're," she said with a scrunched nose, "sheep."

Mary Jane laughed. "Yes, ma'am. And that's only one of four bands we have here."

They rode for a moment in silence, then the young woman turned to her with scrunched eyes.

"You want me to be a sheep farmer?"

With a slight chuckle, Mary Jane remembered that sentiment all too well.

"Do you want to be a sheep farmer?" she asked. "With a roof over your head, food to eat, money to spend?"

Judith thought for a moment, likely evaluating her alternatives.

"What would I have to do?"

"That is a great question for Lucy Deardon." Mary Jane nodded toward the woman who had just stepped out onto the front porch of the homestead, clad in denims and a wool button-down shirt.

"Deardon, as in the Mr. Deardon we just met in town?"

"Cousins."

"Ah."

Lucy skittered down the steps and met them with a huge smile and a wave.

"Welcome, Judith." She reached up to the newcomer to

help her down, then placed her arm around her shoulders as she guided her into the house.

Lissa, another of the hands, and Mona both came out to help Mary Jane unload the wagon.

"What in heaven's name does she have in this thing?" Lissa asked with a grunt as she attempted to retrieve the enormous trunk from the back.

The efforts of all three women were needed to get the case down and carted over to one of the empty rooms in the oversized and elongated bunkhouse that sat adjacent to the homestead. The long building consisted of eight bedrooms, each with its own, entrance. Lucy had once told her that men and women were different in many ways, and acceptable sleeping accommodations was one of them.

Each of the female hands hired on to work at Happenstance was given access to and responsibility for her own room in the elaborate bunkhouse. Mary Jane had never seen or heard of such a thing anywhere else and appreciated the thought Lucy had taken for all who came to stay. She hadn't been in those accommodations long, though, as she'd moved into the larger homestead when she'd been selected as foreman.

Mona, still strapped with her back scabbard and shotgun, awkwardly pushed open the door to Judith's quarters with her foot, and they heaved the large trunk inside and set it on the floor. Each of the bunks had been furnished with a bed, washstand, wardrobe, small desk with a stool, and a large window at the back of the room adorned with curtains and shutters. A modest pot-bellied stove had also been placed in each of the occupied rooms for warmth in the wintertime. The accommodations were not overly large, but they were comfortable and extremely generous.

"What do you think?" Lissa asked, leaning against the doorframe and appraising the newest addition as Lucy showed her around the grounds.

"Oh," Mary Jane said, "I think she's just like the rest of

us—confused, scared, apprehensive. She'll be fine once she gets cleaned up and has some food in her belly. It'll be an adjustment for all of us. It's been a long while since we've had someone new."

"I don't think I've ever seen so much luggage that belongs to one person," Mona piped in. "I just hope she'll be willing to pull her weight. We've already lost three in this last year."

Mary Jane had been at the ranch longer than any of the other displaced brides. Most of the women found Happenstance to be a welcome opportunity in the face of their adversity and stayed on the ranch to work the sheep, but Lucy was no stranger to matchmaking, and she'd found suitable matches for most of them within a year.

"Radford Steele has sure been coming to visit a lot lately," Lissa said as she reached forward and pushed on Mona's shoulder. "It seems you just might be leaving us too."

Color flooded the young woman's face. "He's a very nice man."

The alarmed scream of a llama brought the women to their feet in an instant and Mona was out the door, shotgun in hand.

"The flock!" she yelled back as they all took off after her.

Mary Jane stopped at the wagon to retrieve her rifle.

Coyotes had been stalking the sheep and Carl, the llama that had bonded with the sheep in the first band, had been working overtime to protect them. His alarm was generally enough to scare off the predators, but sometimes he needed a little assistance. The ewes would be particularly vulnerable right now as it was tupping season.

Mona threw open the paddock gate. Carl had all of the sheep corralled into the corner closest to the homestead. Two coyotes had gotten into the enclosure and now loomed less than fifty feet from the herd, but each time one of them attempted to take a step forward, Carl bolted toward it, kicking and prancing, pushing them further back.

CRACK!

"Nice shot, Mary Jane," Lissa praised as the coyote furthest away from them dropped in its tracks.

BOOM!

Mona stood up straight and lowered her shotgun to one side, then leaned it up against the fence post. She'd got the second one.

"Whoa, boy," she coaxed as she gingerly approached the herd. At the sound of Mona's voice, the llama's ears slowly perked up from their laid-back position.

It would take a little while for the sheep to calm down completely, but Carl seemed to be contented now that the immediate danger to the herd had been eliminated.

"When are we going to get those dogs?" Lissa asked.

"Hank told me the boys dropped off two Great Pyrenees with Evaline and the third band in Meadow Creek last week," Lucy said as she caught up to them with a huffing Judith trailing behind her. "Seems Otis got into some Black Locust trees and has himself quite a bellyache so they thought she could use the extra protection over these next two weeks as she leads her band back home for breeding."

Normally, with the number of sheep they had at Happenstance, the herd would all stay together, but in order to keep track of everything during breeding season they'd been broken off into four smaller bands and separated onto different grazing lands.

"What. Is. That?" Judith asked, pointing at Carl—one of four llamas in all of Montana.

Mary Jane had never seen one before coming to Thistleberry either, nor had she even heard of one, but Carl and the others were a godsend. One of the Deardon family's close friends had brought them up on a drive through South America as a gift for Hank and his brother Sam.

He'd claimed the animals were natural protectors of livestock against predators. Over the years, it had proven to be true as the odd-looking animals bonded quickly with the sheep and lambs. Because they had been accustomed to living up in the peaks of the Andes mountains, living in the highlands of Montana had not been too much of an adjustment for them and they seemed quite content with their surroundings.

"It's called a llama, dear," Lucy said with a smile as she reached out to pet the animal. "His name is Carl. Isn't he wonderful?" He snuggled his face up against her shoulder.

Judith's face did not show wonder, but instead, her features contorted into something akin to disbelief and disgust. Her mouth stretched downward, and her head pulled back with wide eyes.

When Lucy decided to start Happenstance as a refuge for displaced women from failed correspondence courtships, Hank, the patriarch of the Deardon clan, had given her the llamas to protect her small and more fragile lambs. Now, each of the four bands was guarded by one irreplaceable llama. They all shared Otis, their black and white border collie, but the addition of two more sheepdogs to their ranks would be most welcome.

"Lucas and I are heading over to Virginia City in the morning to inquire on a couple more border collies," Lucy said as the women made their way back toward the main house. "In the meantime, I will have my husband contact his trapper friend and he'll be around to dispose of those coyotes."

Mary Jane suspected that her boss was looking to grow the ranch and bringing on additional herding dogs would be a natural step in that progression. Though Lucas was a cattle rancher, he'd been very supportive of his wife's venture into the sheepherding business. He—well, all of the men in his entire family really—were the kind most women would want in their lives.

While the majority of eligible ladies in Thistleberry, and the surrounding towns, primped and primed, preening themselves at every opportunity in various attempts to catch any unattached Deardon man's eye, Mary Jane had no romantic interest in any of them.

"I'll let you know when I return," Lucy said on her way over to the stables to collect her horse.

The weather had turned a little chillier over the last hour, but Mary Jane had hardly noticed. She preferred the cool crisp air to the heat of summer and was looking forward to a nice autumn and winter season.

"Oh, and Mona," Lucy called back, "you might not want to keep Mr. Steele waiting too long." A grin spread across her face as she glanced over at the gate where a nice little black surrey had appeared.

Mona's eyes sparkled when she waved to the man who'd come to call.

Mary Jane was happy for her friend. It wouldn't be long before Mr. Steele would propose, and the young hired hand would join the Mrs. Society.

You are just too picky, Mary Jane, she could hear her mother's voice in her head. *You'll never find a man who'll marry you if you don't learn to be amenable.*

"Well, you were right, Mother," she said aloud, but under her breath. "I haven't found the right man to marry. Yet," she finished with a notion he could be out there.

Somewhere.

She just didn't dare hope.

CHAPTER THREE

Tessa Hawthorne – Two Weeks Later

"It was right there, Tessa." Malcolm Longhurst shoved his fingers through his too-long hair as he paced the pocked wooden floor of their simple mining cabin, tucked into a large copse of trees in the middle of nowhere. "A photograph of Rafe Redbourne and his family on Lucy Deardon's mantlepiece. Haunting me. Following me. Why can I not escape them?"

Tessa Hawthorne wasn't at all surprised. She'd almost been a part of the Redbourne family once and had learned quickly that they had friends everywhere. It was hard to believe that more than eight years had passed since she'd left Rafe for Malcolm on their wedding day without a word. She couldn't help but wonder how things would have been different had her little sister not walked in on her kissing the best friend of her betrothed.

"Why are you so upset, Mal? It's not like the Redbournes live here in this little town in the backwoods of Montana. Besides," she said, walking up behind him and sliding a hand up his back to his shoulder as she leaned into him, "we'll be headed back to England soon and none of this will matter."

Malcolm spun around, knocking her slightly off balance, and glared down at her, scaring her a little. She took a step back, away from him. The light from the fire in the hearth cast an eerie shadow on his face, adding depth to his already livid expression.

"You are naïve, Tessa, if you think we can return to England now. My name will be ruined. Your sister and all the Lords Darington will have seen to that. And just when everything was within reach."

Not go to England?

She looked around at the hovel where they stayed.

This can't be what I gave up everything for. It can't.

"You wouldn't really have tried to marry my sister for appearances sake, just to get your precious title, would you? You do still love me?" she questioned, needing to hear the words.

"Of course, I would have married the chit. But," he held up a finger, stifling her objection, "just to solidify our standing on paper in front of an authorized notary. Then, of course, we would have had to kill her right away to have ensured she couldn't have told anyone the truth." He raised a brow and smirked. "Or maybe I would have waited until after the wedding night."

Tessa did not find his sardonic grin or his comment amusing.

"Wait, kill her? My sister? Dead?"

"You know she never would have gone along with our little ruse. Besides," he said, grabbing Tessa by the arm and pinning her hard against him, "she certainly did not have your…vigor." He laughed throatily, then crushed his mouth against hers, bruising her tender flesh with his ardent kiss.

When he retracted, he pulled away only inches, staring down at her, his fingers digging into her arms.

Ouch.

There was something very wrong with Malcolm tonight. He had never behaved in such brute fashion. She had not smelled or tasted any liquor on his breath, so if a mere photograph could send him in such a spiral, she couldn't imagine what would happen had he seen a Redbourne in person. Sooner or later, it was bound to happen as the Redbournes and the Deardons were kin.

He needed to pull himself together. Maybe giving him something positive to focus on would help.

"Mal, we're here, far away from our past. Let's just start over right here. Right now." She dared step forward again and reached out for him, clasping his arms in her hands. "You and me. Together." She squeezed.

He looked down at her, his eyes vacant, cold.

Tessa shivered. She had never seen him like this. For years he had promised her the moon. Had vowed they would marry and have a life full of every luxury imaginable, but here they hid in this little abandoned shanty. It no longer mattered. She could be happy here. With him.

Couldn't I?

He said nothing.

"Don't you see, Malcolm? None of that matters anymore. Just let it go. Let's be happy," she pleaded with him in hopes of regaining his attention. "This…" she glanced around, "…place…is just a beginning. It will grow. This one room will become ten and with the money you get from the mine you won in that poker game, we can live the life we always talked about…Even if it is in America."

Her comments seemed to fall on deaf ears as he sat down in the solitary chair in the room, his fingers rubbing against his chin as he stared blankly at nothing in particular.

"He'll find me here," he whispered as if she had not spoken a single word. "You know he will."

"He has no reason to come after you," she tried to reassure him. "No one got hurt."

"He took everything from me—my father, the respect of my people, my fiancé." He stood abruptly and made the distance across the room to the door in just a few steps.

"But Tayla was never *your* fiancé, Mal. She was engaged to Lord Brick Darington. You were only acting, pretending to be him in public. His things did not become your things just because you wanted them to be. You are not really Lord Darington. Tell me you know the difference."

"No," he said with a slight shake of his head, "I'll have to get rid of him first."

He still could not hear her past the demons in his head.

"Once he's gone," Mal continued, "and his family too, I can start making plans for the future. Real plans." For the first time in several minutes, he looked down at her and actually seemed to be able to see her. "Don't you understand? I will never be free from him until he is gone. Until they're all gone. And that includes the duffer here who thinks he's in charge. I'll show him."

She had to talk some sense into him.

"You are crazy if you think—"

With one swift movement, he smacked her straight across the face, sending her sprawling onto the bed, his eyes curled with the reflection of the hearth's flames.

"Do not call me crazy!" he spat out slowly, the blatant warning in his voice unmistakable, spittle spewing from his clenched teeth. He whipped around, then yanked at the door and strode out into the night.

Tessa held her cheek.

Shock completely filling her.

Her chest heaved with the breath she couldn't catch.

Heat radiated from her throbbing face.

Then, as the past eight years flashed through her mind with precise clarity, she saw Malcolm Longhurst for what he'd been, what he was. A cheat and a liar.

What had she done?

She had to get away. To warn the Redbournes.

She would start with Lucy Deardon.

"When is it going to be your turn, my dear?" Mrs. Smith, the owner of the mercantile in town meant well.

Mary Jane fought the urge to sigh out loud and smiled instead. Mona's wedding had been a small affair that took place in the preacher's home earlier that morning. Only the remaining six displaced brides from Happenstance Ranch, including herself and Judith, Lucy Deardon and her husband, Lucas, had been in attendance along with Mr. Steele's parents and his friend Gus.

"If I left Happenstance, Mrs. Smith, who would package up the cheese and make the candles you sell here in your store?"

"I don't care how old you are, Mary Jane Bennett. You're a mighty fine woman. Some man is bound to whisk you away. And that will be a sad day for Thistleberry."

"Thank you, Mrs. Smith, but I assure you, I am perfectly content helping Mrs. Deardon run the ranch and peddle our wares."

At thirty-one, Mary Jane knew she was well beyond being a spinster—though, in actuality, the term didn't fit her either. The men around here wanted girls that were still practically children. They also found no use for a woman who loved her library more than tea socials and who found using her creativity in making beautiful things to be more rewarding than slaving over a hot stove all day for a man.

Not that she couldn't cook. She could, and was quite good at it, but she found that she preferred to create meals that didn't require extensive hours from the day or exhaustive preparation. There were too many other, and more important things, on which to spend her time.

"I'll take one of those beautiful new churns," Mary Jane said, pointing at the converted small-sized whiskey barrels in the corner, "along with a sack of flour, some molasses, a new lantern, and these." She set down two small bags of lemon drops that she would take to the orphanage on her way home.

As Mrs. Smith wrote up the order, Mary Jane glanced around the store to where several of the women from town perused the Happenstance Ranch goods on display in front of the window. She felt a huge amount of accomplishment and pride at the work the small ranch was able to produce with so few hands.

Her eyes were drawn to a wanted poster hanging on the wall behind the counter. The man looked familiar. Very familiar. If she didn't know any better, she would say that it was most certainly their new neighbor, Mr. Richards, and she was surprised that no one had seen the resemblance. Of course, the man had only been in Thistleberry a few weeks.

"May I have that?" Mary Jane asked the store owner, who looked up from her task and back at the wall.

"Middleton's sheriff came into town yesterday and asked, rather nicely actually, if all the businesses in town would be willing to help catch the varmint," Mrs. Smith said as she reached back and tugged the poster from its nail and handed it to her. "You seen him?"

"I believe so, yes." She turned it around for the shop keep to look at. "Haven't you?"

Mrs. Smith looked at the paper with squinted eyes, then with one eye shut. "I just see my son-in-law every time I look at one of those things."

Mary Jane laughed. "Jed? Really?" She looked at the poster again.

It was most certainly not Jed Gailey.

"Thank you for letting me have it." She folded it up and tucked it into the pocket she'd had Mrs. Fawcett sew into the skirt of her dress.

Lucy needed to see it. Nobody really knew anything about Mr. Richards, but the man had been inquiring about leasing some of the land in the north corner of the ranch, out by the old mine. He claimed he was bringing up cattle from Texas. But she doubted that the Deardons would want to go into business with a wanted criminal.

Fraud, mayhem, and murder were the words that headlined the poster, and a substantial reward had been offered. His aliases were listed as Lord Brick Darington and Malcolm Longhurst. The information on the bottom of the poster read to contact the nearest U.S. Marshal's office or Rafe Redbourne, Bounty Hunter. The Redbournes were Deardon kin. She needed to let them know right away.

"Your things have been loaded into the wagon, M.J.," Mrs. Smith told her. "Shall I take the cost off your inventory bill?"

"Yes, yes, that's just fine." She nodded at the shop keep, still a little distracted by her discovery. She picked up the hem of her skirt and rushed out the door to where her wagon sat ready.

As she reached the edge of town, a fancy black buggy passed her on the way. Her eyes locked with the driver, one Mr. Augustus Richards. He raised his low flat-topped derby hat in greeting. She forced a smile she did not feel. He didn't dress like a cattleman at all—at least the ones she knew.

Mary Jane snapped the reins. If this man was as dangerous as the poster made him out to be, the Deardons needed to be prepared—especially Lucy who'd had dealings with him as recently as yesterday.

When she pulled in front of the Happenstance homestead, Judith was sweeping the front porch. The newcomer was still a little skittish around the ewes—all livestock on the ranch if truth be told—and often opted to focus on the cooking and cleaning rather than on the ranching.

She'd come around. In time.

Once she'd taken care of the wagon and the horses, she ran around the side of the house to Lucy's office. The door was open, and Mary Jane rushed inside.

"Have you seen this?" she asked as she thrust the wanted

poster on the desk in front of her boss. "Does he look at all familiar to you?"

"A good morning to you too." Lucy slid her chair backward. "Mary Jane, have you had the opportunity to meet Miss Tessa Hawthorne? She's going to be staying with us for a while."

With all the excitement, she had not even noticed the woman sitting on the opposite side of Lucy's desk, but now, the mixture of purples and yellows on Tessa's cheek did not go unnoticed.

"Hello," Mary Jane said with a nod. "Forgive my blindness. Sometimes, I get so focused that I forget myself." She dusted off her hand and extended it to the bruised woman. "You will be safe here," she assured her.

Tessa raised a hand to her face.

"This is what *my* blindness has done to me, but today, I am making a choice to stop living in denial." She stood up and pointed at the wanted poster Mary Jane had placed on the desk. "His real name is Malcolm Longhurst. He took everything from me." She sat back down, her hands dropping into her lap. "From a lot of people. He has to be stopped before he hurts someone else."

"Lucy, look at the name on the bottom of the poster."

"Rafe Redbourne? It must be personal. He doesn't usually attach his name to these."

"It's very personal, I'm afraid. Mal saw Rafe's photograph on your mantlepiece and it did something to him. He resents the Redbournes something fierce and is determined to see them…" her voice trailed as she darted a glance between them.

"See them what, dear?" Lucy asked.

"Dead."

Without another moment's hesitation, Lucy handed the drawing back to Mary Jane. "Take this up to Whisper Ridge right now and have Lucas send word to Redbourne Ranch. I'll get Tessa situated."

The Deardon place was only a couple of miles down the road and they had their own telegraph machine right inside Hank's study. With any luck, Rafe Redbourne or one of the U.S. Marshals would soon be on their way.

CHAPTER FOUR

Kansas, Early October

The methodical hum of the train as it slowed its pace nearly lulled Raine to sleep in his car accommodations. He leaned up against the back of the cool metal wall, his legs extended on the mattress and his body propped up with one arm.

He stared at the paper in his hands for a good fifteen minutes before deciding how he would begin. He jotted down a few short sentences, then lay back with the paper clutched in his hand on his chest.

It was no use.

"I had no idea my wife could jabber like she does," Cole said as he slid the door shut behind him. He had joined Raine in the sleeping car they shared so Lily, his sister-in-law's best friend, could stay with Abby. "Of course, bringing her along was probably not my finest decision, considering... Well, sorry for that."

Raine shrugged.

It didn't bother him that Lily had come along to be with Abby. Truth was, he liked the girl. She was sweet as sugar, light on her feet, and an absolute beauty, but what she had to offer was meant for some other lucky devil.

"You can't fool me, Charcoal. I've seen the way you look at your wife. She could talk to you until she was blue in the face, and you would eat it up like a bowlful of Lottie's berry breakfast custard."

"It's that obvious?" Cole sat down on the opposite end of the bed and raised one foot onto the mattress.

"Uh…yes!"

"What about you? It's been a long time since Sarah."

Raine looked down at his paper.

Nearing eleven years.

"I'm the last one to dole out any advice, big brother, but…" Cole glanced over at Raine, who raised a brow. "Ah, never mind."

Raine chuckled.

"I'm sure you know exactly what you want."

He'd given a great deal of thought to that lately. He wanted someone older than these young girls who married just out of primary school. She didn't have to be particularly pretty, but well kempt. Someone who needed him. Someone educated and refined, but who wasn't afraid to get her hands dirty now and then. No, the woman he would marry didn't need his heart, just the stability he could offer her in exchange for stimulating conversation and devoted companionship.

"Yep," was his only response.

Cole took off his hat and leaned forward, resting one elbow on his knee. "A lot has changed since we've been home."

It was true. And Raine was sure it would be no time at all before his mother would start arranging for every eligible woman in the territory to dine with them at Redbourne Ranch. She'd done it often enough when her boys were younger and unattached. But now that he would be the only unmarried of the bunch, he figured all of her matchmaking attentions would be directed solely at him and he was not looking forward to whatever schemes she had planned.

"What ya got there, big brother?" Cole reached over and grabbed the paper from his hands. "What is this?" he asked, glancing down at Raine's scribbles.

"Nothing you need to concern your pretty little head with," he retorted, sitting up and swiping for the note.

"A law-keeping bachelor with strong moral character, thirty-two years of age, desires to correspond with an educated, church-going woman in mid to late twenties. Companionship desired. Object matrimony." Cole read his note aloud and by the look on his face was mortified at the idea.

"You can have most any woman you want. Land sakes, Lily would be first in line if you stood on the church steps offering marriage," Cole chuckled, "but you still feel the need to advertise for a wife? What? In a paper? A marriage broker? What's gotten into you?"

Raine shrugged. "I've already had the love of my life. I'm just looking for companionship and good conversation. Is that too much to ask? Lily will have plenty of offers from suitors more her age. She doesn't need the likes of me. She deserves someone who will love her. Cherish her."

"And you can't do that?"

"I don't *want* that. That kind of love only comes around once in a lifetime, but I'll admit, watching all of you settling down does make me think about finding someone of my own. Maybe a spinster or widow woman who just needs…me."

"Or your money."

"Would that be so bad?" he asked.

"Not if you're looking for a woman like Tessa Hawthorne or Norah Hutchinson."

"I'd like to think I'm a better judge of character than that. No cheats, no murderers, no shallow gossips or high society travelling singers. Just a good woman. And maybe one who can cook." He smiled.

Cole smacked him on the arm with the back of his hand.

"My wife can cook," he said. "Just not very well."

Raine laughed.

"Well, good luck with finding everything you're looking for, big brother. But, with a heart like yours, you are *doomed* to find love again." Cole laughed loudly at his own jest.

Before Raine could protest, the train whistle blew as it pulled into the station. Stone Creek was still several hours away, so they would likely stay the night in town and head out early in the morning. He slid his legs out from behind Cole and stood up, swiping his advertisement from his little brother's hands.

Cole chuckled again and got to his feet.

They each grabbed their traveling bags and Raine pulled the sleeper room's door open. The train jerked some as it came to a halt, and he braced himself against the frame. As he stepped out into the hallway, he half expected to turn around and see their brother Levi standing in the corridor, as his job with the railroad still involved a significant amount of travel for him. And, like Rafe, he had a way of just showing up when least expected.

No Levi.

Not yet anyway, he thought with a laugh.

There were several livestock cars with slatted sides coupled behind the locomotive, trailed by a few passenger cars and a dining car, then finally, the sleepers pulled up the end near the caboose. It was still hard for him to believe that trains made it possible for them to travel across the country in such a short period of time. And being able to sleep, talk, read, and walk around while moving steadily toward their destination was truly an amazing blessing.

His rump was grateful he didn't have to spend weeks or even months in the saddle—especially with women in tow. Not that Abby would have minded much, but Lily just wasn't accustomed to being on a horse for any length of time nor being without certain luxuries.

Their mounts would be restless from days of being cooped up. Cole paid the man who'd fed, watered, and kept their stalls clean during the trip—although he, Cole, and even the ladies had taken their fair share of turns checking in on the animals, making sure the man had been doing his job.

When the large door to the livestock car was lowered, Maverick, Cole's big black Arabian, snorted and twisted his head, obviously anxious to get off the train. The others in the same car followed suit and soon the platform was abuzz with neighs, nickers, and snorts in a variety of tones accompanied by the swarms of flies that surrounded them. The other livestock cars also began to unload their cargo which just added to the excitement.

Raine leaned against a post on the fenced boardwalk and waited, his bag slung across his back and his arms folded. After a few minutes of watching animals and goods being unloaded, something nudged his arm, pushing him forward.

What in the…

He glanced over his shoulder to find the most beautiful palomino he'd ever seen. Its muted wheat colored coat was void of the yellow tones he'd seen in most Quarters of that coloring, but it was a far cry from being gray. As the evening sun descended in the sky, it shone through the animal's brilliant white mane and Raine was immediately taken by it.

"Well, hello there," he said, turning to face his remarkably affectionate new friend, and was greeted with a soft nicker. He trailed its lead to a burly man with a long scruffy beard heartily engaged in conversation with a gentleman in a suit, unaware of the horse's actions.

"How was the ride…" he tilted his head, bent down to look beneath the horse then righted himself with a smile, "girl?" he finished after determining the horse was a mare.

She nudged into him again, evoking a laugh, and he lifted his hand to rub just under her jawline. The horse raised her head slightly, leaning into him a little more and he extended his scratches to the throat and neck as she rested her head on his shoulder. He had never before experienced such affection from any animal—unless he counted Seamus, the family's giant, fluffy sheep dog.

"Whoa," Cole said with a chuckle, "looks like you've made yourself a friend." He took a moment to look her over. "You said you were looking for companionship." He laughed again as he appraised the mare. "She's a beaut, though. Strong with a good muscular frame. Quarter horses are quite versatile. Fast too. I'll bet she'll fetch close to a hundred dollars or more at auction."

"Have you ever seen a horse do this with someone they've never met before?" Raine asked, still stunned by the mare's warmth toward him.

"Never."

"Then, how do you explain it?"

"Can't."

"Oh, you're very helpful," Raine said glibly.

"Looks like even horses of the female variety are standing in line to be with the likes of you," Cole teased.

All his brothers had horses that they had bonded with over the years, but that had never happened for Raine. He knew the temperaments of all the horses at Redbourne Ranch and knew which ones he could count on for which activities, but he often changed up which horse he would ride.

"Our horses have all been taken over to the town livery for a good grooming and watering before we head out for home." He motioned over to the two women who sat on a shaded bench in front of the station building. "The ladies are hungry. I thought maybe we could get something to eat while we wait. Looks like there are two restaurants in town."

Raine nodded. "I could eat."

"Come on, girl," the burly man holding the mare's lead called, followed by a click of his tongue.

The horse resisted for a moment, then turned to follow the man, her head still slightly turned as if looking back at him.

"Are you seriously just going to let him leave with her?"

Cole asked from behind Raine, placing a hand on his shoulder as they watched the odd duo walking away.

"Patience, little brother. Like you said, she's being sold at auction. I'll get her there."

"You really going to risk it? A lot of things can happen between now and then."

It was true.

He couldn't just let them go.

There was something special about that horse and Raine was excited about the chance to find out exactly what more that entailed. Without another moment's hesitation, he lunged forward in an awkward half skip and a run.

"Excuse me, sir," he called out to the man with the mare's lead.

In all the commotion of the station, the man hadn't heard him. He trotted after him, and once he caught up to him, he reached out and placed a hand on his arm.

"Excuse me," he said again.

"Well, don't you look a might determined? How can I help you, son?" He wrapped the mare's lead around his hand a couple of times and reached up to scratch behind her ears.

"Is this your horse?"

"She's right purdy, isn't she?" the man said with a grin. "Going up on the auction block in half an hour."

"She's extraordinary, actually," Raine said, realizing that probably was not the best thing to say when looking to negotiate.

"She'll make some cowboy mighty happy I reckon. Got another dozen or so too, not quite like her, mind you. But I imagine they'll each bring in at least a hundred or so. Maybe one twenty-five—"

"I'll give you one fifty for her right now," Raine jumped in, barely allowing the man to finish his sentence.

The mare pushed into his arm again, evoking another smile.

The man's eyes travelled between Raine and the horse.

"You know this horse?" he asked, scratching at his chin.

"No, sir."

"Do I know you? You look awfully familiar. Name's Boster Craven," he said with a nod.

"I don't believe so."

The mare raised her head and nibbled a little at Raine's neck.

The man's eyes narrowed. "One seventy-five."

"Sold." Raine pulled his travelling bag from his shoulder and reached in to retrieve the remaining funds he'd stashed for the journey home. A knot formed in his stomach as he sorted through his remaining coins. He was short—not by a lot, but enough to thwart the deal he'd just made.

The man must have realized the problem as he placed a hand on his shoulder.

"Don't worry, son. She'll be up on the auction block soon and you might get lucky."

Raine had not been prepared to make such a purchase on the trip home, but he cursed himself all the same.

"I could wire you the money," he said, effectively stopping the man's retreat. He glanced over his shoulder to look at Cole, who stood watching from back on the boardwalk, his arms raised with a shrug.

Raine held up one finger to the man to wait—maybe Cole had some extra cash on him, but as he turned around, a familiar voice stopped him in his tracks.

"Hey, Boster," Ethan Redbourne called out, "I see you've met my brothers here."

The man's eyebrows raised in understanding. "That is why you look familiar to me. Why didn't you say something?" he asked.

"I didn't know it would make a difference," Raine said, holding out his hand.

"You're a Redbourne," Mr. Craven said as he handed the lead over to him. "Horse is already yours."

"Thank you, kindly." Raine tipped his hat. "Wait, what?" He took the lead from Boster and the mare cuddled up right behind him, nudging him forward, and then propped her head over Raine's shoulder, nuzzling her face against his.

Everyone laughed.

"I wouldn't have believed it if I hadn't seen it for myself," Ethan said with an awed shake of his head.

Raine reached up and rubbed the mare's cheek. "You're a good girl, aren't you?" he said in the type of voice he usually used with his nieces and nephews, then remembered he had an audience and cleared his throat and turned to the man who'd handed him the horse. "I'm guessing Ethan knows how to get a hold of you?"

The man snorted. "He ought to, seeing as I work for him and all. At Redbourne Ranch."

He and Cole had been gone a good bit from Stone Creek, but Raine didn't think they'd been gone so long he wouldn't recognize the people living at the ranch, and he had a feeling there would be a lot to catch up on.

Horse is already yours, Mr. Craven had said. Now, it made sense.

Raine handed the man a ten dollar note. "Thank you for your trouble, my good man."

Boster's face lit up. "Thank you, sir."

"It's Raine. Raine Redbourne," he added with a chuckle and a wave.

The hired hand nodded. "Well, I've got work to do. If you'll excuse me."

Instead of Levi, it had been Ethan to show up when least expected.

"What are you doing here?" Raine asked as he pulled his younger brother into a bear-sized hug.

Cole closed the distance between them in just a few strides and joined the reunion.

"Did you know we were coming in on the train?" Raine

asked. It only took him a moment before he realized the only logical response.

"Auction," both he and Ethan said in unison, then laughed.

"*And* I may have known that you were coming in on this evening's train. Mama has a way of knowing exactly where her children are—especially when they're coming home."

"I don't believe my eyes," Abby said as she and Lily approached. "You are definitely a Redbourne what with the height, the chiseled jaw, and dimpled smile."

Cole grabbed his wife's hand and practically dragged her over to Ethan.

"This is Abby."

"Of course, it is." Ethan bent down and kissed her on the cheek. "You must be one incredible woman to be putting up with the likes of this one," he said playfully, wrapping an arm around her and squeezing her into his side.

"He's not all that bad," Abby said with a wink at Cole.

Ethan turned his attention to Lily. "And who might this be?" he asked with a nudge to Raine's arm.

"I'm Lily Campbell," she said, stepping forward and extending her hand.

He let go of Abby and reached out with a firm handshake. "Well, the pleasure is certainly mine, ladies. I must admit, I feel like I know you already. Hannah has told me a lot about you both. It will be wonderful to have you at the ranch."

Lily glanced at Raine, and he mustered a smile, which she returned warmly.

"That is one beautiful horse," Abby said as she ran a hand over the mare's neck and shoulders. "What are you going to call her?"

He figured *The Palomino* wouldn't go over very well.

"Don't know, but I'm open to suggestions."

"What about Rosebud or Daisy or Buttercup," Lily suggested, stepping forward eagerly to also pet the horse, but the mare immediately lengthened her neck, pulling upward, her ears laid back and her eyes wide.

Lily backed away. Raine stepped between the two.

"It's all right, girl," Raine coaxed, reaching out to scratch just beneath the forelock of hair draping down over a long white stripe that spanned the length of her nose.

"If I didn't know any better," Cole said, snatching his wife back into his arms, "I would say that horse is jealous."

"Of me?" Lily asked, her own eyes wide. "Do horses even get jealous? And why would she be jealous of me?"

The question hung in the air without a response for quite some time before Ethan broke the silence. "All right," he clapped his hands together. "Why don't you all go get something to eat while I take care of business. I'll meet you at the hotel, then we can all ride home together in the morning."

"You going to be long?" Raine asked.

"We just have these dozen or so horses Tag brought with him to auction off, then we'll be headed back. Why?"

"Tag is here?"

"Yup. Well, at the ranch. Will too?"

The news filled Raine with excitement. It had been too long since they'd all been together.

"Brenna and the kids too? Elizabeth?"

Ethan nodded. "All of them."

"Has anyone heard from Levi?" Raine asked.

"Not yet, but the wedding won't be for a couple more days. He's got time." Ethan put on his hat and took two steps toward the auction block where horses had been lined up for display. "The Little Pete restaurant has the best chicken dumpling stew for miles. Rose is almost as good a cook as Lottie. I heard she just pulled a fresh peach cobbler from the oven. If you get over there before it's gone, save me a piece."

Raine's stomach rumbled loudly at the mention of food, causing Lily to giggle.

"Sounds good to me."

After dropping the new palomino off at the livery, it didn't take them long to find the restaurant Ethan had suggested. Huge signs tented on the boardwalk had written specials and at the mention of fresh hot cornbread, Raine's mouth began to water.

They walked in and were immediately greeted by an older woman with dark hair pulled back at the nape and donned in a well-worn apron.

"Welcome! I'm Rose," she said, looking up and scanning the four of them with a smile. "Sit anywhere you'd like, and I'll have someone with you in a moment."

The small group settled into their seats at a table at the far end of the dining room, nestled up against the corner with windows on each side. Oversized paper menus lay at each place setting next to a neatly folded cloth napkin with shiny, but well used utensils sitting on top.

Though The Little Pete had only been built in the time since he and Cole had been gone, by the descriptions on the menu it was obvious that Rose was well versed in cooking for large groups of men. Raine wondered what else had changed in the short time they'd been gone. While he was grateful the little town had grown and they would have a place to stay for the night, it was also good to know they were so close to home.

He looked forward to seeing his family. All of them.

"It's so nice to see such lovely couples come through," a younger woman with ringlets in her brown hair and a decorative full body apron said as she approached them with paper in hand and a pencil behind her ear.

Raine looked over at Lily who sat across from him, and heat immediately emanated from his collar. He smiled but didn't correct the woman. He guessed it was natural for people to assume that two men and two women travelling together would be married. Propriety would have demanded the same, but they had taken precautions to avoid speculation.

"All we really get right now are the cowboys who come to sell their cattle at auction and a few of the townsfolk." She leaned down and rested her elbow on the ledge just behind

Raine. "Not that I'm complaining, mind you."

"I'd like some of that cornbread you're advertising," Raine said without hesitation. "And some water," he added, with the hope that a refreshing beverage would sooth the lump in his throat.

Cole glanced at Lily, then at his wife who nodded. "And dumplin' stew for the four of us," he said. "We hear it's the best around."

The woman's face brightened even more. "Ah, I thought you looked familiar," the waitress said with a grin. "Redbournes, right?"

"Yes, ma'am," both Raine and Cole said at once.

"Dumplin' stew and cornbread." The pencil remained behind her ear, and she dropped her hand with the paper to her side. "Easy enough. Can I get you any cobbler? Rose just pulled a fresh one from the oven."

Raine laughed.

"We'll take the whole thing."

"Now, this one," she patted Raine on the shoulder, "I like. You are one lucky woman," she told Lily.

Color rose in the girl's cheeks.

"It'll take someone really special to capture his heart," Lily said with a genuine smile, "but unfortunately, that someone is not me."

Raine looked at her in surprise. Abby had hinted more than once how wonderful it would be to have Lily a part of the family and he'd assumed the young woman had felt the same. Relief washed over him, and he relaxed against the back of his chair, then smiled back at her with a wink.

"Awww, don't let her fool ya. Miss Campbell is too good for the likes of this old cowboy."

"Single?" The waitresses' eyebrows raised, and the corners of her mouth upturned.

"Don't get your hopes up, ma'am'," Cole chimed in, "he's a right confirmed bachelor."

They all laughed.

"Not if Mama has anything to say about it." Raine thought of the scribbles in his pocket. If he was going to get married again, it would be on his terms.

They spent the night in town but were up with the sun.

Raine had arisen even earlier, anxious to brush down and saddle the palomino.

"What am I going to call you, girl?" he asked as he tightened the cinch, then rubbed and patted her neck with his hand. Of course, the horse had already been saddle-broken, she came from Redbourne Ranch. Ethan would not have had it any other way.

The horse nickered and Raine chuckled as he slipped half an apple into her mouth. "Don't worry, it will come to me." Not just any name would do.

Once the others' horses were saddled and ready to go, they waited in the livery yard for Ethan.

"Let's get a move on," their brother's voice called from behind him. He and Boster were already mounted and ready to head out.

The journey passed quickly as Raine's mind was occupied with questions of his future. As he crested the last hill, Redbourne Ranch came into view and his heart swelled at the scene. The colors on the trees had already begun to change and the pond just to the east of the homestead reflected the shimmer of the still rising sun climbing in the sky.

He could almost smell Lottie's mouthwatering peach muffins swirling with the late morning air. Cole and others rode on ahead, but Raine paused for a few minutes to take in the beautiful landscape. Then, with one last deep breath, he descended the knoll and rode into the yard.

As he walked the palomino into the stables, he noted several additional horses. The working herd was generally kept separate from the family's horses. Then, it dawned on him. They had more visitors for Rafe's wedding. Everyone was home for the big event.

While he was anxious to see everyone, he took his time brushing down and feeding his beautiful new mount.

"Who do you think's all here?" he asked the mare as he placed a bucket of water on the hook just inside the stall for her. "Do you think Tag was able to make it up?"

"Talking to yourself, big brother?"

Raine spun around to find Will leaning against the stable door.

With grins on both of their faces, the brothers grabbed each other in a fierce bear-like grip.

It had been more than two years since Will had been back for a visit.

"Elizabeth and the kids?" Raine asked as he released his little brother.

"They just arrived yesterday," Will beamed.

"Who else is here?"

"You and Cole were the last to arrive."

"You mean…"

"Everyone. Tag, Levi, all of us, under the same roof."

Raine shut the palomino's stall gate, slipping her another apple before draping an arm around his brother and walking with him up to the house.

He wasn't prepared for the scene that greeted him. The homestead was usually pretty quiet in the early afternoon as everyone had their chores to do and lists to complete, but today it was abustle with women and children. Elizabeth and Brenna each sat on the couch with the newest additions to the family cuddled in their arms, while Grace bounced a toddler on her knee—not her own, but Cadence's little Gideon.

Raine could hardly believe how much the little boy had grown in just the few months they'd been gone.

Hannah squealed from the kitchen and Raine imagined she was busily catching up with Abby and Lily.

When the door shut behind him and Will, everything

quieted for just a moment while all eyes fell on them.

"Daddy," Will's youngest son ran up to his brother in delight. "You found him," the little boy said looking sheepishly at Raine.

"Yes, I did. And I think we should let him settle in for a moment before we accost him."

"Nah," the little boy said with a shake of his head and a delighted giggle. He leaned toward Raine, then practically jumped from his father's arms into his.

After a tight hug around his neck, the boy squirmed to get down, then quickly rejoined the others who were concentrating intently on something in the middle of the floor.

As he peeked over the heads of several children to find two of his oldest nephews setting up lines and rows of dominoes in various patterns on the floor as the rest of them waited in anticipation for the moment the first domino was triggered to collapse the entire trail one at a time.

"Took you long enough."

Raine turned to see Rafe walking into the room with his bride-to-be in hand. It had been too long since he'd seen a smile like that on his brother's face.

"Married?" Raine said as he strode over to him and pulled him into a hug, then leaned down and placed a kiss on Tayla's cheek. "You have certainly grown up, Miss Hawthorne," he said appreciatively. "I remember when you looked at Rafe with stars in your eyes and you couldn't have been more than what, thirteen at the time? I guess some things don't change," he said with a wink.

Tayla beamed at him.

"It is wonderful to see you, Raine." She leaned in. "Be prepared," she whispered. "Your mother has decided it is her duty now to find someone for you to marry."

He had been afraid of that.

"Another testament to the fact that some things don't change." He chuckled. "Congratulations, you two." He squeezed Rafe on the arm and headed for the kitchen, wanting to make sure his mother did not invite any single women to the wedding solely for his sake or he was afraid she would be sorely disappointed.

CHAPTER FIVE

Rafe Redbourne

"You are a bounty hunter for heaven's sake." Rafe stared at his reflection in the washstand mirror. "You have faced killers and thieves and wild horses. You can do this." He took a deep breath, then shook his head. "No, I don't think I can do this." He grabbed the sides of the basin, then splashed some cool water on his face. "Where is Raine?" he asked, reaching for the towel that hung from a wooden peg.

"You can and you will." Raine stepped into the bedroom with his freshly pressed frock coat and held it out for him to put on.

"I'll look like a fool in that getup," Rafe said as he slipped one arm through the sleeve, then the other. He would have preferred to wear his denims, a nice button-down, and a vest, but his mother had insisted he dress like a gentleman for his wedding. He supposed Tayla deserved at least that.

Luckily, Leah Redbourne had not pushed for an extravagant event this time around. He felt like the townsfolk would come just to see if his bride-to-be would follow through with it this time. Heaven knew that if he'd had to face the possibility of another crowd he would never show his face again in Stone Creek.

What if she didn't show?

Buck up, Redbourne, he chided himself.

He was a grown man who was about to marry the woman of his dreams, yet his apprehensions were getting the better of him.

"She's not Tessa," Raine said as if knowing the exact thoughts that plagued him.

"I know." Rafe readjusted his tie in the mirror and buttoned up the vest, stretching the tight neck of his shirt with his finger. It had seemed to fit perfectly well yesterday, but today it seemed to be closing in around his throat.

She's just Tessa's baby sister.

"She loves you," Raine assured him.

"I know."

"She's waiting."

"I kn…Wait, what?" Rafe turned around to face his brother. "What do you mean she's waiting?" His eyes narrowed at his brother.

"I mean, she knew how hard today would be for you…and she wanted to make sure you knew that there was nothing to worry about. She didn't want you to have to wait for her and wonder. So, she decided to go down first. She's standing at the edge of the pond in front of all your guests in the garden with Preacher, waiting for you."

Rafe took a deep breath.

His heart swelled knowing that she knew the insecurities he worked so hard to hide from the world. How had he been so blessed to have found her?

"This is really happening," he said as if to convince himself of its veracity.

"It's really happening," Raine confirmed.

Rafe had been lost for such a long time after Tessa left him standing in front of the whole town on their wedding day with no explanation for her absence. All he'd had was a simple note from her little sister saying it was for the best. That same little sister who he now would call his wife.

For eight years he had wallowed in self-pity and regret. He'd taken his frustrations out on miscreants and deviants, given up on most everything he'd believed in—except God and his family—and had thrown himself into the most dangerous situations as possible. But he'd been completely unprepared for the girl who'd written that note so long ago to come back into his life and offer him redemption.

He hadn't understood her message on that blasted note all those years ago, but now as he prepared to walk out into the yard and wed the most beautiful woman he had ever known—inside and out—everything came into focus, and he understood better than he ever thought possible.

It truly had been for the best.

He loved Tayla Hawthorne more than words could ever express, and he was going to marry that girl.

Today.

"Well, what are you waiting for?" Raine said, handing him his hat.

When they reached the bottom of the stairs, their parents stood on either side of Lottie. The woman had been like a second mother to all the Redbourne children from before the time Rafe could remember. She was the family's cook and housekeeper—she was responsible for the majority of the delicious meals consumed at the ranch as well as various housekeeping duties, and she was their friend, their confidant.

A mother.

Rafe placed a finger gently beneath the older Spanish woman's chin and tilted her face up to look at him. He studied her eyes and evaluated her constitution.

"You have a little more color today," he said, happy to see her on her feet, but her shallow breathing and heavy lids still concerned him. "How are you feeling?"

"I'm good, niñito," Lottie said with a reassuring smile, though the lines and dark circles below her eyes betrayed her continued weariness. "I will be better once my little Rafe is married to Miss Tayla."

Everyone looked up at Rafe and all began to laugh.

Rafe was the tallest of his brothers and compared to Lottie, who was significantly shorter than even his mother, he was anything but little. He scooped the old woman up into his arms and carried her out onto the front porch steps where he paused a moment and glanced over at the garden. The backdrop of vivid yellows, oranges and red reflected off the pond creating the ideal landscape for such a momentous occasion.

He smiled.

There, standing in the middle of it all, was his beautiful bride-to-be in a simple ivory gown, void of all the frills and fluff so many brides wore, but still ornamented with a touch of lace at her neck, shoulders, and waistline. The flowers in her wheat-colored hair arrayed her upswept crown and her skin glowed pink from the slight chill in the air.

"Ella te espera" Lottie cooed, her voice quiet and tired. "She's waiting," she repeated in English.

Rafe chuckled and made his way down the steps and out onto the garden path. One of the porch benches had been brought down and placed at an angle toward the back. Plush cushions and Lottie's favorite blanket adorned the seat. He set down his precious cargo on the seat and bent down to kiss the top of her head.

She smiled up at him and his heart warmed inside his chest even more.

His mother wrapped the blanket around the woman and sat down next to her.

Rafe stood up even a little taller than usual.

All those in attendance rose as he hurriedly made his way down the path. He knew it wasn't customary to greet or acknowledge guests, but he was amazed to see so many familiar faces. Few people from town had been invited, but those who were the most important in the world were there.

He nodded at each of his siblings and their spouses, amazed that all of them were in the same place at the same time. It had been years since they'd all been together, and he'd never seen all his nephews so well behaved. His gaze shifted to Tayla's parents, her newly discovered twin brothers, Finn and Harrison, and then on Adrien Longhurst—a man who'd also been like a father to him.

Everyone else around him became a blur as his eyes focused solely on his waiting bride.

"You're here," he said with a grin.

"And so are you." Tayla leaned toward him and whispered, "Thank you for not leaving me standing here all alone in front of the entire town and our families." She winked and flashed a mischievous little smirk.

All tensions and fears melted away and he reached out, pulling her into him and kissing her hard on the mouth.

"Well, we haven't quite gotten to that part yet, but…" Preacher started with a laugh and raised his brow, the rest of his sentence never touching his lips.

Rafe raised his head, his soon-to-be wife still clutched in his embrace, and found her eyes with his own. He breathed deeply and loosened his grip, trailing her arms until her hands rested in his and the good reverend began.

It was all over in a moment. Vows had been exchanged before God and family and they now belonged to each other wholly. She was his and he hers.

Whoops and hollers erupted from the small crowd as Rafe pulled Tayla back into his arms to claim their first kiss as husband and wife. He'd never been happier.

"Wife," he said as he pulled away from her and nodded.

"Husband."

"I love you."

"And I you."

Rafe took his bride by the hand, and they headed back through the small crowd. When they reached the back of the garden trail, his eyes fell on Lottie. Her eyes lay closed, her hands limp in her lap, and he stopped, immediately dropping to one knee in front of her.

She was gone.

A soft smile graced her lips, her face peaceful. Tears graced his eyes, and he dropped his head. His siblings and parents gathered around them. Tayla placed a hand on his shoulder as he looked up into all their expectant faces—each full of emotion, waiting.

He shook his head.

She was gone.

"What do you mean Dad slipped it into your pocket at the wedding?" Raine held the telegram Rafe had pulled from his suit coat.

Longhurst in Thistleberry STOP Awaiting your instructions STOP Seth.

Thistleberry, Montana? That was unexpected. What was the likelihood that Malcolm would end up in a town full of Deardons, Redbourne cousins?

"What am I supposed to do now?" Rafe asked, his hands raking through his hair. He paced the length of their father's study. "I just got married. My…wife," he stopped short for a moment and looked at Raine with wide eyes, "that is very odd to say," he shook his head and continued his pacing. "My wife…is in the other room with Hannah preparing for our honeymoon trip as we speak." The couple had planned to head out to Connecticut to see about Rafe re-enrolling at Harvard

Medical School to finish out his last year.

"What do you want to do?" Raine asked. "Cole and I could—"

"No." Rafe stopped him from finishing his thought. "He was my best friend and he betrayed us. I can't just let that slide."

Months before, Cole had drawn up a likeness of Malcolm Longhurst for a wanted poster on a few different carbon papers to be copied and distributed out to all the marshals' offices in the surrounding territories—even though they'd believed him to be hightailing it back to England. They never would have expected him to be in Montana, least of all, Thistleberry, but the posters had paid off.

"I'm still a bounty hunter—and pretty good at that. I can't risk allowing him to hurt anyone else. We ride out first thing in the morning. Tayla will understand." He ran a hand through his hair again. He stopped his pacing long enough to face him. "She will understand, right?"

Raine stared at his brother a moment, wanting to offer some comfort. "I hope, for your sake, that's true." He clapped Rafe on the shoulder—who blew out a long breath and nodded.

"That is, if *you* are up for the ride."

It wasn't surprising that Rafe wanted his company. He was now the only brother without any familial obligations. He hadn't been back in town long enough to go back to work in the sheriff's office and had nothing else keeping him here.

"What about Lottie?" Raine asked. "We were her family after all."

"At first, I was arrogant enough to believe that everyone could miraculously be here because I was getting married, but now I know that the good Lord made it so we could all be here together for her. We should do something to pay our respects. Maybe Malcolm will stay put for a few more days."

"I'll talk to Mama. I'm sure we can have a small service for her before we leave. Go talk to your wife and I'll speak with the others about preparing a resting place for her."

"Are you sure you're up to another ride? You just traveled across two states."

"Wouldn't miss it." Raine had known that coming back to Stone Creek would provide him with the stability of his old job as deputy, but, somehow, that just didn't seem fitting for him anymore. Maybe a trip to visit family up north would be just what he needed. "Besides, I've never been on a steamboat. I imagine it will be quite an adventure."

"That's right," Rafe chuckled. "I guess the railroad hasn't exactly made it into Montana Territory yet. We should talk to Levi about that."

"I don't know how much pull he has with the Northern Pacific, but we can try."

If they would be leaving soon, it only gave them a short while to catch up with those siblings who'd been away from Kansas for a long time, so they'd better make the most of it.

"I'll go break the news to my sweet wife. Pray for me."

Raine laughed as Rafe headed out the door.

Godspeed, little brother.

A photograph on the bookshelf behind his father's desk caught his eye. He pushed the chair under the desk and picked up the frame, one finger tracing the side with a beautiful young woman standing next to a boy who'd believed he had the world at his fingertips.

Lavender, he remembered all too well the color of her dress on their wedding day.

"Thistleberry?" The door to the study burst open and his dad stepped into the room. "Rafe tells me the two of you are heading up to Montana after Malcolm."

Raine put the photograph back on his father's bookcase.

"Yes, sir."

Jameson took his hat off and hung it from the rack on the wall. He walked over to stand at his eldest son's side and looked lovingly at the picture Raine had replaced on the bookshelf.

"I still think about her too, you know," his father said.

"It was a long time ago."

"I suspect it doesn't matter just how much time passes, she'll always be a part of you."

What his father said was true. Sarah had her own place carved permanently into his heart.

"Yes, sir."

"You've been on my mind a lot today, son. When I first learned that you would be coming home, I spoke with the sheriff and told him you wouldn't be returning as deputy in Stone Creek."

"Why would you do that?" Raine stared at his father in disbelief.

Other than ranching, being a lawman was really all he knew. And he was good at it.

"You have always been there for your siblings, for this town, for everyone else, but when is the last time you stopped to consider what it is you want or need for that matter? You deserve a life, Raine. A family. Children. It's time for you find your place, son. To do something for yourself."

True to form, his father always knew what he was thinking. It was frustrating at times, but he was glad to have someone who would listen and understand.

"I have been considering those questions more often lately." Raine dropped into the overstuffed chair next to the desk and exhaled slowly. "Everybody has grown up and don't have much need for their big brother anymore."

"You know you always have a place here at Redbourne Ranch. And your siblings will always need their big brother. We all need you."

"I know, and thank you, but—"

"But," his father cut in, "I've got a sneaking suspicion that your future lies somewhere else, much to your mother's chagrin. You've been gone a lot—helping Tag in Texas, Cole in Colorado. Where do *you* think you're supposed to be?"

Raine contemplated his father's question for a few

moments before responding.

"I don't know what is in store for me. I just need to finish this job with Rafe and then I'll have some time to figure it out. I doubt there's much of anything in Montana. It's been a while since we visited Whisper Ridge, but if memory serves, all the women there were either children, married, or spoken for."

"Who said anything about a woman?" There was a gleam in Jameson's eyes that beamed at his jest.

"And it's cold," Raine said, avoiding the obvious bait. "I don't want to live in a place where my hat freezes to my head or where the risk of being snowed in is an everyday possibility."

His father laughed, knowingly.

"It gets cold here."

"Not the same."

"So, you're thinking down south with your brother then? I'm sure there are plenty of jobs available in Texas. You could be a ranger."

"Miserable heat or freezing cold. Not much of a choice if you ask me. What's wrong with Kansas?"

Jameson looked at him long and hard, then stood up and walked back to pick the picture of Sarah up from his bookshelf. He handed it to Raine.

"Nothing. In fact, there are a lot of good things about Kansas. For me, it's my present and likely my future. Your mother is here and wherever she is, is home to me. For you…"

Raine waited.

Nothing.

"For me what?"

"Well, I hear Mary Beth Hutchinson is back in town," his father said with a wink.

"Now, don't you start too. Just what you always wanted—Norah Hutchinson's daughter to be a part of the family."

The smile left his father's face at the mention of his old flame who'd shot Cole in attempt to stop him from marrying Abby and marry her daughter instead.

"I can see the wheels turning in Mama's head now that she only has one unmarried son left." Though he highly doubted that Leah Redbourne would approve of such a match as one with Norah Hutchinson's daughter.

Raine considered his parents and how they had never been ashamed or embarrassed to show their love for one another. They loved each other and it was no secret to anyone who knew them—and much of the time even to those who didn't. He'd wanted that kind of relationship with Sarah. His chance was gone. Even though he hoped to find someone worthwhile to chase away the loneliness, he doubted there was room in his heart to love anyone else like that again.

"How is Mama?" Raine asked, righting himself in the chair, then leaning forward with his elbows resting on his knees.

"She's in with Hannah, Grace, and the others now. They are…um…" there was a slight catch in his voice, "looking after Lottie."

"I was thinking about the large walnut tree with a view from the kitchen window. She used to love watching that tree sway with the breeze and always commented on how it changed with the seasons. She used to say, 'Mi hijitos," he did his best to imitate her Spanish accent, "you can learn a lot about life from a tree, you know. It's full of endings and new beginnings, but every stage is beautiful if you are paying attention.'"

"She was a good woman."

"I was thinking maybe we could bury her beneath that tree."

"That would be right fitting, son. She'd like that."

Raine jumped up from the chair. "I'll talk to the others. We'll get it done before dark."

He made his way through the hallways until he reached the big family room where Tag, Will, Cole, and Ethan sat reminiscing about their childhood.

"Do you remember Genesis?" Will asked the others, referring to the lizard the twins had stuck in Hannah's bed to scare her.

"Do you remember how disappointed we were when we put him out on the table for Emma to find the first time Jonah brought her by and she ended up playing with him instead?" Tag grinned.

"What did I miss?" Levi said as he came into the room, eating one of the last pieces of Lottie's sponge cake.

"Is there any more of that bizcocho?" Will asked, perking up from his seat on the oversized armchair by the hearth.

When Rafe joined them, it would be the first time in several years that they had all been together in the same place at the same time. He wondered if he might be able to persuade Grace to take a photograph of them with the camera Ethan had given her last Christmas.

Tag was the first to notice him standing there. He jumped to his feet and, in three long strides, closed the distance between them. Raine pulled his little brother into a hug and was joined by Levi, then Will and Cole, followed by Ethan until they all were in a large ball of Redbourne men.

"I want some of that," Hannah said as she wiggled through them until she was at the heart.

Raine beamed. His family was everything to him.

Will and his little family still lived in England, Tag in Texas, Rafe would be moving to Connecticut soon, and Cole was in Colorado. While Ethan, Hannah, and Levi all had homesteads here around Redbourne Ranch, he couldn't help but consider his dad's words in the study.

Your future lies somewhere else.

His heart was conflicted.

Where was somewhere else? Thistleberry? Silver Springs? With Tag in Texas? Or somewhere further west venturing out on his own?

Lily Campbell's face popped into his head. They had spent a lot of time together in Silver Springs, her being Abby's best friend and all, but there had been something missing. He liked the girl quite a bit. She was smart and funny, light on her feet, and loved his sister-in-law something fierce, but it wasn't enough. It was almost like she was another sister to him, someone to enjoy spending some time with, but there was no deeper connection.

As they broke apart, each of the Redbourne siblings retired to their places on the couch, the chairs, and the floor.

"Dad said that you all were going to prepare a place for Lottie under the old walnut tree," Hannah said, still snuggled under one of Raine's arms.

"I hadn't mentioned it to them yet, but…" He scanned the faces in the room with the unspoken question and all nodded agreement.

"It's so hard to believe that one day could be filled with so much happiness and so much sadness at the same time," she said solemnly.

Raine pulled her in tighter and squeezed. They all sat there in silence for a few minutes until his only brother-in-law opened the front door. Hannah looked up at Eli with a grateful smile, then left his embrace for her husband's.

"It's ready, Tag," Eli said, glancing over at one of the twins, "I've finished building Lottie's burial case. It's just out in the barn."

Of all the men who could have won Hannah's affections, Raine was glad it had been Eli. The former lumberjack made no secret of the fact that he loved her and their little girl more than anything. He was strong and patient and kind. They were lucky to have him amongst the Redbourne ranks.

Tag had been working with Cole on some designs that he could carve into Lottie's casket. His talents with design often paralleled what he could do with horses. His woodworking skills had entertained many children—some older than others—and had brought great joy and comfort to those around him. He had even built the benches that adorned the porches at the ranch. It was fitting that he would create something special to hold their beloved housekeeper, mother-figure, and friend at burial.

He arose from the couch where he had been lounged next to Levi, nodded at Eli, and left the house.

"Uncle Raine! Uncle Raine!" His nephews Luke, Oliver, and Jamie all came running into the living room. They easily brightened the solemn mood with their sunshine smiles and innocent voices. "There's a bad man out by the chicken coop."

Raine dropped down on his haunches. "Is this a real bad man or is it a part of your game?" They didn't look too scared.

Luke, the oldest of the three leaned into him close. "It's Henry. He's just pretending," he whispered.

The imaginations of the children never ceased to amaze him, and he stood up with a nod.

"Just let me get my badge and gun. We'll get the rascal."

The children squealed with delight as they ran back out the front door.

"We'll have plenty of time to catch up after dinner," Levi said with a nod. "You should probably go catch my son, the real bad man, before he steals all the eggs."

Everyone laughed.

As the day came to a close, Raine sat on the porch swing looking out over the land. Redbourne Ranch was a beautiful place. Their parents had worked hard to make it into a prosperous and beautiful home for their family. A large mound of dirt sat beneath the old walnut tree and Raine's heart broke a little as he mourned their loss. The pain was all too familiar, and he fought the emotions that threatened.

"Do you mind if I join you?" Jameson handed Raine a quilt as he sat down on the swing next to his son. "There's quite a chill in the air tonight. Your ma thought you might get cold out here."

Raine placed the quilt over his lap with a grateful nod but didn't say anything. He knew he was missing out on time with his siblings, but he just needed a moment longer to collect his thoughts.

The two men sat there for several minutes in comfortable stillness.

"Heard from Hank last week," Jameson broke the silence. "Said he's written to you on several occasions about taking a job as sheriff in Thistleberry." He picked up right where they'd left off in the study.

"He has. But Cole needed help getting his ranch on its feet. The timing just wasn't right."

"What about now?" His father leaned down, resting his elbows on his knees and looked out into the yard. "I don't think it's coincidence that Malcolm headed up that way and now you just happen to be available to go with Rafe to collect him. Once that job's done, maybe you should consider staying a while. Hank's offered a place for you to stay at Whisper Ridge."

"He's written to me several times, and it has crossed my mind, but I don't know."

"What's holding you back, son?" Jameson turned his head toward him.

"The cold." What was he supposed to say? That it just still hurt so much? That the thought of settling down in one place terrified him?

"I know you better than that."

What *was* holding him back?

Raine thought good and hard about that question. It was hard to answer. He loved the law and was grateful for the opportunities that had often come his way to use the talents with which the good Lord had blessed him, but it seemed unfair somehow to Sarah that his life could go on without her.

"Will it ever go away?"

"What's that?"

"The gaping hole in my chest where my wife used to be."

And...the rest of the words were on the tip of his tongue, but he quickly shook his head. He'd tell them all one day, but he couldn't bring himself to do it—not even now. It was still for him and Sarah to keep.

"I imagine not. But that doesn't mean there's not room in that big heart of yours for someone else."

Raine rolled his eyes.

"Seriously, where is she? Mama, I mean." He glanced around as if his mother would be hiding behind the windowsill. "Mama, come on out," he called, knowing she wasn't really there.

"It's not your mother putting me up to anything. I just see you punishing yourself like you believe you don't deserve to be happy again."

"I'm happy."

For the most part that was true. He wasn't unhappy.

"When is the last time you did something for yourself?"

"I feel like everything I do is for me, to make up for the guilt."

"What do you have to feel guilty about? Sarah's death certainly wasn't your fault, Raine. Sometimes bad things happen."

"I know, but if I had just been home or if I had just chopped up that blasted tree and taken it into the house like she'd asked me several times before…"

Jameson sat up and turned to look his son directly in the eye. "It was not your fault."

He'd tried to rationalize it in his head many times throughout the years, but the idea he could have prevented the accident still haunted him. She'd fallen through the ice. Maybe if he'd been there she wouldn't have even been out by the pond. He still had no idea why she'd been out there in the first place.

"What is it that you want, Raine?"

He sucked in a deep breath.

"I don't know. I think it's just been so long since I thought about what I want. It's been easier that way."

His father didn't say anything more for a long while, he just sat and listened.

"When I focus on helping everyone else, the pain, the bad

memories, they all seem to fade away."

"And now?"

"And now, I suppose it's time for something a little different." When he spoke the words aloud, Raine knew they were true. "It's time to find out what that is."

CHAPTER SIX

Thistleberry, Montana, Mid-October

"These are just beautiful, Mary Jane." Mrs. Smith ran her hand over the dyed pattern of the new woolen blankets she'd brought in to sell. "As the weather continues to get colder, I am sure we will require as many as you can offer. For now, why don't you put me down for a dozen or so."

With their numbers quickly dwindling at Happenstance Ranch, Mary Jane had taken on many responsibilities beyond her usual foreman duties. She found herself sitting at the loom more often, weaving intricate patterns out of the brightly colored wool, overseeing the packaging of blankets, winter wear, cheeses, and more. Breeding season was coming to an end and their previous plans to purchase another fifty ewes to help grow the herd had been postponed until spring. Come lambing season they expected to yield close to another hundred lambs, which would also increase the workload.

She caught a glimpse of Andrew Deardon out the large store front window.

He just can't help himself, she thought as she closed her coin purse and returned it to the hidden pocket in her dress.

"Will you excuse me, Mrs. Smith? I will be back next week with a few more." She lifted the skirt she had worn simply for the trip to town and rushed past several townsfolk on her way out of the store.

"Mr. Deardon," she said as Andrew lifted one of her several crates from the boardwalk and loaded it into the back of her wagon. "I know you are just being chivalrous, but surely, you have better things to do than load my wagon. I know just how busy you are, and you know that I am perfectly capable."

Andrew raised his hat. "It seems like we have this conversation every time you come into town, Miss Bennett." He picked up another crate and set it in the back of the wagon.

Mary Jane wished she had on her britches instead of the cumbersome dress she wore, but she grabbed her hem and, as gracefully as she could, descended the four stairs leading down to the street.

"Really, I can take it from here, thank you," she said as she sat down on top of the last crate with any actual goods in it to take back to the ranch with a satisfied smile.

"And this one too, I am assuming," a strong baritone voice boomed from behind her.

Without warning, the crate raised upward, and Mary Jane threw out her arms to brace herself against the sudden movement, but instead, fell backward into a man's firm chest, the back of her head landing on his shoulder, her face so close to his she wasn't sure she could breathe.

"Howdy, ma'am," the stranger said with a smile.

In a moment's time, she found herself in the back of the buckboard, sitting upright, along with the rest of the crates. She craned her neck around to see who had accosted her and was unprepared for the handsome grin that greeted her.

She quickly stood, but she was blocked from walking around the crate on either side. With a sigh, she sat back down on the crate, lifted her feet—careful her dress covered her completely—and spun around, as lady-like as possible to face the man. With hands on her hips, she looked down on the two very handsome men, brushing her hand at the crumples that now appeared on her dress. She shook her head, biting her lip to suppress the smile that threatened.

"Mary Jane Bennett," Andrew said, barely concealing the smirk on his own face, "meet Raine Redbourne. He's come all the way from Kansas on account of you."

When she glanced over again at the stranger, she wanted nothing more in that moment than to wipe the self-satisfied smile off his too-good-looking-for-his-own-good face, but the name caught her attention.

"Redbourne?"

"Yes, ma'am. It's a pleasure to meet you." He raised his hat in a most irritatingly charming way.

He didn't look like any bounty hunter she'd ever met. She imagined most of them to be gruff and angry, like they had a chip on their shoulder.

"I suppose you are here about Malcolm Longhurst being here in Thistleberry?"

The man's expression changed in an instant and his playful demeanor suddenly became very serious.

"Has he been causing any trouble around town? Do you know where he is?"

"Not exactly," she started, but when he raised a single brow in question, she stood up a little straighter. "The only trouble he's caused so far was to his lady friend, er, the woman who accompanied him into town. I don't know who she was to him exactly, but she's now staying with us at the Happenstance Ranch. I'm sure she will be more than happy to tell you where to find him after what he did to her."

Andrew and Mr. Redbourne exchanged a look she couldn't quite read.

"Is your friend all right?"

"I didn't say she was my friend. I haven't known the woman

all that long, but…"

Raine Redbourne?

"Hold on. I thought the name on that wanted poster was Rafe Redbourne, not Raine," she said, just registering the difference.

"It was." Another stranger joined them at the back of the wagon. "Is." This one did not wear a smile and stood just a hair taller than the other. "I'm Rafe." A white-handled revolver adorned each hip.

Despite his good looks, *he* definitely looked and acted more the part of the bounty hunters she'd encountered. At least the scowl was familiar. She felt sorry for anyone who dared cross him.

Her eyes flitted over to Raine.

Good heavens, she thought, glancing back between the two highly attractive men. *Brothers.* They were as handsome as any she'd ever seen—though they seemed to lack even the most basic of manners.

Heat flooded her face at the thought of falling backward against Raine's chest. A true gentleman would have…

What would he have done, Mary Jane? she asked herself with no good answer.

But, if both were lawmen, it would explain the guns slung across their hips. Why did the handsome ones always spell trouble?

Mary Jane silently chided herself for allowing her eyes to linger on Raine's beautifully carved face.

"Are you a bounty hunter too? Or a territory Marshal?" she asked him.

"No, ma'am."

"He's a sworn in deputy," Rafe snipped. "Now, who is the woman who came with Malcolm?"

"Forgive us. Where are our manners?" Raine said as if having read her mind. "We just rode into town and are still a little tired from the trip—though I realize that is hardly an excuse. Miss Bennett, was it?" He turned to look at Andrew for confirmation.

He nodded.

"Miss Bennett, if you would be so kind as to direct us to where we might find this woman you've spoken of, we'd sure be mighty grateful."

She narrowed her eyes at him. He was part of Lucy's family and every Deardon she knew was trustworthy, but maybe the Redbournes were different. Most of the lawmen she knew had turned out to be scoundrels of one sort or another.

"She works with Lucy at the Happenstance," Andrew filled in for her. "New girl's name is Tessa. Hawthorne, I think."

The color drained from Rafe's face, and he swallowed hard. His jaw flexed and his nostrils flared.

Raine moved closer to his brother and facing him, placed a hand on his arm and leaned toward him. "Maybe we should get some food in your belly before we go storming the castle," he said quietly, but still loud enough for Mary Jane to hear.

Why would they react so to Tessa?

She'd had her own apprehensions about having Tessa stay at the ranch—at least at first, but she understood all too well the pain that could be caused by a man who could hurt and betray a woman. So, she'd taken the newcomer under her wing, and she seemed to be thriving—taking easily to the work unlike Judith who still struggled to even pet a sheep.

"Well, what are we waiting for?" Rafe asked as he strode across the street down by the post office where a huge roan mare and a beautiful palomino had been tethered. "I'm guessing you know the way to this Happenstance Ranch," she heard him say, but had no idea to whom he was speaking.

Before she knew it, Andrew had already crossed the street and climbed up onto the front seat of his full wagon of feed and grains, and the two strangers she'd just met had mounted their horses.

Mary Jane stood there, realizing she still stood in the back of her wagon. She growled to herself. If they were going to be such gentlemen, the least they could have done was help a lady down.

This would have been so much easier in britches.

"See you later, Miss Bennett," Andrew called as he rounded the pavilion in the center of town and passed her, slapping the reins of his team.

Raine raised his hat as he rode past, following their cousin.

"Arggg."

Mary Jane felt bad she wouldn't have enough time to warn Lucy or Tessa about the impending intrusion. Whisper Ridge had its own telegraph machine, but there was no way to communicate with the Happenstance without a courier, and she guessed Lucy would be in her office instead of at home.

Satisfied no one was paying much attention to her, Mary Jane lifted her skirt as much as she dared and clambered back over the crates and then the front seat, rushing to sit down. After another glance around, making sure she hadn't been seen, she picked up the reins and headed toward home.

When she arrived, she was surprised to see that neither the strangers' horses nor Andrew's wagon were in sight. They'd obviously gone to Whisper Ridge first—likely to unload their things and to get something to eat.

As she pulled through the gate, she spotted Lissa hunched over a broken fence post with a pair of wire cutters jutting from her mouth. The two-year seasoned ranch hand stood up straight from her task and strode over to Mary Jane at the wagon.

"You look a little flustered, M.J., what's happened?" She reached up and rubbed the horse's neck closest to her.

"The bounty hunter made it to town. And he brought a brother."

"Are they handsome? Married?"

"I didn't ask," she said with a flip of her hand as she climbed down from the buckboard seat. The scene where she fell against Raine's chest kept playing over and again in her mind. She had to focus on something else.

Anything else.

"Too bad," Lissa said with a smile.

"They are looking for our good neighbor, Mr. Richards, Longhurst, whatever we are calling him these days, and I think they want to speak to Tessa. May even have history with her. They left town ahead of me, so I thought they would have beat me here. Has anyone stopped by?"

"Just Mr. Deardon who stopped by to check on Carl this morning."

There were so many Mr. Deardons now, it was nearly impossible to keep them all straight, but if he was checking on Carl, Mary Jane deduced, it must have been Hank, since all the llamas actually belonged to him.

"I'll take care of the wagon," Lissa said as she patted down the horse closest to her. "Lucy headed up to Whisper Ridge about an hour ago. And Evaline took both Tessa and Judith out to the west pasture to teach them how to turn out a ram."

"Bless Evaline's heart. Judith too?" The newest addition had barely learned to stay upright on a horse, she couldn't imagine how jumping right into breeding season would go over.

"I offered to have one of them stay behind and help me with that fence," she motioned back to the broken post she'd been working on when Mary Jane had arrived, "but they were much more interested in the sheep. Even Judith."

Evaline was the most seasoned hired hand at Happenstance. She'd taken her band of sheep up the mountains past Deardon land for some seasonal grazing and had just returned a few days ago, but the woman never stopped working. She seemed to actually prefer the sheep over people.

Since losing Mona and several others over the last year, it had been hard to keep up with all the responsibilities needed to run the place. Lucy had envisioned the ranch as a place for women who had been displaced by correspondence courtships gone awry, but it had proven to be difficult to maintain the level of productivity they required with so few of them.

As they approached the winter season, they wouldn't need as many hands, but come spring, they'd have to hire on more women from town to lessen the load. She'd already opened it up for Tessa, there could be others like her out there who needed a place like Happenstance.

"Let me get changed, Lissa, and I'll come help with the fence."

Luckily, Evaline's band of sheep was the last of the four to be bred. Once tupping season was complete, it would be time to prepare for the Harvest Fall Festival at the end of the month. Other than caring for the sheep, they would prep the newest rams for auction, and focus more on utilizing the wool to spin yarn, weave clothing, blankets, and fine materials for the milliner, haberdashery, and General Store, and make butter, cheeses, lotions, and other products to market and sell in and around town.

It felt good to get out of her dress and into some denims and a button-down shirt. Working in the men's style get-up was a lot easier when traipsing through mud or riding a horse. She'd learned a lot over the last few years about how to run a small ranch, and dreamed of having her own little place one day—maybe something a little smaller like Mrs. Isaacson's farm just to the south of Happenstance. The woman had been considering moving away to be with her daughter, and Mary Jane had been saving every penny she could spare to save enough to cover the amount required to get a loan for the place from the bank.

After shrugging on her tall working boots, she joined Lissa out at the gate. One of the rams in the last tupping had gotten a little unruly and three fence posts had suffered the consequences.

A single rider approached.

Seth Deardon, Hank's eldest, came into view.

"M.J.," he called out, "Lucy needs to talk to you and asked

that you come to dinner up at Whisper Ridge."

Odd.

Mary Jane could only suspect what was on Lucy's mind. The woman had been playing matchmaker ever since she'd known her, and two handsome, seemingly eligible men just rode into town.

"Can I decline?" she asked, half-jokingly.

"I suppose you could, but I would never hear the end of it, so please just come."

"What time is it?"

Seth glanced at some gadget on his wrist. "It's half past four."

Supper at Whisper Ridge was usually served at five o'clock.

"Okay," she said, brushing back the stray tendril that had fallen in front of her eyes with her gloved hand. "But I'm coming as I am." She turned to Lissa. "Will you be okay for a little while?"

"We're almost done anyway," Lissa said with a wave. "Go. When Evaline is finished, I'll take the girls up to the north pasture to work on the barn."

"Good. I'll bring you back some of Alex's honeyberry preserves."

"I'll hold you to that. And I wouldn't argue if you were to bring me something else even sweeter. Man-sized maybe."

Mary Jane smiled.

It had taken Lissa a long time to get over her marriage mishap, but in the last few months she'd shown that she was ready to move on and start over again.

"I'll wait," Seth called after Mary Jane as she headed to the stables to get a horse.

It took her ten minutes to get a mount saddled. She probably could have done it faster, but was not looking forward to another of Lucy's matchmaking ideas.

"Andrew said you met our cousins in town today," Seth said with a smile.

Heat rose in Mary Jane's cheeks at the memory. "Quite impertinent if I remember correctly," she said with a laugh. "I don't know why the men in your family all think us womenfolk incapable of handling ourselves."

"It's quite the opposite actually. We are accustomed to strong women, we've been raised by them, but we have also been taught that women deserve to be respected, doted on, and appreciated."

Mary Jane didn't say anything. She'd had to be tough and had learned that she couldn't count on a man to take care of them, but she filed Seth's words in her mind to ponder and mull over later and mentally added 'doting' to her list of qualities necessary in a man.

When she rode into the Whisper Ridge stables, she immediately recognized the two horses from town. The Redbournes were most certainly Lucy's guests—at least until they caught up with Malcolm Longhurst. Despite her attraction to Raine Redbourne, she reminded herself that he was a lawman and was not to be trusted at any cost.

CHAPTER SEVEN

"When I get home, I am going to wring his little neck." Raine stared down in disbelief at no less than two dozen envelopes, all addressed to him, spread out across Uncle Hank's desk.

"I thought you would be happy about having so many responses," Lucy said, her brows scrunched together, obviously not understanding what had crawled under his hat.

"Are you sure it was Charcoal, big brother?" Rafe asked. "It sounds more like something Mama would do. Or Hannah."

While it was true, it was something Leah Redbourne would do to try to marry off her last unwed son, the only person who had known about his scribbles was Cole.

"Oh, I'm sure."

"Lucy, this is all very flattering," Raine said, "but I did not place that ad."

"If you didn't write it, then who? It came directly from Redbourne Ranch," she protested.

"I mean, I did write it." He ignored his brother's raised brow. "But it was never meant to be seen by anyone."

Undeterred, Lucy picked up the first one.

"Let's just see what they have to say."

"Let's not," Raine sighed, knowing he wasn't going to win.

"Oh, let's," Rafe said, smiling for the first time since leaving Redbourne Ranch. He swooped over Raine and picked up a small handful of envelopes, then sat down on the double settee couch at the edge of the room beneath the window.

"Lucy," Lucas said with a playful warning, "leave the man alone. If he doesn't want to get married, I'm sure he has his reasons." He pulled his wife down onto his lap and she giggled.

"I remember a time when you were dead set against the notion, Lucas Deardon. It only took a few days for you to change your mind."

"Ah, but the odds were stacked against me. You came to Whisper Ridge. I was done for after that. I highly doubt there is another Lucy Russell hiding somewhere in that correspondence."

"Don't forget, my darling husband, I came to Thistleberry as a mail-order-bride too."

"All right, let's read."

"Traitor," Raine said with playfully narrowed eyes. "I think I'll just head out now."

"You'll do no such thing."

As he watched Lucas and Lucy, he admired their strength. They had been married nearly fifteen years now and had yet to be blessed with a child, but their obvious love for each other was still highly tangible.

A low, hearty whistle accompanied Rafe's first opened letter. He held up a picture of a very respectable young woman, then flipped open her letter to read.

"Dear, Mr. Redbourne. I understand you are looking for a wife …"

Raine groaned, sat down on an upright chair and shook his head. "Please stop," he begged. It had been one thing to entertain the possibility of placing an ad, but something entirely different to actually do it.

"I am a woman of some means, taller than most women, but strong and willing to work hard. If interested in further correspondence—"

Raine grabbed the letter from Rafe's hands.

"This is ludicrous."

The study door opened, and the family's cook stepped inside. "Mr. and Mrs. Deardon, dinner will be on the table in five minutes."

Lucas curled his arms around his wife and hugged her close to him.

"Thank you, Tillie," Lucy giggled again, struggling to get up from her husband's lap. She turned back to look at him. "Dinner awaits."

"Come to think of it, I am pretty hungry," Lucas said, patting his stomach.

The railroad was still a far cry from being completed into the northern territories, so their journey from Stone Creek to Thistleberry had been a new experience for Raine—long and somewhat arduous. They'd been lucky there had been room in the lower decks of the steamboat to transport both of their mounts as they'd had to complete the remainder of their trip from Fort Benton to Thistleberry on horseback.

Thistleberry.

When they'd finally arrived, Rafe hadn't wanted to waste any time in finding Malcolm, and it had taken quite a bit of convincing to get him to stop, get some rest, and eat.

Raine imagined it had been difficult to leave his bride after only one day of being married, but he also understood that his brother felt responsible to bring his childhood friend to justice. Unfortunately, Mal had changed into someone they didn't recognize anymore over the last few years. Because of his greed, at least two men were dead, and he'd nearly killed Tayla.

Rafe needed this.

And Raine needed to be there for his brother, but at the moment, he agreed with Lucas. His stomach also protested hunger.

"Let's eat!"

He was the last one to leave the study. With a single backward glance, he threw the opened letter on top of the others and scoffed. Writing an ad had been a horrible idea. As he moved to close the door behind him, he stopped, looked back at the desk, then strode over and wiped all of them off the side into the wastebasket.

With a satisfied smirk, he closed the door behind him.

The smell of freshly baked bread and savory meat filled the halls as he followed the others through the house and into a dining room which opened up into a space larger than the size of most homes in Silver Falls. As he stepped into the room, Raine's gaze fell on the enormous table in the center which could easily seat twenty people.

Andrew, who was Uncle Hank's youngest and nearly eight years Raine's junior, popped in through the side door and waited for Lucas, Lucy, and Rafe to pass before joining him.

"Granddad built this room because he wanted his whole family to be able to meet together and share a good meal. I don't know that he expected us to grow so quickly. With all the young'uns now, we have more than forty living at Whisper Ridge and we still have to bring in more tables to accommodate everyone for Sunday supper and holidays."

Raine wished he'd had more opportunities to know his granddad. The man had passed away when he was just sixteen, but he was certainly grateful for the inheritance that he had provided for his grandchildren. There had been one stipulation for each of them and that was that they had to be married before their twenty-sixth birthday.

His wedding to Sarah had assured that he would see that inheritance, but he would have gladly given it all up to have his wife and unborn child again by his side. Granddad may have had his quirks, but he'd been a good man who'd loved and wanted the best for his family. He was the kind of man that Raine only hoped to live up to.

"There will only be a few of us tonight, so we'll just eat in here," Andrew said as they passed through the dining hall and into the kitchen. "During the week, everyone usually eats at home."

Raine had forgotten just how many cousins he had on his mother's side. While Leah Redbourne had chosen to move away with his father, Uncle Hank and Uncle Sam had stayed in Thistleberry where they'd each raised four children of their own—all boys. And most of those boys were grown with families of their own and had stayed at Whisper Ridge, building their own homesteads on the vast acreage the property provided.

He thought about his own siblings and imagined it wouldn't be long before they would need to expand Redbourne Ranch in order to accommodate all of their growing families. Levi, Ethan, and Hannah had each already built homesteads of their own on the property, but Elizabeth had hinted that she and Will were looking to return home with their little Calvin, and Rafe and Tayla wanted to be near family once medical school was completed.

"So," Uncle Hank said, walking into the kitchen with Aunt Mara right behind him, "we've had people keeping tabs on this Longhurst fellow." He didn't waste any time as he sat down at the dinner table and leaned back in his chair, folding his hands together on his belly in front of him. "It's a rare occasion to see your name on a wanted poster that comes through here, son," he said. "Sounds like there's a story in there somewhere."

"Yes, sir," Rafe responded, sitting down next to the man.

Lucy caught Raine's eye and then looked at the seat next to her. He chuckled inside, knowing what was in store for him, but he went anyway. He liked Lucy. He'd been forewarned that she'd become an avid matchmaker and fully expected to be coerced into reading each and every one of those letters after dinner.

Once he sat down, Lucy turned in her seat to face him. "So, Uncle Hank tells me that you may be considering taking the sheriff's job here in Thistleberry. Heaven knows we could use a man of your talents—not that there is generally a lot of crime here, but for one reason or another, we can't seem to keep the position filled since Sheriff Jeffers passed on."

To avoid straining his neck to talk back to her, he adjusted his seat enough that he could look at her.

"I'll admit, the idea initially intrigued me, but I don't think this is where I belong. It's too blasted cold up here. It's only October and I saw my breath in full sunlight when we pulled into the ranch. I don't know how you all have survived for so long." He shifted in his seat. "However…"

"I love that there is a 'however,'" Lucy said smiling and leaning in closer.

"However," he started again, "purely out of curiosity, what exactly happened to all the others?"

"Honestly, I think Hank's just picky. Most get fired. He's the head of the town council you know, and he expects a lot out of our civil servants. We've had six in the last four years."

"I would expect nothing less," Raine said. "And what happened to the last one?"

"He's now a territory Marshal," she said with a grin. "Although, in all fairness, before that, he was the deputy for a few years around here."

Raine raised a brow. "Well," he said after a moment's consideration, "for now, I am just here to help Rafe with Malcolm Longhurst. Once that is done, we'll see if a more permanent situation is warranted."

"Fair enough." She nodded emphatically. "So, Mr. Richards is what he calls himself. Mr. Longhurst, I mean. He has been spending a lot of time out at the old mine just behind the MacPherson place."

"And may I ask exactly how you know that?" he asked.

"I have my ways."

Of that, Raine had no doubt.

"He tried to intimidate the MacPherson's into selling him their property and he's come around on more than one occasion inquiring about trying to lease a portion of the land behind Happenstance."

"What would he want with all that land?" Rafe had obviously overheard at least a portion of their conversation and wanted some answers. He leaned forward, his elbows on the table and his hands extended in front of him.

"He claims he's bringing in a herd of longhorns from Texas to cross with local breeds to make a more robust variety," Seth said, "but what Longhurst doesn't realize is that we are a close-knit community, and we all talk to each other."

"And the mine?" Raine asked.

"Word has it that he won it in some poker game," Andrew told them.

"Nothing valuable has come out of that mine in a decade," Hank said. "Don't know what he or anyone else would want with it."

"Isn't that where Cochran and his gang used to hide out?" Andrew asked.

"Those fellas have been gone a long time," Hank said, "though some ruffians have been seen lately in town drinking and causing a bit of a ruckus."

Tillie set a basket full of biscuits on the table in front of Raine and his stomach rumbled again. The buttery warmth wafted into Raine's nostrils, and his mouth began to water. Within moments the entire table was filled with hot shucked corn, fried chicken, potato salad, some sort of meat pie, and custard.

"Do you all eat like this every night?" he asked.

"Nah, sometimes we also have steak or pork cutlets and fresh honeyberry jam."

As if Tillie knew what Andrew was going to say, she brought a bowl of the preserves to the table with a knife and set it down in front of him.

"Ask and ye shall receive, cousin. Ask," Andrew picked up the knife, "and receive." He winked at the cook, who just shook her head with a smile, and then he scooped up a large portion of the jam and smothered it on top of a buttery biscuit.

Rafe returned to his conversation with Uncle Hank and Aunt Mara.

"Lucy," Raine said, "Lucas told me that you are the one who came up with the idea for Happenstance Ranch. I would think that you would all have plenty to do here at Whisper Ridge. Why did you want to start a competing ranch? Tell me more about it."

Lucy beamed.

"Oh, boy," Lucas said with a grin, "now you've done it."

Lucy hit him in the chest with the back of her hand.

He leaned over and kissed his wife on the tip of her nose. "But you are so cute when you talk about it. You just light up, so, by all means, tell the man."

Truthfully, Lucas had expressed how proud he was of his wife, but in the few minutes they'd had to chat, he hadn't wanted to go into details about his wife's new venture, saying he would leave that to her.

"You know our story." She reached out and squeezed Lucas's hand.

Raine nodded. He'd heard his mother recount the story from her letters several times over the years.

"Well, a few years after we were married, I was in town, and I saw an unfamiliar woman, broken down in tears, resting in front of the steps of the General Store with three large travelling cases sitting next to her. I felt bad for the poor thing and when I approached, I discovered that she was from a place called Hartford, back East and she had come west with the promise of matrimony from one of the good citizens in Thistleberry."

"He probably doesn't need *all* the intricate details of the story, my love," Lucas said, leaning forward with an apologetic smile.

"Fine," she said, taking a deep breath and returning her focus to Raine. "You obviously have heard of correspondence courtships or mail-order brides as some are calling them?"

"You know I have," Raine said wryly.

Lucy giggled. "Well, they don't always work out as expected and sometimes that leaves women without means to take care of themselves. Happenstance Ranch provides the displaced girls with jobs, a roof over their heads, and food to eat."

"So, it's a philanthropic venture?" he clarified.

"No, not at all. The ranch is self-sustaining. All of the hired-hands at the ranch are displaced brides or women who have nowhere else to turn."

Raine was trying to envision a group of women trying to take down the bull that had gotten loose from Cole's place a couple months back.

The side door of the house opened, and Seth strode inside, then directly over to his wife who sat at the far end of the long table. He kissed her firmly on the mouth then sat down between her and his mother.

"Did you bring M.J.?" Lucy asked.

"Who's M.J.?" Raine thought he'd had a big family at twenty-five including all the little ones. Whisper Ridge had three families and multiple generations all living at the property. Sometimes it was hard to keep them all straight, but he didn't remember anyone named M.J.

"My foreman," Lucy said with pride. "There's no one better at keeping everything on track and the sheep healthy and happy."

"Can't wait to meet him…er…her. Wait, did you say sheep?"

He had certainly not expected sheep. Most of the cattlemen that he knew wouldn't associate with sheep ranchers if their life depended on it.

"Do you have a problem with sheep, Mr. Redbourne?" The

woman's voice was familiar, but he couldn't place it.

He opened his mouth to answer, but Lucy spoke first.

"Raine, I'd like to introduce you to the foreman at my ranch. M.J. Bennett."

He turned, fully expecting to see a rough burly woman with broad shoulders and a permanent grimace on her face with a thick moustache and a six-gallon hat.

Boy, was he wrong.

There, standing in front of him in denim britches that curved in all the right places, her hands on her hips with a raised brow and narrowed eyes, was the woman he'd lifted on the crate earlier in front of the General Store. His mouth suddenly went dry. Not only did Mary Jane Bennett live at Happenstance Ranch, she ran it.

Impressive.

"M.J., I take it you have already met our cousins Rafe and Raine Redbourne."

"It has been my pleasure, yes. We met in town this afternoon. They were gracious enough to um, load…the back of the wagon."

Raine met her eyes. He could tell she wanted to say something more, but refrained by folding her lips together, then releasing them.

He liked watching them move.

Andrew covered his mouth to hide his chuckle.

Raine pushed his chair back and stood up. "Ma'am," he said with a nod. "It's nice to see you again. I see you made it home all right."

Since the only seat left at the table was the one directly next to him, he pulled the chair out and waited for her to sit. Andrew had warned him that Mary Jane wasn't very keen on chivalry and that she had tried to prove over and again that she didn't need anyone's help—especially a man's, but he couldn't stop himself. His mother had ingrained in him over the years just how a gentleman should act. He knew what he was supposed to do, even when he didn't do it.

"I see you've changed into something a little more…comfortable." Raine raised his glass to wet the cotton that had suddenly formed there.

"Would you have me mending fences and breeding sheep in a dress, Mr. Redbourne?" She wasn't cool exactly, but from her tone he felt like he needed to lighten the conversation.

"On the contrary, Miss Bennett, many of the women in my family prefer to wear trousers and a good button-down while they're working out on the ranch. Believe me, I don't mind one bit."

She glared at him.

He imagined that she had likely expected him to be shocked by her appearance, but it was just the contrary. It gave him a new appreciation for the woman and her mockery of social norms. He liked her.

"Andrew," Hank interrupted whatever little exchange was going on at their end of the table, "would you say grace?"

Once the prayer on the food had been said, Raine was not shy about filling his plate. He was grateful for the opportunity to eat a homecooked meal. One of the drawbacks of being on the road was the lack of culinary variety—although, he had to admit that the food on the steamboat had been better than he'd expected.

Usually, fruit jerky and meat jerky, beans, and an occasional stew were their staples as they rode across the country, but the abundance of food on the table now humbled him and he silently said his own little prayer of gratitude.

He raised a fork to his mouth, the savory aroma of the meat filling him with anticipation as he took his first delectable bite.

"Raine," Lucy said, "Did you know that M.J. came to Thistleberry for much the same reasons I did?"

He looked from one woman to the other, chewing his recent mouthful a little faster.

Mary Jane leaned forward in her chair and threw a look of

warning over at his cousin's wife, but she wasn't deterred.

"She answered an ad much like yours."

Raine coughed, choking down the last bite of meat.

"And look where that got me," Mary Jane said like a true cynic.

He was starting to feel like the foreman had not been invited to dinner for work-related reasons and shifted uncomfortably in his chair. Truth be told, he liked to see independence in a woman, and she was beautiful, he would give her that, but if he was going to get married, it would not be to a woman who didn't want or need him around.

Raine looked over the table where more than a dozen sets of eyes now fell on him.

"What?"

He wanted a plain woman who could provide good conversation and friendship, not someone with whom he would be in a constant battle with or who couldn't let down her guard for five minutes enough to allow a man to help her put crates in a wagon without spewing on about how capable she was on her own. Attractive or not, let her be on her own.

CRACK!

Everyone froze.

CRACK!

"Rafe Redbourne, are you in there?" someone bellowed from outside.

His brother jumped to his feet, his eyes narrowing as they met Raine's.

"Malcolm." He threw his napkin down on the table and pushed his chair back. "Everyone stay inside," he barked as he headed for the front door.

"If you'll excuse me," Raine said with a nod. He reached for his hip, grateful he'd listened to his gut earlier and left his gun holstered. He slipped out the kitchen door, a frosty wind biting at his coatless body. He shook off the chill and quickly made his way around the house.

As he approached the front corner of the homestead, he leaned back against the building and drew his gun.

"Malcolm," Rafe called out from the front door. "You don't want to do this."

His brother's lifelong friend sat mounted on his horse, a rifle in his hand, at the edge of the gate leading up to the house.

"I heard you'd come for me. I figured I could run. Again. Or I could face you like a man."

"Just come home with me, Mal." Rafe had stepped out of the house, his hands raised waist high in front of him, his guns both resting at his sides.

Something wet landed on Raine's cheek and he looked up. Tiny snowflakes drifted on the air, slowly making their way to the earth.

"Where? Redbourne Ranch? That's not my home. Never was." He raised his rifle and Rafe stopped.

Something wasn't right. Mal would never confront his brother straight on without a plan.

A gun cocked behind Raine. The cold metal pressed against the side of his neck sent a shiver down his spine. He started to turn.

"Uh, uh. Stay!"

CHAPTER EIGHT

Everyone scrambled from the table. Seth, Andrew, and Hank each grabbed one of the shotguns or rifles from the rack next to the stairs and after a brief council headed to different parts of the house.

One gun remained on the rack and Mary Jane headed for it.

"M.J., I know you're a good shot, but it's only one man," Mara said with a quieting hand on her arm. "Let them handle it."

"Why? Because they are men? If it's going to take five men to bring down one, I don't think it will hurt to have an extra pair of hands." She didn't have time for this. If she could help, she would.

"Think about Sarah Jane."

"I am." She turned to her boss, "Thank you for inviting me, Lucy. I'll see you later." She went out the same door as Raine. Snow bristled the air. Grateful for her choice of shirts, she shrugged her shoulders for a little added warmth, then headed around the side of the house.

"Uh, uh. Stay!"

She knew that voice.

She stopped a moment to force herself to breathe.

He's dead, she reminded herself. *But his cronies aren't.*

They'd been gone a long time. Why return to Thistleberry now?

Mary Jane gingerly placed one foot in front of the other, careful not to crack a twig or kick a rock that may alert Moses Rigby to her presence. When she stood a mere three feet from the man, she cocked her shotgun and raised it shoulder level, pressing the barrel into the lout's neck.

"What are you doing back here, Moses?"

"Do I know you?" he asked as he raised his hands and whipped around to face her.

Raine relieved him of his gun. "I thought you were told to stay inside."

"Then where would you be?" she shot back.

"Well, if it isn't Mrs. Lionel Cochran." The stench of stale whiskey and malodor stung her nose, and a familiar pulse in her neck spasmed. She hadn't heard that name in a long time and would be just as happy to never hear it again.

"It's Bennett," Mary Jane spat. "I thought you were dead, Rigby. Last time I saw you, you were bleeding pretty good."

"I take it you know this man?" Raine said as he grabbed the man's arm and twisted it behind him.

"Turn around, Rigby," she said, knowing full well he would go wherever Raine moved him now. "You're not getting away this time." She jerked the gun slightly to the side of him, urging him into the front yard.

The musical hum of cocking guns reached her ears. She scanned the yard and saw three ruffians at the mercy of Deardon rifles and was pleased to see Meg and Dahlia, Daniel and Garrett's wives, amongst the men with their weapons all aimed at Malcolm Longhurst.

"Stop here, Rigby," Mary Jane said as she watched the bounty hunter walk slowly toward the man who'd threatened them all.

"Don't do this, Malcolm," Rafe pleaded.

Mr. Longhurst glanced calmly around at all the weapons aimed in his direction. He raised his hands, swung one leg around the back of his horse and slid down. He stared at Rafe, his jaw firm, his eyes scrutinizing.

"Put it down, my friend," Rafe said. "These people don't know you like I do. Don't make it any worse than it already is."

Longhurst, with his hands still in the air, tossed his rifle sideways to the ground. Meg bent quickly down to retrieve the discarded gun.

Rafe walked toward him, his guns still holstered.

"It's not raining this time," Longhurst said.

"And you don't have my wife as a hostage. I don't want to fight you."

"Yes, you do. I've betrayed you. Betrayed my people. You need to fight me."

"Your brother is going to get himself killed," Mary Jane gasped, her shotgun still trained at Rigby's back. "Isn't he supposed to be one of the best?"

"He is," Raine stated, unperturbed. "Watch and learn."

As Rafe took the last step toward the man, he pulled Longhurst into a brotherly hug. The man reached down for the bounty hunter's guns, and then it was over. In the time it took her to blink, the villain lay belly-down on the ground, his arms behind him, and Rafe's knee pressing into the center of his back.

"And *that* is just one of the many reasons he is the best at what he does."

Raine congregated with the others in the center of the yard, pushing Moses ahead of him.

"So, if you don't have a sheriff in town, what do you do with the criminals you catch?" he asked Seth as he guided Rigby to his knees.

Mary Jane kept her shotgun at the ready as she joined the Deardons guarding and binding the hands of the three other ruffians.

"Wire the territory Marshal. Dad has keys to the jail. I suppose we could cart them all into town and keep them there for the night." Seth threw a length of rope to Raine who quickly proceeded to bind Rigby's hands behind him.

"Anybody else feeling like that was a little too easy?" Raine asked as Rafe heaved Mr. Longhurst up from the ground and joined the others.

BOOM!

BOOM! BOOM!

Everyone instinctively ducked, except for Longhurst, whose grin spread wide across his face.

BOOM!

"What in tarnation?" Moses screamed as he hunched down again.

BOOM!

Immense clouds of dust and debris filled the darkening sky to the north.

Longhurst snickered.

"What have you done, Malcolm?" Moses spat.

Mary Jane's throat sunk into her chest, and it took her a moment to find her voice.

Sarah Jane.

She looked up to see Sam Deardon, Lucas's uncle, who had just ridden into the yard past several Deardons as they scattered to the stables for their horses.

The children are all safe with Alex at Whisper Hollow up the road, she reminded herself again, willing her heart to stop racing.

"The children are fine," he confirmed her hope as he met Mary Jane's questioning gaze with a firm nod.

She closed her eyes, breathed out a heavy sigh, and lifted her head heavenward.

Thank you.

"Sounds like someone's blasting up at the old mine," Sam growled as he inspected the unlikely group of hoodlums all clustered together.

All were quiet, exchanging nervous glances with one other, except Longhurst, who appeared calm and collected as he stared blankly in front of him. He didn't say a word, just stood there with a smug smirk on his face.

"Longhurst!" Sam nudged his mount around to face the man.

The criminal glanced up and met his stare, a wry smile still haunting his features.

"I understand you own the rights to the old mine," Sam said, "but would you mind telling me exactly what kind of crazy you have to be to be blasting at this time of night?"

The man's expression converted to a scowl in an instant and he thrust himself toward Sam. Rafe swiftly grabbed him by the arm, halting his enraged friend.

"I'm not crazy!" the man spat through gritted teeth, spittle spraying in front of him.

"Whoa now, Malcolm," Rafe said, his voice low and calm. "What has gotten into you? If you say you're not going mad, then stop acting like it. Answer the man."

Longhurst shot his old friend a look that chilled Mary Jane's bones, but he didn't speak. His brows turned inward, and his lips tightened, his shoulders hunching forward.

"I don't suppose any of you know what's going on?" Sam directed his comments at Moses and his associates.

"Sure do," Moses said, his voice rising slightly in pitch. "We was just being all neighborly like and came out for a visit. I believe our intentions have been gravely misunderstood."

"I mean with the mine." Sam's jaw flexed and an eye twitched.

"Mine?" The two-bit liar asked with scrunched shoulders. "I thought that old thing was closed up ages ago."

Something more was going on than it seemed. Raine was right. Capturing these men had been too easy—especially since the only shots fired had been the first two Mr. Longhurst had discharged to get their attention.

Sam turned to Rafe as he pulled his horse around. "I take it you've got this under control?"

"Yes, sir."

"Good, I'll leave it to you, then."

The huge clouds of debris from the blast lingered on the darkening sky, mixing with the small snowflakes that continued to fall.

"The barn," was all she could force herself to say aloud.

Several mine corridors ran beneath the land on the north end of Happenstance where the women had been working to construct the new winter outbuildings for the sheep. Lissa had been taking the greenhorns up to work on the barn this afternoon. It would have been past quitting time and she prayed that Casey and Astrid had already moved the last flock out of those surrounding fields, and that everyone was all right.

Raine leaned back. "What is it, Mary Jane," he asked, his brow furrowing, his interest genuine.

"We've been working to build the barn." She offered him a little half-smile as she turned to Sam. "I have to check on the girls. I know they usually finish up well before the sun sets, but you know Lissa."

Sam nodded. "I told Philip to head up that way. I'll send him back and he can pick you up."

"I'll take her," Raine offered.

Mary Jane's eyes widened. The idea of riding so close to him terrified her.

"I have my horse—" she said with a step toward the stables.

"No, you don't," Sam said, cutting her off. "It appears these brutes opened all the stable gates here at Whisper Ridge and most of the horses bolted at the sound of gunshots. Looks like Ryder and the boys are working on rounding them up now. I'm afraid those two are the only ones that didn't scatter," he pointed at the two Redbourne mounts that had come out of their stalls, but stood with their ears perked at the gate in front of the house.

Of course.

"It's amazing actually that they stayed put. It would be nice to get some Redbourne-trained horses up here."

She didn't have time to waste. Running to the north pasture beyond Happenstance would take her hours. Thoughts of her friends being hurt pricked her mind.

No time for pride, Mary Jane, she chided herself. *Let him help you.*

"I'll just go with Philip. I don't have time to wait for you to…" her voice trailed when she turned to find Raine emerging from the stables, his saddle in hand.

"All right, Sam." She handed the shotgun she carried up to him, fearing it may go off accidently while she made pace up the road. "Will you tell Mr. Redbourne that I'll be over at your place?" Grateful she had stayed in her working clothes, she started to run. "He can pick me up there," she called back.

By the time she reached Whisper Hollow, Sarah Jane stood on the porch next to Sam's wife, Alex.

"Mama!" the little girl squealed and ran to greet her.

Mary Jane dropped to one knee, her arms wrapping heavily around her four-year-old daughter.

"Mama," she said after a moment, "you're squishing me."

With a relieved laugh, she pushed her little girl away from her just enough that she could kiss all over the child's face.

Sarah Jane giggled wildly until Mary Jane pulled her close for one last squeeze before letting her go.

"Did you hear that boom?" the little girl asked with wide eyes. "It shook the whole…" she opened her arms, stretching as far as she could, "…house, and I wasn't even scared," she said, shaking her head. "Sebastian said that he would protect me." She nodded emphatically. "And I believe him because he's really strong and smart and I think he loves me."

"Oh, you do? Well, then you are both very lucky people."

She loved that Alex's grandchildren had embraced Sarah Jane and made her feel loved—especially little six-year-old

Sebastian.

"Uh, huh."

"Guess what? Aunt Alex let me make my own little scarecrow, but I left it inside. It's not done yet."

Alex had insisted little Sarah Jane call her Aunt Alex like the rest of the children—at least those who didn't call her grandma.

"I'm going to leave you here with her for just a little while longer, okay? So, you can finish. Mama still has a little bit of work to do, but will you show me your scarecrow when I get back?"

The child nodded. "That's okay, Hayden and Sebastian are making paper boats and said they would teach me."

"Good girl," Mary Jane said, reaching out and caressing the ends of the little one's braids.

"Love you, Mama."

"Love you, my angel," she said as she rose to her feet and watched Sarah Jane skip up the steps and past Alex into the house.

Thank you, she mouthed to Alex.

Gratitude consumed her that the children were all safe. Now, she just needed to know her friends were safe too.

Where is he?

She looked down the road anxiously.

Their morning chores at Happenstance came first—feeding, watering, and caring for the sheep. The evening tasks often included cleaning, carding and spinning the wool to be used for making many of the products they sold in town. It was their afternoon responsibilities out at the north pasture that may have put them in harm's way—which was what weighed heavily on her mind.

"Come on!" she said aloud with a little impatient stomp of her foot.

Seconds later, the familiar click of a galloping horse filled the space behind her, and she turned. It didn't look like he was going to slow down much as he extended an arm downward.

Did he really expect that he could lift her up behind him one-handed?

As he reached her, she took a step back.

He pulled around, dismounted, then stepped backward, waiting for her to mount.

He learns quickly.

With a foot in the stirrups, she heaved herself upward only to have the boot slip from beneath her. Before she could hit the ground, he was there in an instant to catch her.

Heat rose in her cheeks as his arm cradled around her.

How are you supposed to show you are capable, Mary Jane, if you can't even keep your foot in a stirrup?

"Are you all right, ma'am?" Raine asked with a voice that could melt butter.

She cleared her throat.

"Yes, I'm fine. I just…" She made the mistake of turning to look up at him. That was twice in a single day, and she had to stop herself from blowing out the breath that caught in her chest.

"Sorry," Raine said, first making sure she was upright, then backing away to give her some room, his hands palm out and up near his shoulders.

Had she really become so closed-minded that she couldn't allow herself to appreciate a man who'd stopped her from falling on her rump?

A lawman, she reminded herself and stuck her foot once again into the saddle, swinging a leg up and over the palomino.

He's a lawman.

Before she could think better of it, she squeezed her knees together and gave a little nudge with her heels to prod the horse forward.

The mare reared, squealing loudly. Mary Jane had to grasp the horse's neck just to remain upright as she leaned forward, nearly in a standing position in the stirrups.

"Shhhh," Raine rushed forward, holding his hand out to the

mare. "Shhh, it's okay, girl. She's not going to steal you away from me to go out on her own into a potentially dangerous situation. No," he said, reaching up to brush the side of the mare's neck. "No woman in her right mind would do that, now would she?"

He did not look at her, but Mary Jane knew exactly what he was trying to say.

The mare touched down and reared again.

"Whoa, girl. Hey. Shhh," Raine coaxed again, taking in an exaggerated breath and exhaling slowly as he reached out for the cheek piece. Finally, the mare's feet touched down to the ground and stayed—though her head bobbed a few more times before she settled completely.

"Stay right where you are, M.J.," he spoke quietly, in a soothing voice, but there was no mistake in his warning.

She stayed.

He blew softly into the mare's nostrils.

Mary Jane raised a brow.

"My sister-in-law taught it to me," Raine said without looking up as if he was used to people questioning his odd tactic. "Don't worry, we'll get her accustomed to your scent soon enough.

She wasn't at all sure she wanted this particular horse to 'know her scent.'

With a gentle pat on the mare's face and jawline, Raine slipped a hand down to the reins and allowed them to slide through his fingers until he reached the stirrups. A moment later, he had pulled himself up behind the saddle, and slipped his arms around her to grasp the leather straps tightly.

Mary Jane reached for the reins, their hands connecting, but he held firmly to the straps. She had to remind herself that this was his horse, and she was merely a passenger. Vulnerability was not one of her strengths and she bit back the need to be in control.

Decidedly, the wellbeing of her friends was more important

than her stupid pride right now. However, in order to avoid leaning back against the stranger, she tried sitting up as straight as possible, but after a few minutes at a decent clip, she found herself thrust backward several times into his firm chest. Finally, she conceded to use him as a physical support, but couldn't help the butterflies that taunted her stomach.

As they approached Happenstance, she pointed to the covered archway leading into the ranches drive, and Raine took them through the gate. The sun had all but fallen behind the mountainside and it was becoming more difficult to make out their surroundings in the growing darkness. She breathed a little easier when the light from a single torch came into view, lighting the south paddock where Evaline's flock was huddled together.

The sound of the shepherdesses singing floated softly on the air as she tried to comfort the sheep.

"It's important that they can see and hear you," Mary Jane said, enjoying the feel of his arms around her, "especially when they are scared."

They had slowed their pace significantly over the last few minutes as they carefully made their way in the dark to avoid endangering his horse.

Why hadn't she thought to grab a lantern?

"I imagine it is very similar to the way you spoke to your horse. We can speak or sing softly to help them feel secure and after a while, they recognize our voices. Wick does that too." She strained her eyes to find the llama assigned to Evaline's flock.

A loud alarm cry sounded even closer than she had expected. They had gotten too close to the paddock fence for Wick's comfort.

"What in the—"

Mary Jane giggled as she leaned forward.

"No harm here, boy," she called out with a sing-song tone to her voice. "I've got a…" she cleared her throat, "friend with me."

She wasn't sure if it was just her imagination, but when he leaned forward, it seemed he squeezed her a little tighter.

"It's just Wick," she assured him. "He's a llama and it's his job to protect the sheep. They make that sound when they sense there may be danger. It's loud and obnoxious, but it gets the job done."

"Who's out there? I'm warning you, I'm armed." While the shepherdess's voice was calm and even, her words betrayed her apprehension.

"It's me, Evaline. M.J!" she called back as loudly as she dared without startling Wick.

"You have llamas here?" Raine asked incredulously, pulling the horse to a stop. "I don't know that I've ever actually seen one. I didn't realize there were any living this far north." His warm breath on the back of her neck sent gooseflesh sprawling down the length of her body.

It took her a moment before she could focus on his statement. When he pulled to a stop, he dismounted and held up a hand for her. She ran to each of the bunkhouses, to the stable, into the main house.

"Empty, all of them."

"M.J.," Evaline reached them with winded breath. She spoke very quickly—though still in quiet, low tones, "Lissa wanted to show Tessa and Judith the progress we've been making on the barn…" she trailed. "They should have been back by now. And—"

She stopped suddenly and stood up straight, glancing between M.J. and Raine.

"Evaline, this is Mr. Raine Redbourne. It's a long story."

"Ma'am," Raine said with that low, rich voice of his.

"Have you seen or heard from Casey and Astrid?"

"Nothing. Last I knew, they were staying out with the rest of the sheep in the north pasture. What's happened, M.J.?"

"It appears that someone is blasting up at the mine. We're headed over there now."

Philip rode up behind them, a couple of lanterns and a lit torch in tow.

"My brothers and a few of the others will join us shortly. It'll be hard to determine the amount of damage that was done in the dark, but we just need to make sure there are no injured cattle." He turned to Mary Jane. "Or sheep," he said with a wink. He lit one of the lanterns and handed it to Raine.

"That sounded like more than just blasting at the mine, M.J. Is everyone all right?" Evaline asked, her demeanor had calmed some.

"That is what we are going to find out, Ev."

"The barn—"

"I know," she said, with a nod. "We'll be back. If Casey and Astrid return with the sheep, have them move the others into the east paddock away from the breeding band. Tell them to stay put and we'll talk when we get back. Stay alert." She climbed back up onto Raine's horse this time without any problems and held her breath for a moment when he swung up into the saddle behind her.

Philip handed her one of the lanterns he'd already lit, and Mary Jane held it out, trying to figure out the position that would offer the most light.

As they turned around, Wick had moved himself between them and the sheep, his ears cupped as he continued to evaluate any threats.

"Good boy," she said as they started back out onto the road toward the barn.

"Where did you get the llamas?" Raine asked as they rode.

"Well, your family, as I am sure you are completely aware, is often blessed with knowing people from all over the world. When he was young, your uncle Hank helped out a man from Peru who was down on his luck. Years later, that man became a wealthy businessman, but he never forgot what Hank had done for him. Every year at Christmastime, he sends unique gifts to the family."

"A llama is certainly unique," Raine said appreciatively.

"The same year I came to Thistleberry, *four* llamas were delivered by some vaqueros from the southern Americas. Hank gave them to Lucy to use at Happenstance and we haven't looked back since."

"Llamas," Raine said, "hmmm," a hint of wonder in his voice. "Who would've guessed?"

It didn't take long to reach the north paddock.

"Whoa," Raine said, pulling the horse to a halt.

Philip followed suit.

"Why are we stopping?"

Raine slid down off the horse, but kept hold of the reins.

"Just how far did the tunnels of the mine run?"

Philip joined him on the ground. "Hard to say, really. It used to produce quite a bit of coal and was busy with miners in and out for a few years, but just about the time Hank and Dad bought the land for Happenstance, there wasn't much more to be had. Miners moved on and within a few months the operation had been abandoned. Why?"

Mary Jane dismounted and joined the men, interested to see what had caught Raine's attention. She couldn't quite make out the barn's frame from this distance in the darkness, but she knew it had to be close. While the soft, whistling breeze carried the snowflakes gently to the ground, she heard a higher-pitched methodical sound that didn't quite fit into the night and she paused to listen more intently.

"I wish I knew how far these tunnels ran."

"Some folks say one goes all the way into town."

"But that would be miles aw—"

With a hand on Raine's arm, Mary Jane turned to him.

"Shhh…Did you hear that?"

They all fell silent to listen.

"Is somebody out there?" It was faint, but definitely the sound of a woman calling out to them from somewhere in the distance.

"Lissa!" Mary Jane yelled as she rushed forward in the direction of her friend's voice.

It has to be.

Raine reached out and caught her by the hand and pulled her back.

"See those cracks in the ground?" He held the lantern lower and pointed to a place just a few feet ahead where several fissures in the ground extended into the darkness, looking as if the earth had split apart like an old pair of trousers.

"The only explanation for that is if we're standing right on top of one of the shaft tunnels. The explosion appears to have compromised the dirt. One wrong step and you could find yourself inside an unstable mineshaft." Raine backed away, pulling Mary Jane along with him until they reached his horse.

When he let go of her hand, she raised it to her chest, surprised by the sudden chill that followed.

"Just how big a blast did this Longhurst fella set?" Philip asked.

"He must have placed charges down several different shafts to cause this much damage." Raine set his lantern on the ground.

"M.J., is that you?" the voice called out again on the wind.

"We're here," a small chorus of voices rang together.

"Mr. Redbourne," she started, taking a step toward him. "Raine, please, I can't just sit back here and do nothing. We have to help them."

"I know." The light from her lantern reflected in his eyes as they met hers—his jawline pulsing, but the corners of his mouth upturned in a heartening smile. "We are going to help them," he assured her.

She believed him.

"But we won't be any good to them if we just rush in without knowing what we're up against." He untied his rope from the back of the mare. "Philip," he called back to his cousin, I'm going to need your help and your rope."

Philip dismounted.

Raine handed the man the bulk of his rope, retaining one end in his hand, then reached into his saddle bag and retrieved what looked like an old harness ring. He tied a knot around the metal hoop, then stretched out his arms, pulling twice the length around him, then secured it back around the ring at his chest. After a quick twist of the rope in each hand, he pulled the corded loops he'd created on each side up and over his shoulders and head, effectively making a harness of sorts around his chest with the supporting ring in the center.

His ingenuity amazed her.

Mary Jane found a shorter length of rope in the mare's saddle bag and attempted to follow his exact movements as Raine proceeded to do the same around his waist and legs using his belt buckle for leverage, but he went too fast for her to replicate it properly.

Once he'd connected the bottom portion of his harness to the top, Raine nodded at Philip, who strung his own rope through the ring at his cousin's chest, knotting it securely.

"Are you sure about this?" he asked.

"M.J.?" Lissa called again, fainter this time.

"We're still here. Who's with you?" Mary Jane called loudly.

"Tessa and Judith!" the two women called out their names in unison.

"We're trapped in the barn," Lissa said. "I've hurt my leg."

Trapped in the barn?

How was that even possible? The building had no enclosed spaces yet. It should have been easy for them to get through various points where the framework was still open. She raised her lantern again and looked around, finally finding what looked like the silhouette of the half-constructed building in the dark.

"Over there," she said to the men as she pointed toward the structure.

Raine looked in that direction and nodded.

Philip let out his rope completely and with the other end, he wrapped it around his waist, then around each of his legs, also creating some sort of harness around his body.

"Tessa, Judith, are either of you hurt?" she asked.

Keep them talking, she reminded herself.

"No."

"No."

"Okay, tell me what happened out here."

Without a word spoken between them, the two men simply nodded at each other and walked forward slowly, but with a wide girth away from the fissures they had come across earlier.

Without warning, the light from Raine's lantern faltered as he staggered. From her position near the horses, it appeared like one of his feet had sunk into the ground and Mary Jane's breath caught in her chest. She didn't know anything about mines or how they worked, except that the miners dug giant tunnels beneath the surface looking for gold, silver, or any other precious metals. Surely, they would not build two shafts so close to each other.

"I'm all right," Raine said loudly. "It's just a depression of some sort. Probably a wagon rut."

She exhaled loudly, relief washing over her. Then, it dawned on her. She and the other women at Happenstance had worked for several days in an attempt to remove a huge boulder at the south edge of the barn's yard, but they had been unsuccessful thus far, only managing to dig mounds of dirt from around it. She'd known it would require the assistance of the Deardons oxen, but had been unwilling to ask for their help. And now, Raine had fallen into one of their trenches. Her face burned with embarrassment, but at least she had pointed them in the right direction.

"What's happening, M.J.? What are you waiting for?" one of the women called out to her.

It was becoming increasingly difficult to make out the words through the progressively intensifying wind.

Snow now came down in blustering sheets. What had started out as small, glistening flakes earlier in the evening continued to grow thicker and wetter with the passing minutes, blanketing the earth in layers of white. Before long, it would be harder for the men to see any of the cracks on the ground in front of them.

"Here it is," Philip said loudly.

Mary Jane held her flickering lantern up a little higher in the hopes of seeing to what Mr. Deardon referred. With an additional ten steps forward, she was able to see the men more clearly, even as the snow hampered her vision.

Raine stood and sidestepped the rut he'd fallen into.

"We're far enough from the mouth of the mine, I don't think there will be another shaft running too close, so, if we just keep moving forward and avoid the width of that shaft, we should be fine," Philip said. He walked around the boulder with his rope to gain the leverage he needed to lower his cousin down into the shaft.

"M.J.," Raine called back to her without turning around. "I need you to keep them talking so I can follow their voices, can you do that?"

She nodded.

No response.

"M.J.?" he called again, glancing over his shoulder.

He can't hear you nod, silly.

"Yes," she blurted awkwardly, then cleared her throat to speak a little louder. "Yes, I can do that."

Dogs barked.

The sheep.

Casey and Astrid were likely out here with the new pups and the other three llamas trying to herd the sheep. They would be completely unaware of the danger in front of them. She needed to warn them not to bring the flock any closer to the barn. A tunnel collapsing beneath them would be disastrous.

"Tessa! Lissa! Judith!" she yelled each of the women's names, hoping it was loud enough to be heard. "We need you to make noise."

Moments later, the women screamed and clapped and banged against something.

Mary Jane strained to see beyond the glow of the lantern she carried and into the darkness. She hoped the new dogs had already been trained the same as the others. She placed two fingers over the edges of her mouth and sounded two short-burst whistles—telling them to stop herding.

"What in tarnation?" Philip exclaimed, obviously more than a little startled.

"Sorry."

Within moments two large white Great Pyrenees dogs came bounding into view, then, almost as quickly as they'd appeared, one disappeared with a yelp against the sound of rocks and dirt caving in.

She gasped, bringing a hand up to her mouth.

Raine paused for a moment and called back.

"Not helping!"

CHAPTER NINE

The snow came much heavier now, but Raine could see a vague outline of the structure he guessed had been the frame of the new barn. He hoped they'd moved far enough away from the cracks they'd found that the earth beneath him would be stable enough to support his weight. It didn't appear that there were any more gaps in the dirt, but he traversed slowly and with extreme caution.

How was it possible to be this cold in October?

He wished he had grabbed his coat on the way out of the house, but he'd been in such a hurry to help Rafe that he'd just ignored the chill, and it hadn't seemed like much of a priority as he was saddling the mare to come up here.

Now, he regretted that decision.

By the time he reached the construction, he held up his lantern to assess how to proceed. While the first few feet of the barn appeared to be intact, the rest lay angled in a dilapidated heap that had fallen into a sinkhole.

"M.J.," one of the women breathed relief.

"Sorry, ma'am, I hate to disappoint, but my name is Raine Redbourne. How many of you are there?"

"Raine, is that really you?"

Tessa.

The Redbourne family had no love for the woman who'd left Rafe on his wedding day, but there wasn't time for past hurts to get in the way of his tasks now.

"Are you all right, Tessa?"

"Oh, thank heaven," she sighed. "It'll be all right, girls. I know him. Knew him."

"Judith and I are fine, but when the backend of the barn collapsed into the ground, Lissa hurt her foot. We've tried to climb out of here, but the walls are too steep and there aren't enough wood pieces to stack."

"And, it's getting cold," another woman said.

"Judith," he assumed, "is that right?" he asked.

"Yes, sir."

He pushed aside a few fallen boards and made his way toward them, testing each step as he went before fully committing. He stopped a few feet from where the floor had given way. He leaned forward, shining his lantern down at them.

Dirty faces with relieved smiles greeted him.

"Thank the good Lord."

He raised the light to look at the woman who now sat on the bottom, leaning against the rubble.

"If you are either the bounty hunter or his brother, I'll marry you right now."

Raine laughed.

"Can you stand?" he asked.

"Of course, I can," she said with determination as she attempted to push herself up from the ground.

"Good. Now, I need you ladies to tell me what you see around you."

They all looked at each other.

"Dirt," one said.

"Rocks and wood."

"Which way does the tunnel run?"

They all looked back and forth at each other.

"What tunnel?"

"It's a hole in the ground, Raine. A big hole, I'll give you that, but there isn't any type of tunnel."

The only explanation for the sinkhole they were in was that the barn had collapsed into one of the blown shafts. However, he guessed the rubble could have formed walls to block off any openings. They were lucky they'd only fallen as far as they had. Most of the mineshafts he'd been in reached far deeper.

He set his lantern down at his feet.

"Are they all right?"

He spun around to find Mary Jane behind him. Unprepared for her closeness, he nearly tumbled backward, but reached out and caught her by the arms to steady himself.

I'm going to strangle Philip, Raine thought as he closed his eyes and took a deep breath as he righted himself. He found he was doing that a lot lately with her around. She was as determined as any woman he'd ever met. He figured he could hardly blame his cousin. She likely would have followed him out here with or without the rope. He dropped his head.

"Mary Jane." What else could he say?

"What?" she said looking up at him, her eyes glowing softly in the lantern's light. "I got myself tied all up," she pointed down the rope secured around her belt. "Once we were able to help the new herding dog out of that hole he'd fallen into, I did what you did with the rope and followed you," she held up a hand as if to quell any protest on his part. "I was careful to step exactly in your tracks. I knew it was safe because, well, you haven't fallen in."

Being out here right now, with him, was anything but safe.

"M.J.?" the women cried from below and, suddenly, the beautiful lady foreman abandoned his arms, falling to her knees, and looked over the edge down at them.

"I'm right here," she said, extending her hand. "We're going to get you out of there, aren't we, Mr. Redbourne?"

"Well, that *is* the plan," Raine said sarcastically as he climbed down onto the splintered floorboards next to her and picked up the lantern, holding it out to assess their options. The sinkhole wasn't very large, perhaps eight by ten feet at most, the floor a jumble of dirt and a few broken wood planks from the collapsed barn.

While they were still fairly close to the surface, the length between Mary Jane's extended hand and Tessa's raised fingertips was still a good foot or so. The women were just too far down to simply reach in and pull out.

"I'm going to have to go in after them."

"I'll do it," Mary Jane said, turning around without hesitation.

Stubborn woman.

He was accustomed to strong women in his life, he preferred them that way, but Mary Jane was something different. She wasn't just strong willed or capable. She was determined to prove herself at every turn.

"I don't think so." He pushed himself to his feet, then bent down, gripping the rope at her waist in his hand and pulled her into a standing position. "Mary Jane?" he said, trying to get her to look at him.

"I'll just—"

"Mary Jane," he coaxed again, this time with a finger below her chin, raising it gently upward. He waited until she met his eyes. "I know you are strong and that you feel responsible for these women."

"Of course, I do. It's my job. And they're family."

"I know." He spoke calmly in much the same way as he spoke to the spirited mare. "But physically, I'm stronger and can get them to safety faster. Let me help you do your job."

She bit the side of her mouth.

"They are going to need you."

With a quick dip of her head, she relented.

"Philip," Raine called, not taking his eyes from M.J.'s.

"Talk to me," Philip called back, "you all right?"

"Yes, but I'm going to need a little help getting these ladies out safely."

His cousin reached the edge of the barn, wrapping the excess rope across the length between his elbow and hand.

"There's not much here to brace against. Are you going in?"

Raine finally pulled his eyes away from Mary Jane and chuckled as the mare moseyed up behind Philip with a soft neigh to let him know she was there.

"Not you too," he said, taking a step toward her. But on the idea of leaving M.J. unattended, he stepped back, placed an arm around her shoulders and guided her to where Philip stood.

"And keep an eye on this one. She is not coming into that hole."

"Understood," he said, holding onto the rope connected to her and smiled.

Raine laughed.

"I'm not going in," Mary Jane reaffirmed with an exasperated raise and drop of her hands.

"Let's not waste any more time. It doesn't look like that snow is going to let up anytime soon." He strode back over to the hole. As he assessed the best way to get down there to help, he realized that the splintered wood from the cracked floorboards might cause a problem for them when they were pulled up. The last thing they needed was for someone to get impaled instead of rescued.

As if Mary Jane understood what he was thinking, she handed him a saw.

"It was with the other tools in Lissa's bag." She pointed at the satchel sitting up against the still solid door frame at the front of the barn.

"Thank you kindly, ma'am." Raine nodded. "Cover your heads, ladies," he told them as he began to saw off the jagged edges.

Philip walked around to the only studded corner that was still even remotely stable and waited.

Once the pointed splinters of the floor had been removed,

Raine attached the still lit lantern to his belt, then turned, backing up slowly to the very edge. He leaned backward enough that he could brace himself up against the side with his feet as Philip carefully lowered him down into the hole. Rubble and mountains of dirt comprised all sides of the hole. It would be difficult to determine which direction the shaft extended in the dark or without digging or prodding. His task right now was simply to get these ladies to safety.

When his feet hit the ground, he called up to Philip.

"Now, just give me a little more slack."

He untied the knots that had attached his cousin's rope to the harness ring at his chest.

"Judith, I presume?" he said to the unhurt woman standing next to Tessa. "Why don't you go first." She was the smallest of the women and would be the easiest to raise up.

She looked down at Lissa, who smiled and nodded before wincing in pain as she sat back down on the rubble.

Raine proceeded to tie a quick harness around Judith's chest and shoulders that would allow Philip to raise her easily without hurting her too much if she were to slip.

"Did you see how I climbed down here?" he asked.

"Yes."

"Okay, my cousin Philip up there, is going to raise you up, but he is going to need your help."

"What do you want me to do?"

He took a pair of gloves from his back pocket and slipped her hands inside.

"Take this rope right here in front of you in your hands like this." He demonstrated.

She did as she was told.

"Now, hold on tight and you are going to walk up the side of this hole." He was grateful that these women were in britches instead of skirts. It would make climbing the walls much easier.

"I don't know if I can do this. The gloves are too big."

"Of course, you can. You are a ranch hand at the great

Happenstance ranch. I'm told you women can do most anything. It doesn't matter if the gloves don't fit perfectly, you just need to be able to grip the rope, can you do that?"

Judith breathed an uneasy giggle but nodded her willingness to try, then tested her grip as she placed one foot up on the wall.

"Now, lean back just a little bit and pull, so Philip there knows you're ready to climb, all right?"

"All right." She leaned back just enough, one booted foot firmly planted against the wall, and pulled on the rope.

Her foot slipped on the rubble, and she tumbled forward, but did not hit the side.

Raine reached out to steady her.

"Let's try again," she said, immediately returning her foot to the wall.

Her gumption surprised him.

With one foot climbing over the other, it wasn't long before she reached the top.

"Now what?" she asked, still leaning backward.

Philip grabbed the knot where the harness rose on the rope and pulled her up and out of sight.

"Judith, I'll need you to toss me down those gloves for the others."

"Is Rafe here?" Tessa asked while they waited.

"He is." Raine did not want to have this conversation.

He caught the gloves mid-air when Judith threw them down.

He watched the top of the hole, waiting for the rope.

"Do you think he will ever be able to forgive me?"

"For what, Tessa? Leaving him on your wedding day? Being disloyal to him with his best friend? Or hanging your own sister out to the wolves?" Raine closed his mouth. He hadn't meant to be so harsh with her.

Philip tossed the rope back down to them.

Tessa remained quiet while he tied a harness around her.

"You know what to do?" he asked with even tones.

She grabbed onto the rope and secured a foot on the wall just like Judith had done, but before she began to climb, she turned to him.

"All of it, Raine. I'm sorry for the hurt I caused Rafe and your whole family. And mine. I truly am. There is no excuse, I just hope that one day, we can be friends again. Family."

Good luck with that.

He thought about the years Rafe had wandered aimlessly, searching for purpose, for acceptance, for meaning.

"Absolution is not mine to give, Tessa. You hurt a lot of people, but if you are sincere, I wouldn't count my brother out."

She gave a sort of half-smile, then pulled on the rope.

"Now," he said, turning to the last of them. "I don't think that way is going to quite work for you."

"I can do it," Lissa said, once again pushing herself up with the help of a wooden plank wedged in the ground.

The motion dislodged the broken wood out from the compacted dirt floor, opening a hole. Lissa gasped as dirt and rocks rushed into a deeper hole below.

Raine braced himself best he could, but the ground was deteriorating quickly beneath them.

Time was running out fast.

He grabbed a piece of wood protruding from the wall to his right, and then another. More dirt and rocks fell through the widening gap now in the center of the shaft.

"What was that?" Philip called to him as he tossed the rope back down. "You all right?"

"We're just fine," he said, hoping to assure the woman whose eyes had already widened significantly even as he fought to retain his footing on a wood beam.

"Tie that thing around us both," she said with false bravado. "We can do it." Even as she spoke, she sucked in a breath when her foot touched the ground beneath her.

It was a good thought, but after rubbing on the edges of the sawed planks, Raine worried that the rope may be compromised too much to hold the both of them. He would rather get Lissa to safety, then he could focus on how to get himself out.

"I'm going to need as much slack as you can offer," he called up to Philip.

Several more yards came down on them.

Raine held out a hand and motioned for Lissa to join him. The injured woman grabbed onto him, gingerly attempting to maneuver over to his side, biting her lip in obvious pain.

With three boards to use, Raine made quick work of lashing them together into a makeshift chair—one for her to sit on and two to protect her back as Philip pulled her up the side. With a rope on either side of her and secured back together a foot or so above her head, he figured it would be the best option.

His cousin peered over the edge and tossed his gloves back down to him.

"Lissa can't walk up the same as the other two," he told him. "Get the mare," Raine instructed. "It'll be easier that way." He tucked his gloves back into his pocket.

Philip disappeared.

The man was a Deardon rancher, he would know what to do.

"You are going to have to hold on with both hands," he told her, showing her the best places for her to grip. "I'm not going to lie, they may get a little scraped up, but this'll work. You'll see."

"Thank you," she said with a hand on his arm. "And about that marriage comment earlier…"

"Let's just focus on getting you out of here." He held the crude chair, bracing it against his knee. "Okay, now I need you to sit down and hold on."

As soon as she was sitting firmly on the seat board, Raine called up to Philip.

"Okay, I'll raise her up as high as I can. You'll have to take it from there."

"We're ready," M.J. called down to him.

Raine tugged on the rope before heaving the woman up to his chest, then onto one shoulder. With the help of those up top and the mare, he found it easier to lift and guide the chair. He raised her above his head and guided it away from the wall for as long as he could manage—until she was completely out of his hands. As the wood scraped against the rock and other debris, dust and unwanted fragments of dead foliage and soil plunged down on top of him. He put up his arms to block most of it from landing on his face. Once the onslaught stopped, he shook the dirt from his hands and brushed at his hair.

Lissa disappeared topside and he let out a long breath in gratitude.

Seconds turned to a minute, then more.

Raine looked down, watching as the floor continued to slowly deteriorate beneath him. Unsure why it hadn't already given way, he perched up as close as he could to the one wall that had proven to be sturdy and waited.

Something was wrong.

"I could sure use that rope down here," he called after a while.

A shadow appeared above him, the light surrounding her from behind casting a glow through her hair. From the silhouette, he knew immediately it was Mary Jane. He shifted enough that the light from the lantern still hanging on his hip illuminated her now dirt-streaked face.

"Is Lissa doing all right?"

"The rope broke."

No fuss, no beating around the bush. Just straight up.

He liked that, just not what she had to say.

"Raine," Philip called, "how is it coming down there?"

"Not too good. There's no other way up," he glanced at the dark, ever-widening hole where Lissa once sat, "and down is not exactly a great option."

"Daniel and Seth should be here soon. I'll ride out to meet them and we'll be back as soon as we can. Just hang on."

Hang on? There was nothing to hang on to.

He shifted uncomfortably and immediately regretted it as his perch collapsed, dirt and rubble rushing around his legs and boots as he swiftly slid towards the gaping hole below. Pushing hard against the flow of soil with his hands he dug into the wall to slow his descent, his heart pounding as he heard the earth and debris hit the ground at the bottom of the black chasm before him. Raine locked his legs as soon as the heels of his boots found the beam he had stood on earlier, panting as he leaned back against the wall. At least he knew the shaft had a bottom now.

"Philip, maybe if we—"

"Mr. Deardon put the girls on the horses and is headed back to Whisper Ridge for help."

"It'll be too late." He squinted, trying to gauge just how far down the floor of the mineshaft sat.

"I have an idea," Mary Jane said, disappearing from sight.

Oh, boy.

What could she possibly be up to now?

A few minutes later, a rope dangled in the air above him and he reached up, barely able to touch the frayed ends with his fingertips. If he jumped, he might be able to grasp the bottom, but he feared there would not be enough lead to allow him to gain any type of real hold. And there was no way Mary Jane would be able to hold his weight, even if he did catch it.

"Thank you for trying, M.J. It's just not long enough."

"I'm not done yet."

He heard the words but couldn't see her. The rope disappeared into the darkness as she pulled it back up.

Before long, the rope dangled down over the edge above, but this time it kept getting longer and longer until the end coiled in a pile at his feet. Raine looked up, turning until the light from his lantern allowed him to see what Mary Jane had done. Just below the sawed floor, was a series of knots. She had tied the two rope pieces together.

"Do you have enough now?" she asked. "Philip took most of the other line with him since it was still tied around his waist. This is all I could salvage from your rope and my harness."

Raine didn't waste any time. He attached the end to the harness ring at his chest.

He yanked on the line, but the slack brought the rest of the rope down on him. He said a quick prayer of thanks that he had tied the rope to himself as he watched the gaping abyss below devour the rope. He wiped the sweat from his brow and pulled the gloves from his back pocket, putting them on before he began to reclaim the rope from the depths of the shaft.

"I wasn't ready yet," Mary Jane said, peeking back over the edge. "Now, throw it back up to me."

"You aren't going to try to pull me out on your own, are you?" He wouldn't put it past her.

"No. Toss it here."

With a secure loop at the end of the rope for added weight and accuracy in throwing, he tossed the line up and she caught it on the first try.

"Now, don't pull until I tell you."

"Yes, ma'am."

Raine glanced around at his immediate surroundings. He needed to settle in for a bit but didn't dare move. The more earth that slipped through the widening cracks, the more he could see that the large support beam on which he stood along with another about four feet from his position were all that stood between him, and a good eight-foot drop into the shaft below. Though grateful for the miners who had shored up this section of ceiling, he couldn't help but wish they'd done a little more.

Crack. The beam beneath his feet splintered, ringing like the sound of a distant gunshot in Raine's ears.

Maybe if I distribute my weight a little more onto the other beam…

He didn't have time to finish that thought as the slack tightened.

"Are you ready?" he called up.

"Yes." Her head appeared over the ledge again. "But I don't have anything or anyone to help me lift, so I secured it to the support studs at the front of the barn. You will have to climb the rope and the wall."

He could do that.

"I can do that."

With the rope securely in his grasp, he took the first step up the wall. Hand over hand he climbed, making significant progress, until he'd nearly arrived at the top. With no one to raise the rope to chest level, he wouldn't be able to walk himself out.

Every step loosened a little more dirt and debris beneath his feet, but his body was just too far away. The closer he pulled along the rope, the harder it was to maintain his footing. He was running out of time. With a firm grip on his lifeline, he took a deep breath, lunging forward to gain some leverage with his arm on the ledge, but the accumulated snow made it too slippery to gain any traction. His feet lost their hold, and he clung to the rope even tighter as he swung away from the barn floor.

Mary Jane grabbed hold of his shirt and pulled him toward her.

Creak.

Raine's eyes followed the rope to the stud where she had secured it. It was bent under his weight and looked like it may snap at any moment. He lunged at the barn floor again with his arm and scrambled to get his foot up over the ledge, but even with her help, it was just not enough.

Crack. The stud broke.

It was no use.

He could not maintain his grasp on the floorboards and slipped.

Mary Jane screamed as she clutched tighter onto his shirt. By some miracle she was able to hold him in place—until the large stud slammed into the back of her, sliding her across the floor, and she tumbled over the edge with him, clinging to his body.

At least I will break her fall.

He closed his eyes.

Seconds passed like the world had slowed to a stop.

Wood splintered.

The partial barn roof crashed to the floor.

Walls and beams and trusses from the remaining sections of the barn collapsed in on top of them as they fell.

Raine wrapped his arms around Mary Jane, hoping to offer some last moments of comfort in their dire predicament.

They barreled through the shored-up support beams, the impact thrusting the air from his lungs as they continued to fall.

All in a moment, pain seared through his underarms and chest as they were brought to an abrupt halt.

He couldn't breathe.

He leaned backward, opening his eyes to the tunnel walls rising around them, still illuminated by his lantern's light.

They were alive.

He didn't know how that was possible, but he immediately closed his eyes in a prayer of gratitude as he willed himself to breathe. It took a moment for him to gain his bearings as air suddenly flooded his lungs, but the action stabbed at his chest with each intake of breath.

He exhaled raggedly and looked upward.

It appeared the span of the support beam to which Mary Jane had tied the rope was wider than the opening to the crevice and served as an anchor, preventing them from falling any farther than the length of the extended rope, stopping just short of the mineshaft floor. The beam was cracked in the center where the rope had been secured, but it had not broken.

Raine's legs dangled below him, his arms wrapped fully around Mary Jane who gripped him even tighter. He reached up and brushed a strand of her hair away from his nose, noting how snugly her face had buried into the gap between his neck and shoulder.

The light illuminated a section of fraying rope just below the knot that Mary Jane had tied. He glanced down to gauge the distance of the next fall. Already surprised the lantern still held its flame, he noted how important that light would be in the depths of the mine. With one arm still around the woman, he reached down for the base of the lantern at his side with the other and cradled it in one gloved hand as he raised it as high as he could manage.

Snap.

The rope broke.

Thud.

"Ouch," he said aloud as he landed on his rump but started to laugh as he set the lantern upright, then leaned back against the ground and sprawled flat. Every movement hurt, every breath threatened to be his last, but they'd fallen another foot.

One foot.

The rope had stopped them less than one foot from the ground.

Mary Jane sat upright, roaming her hands over her arms, her legs, her torso.

"Certainly, this can't be heaven?"

"Nope."

"We can't be—"

"Yep."

"But, how?"

Raine pointed up at the beam that now crossed the hole, preventing the roof and rest of the building from tumbling down on top of them.

"God must think you're something pretty special," he said, wincing at the pain even his speech produced. Mary Jane wasn't wearing a harness. She had nothing to protect her in a fall. Except him.

"I wish that were true." There was a slight catch in her voice.

All humor left him, and he propped himself up onto his elbows.

"From what I've seen," he said, "I know it is," he said with a pained groan.

"You're hurt!" Mary Jane exclaimed, scooting closer to him.

"Ah, it's nothing a hot bath and a good night's sleep won't cure."

She swatted playfully at him with the back of her hand.

He chuckled lightly.

"Ow," he grunted again.

Mary Jane dropped her hands into her lap. "Well, what do we do now?"

Raine laid back again against the ground. "I figure we wait until help comes or find our way out."

"What do you mean?" she asked. "How are we supposed to find our way out?"

He attempted to sit up, but it nearly clipped his breath again, so he focused on his breathing—in and out several times—before his next effort. With a loud exhalation, he braced himself for the burst of agony that was sure to follow, and with a determined grunt, sat up. His knees were bent, his arms supporting him with fists pressing fervently into the ground.

"At the risk of sounding like an incapable fool, I have no idea exactly what to say or exactly what to do right now," she said, turning to face him. "I *don't* know exactly what to say and I *don't* know exactly what to do."

"Well…darlin', that makes two of us," he admitted, throwing the stick he'd been playing with on the ground.

"Thank you for helping me."

A few moments of silence passed between them.

"Was that hard to say?" Raine asked with a grin.

"Excruciating," Mary Jane laughed. "Seriously, we could have died tonight, but here we are." She glanced around. "Wherever this is."

"The night is still young."

CHAPTER TEN

"Any ideas on how we're going to get ourselves out of here?" Mary Jane asked, her eyes searching his for any hint of his ingenuity, though the limited lantern's glow made it difficult. "And how on earth are we not dead?

"I told you, God—"

"It's not that I'm so special, Mr. Redbourne, but He did give me something mighty special to hold on to. To live for." Sarah Jane's face filled Mary Jane's mind and she glanced upward.

Thank you. Again.

"Now," Raine said, struggling to get to his feet, "what do you say we move before that beam up there can't stop the roofing from caving in on us?"

"But if we move, how will they ever find us?"

"Have a little faith, M.J." He removed his gloves and reached up to untie the knots of the harness, but from the sudden wince, she guessed him to be in a lot of pain.

"Here, let me help." She smiled to herself as she thought about what she would have done had the roles been reversed. Would she have allowed him to help?

Probably not.

She barely knew the man. No lawman she'd ever known had been trustworthy, so why did she trust him? And why did he affect her so?

Her fingers trembled slightly as she reached up to undo the first knot. The cold had stiffened her fingers and she found it difficult to bend them adequately enough to complete her task. After a few moments of fidgeting with the knot, Raine placed his hands over hers.

"Leave them be. We'll remove it when we get out of here." He cupped her hands in his, raised them to his mouth, and breathed warm air onto them. "Your hands are freezing."

She'd hardly noticed until she'd tried to do something with them.

"Here." He reached into his back pocket to retrieve his gloves, then slid them onto her hands. "They may be a bit large for your hands, but they will protect them from the crisp night air."

Speechless.

Even though the Deardon men were all cattle-ranchers, they'd always been the chivalrous type. She had no doubt that any one of them would have done as Raine had in helping Tessa, Judith, and Lissa get out of that hole, but there was something about him that intrigued her.

Alarm bells sounded in her ears, but tonight, she would choose to ignore them. She liked Raine Redbourne—was grateful to him at least—and figured he deserved her respect, if not her trust.

At least until he proved otherwise.

A lawman. She snorted.

"Did you say something?" he asked as he wrapped the remainder of the rope around his waist.

"No, nothing."

He removed the lantern from his belt, holding it up with one hand, then grabbed hold of hers with the other.

"Shall we?"

She hesitated, then looked back up at the opening where they had fallen in. The last thing she wanted was to wait for the rest of the barn to fall in on them, but she couldn't help but wonder what dangers lurked inside a tunnel that had just been blown up.

"I'm right here with you." Raine reached out and took her by the hand, guiding her through the tunnels. As they passed through the first narrowed hallway, the acrid stench of smoke and gunpowder filled her nostrils. Mountains of rubble and fallen supports lined what was left of the mineshaft.

Small fires burned randomly around every corner.

"That's good," he said, motioning to the flames. "It means air is reaching these corridors." He held the lantern a little higher, then glanced from one direction to the next.

"How is it even possible that the lantern didn't break in the fall?"

"Lucky, I guess," he said, plowing ahead.

'Thank you for not saying that other thing."

He looked down at her and smiled.

"I am afraid, however, that our luck is about to burn out." Raine stopped and held up the light—the flame growing in spurts, then fading to a dull glow. "The glass may not have broken, but I'm guessing this lantern hasn't been refilled in a while."

"So, are you saying we are going to be stuck down here in complete darkness?"

"I'm saying we need to move a little faster while we still can." She could hear the worry in his voice.

"Maybe we should just turn back," but even as she said it, a thundering crash sounded from somewhere behind them.

"Was that—?"

Raine raised the lantern again, inspecting the walls of the tunnel. "Why don't you sit down here for a moment and rest? We have to be getting close."

"No. You're right," she said, raising her chin and straightening her shoulders. "We need to get out of here. Sitting down and waiting for any length of time is not going to help us do that."

Something slithered past her foot sending a cold chill down her spine.

"Let's move a little faster, shall we?" she said, imitating his earlier choice of words.

Raine stopped and leaned up against the wall, pulling Mary Jane with him and pouted his lips at her in a hushing manner as if to tell her to stay quiet.

A dull, yellow light came from just ahead.

Raine extinguished theirs.

"What in tarnation happened in here, Mundy?"

"It had to have been Longhurst, boss. He wasn't too happy that you double-crossed him."

She wanted to protest that the men may be able to help them get out of the mine, but at the mention of Longhurst's name she froze.

"Who are they?" she whispered.

"AAAAAAAAARGGG," a man shouted. There was a small crash and then another. "It's gone. It's all gone."

The hollow sound of metal clanked against the walls as if things were being thrown around the chamber.

"Longhurst will pay for this. Where did you say he went?"

I know that voice, Mary Jane realized, but she couldn't place it.

Raine looked back at her but didn't say a word.

"He took Moses and a few others to go call out that bounty hunter who came into town today."

"What bounty hunter?"

"Reef or Rawfay. I don't really remember. It's the one who's been after him for a while."

"Rafe Redbourne is here? In Thistleberry?"

"That's what he said, boss."

"And just where is our good friend, *Mr. Redbourne,* staying?" the man asked.

Good friend? Mary Beth glanced at the back of Raine's head, apprehension filling her belly. She assumed by the man's tone he was not at all friends with anyone, but she'd been burned by assumptions before. She knew nothing about these Redbourne men—other than they were Deardon kin, but she'd known too many black sheep to put much stock in that.

What are you thinking, foolish girl? The man just saved your life.

"Whisper Ridge, I reckon."

Mary Jane gasped, then quickly covered her mouth.

"What was that?" the man asked, the sound of a cocking gun accompanying his question.

Raine drew the revolver holstered arm's length down his right leg and held it up near his face.

She needed to get home, to warn them. Her family. To protect her daughter.

"Holes is opening up all over from the blast, boss, and everything is collapsing into the tunnels. Just like that crash we heard a few minutes ago. With the weather like it is, the wind has been blowing through this and whistling through that—playing havoc on all of us. Sounds like ghosts."

Silence followed for some time.

"The only ghost in here will be Cletus's, poor fella. Too bad you had to go and throw that coal torpedo into the fire, Cletus. Blew up more than half the mine." The man tsked. "Looks like it hurts."

A dreadful groan was the only response.

Mary Jane's mind raced as the realization hit her—someone had been in the mine when it exploded. And had lived.

"Can't exactly leave him here to tell anyone, now can we?"

CRACK!

Mary Jane silenced the scream in her throat. She slipped her hand from Raine's and placed it on top of her other one over her mouth for extra caution that any whimper would go unheard.

"Do you think Longhurst will talk, boss?"

"I think he's dug his own grave, but I wouldn't be surprised if they encounter a little trouble in their travels."

"What do you want us to do?"

As they spoke, it sounded like they were getting farther and farther away.

"What about the payday, boss?"

"Unfortunately, we just lost any clue we had to it's whereabouts and the only man who knew its location is singing in the devil's choir with Cletus there. We'll have to find it another way."

"If Moses and the others got caught, we'll be down to just the four of us."

"Then, we'd better get to work. First thing tomorrow, come back and get this place boarded up. Or blown up if you prefer. It's too dark to do much about it tonight. Now, come on. We've got work to do, boys."

As the light began to move, Raine slipped his hand over hers once again—its warmth contrasting heavily with the icy chill of hers. Her chest tightened at the thought of being enveloped in complete darkness.

In moments, the men and all their precious light was gone. She'd never been in dark this tangible and it weighed her down with thoughts of gloom. Choking down a sob, she leaned against Raine, desperately clinging to his hand as she closed her eyes and took a deep breath to calm herself.

Someone will come, she repeated. Please, God, send someone. Anyone.

It was impossible to tell how long they'd been waiting there. Mary Jane fought the exhaustion that now seemed to be penetrating even the deepest recesses of her soul. Her legs cramped, her feet hurt, and she needed some air.

When she glanced up to where Raine was, she realized how much he must be struggling. He'd taken the brunt of their fall, but had still managed to get up and walk away.

The way out had to be close—a crisp, cool breeze rushed down the tunnel in waves, pushing her hair back away from her face.

Raine let go of her hand.

She hadn't realized just how much comfort his warmth had offered her.

A flicker sparked the air, but extinguished as quickly as it had appeared.

There it was again.

"The lantern won't light," he whispered back to her.

A warm, yellow glow slowly crept into the mineshaft, chasing the oppressive blackness away. Men's voices echoed faintly in the corridor, growing louder with every passing moment. Mary Jane took a step out from where they stood, but Raine reached out to pull her back. Through the dim light, she could now make out his features. He placed a finger over his mouth as he took a step forward, his gun drawn as he pulled her along behind him.

Mary Jane appreciated that he acted with caution and had no doubts that he would do everything in his power to keep her safe from whatever loomed ahead.

"Over here!" someone shouted.

They were very close now.

Raine extended an arm to nestle her up against the wall behind him. She nearly tripped over something at her feet but was still able to keep herself upright.

For a moment, Mary Jane wished she'd held on to that shotgun instead of giving it to Sam—though, it never would have made it this far. Distinguishing between what was just rubble or not was nearly impossible with just the low light from ahead. She supposed that even a rock could come in handy under these circumstances if she needed to defend herself, so she quickly dropped down on her haunches and began to feel around.

"Are you all right?" Raine asked in a whisper.

"Yes."

Most of the pebbles were too small to be of any consequence, but with a slight movement to her left, she grazed something more substantial. It felt like wood. A plank maybe? It was too small to be a beam. She ran her hand along the smooth wood finish until her fingers tapped cold, hard metal—she discovered a blunt edge on one side and a pointed edge on the other.

A pickax.

She wrapped her hand around the handle and slowly stood back up, holding it at the neck against her body. Raine nodded at her approvingly and moved slowly and cautiously toward the light and voices ahead.

A new torch sizzled to life and a warm light moved its way toward them.

Raine's body tensed in front of her, and Mary Jane gripped her weapon tighter. The light stopped advancing. They slowly crept along the wall, stopping at the corner of the crossroad.

"He's dead."

That's Lucas.

Relief washed over her.

"Looks pretty burned up."

"But I don't think that's what killed him." This man's voice was similar to Raine's. It had to be his brother.

Mary Jane relaxed her hold on the ax and allowed it to slip through her fingers to the floor, wincing as a sliver of the wood embedded in her finger with the action.

"It's Lucas," she repeated aloud, leaving her place behind Raine and stepping around the corner into the lighted tunnel.

The near deafening clicks of several guns cocking froze her to her position.

"Stop!" Raine said, jumping in front of her, his revolver holstered, his hands in the air. "I don't think your wife would appreciate losing her foreman this way."

Seconds later, Rafe grabbed his brother and enveloped him

in a bear-sized hug.

"I knew it!" he said with an actual smile on his normally scowling face. "I knew you'd find a way out."

Raine grunted.

"Did you see them?"

Rafe pulled away.

"You're hurt." He glanced over at Mary Jane for confirmation.

She nodded.

"Did you see them?" Raine asked again.

"See who?"

"There were at least two men. They left minutes before you got here. One of them did that." He pointed at the dead man lying in the passageway. "I'm surprised you didn't hear the gunshot."

"Oh, we heard it all right," Andrew said, stepping up from behind Rafe. "This one couldn't get here fast enough after that. But we didn't see anyone."

"They can't have gotten too far, but I don't have my horse."

"It's dark," Rafe said. "You're hurt. Let's get you back to Whisper Ridge where I can take a better look at you." Concern etched the bounty hunter's brow.

"I'll be fine. It's nothing a good night's sleep and a hot bath won't cure."

He can't be serious, Mary Jane thought. She'd heard him say the same thing once before, but realized he was deflecting.

"I think he may have broken a rib. Or worse," she said. "Shouldn't we at least call on the doctor?"

The men all looked at each other and chuckled.

Odd response.

Raine gingerly reached back toward her, his face contorting slightly in a wince, and placed an arm over Mary Jane's shoulder. "It's a long story," he said with a tired smile. "I'll tell you on the way."

She wasn't sure exactly how he expected to do that. He was

certainly in no condition to walk all the way back—even to Happenstance—especially in this weather, and Philip had taken his mare back with the girls.

The sheep.

Suddenly, Mary Jane realized that three of their four bands had been scattered.

"Oh, and M.J.," Andrew said, "Dad and Lucy are working with Casey and Astrid on rounding up the sheep and getting them to safer ground along with Carl and the other llamas. Just thought you'd want to know."

If she didn't know any better, she would swear that the Deardons all had a knack for reading minds.

"Casey and Astrid are safe?"

"Yes."

"And the new Pyrenees?"

"Philip said one of them fell into a hole but, thanks to your quick thinking, didn't appear to be hurt."

That was good to hear.

"Dropping a wide board for him to crawl out was brilliant."

"Thank you."

Raine squeezed her shoulder, and started toward the entrance behind Rafe, but she paused where Lucas knelt.

"We'll take care of this," Lucas said, motioning to the body.

She didn't want to look. Couldn't. What if she knew him?

"Get M.J. on home."

Raine nodded.

As they passed, it was the man's boot that caught her eye.

She knew those boots.

He'd been there.

That night.

He'd been with Moses and Lionel, when Lionel…

She shook her head against the memories.

The name Cletus hadn't rung a bell before, but she would never forget those boots with their red strap and carved designs.

Why are they back?

"I'm telling you, Raine," Hank said as he pounded another nail into a new fencepost. "You are the right man for the job. There hasn't been a lot of crime here—not for several years, but if this mine character, who could just kill a suffering man like that in cold blood, isn't just passing through, there could be a real danger to the folks here."

Daytime had shed some light on the realization of just how much damage had been done by the explosion. Several brand-new ravines of different depths and widths now extended out from the mouth of the mine into the surrounding properties, including the north pasture of the little sheep ranch, and up onto the base of the mountain.

Many fences, trees, and other structures like the barn had fallen victim. It would be impossible for them to see the extent of it until the snow melted—which wasn't likely to happen until spring, or so he'd been told. For now, they would have to attempt to put fences up around the holes to prevent livestock from getting hurt.

Raine looked up at his uncle, whose unspoken question still lingered on the air.

"It gets awfully cold up here," Raine said, pulling his coat a little tighter around him—wincing at the pain even the slightest movement caused to his chest and shoulders, but shrugged it off as he walked over to the large pile of posts they'd hauled in with the horses.

"It does at that," Hank said, firmly shaking the post he'd just finished setting. "But Thistleberry does come with other benefits."

"You know I don't care about the money."

"I wasn't talking about money."

His uncle patted him on the shoulder, somehow knowing what was on his mind.

Ouch.

"I saw the way you looked at M.J. Bennett last night when you dropped her off up at Happenstance."

"And how was that?"

"Like she was the only star in your sky."

A lawman.

In Thistleberry.

Raine ran through several reasons why moving up to Montana would be good for him and then weighed those against the reasons it wouldn't. After hours of laying new fence, it shouldn't have surprised him at the effort it now took for him to carry a single log to where his uncle had begun to chip away at the cold ground for the last post of the day.

By tonight, he likely wouldn't be able to move.

Who would want a sheriff like that? He didn't feel like he could do justice to the badge in his current condition, so, if he could just continue to avoid the question, maybe Hank would forget the notion.

"So, how 'bout it?"

Raine shook his head, it was never like his uncle to beat around the bush.

However, the cold and his injuries were not the only issues. A certain woman with dark cinnamon brown hair and eyes the same color as today's wintery sky had somehow gotten under his skin, which just made it plain uncomfortable.

"Don't you think you need someone who can haul more than one measly stick over to build a fence?"

"Eh, you're just sore is all. You'll heal. Word is around town, you're a hero."

His bruises were quite extensive all along his shoulders, back, and chest, and every muscle in his body protested all movement. He wished he could get to the healing part already.

"I'm no hero. Just in the right place when they needed some help is all."

"There are several women back at Happenstance who'd beg

to differ." Hank breathed a chuckle as he took the 'stick' from Raine and shoved it down into the hole to check the fit.

"I think at this point, you'd have your pick."

"Of what?"

Hank placed a hand on top of his post and looked at him with a raised brow.

"What?"

His uncle's eyes bored into him.

"Truth is, I *had* entertained the idea of getting married again, but—"

"Lucy showed me all those letters you've been gettin' in response to your ad." He returned to his work, a smile touching his face.

Raine rolled his eyes. If Cole only knew what he had coming to him.

"That's just it. I tossed around the idea but realized that I don't have what they want."

Hank stopped what he was doing and stood up straight to look him in the face.

"Now, I don't know what imaginings you've had in that pretty little head of yours, but the women around here are acting like pups at feedin' time. You have exactly what they are looking for…money, a decent face, moral character. What more do they need?"

"Love." The words nearly got caught in his throat. "Someone to adore them like you do Aunt Mara or like Dad does Mama."

"I've known you your entire life, Raine Jameson Redbourne. No one has demonstrated love more than what you have for people. You're one of those men who make it that much harder on the rest of us." Hank reached down and grabbed a strand of wire from the large bolt at his feet.

What was he supposed to say to that?

"Don't make it awkward, son."

Raine laughed.

"My mama taught me to be a gentleman is all."

"I would like to settle down in a place of my own. Maybe not somewhere with this much snow in October, mind you," he added with a chuckle, "but somewhere."

"And why can't that somewhere be here?"

"It's—"

"Cold, I know. One of these days you're going to have to stop making excuses as to why you're not living and live."

"I guess they do all sound like excuses. Sorry." Raine sat down on the stump they'd been using to trim the fence posts. "I thought it would be easy just to marry for companionship. These women who enter into a correspondence courtship have lofty dreams of finding true love only to have their hopes squashed for one reason or another. Isn't that why Lucy created Happenstance. A place where those women with crushed dreams could start over and make a way for themselves in this world without a man?"

"And M.J.?"

"She is strong and beautiful and…" he laughed to himself, "capable. She deserves someone who will…"

"Look at her like she's the only star in his sky?"

Even as he opened his mouth to protest, he knew it was no use. Hank was right. Mary Jane was just the kind of woman he would want. The kind Sarah might even have approved of.

"Well, I think Andrew would marry her tomorrow if he could." He glanced up at the opposite end of the pasture where Seth, Lindon, and Andrew were working on constructing that side of the fence.

"It's a wonder my youngest son is yet unattached—not for lack of trying on his mother's part. Or Lucy's."

Raine breathed in deeply, the crisp air filling his lungs with much needed refreshment.

"I'll do it." His voice was quiet. He could hardly believe he'd said the words aloud.

"What was that?" Hank asked.

Certain his uncle had heard him the first time, he raised a brow.

So did Hank.

They stared at each other just a few moments before Raine gave in and restated what he had tried to say before.

"I'll come on as sheriff in Thistleberry—at least through Christmas." He figured if he hadn't found what he'd been looking for by then, it was time to look someplace else. "I think we can rid this town of a few ruffians in that time."

Hank looked as if he might counter, but a huge grin broke across his face instead.

"I think you'll find that it's not just that Thistleberry needs you, but that you need Thistleberry too."

"Don't make me regret the choice before I've even started."

Hank laughed.

"I know you said that you had a place for me at Whisper Ridge, and I am mighty grateful for your generosity…"

"But you don't want to stay there?"

It was counterintuitive, he knew, to be away from his family—especially since he'd likely only be in town for a couple of months, but something told him there was a reason.

"It's funny that you feel that way. Mrs. Isaacson owns the farm just southwest of Happenstance. She's getting on in years and has decided to go visit her daughter in the Arizona Territory for the winter. She's been looking for someone who might take care of the place and her animals while she's gone. You interested?"

"I'd like to look at the place first, but it sounds like this Mrs. Isaacson may have a new tenant." He stopped for a moment. "Just how many animals?"

"The Isaacsons used to have one of the biggest cattle herds in the territory, but once Gerard passed away and their only daughter moved away after she married, Mrs. Isaacson sold off all her stock except for a dairy cow, a dozen or so chickens, a pig named Fred, a pair of goats, two horses, and she may still have a few…" he cleared his throat, "sheep."

Raine raised a brow, but didn't say anything.

"The house is in good condition, but there are some things you'll have to do for winter."

He looked at Hank, his eyes narrowing.

"Just what's in this for you?" he asked.

Hank scratched at the growing beard on his chin. "Well, I get you to stay in town."

"And?"

"And…now I don't have to take care of those blasted sheep. When Ida couldn't find someone to watch the place, she left it to me and Sam to look after. Now, we won't have to." He shrugged.

Raine laughed loudly.

The rivalry between cattlemen and sheepherders was no secret in any part of the country. The cowboys often complained of decimated grazing land and barren landscapes where the smaller, closely congregated animals had devoured the sprouting grasses and shrubbery before they'd had a chance to take root—a sentiment the sheepherders did not share.

"How many is a few exactly?"

"Oh, not a lot. Less than a dozen I'd say."

"Why don't you just bring them up here to be with the other sheep?"

"Well, now, you'd think that would be a good solution, but apparently, there are different types of sheep with different types of wool and…I guess it's a little like cattle ranching. You don't want to mix our Angus herds with the Herefords if you want to bring in top dollar."

A loud groan gurgled in Raine's stomach.

"I'm sure we can discuss all the details later. What do you say we get back up to Whisper Ridge? Lucy said they are going to have hot stew, fresh rolls, and a variety of pies for us tonight before we…before Rafe," he corrected, "leaves in the morning with Mr. Longhurst."

Sheriff in Thistleberrry. Montana.

As a sharp gust of wind whipped by his face, he scrunched his shoulders, and immediately regretted the action. Pain was quickly becoming like an unwelcome companion.

"What am I doing?" he said aloud.

"Making a difference," Hank called back to him. "You're making a difference."

Making a difference, he repeated in his mind. *I like that.*

CHAPTER ELEVEN

Mary Jane opened one eye from sleep to look at the little girl whose fingers kneaded her cheeks and face. Blessed warm light poured in through the front window casting its creamy glow across the greyed wooden floorboards.

"Do you like them, mama?" Sarah Jane asked, stepping backward into the sun's streaming rays.

How had she slept so late?

It had been a long time since she had not awoken long before the sun came up, and she did a quick assessment of everything that needed to be done for the day. After the incident at the mine, she'd been instructed to rest, but today she needed to focus on getting back to work. She wiped the sleep from her eyes and turned, pushing herself into a seated position on the couch.

"Well, good morning, little lady. Might I say that you are the most beautiful little ranch hand I have ever seen?" she told the youngster who'd donned a pair of too-large boy's britches, a dusty red button-down shirt, and black suspenders that had been fastened properly.

Sarah Jane beamed at the praise. The light cast a glow

around the girl's freshly braided hair.

"Did Sebastian lend you some of his clothes?"

"Yes."

"Well, that was awfully kind of him."

"Yes, it was. And Miss Tessa brushed my hair. Do you like it?" She ran her hands down the sides of her pigtails.

"I do."

Tessa and Judith seemed to be recovering from their ordeal quickly, and she was grateful for the efforts they had made on her behalf in watching over little Sarah Jane yesterday and this morning.

Mary Jane noticed that while the trousers her daughter wore were several inches too long for her and had been rolled up at the bottom, little pink toes peeked out from beneath the material.

"What do you say to us finding your boots and covering those adorable little piggies of yours before they freeze to the floor?" Mary Jane rushed off the couch and scooped her daughter up into her arms, whirling her around in circles and evoking the most adorable giggles.

Knock. Knock.

Without waiting for a response, Evaline opened the door and stepped into the house with a small Shropshire lamb at her heels.

"This little lady must have wandered into our field behind the Isaacson place. She looks just like a little shadow following ours around that I didn't notice her mingling with our flock until we arrived in the west paddock."

Sarah Jane squealed at the sight of it and squirmed to get down. She ran over to the lamb, that stood nearly her waist height.

"Thanks, Evaline. I'll see that she gets back over to Mrs. Isaacson's this afternoon. I've told her time and again that she needs to hire a shepherd or a ranch hand to help out around the place. It's just getting harder for her to get out and take care of all those animals by herself."

"I imagine it's even harder with the snow." Evaline stepped out the door but stopped before closing it. "All of our ewes are back together in the west pasture. I've looked them all over and don't see any major injuries, but we're short three."

It had been too much to hope that they would come out of the incident without a loss.

"With Lissa down, we'll need a couple of the others to go back out there, now that the snow has let up, and search for them. It's likely that they…well, you know." She took off her hat and hit it against her thigh and was quiet for a moment.

Of all the women who had come through Happenstance, Evaline had taken the most to the sheep. She was the kind of shepherd that every owner would want to watch over their flocks. She knew them all. Loved them. It was a luxury that being foreman didn't allow.

Lucy had said she'd wanted to keep the ranch small, but in order to best accommodate the growing number of women searching for place and employment—no longer just the displaced brides—they'd had to talk more about expansion.

"The rams have the east paddock to themselves until we can figure out what else to do. I have to tell you, M.J., losing that barn was—"

"I know," Mary Jane said, still unable to fathom everything that had happened in the last couple of days.

At least Mr. Longhurst would no longer be a threat. The Redbournes would be leaving this morning to take him back to Kansas where he was also wanted for several outstanding crimes. She ignored the pang of regret that danced in her belly as she thought about the man who'd saved her life.

Heat flooded her cheeks at the thought of his arms around her as they rode up to the north pasture. How she'd rested against the comfort of his broad chest. The feel of her hand in his as he'd guided her through the unstable mineshafts. And how he'd looked at her that night when they'd said goodbye. She bit her lip at the thought of his smile.

Stop it right now, Mary Jane Bennett. He's gone.

Raine would never know how grateful she was that her daughter would not have to grow up without a mother.

"M.J., are you all right?" Evaline asked, reaching out and touching her arm.

"What? Oh, yes, I am fine. Sorry. Um, thank you for all you do with the flock. I don't know what we would do without your skills and dedication."

"Thank you for teaching me. I don't know where I would be without them. Happenstance saved me and I will be forever grateful."

The tupping season had just come to a close. They'd anticipated a growth in terms of doubling the size of their current flock—taking into account multiple births and loss to predators or other ailments.

"Lucy should be stopping by sometime this morning, and we can discuss our options for rebuilding, though with snow already here, we may have to consider some alternative solutions that will get us by until spring."

Baaaa.

"It doesn't look like the other sheep, mama," Sarah Jane said as she reached out to pet the little one. But then she stopped, her hand mid-air, and looked back at her mother, bringing the tip of her thumb between her teeth and her eyes open wide and pleading as she silently begged permission to touch the baby sheep.

Mary Jane nodded with a breathy laugh, and the child quickly reached out again and rubbed the top of the lamb's head.

"That's because she's newer than all of our lambs around here and a different breed than ours."

Sarah Jane seemed satisfied with the answer as she happily turned back to her new friend.

Happenstance raised Rambouillet sheep for their fine high-quality wool, but this was a little Shropshire Down lamb. Where the wool from their sheep was often used to make the softest of shawls, scarves, and blankets, the Shropshire's wool was spun for use on some of the sturdier wares like socks, gloves, or saddle blankets.

Over the last couple of years, Mrs. Isaacson had hired Astrid and Casey to sheer her flock. The woman had then sold the wool to Happenstance at a considerably discounted rate.

"It's really surprising that one so young could have gotten this far away from his flock without Mrs. Isaacson noticing." Mary Jane crouched down next to her daughter and reached up to pet her too.

The little lamb nudged her hand and wiggled her head until M.J. gave in and scratched behind her ears, evoking a giggle from both mother and daughter.

"Well, aren't you a little escape artist? How did you get away from your mama, hmmmm? Don't you know you'll catch your death out in the cold like this all alone?"

The lamb didn't look like she could be older than a month or two. Something must have happened for her to have wandered off away from her mama and the rest of her flock. It still amazed her that Mrs. Isaacson's sheep could lamb more than once a year. To see one so small at this time of year was unheard of with most breeds.

Mary Jane smiled as she watched her daughter press into the lamb's side and throw her arms around its neck.

"She's so cute," Sarah Jane said in her sweet little four-year-old voice. She looked up. "Can we keep her, mama? Please?"

The little lamb nuzzled up against the girl, clamoring for continued affection.

"Well then, if you'll take care of it, I've got work to get back to," Evaline said.

Mary Jane nodded.

"Thanks, Miss Evvy," Sarah Jane said. "She's wonderful."

Evaline chuckled, patted the little girl on the top of her head. "Best get some boots on those feet, S.J., or you're going to freeze those toes right off," she said with a wink.

"I know you're just joshin'."

The woman raised an inquisitive brow.

Sarah Jane's eyes grew wide as she looked up at her.

"Yes, ma'am," she said quickly, and with one more rub on the lamb's head, dashed into the back room in search of her socks and boots.

Mary Jane leaned down and scooped the baby into her arms, surprised at its light weight. She figured she couldn't weigh more than fifteen or twenty pounds.

"He's shivering. I'll get him some warm milk and a blanket. I'm sure my daughter won't mind if we keep him around for a bit."

Evaline nodded. As she headed back out to the pasture, the two dogs Mary Jane hadn't noticed moments before, stood up and followed her just as if they were a part of the flock. The woman certainly had a way with animals.

"Awww," Sarah Jane exclaimed with delight as she emerged from the bedroom.

"We're not keeping her," Mary Jane cautioned, seeing the excitement in her daughter's eyes. "She doesn't belong to us. But we need to give her something to eat and keep her warm until we can take her home. Can you help me do that?"

The little girl's head bobbed up and down with exaggerated movements. She immediately walked over to and climbed up on the couch, her little boots barely extending past the cushions, and she held out her arms.

When Mary Jane set the lamb on her lap, Sarah Jane reached for the blanket that now draped over the couch arm and wrapped it around the small animal.

It didn't take long to warm some milk. Mary Jane poured the liquid into a glass bottle with a narrow neck and reached into the drawer to retrieve one of the leather toppers that could be secured with twine over the opening for easy dispersal. Satisfied it wouldn't leak onto her daughter, she handed the device to

Sarah Jane, who quickly placed it up against the lamb's mouth.

Within moments the lamb was suckling the makeshift teat.

A flash of color splashed across the windowpane. Mary Jane walked over and opened the door before Lucy'd had a chance to knock. She was surprised to see Sam accompanying her.

"I didn't realize this was going to be such a formal meeting," she said, very aware she still wore the clothing she'd been in yesterday. She could see strands of her hair falling in front of her face and knew she must look a sight.

"Lucy asked for help finding a new location to build a new barn," Sam said, taking off his hat and running his fingers through his graying hair. "And I think we've found the perfect location."

"So, you think we can still build before winter?" she asked.

"Yes. Well, sort of."

For four years now, Mary Jane had prided herself on being able to do anything her male counterparts could do. As much as she wished she and the other women at Happenstance could build a barn before winter really set in, she knew she needed to humble herself enough to accept any help that was offered. It wasn't so much that she was against men as it was that she didn't want anyone to see her as a helpless female.

"We will have to move the site away from the north pasture for obvious reasons," Lucy said with a quick glance at Mary Jane as she moved to the table where she rolled out a large, weathered map that nearly covered the entirety of the tabletop. The name Thistleberry was written in big, pronounced, black lettering that had been centered above the drawings.

Mary Jane had seen plenty of maps before, and was often fascinated by their texture and detail, but had never taken the time to sit down and actually learn how to read them. She'd never had to.

"As we were reviewing the acreage at Happenstance, we were reminded that our lands extend all the way over here." She ran her finger across a large open space on the map with a few lines of different colors. "And, here, smack dab in the middle of this field is an old, dilapidated barn that was built before the Deardons purchased the land."

"Okay, I can see that we are looking at a map of Thistleberry, but I'm not sure what any of these things mean," Mary Jane said, reaching out to touch the ornate drawing.

Lucy smiled her understanding.

"It's been a long time since Lucas taught me how to read these maps. I forget that not everyone understands these scribbles any more than I did. Let me show you."

"Thank you." Up to this point, there had been no reason for Mary Jane to learn. School had offered her many things as a part of her education, but cartography the professors had generally reserved for the boys.

If she was going to purchase her own place for her and Sarah Jane, knowing the details of maps would come in handy, so there was no better time to start learning than now.

"Okay, see this?" Lucy pointed to a small square on the map. "And these?" She swirled her finger at several other small squares in the same vicinity. "Those are the various homesteads at Whisper Ridge. Hank's Place, Sam's, Gabe's, and mine. Obviously, it hasn't been updated to include the rest. But this," she pointed to another square just a few inches from the others and a long rectangular box right next to it, "represents the Happenstance homestead, here, and the row of bunkhouses outside."

Mary Jane nodded. It actually made sense to her.

"And all of this," Lucy waved her hand across a huge portion of the map with clustered lines, pencil shading, and highlighted contours with names of rivers and valleys written across it, "represents our land. Well, most of it. These lines here are property lines and as you can see…"

"Whisper Ridge should have its own map," Mary Jane said with an uneasy laugh.

"Well, that's true." She glanced over at Sam. "Your daddy

did buy up most of the valley when the Deardons first arrived in the territory." She turned back to M.J. "I feel very blessed that Sam and Hank were gracious enough to sell us enough land to give Happenstance a good chance at survival."

"Don't let Lucy fool you," Sam said with a nod. "She can hold her own and be quite persuasive when she knows what she wants."

"I guess that's true too," Lucy responded sheepishly. "And what I want right now is to fix up the old barn that sits in the good one hundred and sixty acres aligning with the northeast corner of Mrs. Isaacson's place."

"One-hundred and sixty acres?" Mary Jane knew exactly how big the Happenstance lands were from riding them so often, but admittedly, she was unsure how her knowledge translated into acreage. "Are you referring to the fenced meadow south of the west pasture?"

"Yes, you know the place." Lucy clapped her hands in front of her, the excitement evident in her voice.

Mary Jane definitely knew the place.

Rumor had it that Mrs. Isaacson was looking to sell her farm. Mary Jane had dreamed of purchasing the place and having Lucy as her neighbor, not her boss. She'd ridden through that pasture many times, often pausing near the fence line to wave at the aging widow. And, on more than one occasion, she had ridden around to help the woman with her chores. But even with saving more than half her earnings every month, she was still a far cry from that goal, unless she could secure a loan from the bank.

"The majority of that section of property," Lucy continued, "actually extends all the way up the mountain, which could be used as additional grazing land for the flock, but there is plenty of space there for another barn, food shelter, and shepherd's accommodations far away from the repercussions of the mine explosion."

Of course, the Deardons own the mountain. She couldn't

be too surprised about that.

"Honestly, just having a place for the flocks to go when the weather is bad will be such a blessing. And if you think that old barn can be fixed up before the next big snow, I say we do it. I'm sure if we could build in quarters for Evaline, she would be ever grateful."

"I'll go speak with Myron Fawcett at the mill about securing the lumber we'll need to get it done," Sam said, returning his hat to his head. "A few of the men are over helping the MacPhersons harvest what's left of their corn and finish up their winter wheat planting."

"The Fall Harvest Festival is in just a couple of days and a lot of folks are worried that their crops may not make it until then."

"This last snow took us all by surprise, but thanks to you," Sam looked down at Lucy, "most of Whisper Ridge's winter stores and preparations were completed weeks ago. So, while we've moved our efforts into helping our neighbors catch up, family comes first." He winked at his niece. "Daniel, Garrett, and Kieran should be back by weeks end from moving the herds into their winter pastures."

Mary Jane had only gotten to know a handful of the Deardon men as her responsibilities usually kept her busy working at Happenstance and spending time with her daughter, except for an occasional trip into town to sell the goods and wares the ranch produced. She recognized the names of the men he mentioned as two of his sons and one of Hank's, but she didn't know any of them.

"Between you and the other hands from Happenstance, all of us at Whisper Ridge, and a few fellas from town, I think we can get that barn put back together in no time—barring any more snow between now and Saturday."

Mary Jane had counted herself very blessed that Lucy had designated the main homestead at Happenstance as quarters for the foreman. It had been a good home for her and her daughter, but sometimes, she had to remind herself that the ranch didn't belong to her.

Someday.

It still amazed her how far a little money, resources, and a whole lot of gumption could get a person. There was no deterring Lucy Deardon from what she wanted—at least the things under her control. They needed a barn, and she'd done everything in her power to make sure they were going to get one.

"I thought we could do it in conjunction with the Harvest Festival," Lucy said. "Everyone was already planning on getting together then and we are always involved in a project of one type or another."

"Two days?" Mary Jane looked incredulously at the woman.

"Yes! Two days."

"With that, I'd better get a move on. I hope the mill will have everything we need." Sam raised his hat at the ladies and walked out the door.

"Will you have some time today or tomorrow to ride out there and see what you think?" Lucy asked. "Maybe you can come up with some ideas on how we will be able to add on come spring."

"I'm already heading out to Mrs. Isaacson's place this afternoon to return her lamb." Mary Jane looked over at the couch to find that Sarah Jane had fallen back to sleep with her arm around the little lamb, whose head nestled snugly in the crook of the sweet girl's neck.

"Oh, now isn't that the sweetest thing I've ever seen?" Lucy's hand rested at her chest.

It had to be hard for Lucy seeing all the youngsters running around the ranch.

She put an arm around her boss and friend. After a few moments, Lucy looked up at Mary Jane.

"How on earth did one of Mrs. Isaacson's lambs get all the way over here?" she whispered.

"That's a really good question. One I hope to find the answer to this afternoon."

Lucy stepped over to the table and rolled up the map.

"Thank you for everything you do here at Happenstance, M.J. You're a true godsend. I don't know if I could have pulled it off in the beginning without you, but because of you, we've been able to help dozens of women. I'm still holding out hope that you will find your happily ever after."

Mary Jane thought about that for a moment.

"I don't want a happily ever after. I want a still-loves-and-adores-you-after-you've-worn-the-same-clothes-for-days ever after."

"Do you still have your list?"

"Yep."

"How long has it been since you looked at it."

After her husband had been killed the day after they were married, she'd made a list of things that a man would have to have or be in order for her to take a chance again.

"It's been a while." Mary Jane paused a moment, then narrowed her eyes at Lucy. "Why? What are you up to?"

"Nothing. Of consequence."

"Lucy Russell Deardon, what *are* you up to?" she repeated.

"Have you made your pies yet for the festival?" Lucy asked, completely avoiding the question.

She'd nearly forgotten that she'd promised the mayor, Hank, that she would enter the pie baking contest. She'd have to bake one to be tasted by the judges and one to be auctioned off at the end of the night.

"Let me know if you have any changes or suggestions for what you'd like to see for the barn plans once you are able to go out and look at the property," Lucy said as she opened the door. "Goodbye." She turned around to face Mary Jane with a mischievous smirk and slowly pulled the door closed behind her.

"Bye," she called after her.

While Sarah Jane slept on the couch, Mary Jane ran into the bedroom to change her clothes. As she caught sight of herself in the mirror, her shoulders slumped and she closed her eyes with a shake of her head, embarrassed that anyone had seen her in such a state.

She reached for the towel on the edge of the washbasin and gave herself a quick spit bath before pulling a pair of denims from her wardrobe. As she went to close the closet doors, a simple cream skirt covered in blue cornflowers caught her attention. She opened the door wide and pulled it out for closer inspection.

Generally, Mary Jane only wore a dress when she went to town, but maybe today would be a little different. She returned the denims to their stack and took down the skirt, pairing it with a pretty blue blouse with three quarter length sleeves Lucy had given her for her birthday. She held it up against herself in the mirror. Her smile quickly turned to a grimace at the sight of her unkempt hair.

With one quick movement, she pulled the tie from the end of her braid and tousled through the curls that had formed before grabbing the boar bristle brush on the shelf below and tugged it through the snarls, brushing until the wisps became too unmanageable to control and pulled it back once again with a tie.

Once dressed, she pulled a wide, plain brown corset belt from the dresser drawer, wrapped it around her waist, and exhaled. With one last glance in the mirror, she pinched her cheeks for some added color and went out to find the lamb evacuating her bowels in small pellets on the floor by the stone fireplace.

"I guess she needed the privy." Sarah Jane held up her hands with a shrug.

"Go get the shovel," Mary Jane instructed, trying hard not to laugh at Sarah Jane's little shoulders hunched over as she walked to the back door before she disappeared outside.

"We're going to get you back home to your mama." A stray strand of hair fell into M.J.'s face and she blew it back out of the side of her mouth. She grabbed the scrub bucket from behind the door and filled it with fresh water and newly batched washing soap.

When Sarah Jane returned, she dutifully scraped up the pellets, her bottom lip turning downward into a self-pitying pout, and gingerly walked back to the door she had left open. She trudged out into the yard several feet, then tossed her small load over the corral fence.

Mary Jane got down onto her hands and knees and proceeded to scrub the small area where the droppings had fallen. Luckily, the lamb was old enough that it hadn't made much of a mess.

"Come on, little one," she called out to her daughter who seemed to be dragging her feet on the way back in. "We're going to go for a ride."

Through the door, she could see the countenance on Sarah Jane's face change in an instant. The little girl ran to the tool shed, then returned with haste.

"Where are we going?" she asked innocently.

"We're going to return the lamb to Mrs. Isaacson." Mary Jane threw the water from the bucket out the back door.

"Thanks."

Mary Jane gasped, bringing one hand up to cover her mouth. Then, her eyes widened in surprise and heat rose in her cheeks.

"What are *you* doing here?"

CHAPTER TWELVE

Raine wiped soapy water from his eyes and spit it from his mouth. Not quite the greeting he had expected from the woman. He retrieved his handkerchief and removed his hat as he stepped up onto the solitary step and cleared his throat.

Mary Jane's eyes widened, and her lips pursed in a poor attempt at concealing her laughter.

Did she know how beautiful she was?

"I'm glad that you find my current predicament funny," he said with a raised brow.

A little girl in britches and braids stepped out from behind her.

"That's because it *is* funny," the child said with a giggle. "Why did you step out in front of the wash water, silly?" She placed her hands on her hips.

Raine opened his mouth to respond, but nothing came. He looked up at Mary Jane who just shrugged with a half-hearted, possibly apologetic smile.

"It's all right," the little girl said, pulling back on the suspenders she wore, "it coulda been worse. It coulda been the lamb droppings I threw out earlier."

Snap. She let go.

As if on cue, a little black lamb appeared next to them, trying to wiggle past, but the girl wrapped her arms around its neck.

Unable to conceal his mirth, Raine breathed out a chuckle. Who was this child?

"Oh, no you don't," she said. "You're going back where you came from."

She reminded Raine of Hannah when she was three or four—bossy and full of spunk.

"Mr. Redbourne," Mary Jane said, clearing the laughter from her voice and biting the inside of her cheek, "I'm sorry, is something wrong?"

"No, ma'am," he said, wiping a rogue droplet of water from his brow with his handkerchief, "I'm just looking for Lucy and I was told she'd come up here to speak with you."

"You always call at the back door?" she asked.

"I just saw that the door was open is all. I apologize, ma'am, if—"

"Please, I jest," she reached out and touched his arm. "You just missed her. I'm actually surprised you didn't see her on your way over. Is there something I can do for you?"

"I appreciate that, ma'am, but I'll keep looking. I'd just like to thank her for her hospitality before heading out."

The lamb broke free from the little girl's grasp and ran out into the yard with the child chasing after it. The snow had all but melted along the pathway leaving a lot of puddles and mud in its wake.

Raine laughed.

"She is plain delightful if you ask me."

"Thank you. She can be a handful, but I like that she's learning to think for herself. Excuse me," Mary Jane said as she leaned to the side to look past him at the girl, "Sarah Jane Bennett, you bring that lamb back in here before you both are covered in mud."

Raine froze and all levity drained from him. His chest pounded with an intensity he hadn't felt in a long while.

The little girl's name was *Sarah.*

"Yes, Mama!" she said, heaving the lamb up into her arms and plodding back toward the house.

And she was M.J.'s daughter.

"All right, well, thank you again, ma'am," Raine said with a light raise of his hat, his mouth dry and his heart racing. "I'll just be on my way." He turned to leave, pausing only long enough to stop his head from swirling and claim his balance.

"Uh, Mr. Redbourne," Mary Jane called after him.

He turned, not sure he could trust himself to stand and face her.

Get it together, Redbourne.

"If I didn't get a chance to tell you the other night," she said, wringing her hands together and biting her lip, "thank you." A genuine smile lit her eyes, contrasting starkly with her dark hair. "Thank you for risking your life to save Tessa and Judith and Lissa." She paused a moment and then looked up at him straight in the face, her voice softening. "And me. Thank you for bringing me home safe to my little Sarah Jane."

A warm, peaceful feeling washed over him, like a reassuring hand had rested on his shoulder and calmed him. He barely even noticed the cold of the wet shirt against his skin, and he wasn't quite sure what to make of it. For years he had carried the weight of loss in his heart and suddenly, in a moment, all that changed. His burden had been lifted—if only for a time.

He didn't know what to say.

"It was my pleasure, ma'am. I'm just glad everyone's all right. Sorry about the barn, though. Wasn't much we could do to save that."

"Not to worry, Lucy always has a contingency plan, and this time is no different."

"Mama," Sarah Jane said, tugging on her mother's skirt.

"Yes, love?"

"Are we still going for a ride?"

"Yes, love."

"Well, I'm sorry to have bothered you, ma'am. There is a lot of work to be done and I best be getting at it."

"Can you say goodbye to Mr. Redbourne?"

"Bye, mister." She rushed forward and wrapped her arms around his legs.

He was speechless.

It had been a long while since he'd been around children, and suddenly he missed playing with his nephews something fierce. They hadn't had any little girls in the family until his baby sister, Hannah, had delivered little Eliza earlier this year. The realization hit him that she was going to grow up in Kansas at Redbourne Ranch and if he chose to stay in Thistleberry, he wouldn't be able to watch her grow up, her first day of school, or her first beau, and it tugged on his heartstrings more than a little. It would just mean that Levi would have to work even harder to get the railroad all the way into Helena sooner rather than later to condense the trip to a few days. Maybe he could even be convinced to move the line even closer to Thistleberry.

"I'm sorry," Mary Jane mouthed as the little girl clung to him.

It hadn't escaped him that his new little niece shared a name with these two beauties.

Jane.

When the little girl let go, she craned her neck back to look up at him.

"You're still wet," she said with a scrunched nose. "You better change into something warm before you catch your death."

Raine and Mary Jane both laughed. She'd obviously heard the phrase a time or two before.

"You are wise beyond your years, young lady."

"S.J., love, if you still want to go for that ride, you'll need your coat."

She sucked in a quick, surprised breath, and disappeared, only to reappear a moment later.

"Goodbye," she said, peeking out from behind the door, and disappearing again.

"Take care, M.J."

"It's Mary Jane. And be safe in your travels, Mr. Redbourne" she said, leaning forward and placing a kiss on his cheek.

When he reached the fence where he'd left the mare, she twisted her head and nickered softly. He rubbed her nose.

"I know, girl. I think it's time to take that risk. What do you think?"

The horse nickered again and Raine chuckled.

"All in good time," he said, patting her on the side, then climbed up into the saddle.

"All in good time."

As he glanced back at the house, Mary Jane leaned against the doorframe and waved.

Maybe, just maybe, he'd get a second chance at love.

It didn't take long for him to reach the Isaacson farm. Hank had provided clear directions and told him that he would stop by later in the evening to make sure he was getting settled in.

It had been hard saying goodbye to Rafe this morning, but his little brother had been anxious to get on the road and home to his new bride. Raine could hardly blame him. He remembered all too well how difficult it had been for him to be away from Sarah.

With someone out there looking to get to Malcolm, Rafe had taken extra precautions and had altered his route home. And Raine prayed his brother's trip would be without incident.

He took a deep breath as he pulled up in front of the large white farmhouse. Hank had given him a laundry list of things that needed to be done around the place and since he couldn't assume his new position as sheriff until all the town voted on his appointment at Saturday's harvest festival, he thought he'd get to work cleaning up the place.

Before dismounting, he sat a moment, taking in the property with its perfect combination of mountain and valley. Vast foliage and towering trees accented the immediate landscape around the house, but it opened up into a large, fenced meadow to the south behind the barn, which most certainly would need some work before the next storm rolled in, and several surrounding acres now dotted with grazing sheep.

Sheep.

He shook his head.

His understanding was that the property comprised a mere fifty some odd acres of land nestled up against the base of the mountainside, but the majority of outbuildings huddled close to the main house. At first glance, he spotted a stable big enough for five or six horses, a chicken coop, a dairy shed, and a large pig pen complete with a shelter that also needed some attention and a good sized black and white Hampshire pig.

"You must be Fred," he said aloud as he dismounted.

Compared with growing up at a place like Redbourne Ranch or staying with family in places like Whisper Ridge, he was used to things being much more spread out, but the quaint scene of this little farmhouse endeared him a little to the simpler view.

Two border collies barked as they ran up to greet him from the fields.

"Okay," he said, scratching one of them behind the ears, "which one of you is Rudy and which is Bo?"

It suddenly occurred to him that he'd neglected to ask about where the dogs slept or what they were accustomed to eating. Seamus, the Redbourne's dog, had his own room out in the barn, but on occasion could easily have been found snuggled up with his sister, Hannah, in her room. But Seamus was not a herding dog. At least not anymore.

After a few minutes of play, they returned to the flock. He'd heard mentioned a few times over the years that some herding dogs lived amongst the animals they protected and couldn't help but wonder if that was the case with Rudy and Bo.

As he made his way over to the stables, he reached up and plucked a single apple from the overhang of a tree. The snow didn't appear to have affected the rest of the crop, but several fruits had fallen to the ground and would need to be cleared out. Once in the stable, two massive Clydesdales greeted him with interest, looking up from their feed and nickering softly.

"Howdy, boys."

As Raine opened the stall gate closest to the door, he found that fresh hay had already been laid on the floor and a bucket of water had been filled and hung from the wall alongside a separate bucket of feed.

"Much obliged, Uncle Sam," he said, brushing the side of the mare with his hand. "Now, be nice to these gentlemen," he told the mare, realizing he still hadn't come up with a name for her. "We don't know how long we're going to be here."

He unfastened his bedroll and travelling bag from the back of the horse, contemplating a good name for her, but when she nudged his hand in search of that apple, he chuckled. "It'll keep." He slipped the fruit into her mouth and rubbed her nose. "I'm off to see exactly what I've gotten myself into."

As he climbed the porch stairs, one creaked and he began making mental notes of things to add to Hank's list. He took note of two rocking chairs that had been placed overlooking the yard on the covered porch that wrapped around more than half of the house.

Raine set his belongings inside the door and did a quick survey of the interior. He could see that Mrs. Isaacson had taken great care in keeping it clean and tidy. Though much of it didn't suit him, with the floral papered walls and pastel colors, he appreciated the structure and design of the home.

His eyes were drawn to a grand piano at the far end of the house, and in moments he found himself sitting down on the bench and raising the fall board. He pressed down one key, then another, plucking out a tune his mother had taught him years ago. Next to the piano sat a beautiful, but worn, violin. It had been too long since he'd played. He abandoned his place at the keys and picked up the small instrument admiring the great detail that had gone into the woodwork.

Moo.

Cluck. Cluck.

Baaa.

The sound of the farm seemed to come to life at that moment and he laughed, setting the fiddle back on its rack. They'd told him that Sam had already milked the cow this morning, so he didn't think she would be ready again until suppertime, but he thought he ought to head out to check on all the animals and assess his newfound responsibilities.

He grabbed a pencil, gloves, and the folded list from his bag that had been carefully written in beautiful handwriting on pink floral print stationary. Mrs. Isaacson must have given the instructions to Hank, having faith he would be able to find someone to stay on through the winter.

As he walked back outside and headed for the porch steps, he did a quick read down the list, adding a few more items as he went.

"Stair, shelter—What in the…?" He scrambled for a moment against whatever had attacked him, slipping on the still frozen section of the porch that was still shaded from the afternoon sun. When he was free of its entanglement, he realized it was just a wooded vine that drooped from the roof over that side of the porch stairs.

When he reached the bottom of the steps, he turned and looked at the roof to see that the vine extended across the entirety of the roof and down one side of the house.

"Get rid of vines," he added to the list.

After walking the perimeter of the house, he'd only found a couple more things that needed any real attention, so he tucked the paper in his back pocket, took off his heavy coat, rolled up his sleeves, and donned his gloves.

"There's no time like the present."

The old tool shed that leaned up against the stables promised to hold everything he needed, and he was not disappointed. It was filled with all sorts of tools—some of which he'd never seen the likes of before. For now, all he would need was a good rake, shovel, and possibly an ax to get rid of those unsightly vines.

A two-horse wagon in the distance caught his eye. Since the road ended at the farmhouse, he decided whomever it was must have not been informed of Mrs. Isaacson's travel plans. While much of the snow had already begun to melt over the traversed terrain, he imagined that before long, a sleigh would be needed in place of a buckboard for visits, trips into town, or in any circumstances where horseback riding would not be sufficient.

With one eye on the incoming visitors, he retrieved the rake and began to gather the apples that had fallen to the ground. Then, one by one, he tossed several of them into Fred's pen. The pig ran to the fence snorting and grunting, obviously excited for the treat. It would feast like a king for the next day or two.

"Ouch." Raine exclaimed as one of the apples dropped onto his head.

He looked up and realized the remaining fruit would need to be picked sooner rather than later or he would risk losing the goods all together. He imagined there were a few bushels full left hanging from the branches. It was a lot of apples for just one man, but he figured he could eat them, dry them, and be downright neighborly and take some over to Miss Bennett and her daughter.

He smiled at the thought.

Three empty stacked bushel baskets sat in the tool shed alongside a tall ladder. He spotted an ax lying next to two different size shovels and decided he would get to those vines on the roof as soon as he was finished. In a matter of minutes, the upper half of the ladder disappeared into the branches of the trees. He propped the ax up next to the stairs, then with a bushel basket in one hand, Raine tested each rung as he climbed up to the top of the ladder where the tree's limbs yielded several clusters of apples.

He bit into one. They wouldn't be any good to anyone if he picked them while they were still frozen, but to his delight, they had sufficiently thawed. The flavor was crisp and slightly tart. Upon confirming they were good, he got to work, claiming those as close to the top as he could reach first.

"Hello up there," someone called from below.

"Mr. Redbourne, is that you?"

Raine glanced down at the bottom of the ladder where little Sarah Jane stood, looking up at him, the little lamb right next to her.

He chuckled as he climbed down.

"Well, you two are the last people I expected to see again today," he said to the little girl's mother as he set the bushel basket with a good peck or so of apples at his feet. "Might I say that color of blue looks particularly good on you?"

He liked watching her face change a shade of pink before his eyes.

"No more so than I was expecting to be seeing you." Mary Jane's brows scrunched together. "You told me this morning that you wanted to speak with Lucy before you left. I thought you were on your way back home."

"That's right. I was worried she might be upset that I was leaving Whisper Ridge to move out here." Noting her confusion, he added, "Not Kansas. Rafe left early this morning with our friend Mr. Longhurst, but I'll be sticking around for quite a bit longer."

Sarah Jane tugged on his pant leg. "Are you going to live at Fred's house now?" Her eyes opened wide, and her brows raised with anticipation.

"Do you know Fred?" he asked, bending down to meet her eye to eye.

"Uh-huh. He's my friend."

Raine reached down and picked up another apple from the gathered pile. "I think Fred likes these. Why don't you go feed him one?"

The little girl nodded her head with vigor and took the fruit from him. Then, she looked up at her mother for approval.

"Can I feed Fred, Mama? Can I?"

"Just be careful, baby."

"I will," she called back gleefully as she ran over to the pig's pen with the lamb on her tail.

"Do you take that lamb with you everywhere you go?" he asked, amused.

"What is this about you moving in here? Where is Mrs. Isaacson?"

"So, you didn't come all the way out here to welcome me to town?" He looked at her, hoping to evoke a smile, but instead, she narrowed her eyes at him.

"You really don't know?" He was genuinely surprised. He thought everyone knew the goings on in a town this small.

"Know what?" She folded her arms.

"Seems the woman who owns the place has been considering a move down to the Arizona Territory to be with her daughter for a long time. Hank said the hard Montana winters have become more difficult on her as she gets older and is all alone. I guess she finally made up her mind."

"And?"

"And…" he shrugged, "she left yesterday."

Mary Jane threw her hands in the air.

"And you've already moved in?"

"Well, I've been here all of about an hour, but yes, this is where I'll hang my hat for the foreseeable future."

Tension mounted in the air, and he was flabbergasted as to why.

"Mama," Sarah Jane called, "look at me."

Both of them turned to see the little girl walking the top of the pen fence with her arms extended out for balance. Raine didn't hesitate but rushed over just in time to catch her as she slipped on the still wet wood. He hugged the child close to him, rocking slightly from side to side.

Mary Jane hurried to his side and wrapped her arms around them both.

"You're squishing me," Sarah Jane said in a muffled voice.

Raine relaxed his hold on the little girl and set her down on the ground. She brushed the hair from her face and smiled up at him. His heart melted.

"I wish I had something to offer you, but it seems I have no idea what I have in the cupboards."

"Yoo hoo!" Three women in winter cloaks approached, each carrying foodstuffs in their arms.

It surprised him that he'd been so focused on Mary Jane and her daughter that he hadn't even heard the women's arrival. He needed to be much more aware of distractions if he was going to be effective in his new job.

"We heard the good news," the tallest of the group said as she held out her arms to him.

"And we wanted to be the first to welcome you to Thistleberry," said another, her lips tight, her skin red—likely from the cold, and her arms also extended over her ample bosom.

"Ladies," Raine said with a raise of his hat and a nod, taking the dish from the first. "This is so…unexpected." He smiled as the second woman placed her dish on top of the first's.

"We hope that you will be participating in the Fall Harvest Festival bachelor auction on Saturday before the dance. I know a lot of women who will pay handsomely for help from Thistleberry's hero," the last one said, her bright cheery freckles dotting her face.

She couldn't have been much older than seventeen.

She piled her dish on top of the other two.

"I made them myself," she said, then flashed a toothy smile and batted her eyelashes at him.

"Thank you so much for these, ladies, but I think you have been misinformed."

Hank hadn't said a single word about a bachelor auction. What did that even mean?

"Cornelia," the tall woman said, addressing the youngest of them with a smile that faltered only a little, "don't you remember, dear. After last year's fiasco, the town council voted to do away with the auction this year."

Whew.

"That's right, Mable" the young woman retorted, "but I'm sure there are plenty of us who would pay handsomely for his services."

Raine coughed.

"Sorry?"

"Ladies," Mary Jane said, stepping between him and the women, "Mr. Redbourne is just settling in. Why don't we give him a little space to do that?" She opened her arms and ushered them back toward their wagons.

"We all know he's looking for a wife, M.J," the second woman whispered, not so quietly. "Didn't you see his ad in the Observer?"

The three women giggled.

Heat rose beneath Raine's collar.

"Cole," he grumbled under his breath.

"If you are interested in the man," Mary Jane said, "then I suggest you respond to his ad by letter. It is supposed to be a correspondence courtship after all."

She knew about the ad. He dropped his head and shook it back and forth.

"What a wonderful idea," Mable said.

"I must get home right away to start." Cornelia looked back over her shoulder and winked at him.

"Goodbye, Sheriff Redbourne," the last one called as she climbed up onto her buggy seat. "We're glad to have you here in Thistleberry."

He raised his loaded arms as much as he could.

"Thank you," he said loudly, grateful they wouldn't be staying.

"Are *you* going to be the new sheriff in town?" Sarah Jane asked.

He hadn't realized the little girl stood so close to him.

"It's looking that way, kid. Do you have any advice for me?"

"Run. My mama doesn't like lawmen."

CHAPTER THIRTEEN

Sheriff?

Mary Jane took in a deep breath and exhaled. It was as if all her hopes had just come crashing down around one man.

Sheriff.

The reality of it began to set in. How had she let this happen? The first man she'd been keen on in a long time was a lawman. And he'd moved into the Isaacson farm. If he bought the place, her dreams would have to change. Again.

"It's time to go, Sarah Jane." She turned around to see her daughter standing right next to Raine with the lamb still by her side.

"Told you," the little girl said. "But don't worry. *I* still like you." She ran toward her mother and the lamb followed.

"She's one of yours," Mary Jane said, pointing down at the little black lamb, then stepped forward enough that she could stuff the makeshift feeding bottle into the crook of his arm next to one of the women's casseroles. Then she took a step back, placing a hand at the little girl's back and they both turned for the buckboard. "You may want to see how she got out. You're lucky a predator didn't get a hold of her."

Raine stood there, looking dumbfounded, holding those blasted dishes of baked goods the women in town seemed to think he needed. Well, her pie was one of the best around and she could have made him one if she'd wanted—had she known he was going to stick around.

But she didn't want to.

Not anymore.

"M.J.," he called after her.

She dared one glance. He set his load down on the porch stairs and ran to catch her.

"Mary Jane," he said, moving in front of the horses and taking hold of the reins up near the bit of the horse on her side of the wagon. "Whoa," he said calmly.

She stared at him coolly.

He allowed the reins to slip through his hands and he rubbed the side of the horse as he made his way to her.

"Miss Bennett," he said, his hands on the wood of the wagon, "I'm not at all sure what happened here today to turn you so cool against me, but I thought we were just becoming friends."

"When were you going to tell me you'd accepted the sheriff's position?"

"It's not a secret. It just didn't come up. I don't make a habit of telling all my business to everyone I meet."

She'd wanted to hear that she wasn't just everyone.

That he'd felt it too.

"You let me believe you were leaving."

"Would you have cared if I had?"

The question took her by surprise, and she had to think on it a moment.

Yes, she cared.

She must.

Otherwise, she wouldn't be making such a ninny of herself.

"Look," he said in a voice not unlike that he used to calm his horse, "I'm old enough that I don't want to beat around the bush. I like you. It's that simple. I like your daughter. Can't we at least be civil to one another? We are neighbors after all."

As much as Mary Jane wanted to hold on to her belief that all lawmen were dishonest, disloyal, and took advantage when it suited their purposes, he was right. She was too old for this kind of nonsense. With a deep breath and closed eyes, she willed the irritation to dissipate.

His candor and vulnerability softened her resolve and for that moment she wanted to believe again in second chances. She glanced over his head at the property she'd hoped would one day be hers and realized he'd had no idea she'd wanted the place. No one did.

"I'm not accustomed to being friends with people like…people in your profession," she clarified, avoiding his eyes, "but…" she paused a moment, then looked down. He was handsome and smart and spoke his mind. She liked that. "But," she dropped her shoulders and smiled, "I like you too."

There. She'd said it.

His grin spread all the way across his face, revealing a pair of dimples she hadn't noticed before.

"Well now, what do you say that you and the little lady here join me for supper tomorrow night? Here?"

Her daughter jumped up from the seat to face her, then she reached up, took hold of Mary Jane's coat collar, and pulled her face down until their foreheads met. She didn't say anything, but she didn't have to. It was apparent that Raine had already made quite an impression on the girl.

Mary Jane pulled back and kissed her daughter on the forehead.

"You're right," she said with a tap on Sarah Jane's little nose, then turned to Raine. "We would be delighted." Saying the words aloud already made her feel lighter than she had in a long time. Her eyes were drawn to an ax that lay at the foot of the stairs. "As long as you are not considering chopping down those beautiful Clematis and Wisteria vines." She motioned to the wooded remnants of the plants growing up the side of the house and rooftop.

He glanced over at the porch, then returned his eyes to meet hers.

"Wouldn't think of it."

She thought about the women she'd just sent on ahead of her and smiled at what she imagined their faces would look like when they found out that he'd taken an interest in her. The outcast. The disgraced.

"It's settled then. It's been a pleasure."

"I assure you," he said, tugging lightly on the front of his hat, "the pleasure is all mine. Say five thirty?"

"We'll be here with bells on!" Sarah Jane said loudly, evoking a laugh from both adults.

Mary Jane nodded. "Five thirty would be lovely," she said with a smile. "Thank you. What can I bring?"

"A hearty appetite," he told her, glancing back at the dishes that now sat on his porch steps.

"That won't be a problem," Sarah Jane said, rubbing her tummy.

"Until tomorrow then," Mary Jane said, still chuckling at her daughter's response.

"Oh, and um, what exactly am I supposed to do with him?" Raine asked, motioning to the lamb that now stood at his feet.

"Her."

"What?"

"It's a ewe lamb. You'll figure it out."

She laughed.

Raine caught her eyes, and it was as if he could see right the past and the hurt and pain of unhappier days, and he lit a spark of something she'd thought gone a long time ago.

Hope.

She snapped the reins and pulled the wagon around.

What just happened?

It had been a long time since Mary Jane had even

entertained the idea of seeing a gentleman, yet Raine Redbourne had blown into town and had been there all of a week and already she wanted to see more of him.

Maybe he wasn't like all the others. Maybe he was everything a lawman was supposed to be. Maybe this time around things could be different.

As she reached the turnoff that would lead them back to Happenstance, several wagons passed with women and their baked goods turning down the path toward the Isaacson farm. Unmarried and married alike. Word of the new sheriff had certainly spread like wildfire, bringing out the good folks of Thistleberry in droves.

The population of eligible women in town had greatly diminished since the mill had opened and men had migrated in from all over the west for work, but Raine's ad for a correspondence courtship in the local paper had brought more in from several of the surrounding towns. Most men looking for a wife in this fashion posted their ads in eastern newspapers, often neglecting or unknowing of the unmarried women living just a town or two over.

Undiscouraged by the sheer number of ladies taking him food, Mary Jane smiled to herself that a man liked her. A good-looking man. A good man.

As they pulled through the overhang into the drive, Lucy ran from the porch and met her at the gate. "It's here! Well, it's in town anyway. Just arrived on a special wagon in front of the mercantile."

"What's here?" she asked, handing the reins over to her daughter.

As she moved to get down, she thought better of it—a frightening vision of Sarah Jane snapping the reins and taking off through fences and pastures and wreaking havoc on the ranch, flashed through her mind. She took the leather straps and wrapped them around the rein hitch, catching Lucy's eye with a smile.

"Can't be too careful with this one."

Once her feet hit the ground, she turned around and helped her little lady down.

"I wanted it to be a surprise, but Lucas and Sam are riding into town to escort them back to Happenstance. I can hardly believe that it's here."

Mary Jane was glad that Lucy reflected her current mood.

"Can I go find Miss Evvy? I want to play with the sheep."

"Sarah Jane, love, how would you like to learn how to make cheese today?"

Sarah Jane's tongue roamed over her lips as she nodded. "Although, sometimes it smells bad in the cheese kitchen." She pinched her nose.

"She's not wrong," Lucy said with a laugh.

For some reason Mary Jane just felt like she wanted to keep the girl close to the house today. Besides, the ewes would be drying up soon, so they needed to make good use of the milk while they could still get it.

"Why don't you go find Tessa. She's supposed to be over there today. Maybe by the time it takes for us to unload whatever surprise Aunt Lucy has for us, you can teach me a thing or two about what you learned and maybe we can even have a taste."

"All right." She wrapped her arms around Mary Jane, then skipped off toward the cheese kitchen.

Down the road, a wagon with a large, covered load lumbered toward them. One rider on each side appeared to be Lucas and Sam.

"Lucy, what on earth did you buy?"

The woman clapped her hands, hardly able to contain her excitement.

"It is really wonderful. I don't know why we didn't think to get one before now."

The driver of the wagon looked none-too-pleased to have had to travel farther than town, but Mary Jane had no doubts that Sam would see that the man was well compensated for his efforts.

Trailing behind them were half the Deardon clan. Whatever that wagon held, it had to be heavy. Lucas directed the wagon over to the looming shed. When they finally came to a stop, the driver climbed up onto the back, untied the ropes that had secured the contraption, and tossed the padded blankets to the side.

A large machine with several large rollers, pulleys, cranks and gears stared back at them.

"Isn't it wonderful?" Lucy asked, rushing up to the wagon to inspect the mechanism more closely.

Mary Jane followed suit.

"What is it exactly?'

"It's a carding machine."

The process of transforming their wool into cloth was both time-consuming and arduous and with their numbers dwindling as more of the displaced brides and other unmarried women employed at the ranch got married, they'd needed to find more efficient ways to accomplish the same tasks in less time.

The two women had perused advertisements in the new Montgomery Ward catalog that boasted the feats of a carding machine. They'd talked about how it would help them to accomplish in a matter of minutes what it now took someone five or six hours to accomplish in brushing and untangling the fibers from the wool so it could be strung into thread or yarn, but with a machine of that size and capability, not only would they need to up their wool production, but they would need to build a power source to run it.

This machine was slightly different than the one they had seen because it appeared that it could alternately be run by crank and be able to forgo the pulley system that would have to be powered by another source—steam or water.

"You do realize, Lucy," Mary Jane said as she watched the men gather around the back of the wagon to unload the monstrosity, "that we have dipped our toes into a variety of different pots, and we are either going to have to hire half the town to keep up with multiple businesses or we'll need to focus all of our attention on just one."

"Yes, I know. We are going to need help."

Without having children of her own, Lucy had wanted to make productive use of her time and had focused most of her energy on Happenstance and her match-making hobby. If Lucas hadn't intervened, Mary Jane was sure the woman would have moved in with her at the homestead.

She didn't want to take away from Lucy's excitement, but part of her job as foreman was to make sure the ranch ran smoothly.

"Even with this beautiful and miraculous machine," she said, "we just don't have enough hands to do everything we have already committed to do. Make the cheese. Spin the wool. Make the blankets and intricate fabrics. And actually care for the sheep themselves during lambing season and breeding season. Not to mention, we will have to add a significant number to our flock, which means…"

"We buy more sheep. I know. We're already working on a deal with a farmer in Oregon."

"How many head are we talking?" Mary Jane asked, worried that Lucy was getting too far ahead of herself for what the current staff at the ranch could handle.

"I know we had originally talked about fifty, but after speaking with Lucas and his uncles, they've convinced me that we have plenty of land to bring on another four hundred or so with plenty of room to grow."

Four hundred?

Mary Jane swallowed hard and took a moment to collect her thoughts.

"That would mean we'd need at least four or even five more Evalines, as she is the best of all the shepherds I have ever seen, and a few more sheepherding dogs. And that is on top of the help we already have with Carl, Wink, Stetson, Buckley, Otis, and the two new pups watching over the current flock." She had to work to keep her voice even not to show her shock at quadrupling their numbers.

Until lambing season, Happenstance had just under a hundred head, and she already anticipated gaining a good hundred or more little ones during lambing season. Since Lucy didn't want to raise the sheep for meat, their numbers would grow exponentially from season to season.

"Let's sit down once the festival is behind us and we can make a plan." Lucy placed a hand around Mary Jane. "I value your opinion, M.J. I hope you know how valuable you are to this place. To me."

She put an arm over Lucy's shoulders. "I know."

It took the men more than an hour to get the carding machine into the looming shed and get it situated properly.

By the time evening came, Mary Jane was ready to crawl into her bed for a good night's rest. Exhausted from a full day of several attempts to learn how to use the carding machine, testing and packaging various aged cheeses to take to Mrs. Smith at the mercantile in town, and teaching Tessa and Judith how to use the new churn for making butter and to mix hand balm and healing salve from the wool lanolin and beeswax.

When she dragged herself into the bedroom, she bowed and shook her head. Sarah Jane was snuggled beneath the covers on her bed, a storybook open in front of her, and she was asleep. Ranch work was tiresome for everyone, but especially for a little girl. Rather than wake the child and move her into her own bed, she traded her skirt and blouse for a thick woolen nightshift and crawled in next to her daughter.

With a light kiss on her forehead, she leaned over and blew out the waning light on top of the night table. Sleep eluded her for the next several minutes as the list of everything that needed to be accomplished the following day ran through her mind. Pies needed to be made. The new fence perimeters on the north pasture needed to be inspected. And on top of everything else, she had to prepare for supper with Raine Redbourne at the Isaacson farm. The last thought brought a smile to her face as she thought about those dimples and the smile that warmed her insides.

The sound of a whimper caused Mary Jane to raise her head and look toward the bedroom door. The moonlight bathed Otis with its soft blue light and the pup leapt up onto the bed, snuggling down at her feet. It was nice to see he was regaining some of his energy.

As she started to drift off to sleep, the startling alarm of the llamas brought her to full awareness, and she shot out of bed. Her daughter stirred for a moment, but did not awaken. Mary Jane shrugged on her trousers and tossed a still buttoned shirt over her head.

KNOCK! KNOCK!

The booming sound at the door had her grabbing her boots and running out into the living area, the cold penetrating her thick woolen stockings.

Mary Jane pulled the door open, hopping around as she pulled on her boots.

"We've got a bear." Lissa stood at the door, bundled up in a thick winter coat.

"How's the foot," M.J. asked as she reached up to the wall and pulled down her favorite rifle.

"I can manage," the hired hand said. The woman closed the few feet between her and their horses with nary a limp.

With only a single backward glance, Mary Jane could see the glow from the moonlight spilling over the form of the peacefully sleeping child. She blew a kiss into the air in her daughter's direction, then pulled the door shut tightly behind her.

A bear. What's next?

CHAPTER FOURTEEN

Baaa. Baaa. Baaa.

Raine tossed in the old lumpy mattress, pulling the pillow over his ears.

The lamb Mary Jane had left with him had not wanted to join the rest of the sheep now under his charge and had stuck next to him the rest of the day as he'd finished cleaning up the outside of the yard, repaired the pig's shelter, and had made a list of the things he would need to pick up in town in the morning.

"Go to sleep," he called out." Having remembered Sarah Jane's earlier comment about her experience with the lamb in the house, he'd been wary of allowing the thing to sleep inside. However, after near a half an hour of bleating, he finally had let the little one inside. He laid a small bed of straw in front of the fireplace, hoping that the animal would curl up and finally go to sleep.

He'd been wrong.

The bed dipped and raised. The little lamb's head nudged the pillow upward as it snuggled up next to Raine. He'd never really been around sheep and thought it odd that the small sheep needed or wanted affection. The bleating had stopped, so he tucked the pillow back under his head and closed his eyes.

It wasn't long before the sound of barking dogs caught his attention.

How in the world did sheep farmers get any rest with so much commotion at night? Hank had given him enough of a run down to know that barking dogs at night indicated there might be a predator nearby, so he turned to roll off the opposite side of the bed than the lamb.

He quickly donned his britches, tugged on his boots, and threw a shirt over his arms and shoulders before grabbing his holster. He realized that he ought to keep his rifle handy as he didn't think his revolvers would be very effective on a mountain lion or a coyote at any distance.

His heavy winter coat hung next to his hat, and he collected them both on his way out the door. It closed behind him as he stepped out onto the large, covered porch. Immediately, the lamb began to bleat.

"You'll just have to stay put for the moment, little one," he said, taking a step toward the stairs. He glanced out at the pasture, straining his eyes to see if he could spot the source of the commotion. The moon glanced off the white wool of the clustered sheep.

He remembered seeing the faded green lantern that hung from the stooped gable, and he stepped forward until he could make out its form. He pulled it down from its nail and reached into his pocket for his flint box.

With a spark, the lantern's wick accepted the flame, and he slid the latch, lowering the glass cage enough that the whole of it filled with life. He held it up—not that he could see very far into the yard. At least the dogs were good at their job and had herded the bands all into one group. He'd counted twenty-three ewes, a single ram, and fourteen lambs during his earlier assessment, the ram being kept in a different paddock as the ewes. It was impossible to see if any had been lost in this light.

He made his way out to the stable. It would be easier and safer for him to get a better look on horseback.

Greeted by a chorus of whinnies and snorts, he opened the stall gate where the mare pranced about. The Clydesdales also appeared a little restless and he spoke to them all in low, calming tones.

Raine contemplated riding the mare out bareback but had never quite mastered the task like his baby brother and with the pain he still had in his chest and shoulders from the harness and the fall, it was probably best just to take it easy for a while. Besides, he hadn't yet attempted it with his new horse and was unsure how she would react—especially while on edge from a potential threat, so he made quick work of getting her saddled, secured the harness collar and lantern around her neck, and within a few minutes had mounted. He pulled his rifle from the scabbard, heading out to look for signs of a predator.

His adventure in the wilds of Montana had been more eventful than he could have anticipated. In the short week he'd been here, he'd helped capture a fugitive, fallen down a mine shaft, taken on a new job, become a reluctant sheep rancher, and had met a woman unlike any other along with her beautiful four-year-old daughter who'd already begun to fill a spot in his heart that had been vacant for more than eleven years.

For the first time since that fateful day, the thought of Sarah and their unborn child did not fill him with despair and loneliness.

Crack!

The distant sound of gunfire, coming from the direction of the Happenstance Ranch, had him riding in that direction. Grateful he had ridden the perimeter of the farm's fence line earlier this afternoon, he knew that there was nowhere he would be able to cross safely, and he would have to revert to taking the main road, which was in terrible need of leveling.

He knew a lot of women who were highly capable and didn't think the women at Happenstance were probably any less, but he couldn't help the protective instinct that crowded his gut as he thought about Mary Jane and little Sarah facing down a predator.

Why did this kind of thing always have to happen at night? While the lantern worked to light the path directly in front of him, they still had to move slowly in order to avoid any hidden pitfalls in the road.

As he approached the homestead, he could see several mounted riders collected in one section of the pasture. He dismounted. Not desiring to be seen, he got down and extinguished the light from the lantern. After a few minutes of watching the female ranchers organize themselves and work to gather in their herd to protect it from any dangers, he gained a new respect for them. His doubts that these women could look after their own dissipated in those moments.

A high-pitched, obnoxious trill sounded not too far from him. From previous experience, he recognized it as one of the llama's alarm cries. He obviously had gotten too close to the flock for the animal's comfort.

"It's just me," he tried calming the animal with the same type of sing-song voice that Mary Jane had used with him before. It seemed to work for a second or two before the llama sounded off again.

Two of the riders broke away from the others and headed toward him. The last thing he needed was for Mary Jane to think he had been spying on them, or worse yet, to think that he was attempting to undermine her abilities in handling the ranches affairs, so he climbed back up into his saddle and urged the mare back down the same road he'd come, leaning down close to the horn, his head out of sight, and quickly retreated.

"Who's there?" the question barely reached his ears.

He didn't raise into a sitting position until he'd turned down the road toward his new home. Whatever had gone after the Happenstance flock would be long gone at this point. He just hoped that it hadn't been pushed toward the sheep he was now responsible for. He took another turn around the property.

Bo and Rudy were on alert, looking after the sheep. He'd taken to the pups right away, and found they'd become accustomed to his scent and his voice rather quickly. It was a good thing that he had practiced some of the commands Hank had taught him, which were not that different than those used by his family to herd their livestock.

They growled.

"Wait. Stay," he said, issuing the commands.

The dogs seemed to recognize his voice as they immediately returned to the flock and held their ground. With no danger immediately present, it was time he got some sleep. Dawn would come too early as it was.

The Clydesdales were calm and seemed to be sleeping peacefully as he walked the mare back into the stable. He removed her tack and collar, relit the lantern, and set it up on the front post near her stall, noticing a shadowed nook in the stable walls that he had not seen before.

"Don't you worry, girl, I'll be right back to brush you down." He picked up the lantern's bail handle, then shut the stall gate before walking around the corner only to discover another section of the stable that had been completely hidden from immediate view.

"What do we have back here?"

He pulled several large, thin, woolen blankets from atop a large object nestled tightly into the small room, unprepared for the stiffness and aching discomfort the action would bring. He rotated his shoulders backward a few times and rubbed his chest in hopes of loosening up the pain.

His attention focused on the body of a buckboard that sat on the ground, wheelless, next to several different pairs and styles of wooden runners. From the looks of it, it appeared that someone had been in the midst of converting the old wagon into a sled. This one was different than the single-seater he'd found in the barn.

The cutter had likely only been used when heading into town for church or to pay visits to neighboring farms and ranches or for attending social functions. This, on the other hand, looked like it would be for carrying larger loads or even people into or around town.

Immediately, his thoughts turned to his brother Ethan who was known for crafting some of the most beautiful sleighs. Not quite in the shape of a typical sleigh, he could envision how pleased his mother might have been at having such a vehicle to travel around in the winter with all eight of her children in tow, singing carols and delivering her Christmas cakes to the neighbors during the holiday season.

Without his brother's blacksmithing skills, he wondered if he might be able to contact the local smithy about adding some metal sheets to the bottoms of the wooden runners to make them sturdier and less susceptible to rot and rapid decline with any type of extended use.

With those thoughts to chew on, Raine threw the coverings back over the deconstructed sleigh and quickly went to task in brushing the mare.

All was quiet as he approached the house. He hoped he would not encounter unpleasantries at having left his new ovine friend alone inside. To his pleasant surprise, when he opened the front door, he saw that the lamb had discovered the small bed he'd made for it on the floor and was now curled into a fluffy little ball.

He took a step inside and froze at the clunking sound his boots made on the wooden floor. Not wanting to wake the lamb, he bent down to take them off, then set them next to the entryway and started across the living area toward the bedroom in his stocking feet. A wintry draft washed over him, and he reached up to rub his arms against the chill. He glanced back down at the little ewe lamb, then tiptoed back to the couch and grabbed hold of the blanket that had been draped over the corner and laid it gently on top of his one-night guest.

Satisfied that she would be warm enough for tonight, he trudged back to the bedroom.

Sleep.

His whole body hurt, and he lowered himself down onto the bed without removing so much as his coat. His mind turned to the flock outside.

Fourteen lambs. Were they warm enough out there?

He decided that finishing the repairs on the barn would be one of his first priorities so that the sheep would have somewhere warm to sleep at night. Gradually, his lids grew heavier and heavier as he reviewed the day and all that needed to be done.

Zzzzzzz…

Baaa. Baaa. Baaa.

Raine opened his eyes and jumped backward, startled.

The lamb's face was so close to his, it took him a moment to collect his bearings. Not more than fifteen minutes could have passed, and he turned around with his back to the animal and closed his eyes again.

Baaa. Baaa. Baaa.

He turned onto his back, his arms spread wide, and looked up at the ceiling.

Cock-a-doodle-doo.

"You've got to be joking." He opened one eye and glanced out the window. The sun had not yet risen over the mountainside, but as he watched the bands of light radiating from a point in the valley between two peaks, he knew it was morning.

The lamb jumped up onto the bed and pawed at Raine's arm until he scratched the top of its head, then it twisted and closed its eyes, enjoying the attention.

"We've got a big day ahead of us, girl. Sam will be here at any minute." He forced himself up out of the bed, changed his shirt, and headed downstairs.

It wasn't long before Sam rode up in front of the house and

dismounted.

"Hope you know what you're getting yourself into, Raine," his uncle said as he wrapped the reins around one of the front hitching posts. He'd come out to the place to give Raine detailed instructions and to demonstrate the extent of what needed to be done on the farm each morning.

"You think I should have turned down the job?"

"No. As a matter of fact, I think Hank was right smart asking you to come up here," he said as they made their way to the hen house. "I was referring to this little ranch. Taking care of all these animals might be a lot for one man to handle along with all the new responsibilities that come with being sheriff." Sam opened the door to the coop, took down the bucket hanging just inside, and handed it to him

Raine shrugged.

"How long can it possibly take to do the chores here each morning and evening?" He walked in and proceeded to collect the eggs like he'd done many times before. While his duties as deputy in Stone Creek had taken him away from the ranching life for the last several years, he hadn't forgotten the amount of work that went into keep a place like Redbourne Ranch running smoothly. "This place isn't that big."

Nine eggs. Nine.

What was he going to do with nine eggs every day?

"It's not the chores you should be worried about," Sam said, making his way across the yard. "Sheep aren't like cattle. Or horses for that matter." He stepped up onto the bottom rung of the fence separating them from the pasture. "They need a constant companion to watch over and protect them, a shepherd, day and night." He rested his arms on the top of the fence and looked out over the open fields.

"I'm no shepherd," Raine said, keeping his feet on the ground. He set the bucket full of eggs down next to him.

"You will be if you stay on here without some help."

"What did you have in mind?"

Sam gave Raine plenty to consider as they talked while they worked and completed the morning chores. Once everything had been finished, Raine let the mare out of the stables and into the pasture to stretch her legs and mingle with their new companions. After what Sam had told him, he'd been hesitant to leave the sheep alone, but it was unavoidable for today. He would inquire about getting some help once he got into town this morning. He hitched the Clydesdales to the wagon and climbed up onto the seat.

"I'm looking forward to Sunday dinner at Whisper Ridge," he told a now mounted Sam. "Thank you for the invitation."

"The womenfolk would have had my hide had I forgotten."

Whisper Ridge had hosted family dinners every Sunday for as long as Raine could remember from past visits. He guessed that was the reason they continued to host them at the main homestead instead of at Hank's Place—since he was the eldest of them living there.

Each of the smaller properties had been named after Liam Deardon's three sons. The main house would have been home to his only daughter, but Leah had elected to move away after she'd married Raine's father.

"I'm sure we'll see plenty of you Saturday at the festival. You know," Sam said as he pulled his horse around to face Raine. "Fred there is a blue-ribbon winning pig. Mrs. Isaacson enters him into the show every year and always walks away a winner. You should consider showing him."

Raine looked over at Fred who was still working on his morning meal.

"I think we'll leave that until next year," he said with a smile. He was anxious to get into Thistleberry. He wanted to see the sheriff's office and jailhouse, pick up his supplies at the General Store, then head out to the mill for some extra lumber to complete his projects for the weekend.

As he rode into town, he noted the construction had almost been completed on a large pavilion in the center of the overly wide street, and several makeshift booths had been erected, presumably for the Fall Harvest Festival that was to begin the next day. A large banner had been strung across the road from the rooftops of the buildings on either side of the pavilion to its large gazebo roof.

Even though the sun was out, a crisp wind blew through the air, and Raine pulled the collar of his coat up around his neck as he traversed the streets, familiarizing himself with the layout of town. Women of all shapes and sizes greeted him with warm smiles, some even stopping him on the boardwalk offering delicious confections and others, invitations for supper or asking to save them a dance at Saturday night's festivities.

He'd traveled through a lot of places, but he'd never quite experienced this level of hospitality in any of them. Of course, this was the first place, other than Silver Falls, where he aimed to stay for any length of time. Returning to the wagon, he placed his armful of delectables in the back alongside the foodstuffs he'd purchased earlier to last him over the next couple of weeks, though if folks kept giving him meals like they were, he'd be eating fat until Christmas.

"I understand you're the man aiming to take my old job."

Raine turned to see a man, still astride his horse, the backlight of the sun obscuring his face. When he dismounted, the marshal's badge was the first thing to catch his eye.

"Name's Tyler. Rutledge." He extended his hand.

Something was very familiar about the man. He'd met a lot of territory Marshals in his line of work and had encountered a few helping Rafe with his, but he couldn't quite place him.

"Redbourne. Raine. M.J. told me about you. Well, she told me that the last sheriff had been appointed a territory Marshal."

"Ah, the lady foreman. I'm afraid I didn't have much occasion to visit with her. Always got the impression she didn't care much for me. Probably on account that I took over as sheriff after her husband was killed. Well, after a few others tried. A real shame."

Mary Jane's husband was the sheriff? Interesting.

"Don't take it personally. I have it on good authority that she doesn't care for lawmen in general." Raine smiled, remembering his earlier conversation with Sarah Jane.

"Redbourne, huh? Any relation to Rafe?"

"Yes, sir. Brothers."

"Rafe Redbourne is as good a man as any I've ever met. Thistleberry is mighty lucky to have someone with your family tree watching over it—though," he nudged Raine's arm, "can't say much ever happens around here. It's not what you'd call the most excitin' of assignments."

There was something off about this marshal. He could feel it in his gut, but he forced a smile.

"And I'm here to keep it that way."

"Well, best o' luck to ya, Redbourne." He tipped his hat, then walked over into the bank.

Raine adjusted his hat in such a way that he could keep an eye on the bank as he moseyed over to the sheriff's office where a bench had been built beneath the covered overhang of the boardwalk. He casually unlatched the snap on his holster, running his hand over the butt of his revolver as he sat down, then leaned back against the wood and crossed his feet in front of him.

Several minutes later, the marshal walked out of the bank without incident, and Raine breathed a little easier as he watched the man climb back up onto his horse. The previous sheriff met his eyes and tipped his hat as he passed at a saunter.

With one more stop and a lot still to do before the Bennett ladies joined him for supper, he gingerly pulled himself back to a standing position and rubbed his chest.

"Get a move on, Redbourne," he told himself aloud.

The mill had been busier than he'd expected. With the Deardon's request for enough lumber to build another barn at Happenstance, he'd been lucky to get what he needed for repairs. The biggest surprise he'd encountered out at the place had been a two-room apartment that had been built into the back of the barn. He thought it odd that anyone would want to sleep out in a place with all the animals, but nonetheless, he included a new mattress for that bed and lumber to repair the broken table he'd found in the corner to his list.

For the rest of the afternoon, he hammered and chopped and cleared out the barn, stables, and underbrush that had grown around and beneath the stairs on the house. As he looked up at the wooded vines growing up the porch stairs and pillars onto the roof, he smiled.

The time.

He glanced down at the wristwatch Will had brought him from overseas for his birthday earlier this year. The Bennett ladies would be there in less than an hour and he still had so much to do.

"Come on, Redbourne. Time to make a good impression."

CHAPTER FIFTEEN

"Sarah Jane," M.J. called for her daughter, "we don't want to be late, now do we?"

The little girl appeared in the bedroom doorway and Mary Jane had to bite her lip to stop from laughing. She wore the simple purple dress that Mara had made for her with primrose-colored flowers embroidered on the collar. Visible beneath the hemline were a pair of boy's denim overalls that had been rolled up on the cuff—which explained the lumpy fit and padded shoulders.

"I think maybe for tonight, we can skip the trousers, sweetheart, what do you say?"

"But what if Mr. Redbourne needs some help cleaning up all those apples from the ground?"

"Then, we'll make arrangements to go back another day to help."

Sarah Jane looked sideways, her lips scrunched and folded together as she thought for a moment.

"Do you think he'd let us feed Fred again too?" Her eyes brightened at the thought.

"I'm sure he'd appreciate your help." Mary Jane tapped the

girl's nose with her finger. "As long as you promise not to climb on the top of the pen," she added, narrowing her eyes playfully at her.

"That's a deal," Sarah Jane said happily.

Mary Jane scooped the child's hand in hers and quickly helped her shrug out of the denims beneath the dress. She would have to talk to Dahlia about the abundance of boy's clothing that had ended up in her care.

With a quick brush of the girl's hair, Mary Jane kissed the top of her daughter's head.

"Pretty as a painting."

She'd spent the majority of the day up at the north pasture putting up new fences where the Deardon men had left off, and baking. As much as she'd hated to admit it, she was grateful for all the work Lucy's family had provided. There was no way she and the other women could have gotten so much accomplished in so little time—especially with Lissa's injury.

The basket full of still-warm sweet rolls sat next to one of the small blocks of her own collection of cheeses that had been aging on the closet shelf for nearly a full year. She hadn't wanted to arrive at the Isaacson farm for dinner empty handed and hoped that Raine was the kind to appreciate a good cheese. Happenstance cheese wasn't like any of the other types of cheese available in the territory.

She smiled to herself. It was good to see the fruits of just how far they'd come at the ranch. With the basket hanging over her arm and the cheese in her hand, she headed to the door, catching a glimpse of her reflection in the mirror to the side of the entryway. She took a deep breath and tried to smile through her nervousness, then pinched her cheeks for a little added color and pinned an untamed strand of hair that had fallen in front of her face behind her ear.

"Are you ready?" she asked the little girl who'd come to her side.

"Are *you*?" Sarah Jane asked wisely, looking up at her.

"Yes."

The answer surprised her. It had been a long time since she'd even entertained the idea of courting, but there was something about Raine Redbourne that intrigued her. It was a risk, she knew, to fall for a lawman, but she was tired of being so guarded all the time. Surely, not every man who'd vowed to uphold the law, would abuse the trust that was placed in him by the townspeople.

She thought of Rutledge Tyler. He'd been good enough to become a territory Marshal. While she'd never really cared for the man or his swaggering temperament, she'd never had any reason to suspect he was anything other than straight-shooting.

The sun descended lower in the sky, but there was still plenty of light as they made their way to the Isaacson farm. As they pulled up in front of the house, Raine leaned against the pillar at the top of the stairs until they came to a stop and in moments was down at the gate to greet them.

Lumber had been stacked out by the old barn, the apples had all been cleaned up, and it looked as if Fred had a brand-new shelter in his pen. The man had been busy.

He reached up to help her down from the wagon. His hands were warm on her waist and lingered well after he'd set her down on the ground. She tilted her head to look up at him, barely able to catch her breath.

How could a man be so handsome? And kind? There had to be something wrong with him, but she didn't want to think about that right now.

"My turn," Sarah Jane said and jumped.

Raine let go of her in plenty of time to catch the girl. The trust her daughter already placed in Mr. Redbourne was growing easier to understand the more time they spent with him. He had a way of making them feel that everything would be all right.

"Ladies," he said, holding out a crooked arm for her and an extended hand for Sarah Jane.

With only a moment's hesitation, Mary Jane accepted his

proffered arm and together they climbed the stairs. He jumped forward to get the door, opened it, and swept his hand in front of them in a welcoming gesture.

"Mama," Sarah Jane said in an urgent and loud whisper, "we forgot the sweet rolls you made for him."

Heat rose in her cheeks. Sarah Jane held the cheese, but the basket was still in the wagon.

"Sweet rolls? For me?" Raine beamed.

"Sweet rolls, yes. For *all* of us," Mary Jane corrected, returning his smile. "Let me just get them from the buckboard."

"Allow me." The door clacked shut as he let go to jump down from the porch, taking several steps at once. He reached over the side of the wagon to retrieve the basket of baked goods from the floor in front of the seat.

He lifted the cloth covering, then leaned down and took a deep breath.

"My mouth is watering already," he said, closing his eyes, evoking a giggle from her.

It only took moments for him to close the distance between them.

He opened the door again.

"Ladies," he repeated with a nod.

The savory smells of buttery crust and meat mingled with the sweet aroma of her rolls and a slight rumble in her stomach reminded her she hadn't eaten since breakfast.

He hadn't appeared to have noticed.

Mary Jane wasn't sure exactly what she had expected, but the interior of the house still looked like it had the last time she'd visited Mrs. Isaacson. Everything was in its place. Somehow, she had expected it to feel more manly, then quickly scoffed at the notion as he'd only been at the place for a single day. There was only so much he could do in that time, and he'd obviously spent a great deal of time and effort outside.

Raine led them into the kitchen where a white linen cloth-covered table had been set as beautifully as she'd ever seen filled with an array of foodstuffs ready for consumption.

Immediately, she recognized the signature dishes of different women from the surrounding farms and ranches.

She laughed, wondering how long it would be before the barrage of meals would cease and he had to fend for himself. She doubted he would starve, as she noted a place on the countertop still covered in random patterns of white flour where he'd likely prepared the steaming biscuits now displayed in a wide-topped bowl on the table.

"I don't know what Cornelia Wilson would say if she knew that you were sharing her traditional meat pies with the likes of me," she said aloud.

His brows scrunched together.

"Maybe we should see if they are even worth their salt before determining if they are worthy of tradition." He raised a questioning brow, pulling out a chair for her to sit.

He set her basket on the counter next to the stack of other casseroles and goods that hadn't yet been touched, and suddenly, she felt a wave of nerves settle in the pit of her stomach. She'd been told on many occasions that her pies were the best around, but she hadn't baked other goods or made big meals for anyone, except Sarah Jane and the other girls, since she'd left her home in Iowa nearly five years ago, and was glad she hadn't volunteered to cook for him.

Yet.

It might take some practice.

"Shall we?" he said as he claimed the seat next to her daughter and across from her.

Sarah Jane handed him the block of cheese she'd been holding the whole way here.

"This is for you too," she said proudly.

"What's this?"

"Happenstance Cheese."

Raine's face contorted. "You mean *sheep* cheese." He winked at Sarah Jane.

He was teasing her.

"It's really scrumptious," the little girl told him.

Mary Jane laughed at her daughter's vocabulary. It was wonderful living around so many women who'd embraced them as part of the family. Mara, Alex, Lucy, all of them were such a big part of their lives. She didn't know how she would have been able to do it on her own. She and Sarah Jane had spent hours reading books from their libraries.

"Thank you," Raine said sincerely. "I look forward to the experience." He set it down on the table next to him, then held out his hand, palm up to her and the other to her daughter.

She wasn't quite sure what he expected, but she reluctantly slid her hand into his.

"Good Lord," he closed his eyes and bent his head, "we are grateful for this bounteous meal that thou hast provided us through the good women of Thistleberry this night…"

Mary Jane also closed her eyes with a silent chuckle. It was refreshing to have a man lead them in a prayer over their supper. Her father had never been particularly keen on God or His goodness, but her mother had still seen to it that she'd read the bible every night after supper and had been an example of faith—even if they hadn't always seen things in the same light.

"Amen."

By the time they had finished eating, the sun had dipped down below the mountainside. Raine lit several lanterns around the house and started a fire in the hearth. The women in town had all outdone themselves. The food had been delicious, but she realized the sheer amount of it must have been a real sacrifice for some of them.

She'd recognized the old green and yellow stoneware dish that had been full of creamed potatoes and made a mental note to drop off a block of aged cheese, a bread loaf, and fresh milk at the Sorensens' home on Saturday morning before the festival began.

The family was new in Thistleberry, and Mr. Sorensen had

just gotten a job with Mr. Fawcett over at the mill. It would likely take a few weeks for them to get settled in. They had eight children, the oldest of which was a woman a few years younger than her and certainly twice as shy, which made it no surprise that Mrs. Sorensen had made such an effort to gain the attention of the newest bachelor in town. The potatoes had been simply delectable.

"Did you know that my mama makes the best apple pie in the world?" Sarah Jane said as she eyed the bushel of apples that sat in front of the now-glowing fireplace.

"Does she now? And I was just dreaming about tasting those right plump sweet rolls you brought."

Sarah Jane jumped to her feet.

"I helped make them," she said as she walked over to the counter and reached up for the basket.

Mary Jane slipped over to help her daughter. She did not want her afternoon's work to end up on the floor like several had in the last batch she'd made. They carried the basket over to the table together and set it down in front of Raine.

He lifted the cloth to peek inside, then quickly dropped it again. He looked at Sarah Jane, ran his tongue over his lips, then peeked inside again.

Sarah Jane giggled.

"Should we try one?"

"Yes, please."

Mary Jane pulled the cloth off the basket with a chuckle.

"You two." She took one out and placed it on a small, unused dessert plate in front of Raine, then cut one in half and set it on the plate in front of her daughter.

"I got cheated," Sarah Jane said loudly, her brows scrunched together and her bottom lip protruding until she looked up at her. "Oh, sorry. Thank you for this small piece."

Raine bent his head and covered his mouth, turning away from her.

Mary Jane swatted him playfully on the arm with the back

of her hand. There would be no harm this one time to give the child a sweet roll near the size of her head. After all the supper she'd eaten, she doubted her daughter would be able to finish two bites of the enormous confection, let alone the whole thing. She slid the other half down onto the girl's plate.

Sarah Jane looked up at her with wide eyes and a newly brightened smile.

"Thank you, Mama," she squealed, leaning onto the edge of the table with her forearms and staring at her treat with anticipation.

"Do young ladies put their elbows on the table, Miss Sarah Jane?"

"No, ma'am." The little girl sat back down in her seat and picked up her fork.

Raine finished his without a qualm. He leaned back in his chair, his hands behind his head, and took a deep breath.

"Why, Miss Bennett, I think you may have displaced my own mother's sweet rolls."

Mary Jane wasn't sure if that was a compliment, having never tried Mrs. Redbourne's sweet rolls, but she was pleased by his apparent praise.

"Wasn't that just the tastiest completion to a meal you've ever had?" he asked Sarah Jane.

Still chewing, the little girl nodded, frosting smeared across her lips and clumped on the tip of her nose.

"Now, what is this I hear about apple pie?"

Mary Jane shook her head. She glanced at the grandfather clock in the hallway. Seven-thirty. She had an early morning ahead of her as she still had two of those apple pies to make, but she didn't want the pleasant evening to end.

"Hank's been after me to enter them into the baking contest tomorrow."

"If they have Hank's approval, they must be good."

Sarah Jane finally finished her bite. "Best in the territory she's told."

"I can hold my own."

"After these sweet rolls, nothing would surprise me."

"Can we make one here, Mama?" Sarah Jane asked.

"Don't you think you've had enough sweets for today, love."

"Yes," the girl said sheepishly, "but Mr. Redbourne looks like he could have some more."

"Oh, I definitely think we need to make one," he piped in. "What do we need?" he asked as he pushed his chair back and stood, heading over to the wall with all the cupboards. "I made a stop in town this morning and picked up a few basics that Mrs. Isaacson didn't already have, and as you can see," he directed his gaze to the hearth where three large bushels sat, "we have plenty of apples."

"You've been busy today."

"Busy enough, I guess. Okay, then you'll probably need some flour," he reached into the cupboard. "Brown sugar, lard, butter. What am I missing?"

Mary Jane watched and laughed. "You two are incorrigible."

Pies would have to be made and she figured it wouldn't matter if she made them here or at home, other than she would be using his ingredients instead of hers. She joined him at the cupboard, but opened the pantry door where she knew Mrs. Isaacson kept her aprons.

"Do you have any peppercorns?"

Raine looked at her and pulled his head back in obvious surprise.

"I didn't think so," she said. "Maybe we'll just have to do this another time."

"No, Mama, please?" Sarah Jane pleaded, her eyes wide, her brows raised.

"Will these work?" He picked up a small ceramic jar from the back of the counter labeled 'peppercorns' on the front and held it up for her to see.

He grinned.

It wasn't looking like she would be able to get out of baking pie tonight. She glanced from Raine to Sarah Jane and back again.

"All right, but only if you allow me to pay you for the supplies."

"How about an exchange," he countered. "A piece of this supposedly delicious pie for whatever items you need. Most of it belonged to Mrs. Isaacson anyway."

She wrapped the apron around her dress, crossed the straps behind her and tied it in the front.

"We'll also need salt, baking powder, nutmeg, cinnamon, lemon juice, and cold water."

Raine clapped his hands, then rubbed them together.

Mary Jane went through the recipe in her head as she rolled up her sleeves.

"Oh, and three eggs." One for each pie.

"I think I can manage that," he said, spinning around her and opening another cupboard. "Maybe not the lemon juice."

Sarah Jane scooted one of the chairs from the table over to the counter next to her and climbed up.

"See, Mama," she said smartly, "I should have worn overalls."

Mary Jane had forgotten how good it felt to laugh.

"And this is for you." Raine tossed a plain white apron on top of the little girl's head, the material covering her face.

"What do you say, love?"

"Thank you, Mr. Redbourne," she said, pulling the apron slowly down over her light curls.

"You are most welcome, little lady." He set the items she requested down on the counter in front of her, including a sealed glass jar labeled lemon juice.

Of course, Mrs. Isaacson had lemon juice in her cupboards. She was known throughout Thistleberry for her flavored lemonades and raisin cookies.

Both Raine and Sarah Jane stood over her, waiting for her to begin.

"Well, you two don't think I am going to be making all three of these pies by myself, do you?"

They looked over at her, then at each other, shrugging their shoulders.

By the way Raine had known which ingredients she would need to get started, she guessed he knew his way around a kitchen well enough and his naivety was for show. She could play along. It still stunned her, and scared her a little, that she now felt so comfortable around this stranger that she didn't feel the need to prove herself to him anymore.

"How many mixing bowls do you have?"

"How many do you need?"

"Four would be sufficient."

They looked through cupboard after cupboard until they'd finally found what they needed. Each of them had a bowl of a different size, but they were all big enough to form the dough for the crust.

"All right, you are going to do exactly what I do. Ready?"

She took them through each of the steps of making the crust dough for the pie. As they finished, she was pleased that all three looked like a viable start. They set them aside and worked for the next few minutes to peel, core, and slice several pounds of apples.

They each took turns adding a new ingredient to the fruit mixture. While Raine measured out the sugar, Mary Jane spread several peppercorns out on the wooden countertop, and using the bottom of a cast iron frying pan, she pushed and rolled them until they reached the right consistency. She scattered them into the mix and Sarah Jane helped her stir until it was well blended.

"So, is that what makes your pie worthy of Uncle Hank's praise?" Raine asked unabashedly. "The peppercorns?"

"Maybe, but I also have a very special ingredient."

"What is it? And please don't say love. My mother always

told us that her secret ingredient in everything was love. You can imagine what happened to my little eight-year-old heart when I found out that the secret ingredient in her best chicken pot-pie was Harriet."

Mary Jane glanced over at her daughter who didn't appear to be perturbed at all by the revelation.

"No," she said with a shake of her head, "it's not love." Her face heated at the word. "You'll just have to wait and see."

It only took another half hour to separate the dough and get all the pie crusts rolled out and strips cut for the tops. Mrs. Isaacson had dozens of pie tins in her house, so it was easy to locate the three that would be needed. She demonstrated how to lay the dough over the tin, poke holes in it, then baste it with a light basting of beaten egg before setting them in the oven to brown.

Once the crusts had toasted slightly, Mary Jane pulled them from the oven and set them on top of the stove.

"Now, we just need to add the filling and our…" she turned to look up at Raine, "the special ingredient." She glanced over at her daughter and nodded toward the table.

Knowingly, Sarah Jane jumped down from the chair and grabbed the cheese round they'd brought.

Raine's brow raised.

"We're going to grate a small block of this cheese." She handed him a knife, then reached into the drawer to the side of the sink and pulled out the grater.

With several small cuts into the round, Raine pulled out a chunk and handed it to her.

Skepticism painted his face as she sprinkled handfuls of it on top of the pie filling.

"Your secret ingredient is cheese?"

"Happenstance cheese," she corrected.

"I cannot wait to taste this pie. Who would ever guess? Peppercorns and cheese."

Mary Jane picked up the remaining strips of dough and

demonstrated how to lay them across the filling in a lattice pattern and secure the edges together. Then, she basted the top of the first pie again with egg and dusted it with sugar. She brushed her hands together in a quick swishing motion, then handed the basting brush to Sarah Jane and Raine, each following their directions perfectly.

She slid the pies into the oven and glanced over at the grandfather clock for the time.

"Now, we wait."

CHAPTER SIXTEEN

"Won't be home for Christmas STOP Sorry, Mama STOP Need sled, girl, age 4 labeled Sarah Jane STOP," Raine said aloud as he scribbled down the instructions for the telegraph operator. He was downright giddy at the idea of surprising Sarah Jane with one of Ethan's sleds for Christmas. With just seven weeks left before the holiday, he'd wanted to give his brother plenty of time to both make and have the item shipped to Thistleberry.

He thought of Mary Jane. Dinner the previous evening had gone much better than he could have expected, and he wondered if he should request something for her as well.

"Mr. Redbourne," a man whose height scarcely reached the top of his shoulders landed a flour-sized potato sack with leather straps and labeled 'U.S. Mail' on the standing desk in front of him, effectively covering the note he'd been making.

Raine had never before met the man, but he reckoned that in a small town like this, it was not usual that the people knew all the goings on.

"These have to stop. Will you just get on with it already and choose one of them to marry?" Without further word of explanation, the odd man walked back through the door to the right of the telegraph operator's window which read, 'Thistleberry Postal Service, Gerald T. Tulley, Postmaster.'

Raine looked down at the mail bag in front of him.

He exhaled loudly.

"Not more letters." He hadn't even read the ones Lucy had given him yet.

He opened the bag and a burst of several different perfumes exploded into the air, invading his nostrils with headache-inducing accuracy and he snapped the bag shut again.

"Whoa." He turned his head, reeling from the pungent fragrances that immediately caused his eyes to water.

After a moment, he felt better prepared and braced for the onslaught. He nudged the opening of the bag to find handfuls of letters of varied shapes and sizes all addressed to Raine Redbourne, care of Whisper Ridge Ranch, Thistleberry, Montana.

Did all the men who placed ads in the paper get this kind of response?

He glanced through them, noting that while only one or two of the letters came from town, most had come from towns back East, one he saw had come from as far as Baltimore.

If Cole put that ad in another paper…

He didn't finish the thought but stuffed the letters back into the bag and strapped it shut.

While he certainly had not come to Montana in search of a bride, it was nice to know that he had options. Honestly, he was surprised that he'd received any responses from women in Montana or any other places out west. He'd always heard that women were scarce in these parts and that men were numbered two hundred to one in some places. That certainly had not been his experience since coming to Thistleberry.

He smiled at the thought of the last of three pies that still sat on the porch railing where they'd placed them last night to cool and the woman who'd taught him how to make it. He didn't understand what was wrong with the men in this town to not see how beautiful and smart she was. And who in their right mind couldn't love her little girl?

Setting the mail bag aside, he added to his note for the telegrapher.

"My large domed dish, STOP." The ceramic butter dish Rafe had given him and Sarah on their wedding day had been one of the first his brother had attempted on an old pottery wheel, and it was big enough to hold near an entire wheel of Mary Jane's cheese. It was time someone got some use out of it.

How had the Bennett ladies made such an impression on him in a matter of days? He figured that he knew more about Mary Jane Bennett than most of those bachelors who courted women through correspondence could glean about their prospective brides from words on a page.

"Post with details to follow, STOP. Raine."

His mother would no doubt be able to read between the lines of his telegram, but he didn't care. Maybe it would satisfy her perpetual matchmaking attempts.

Eleven years was a long time to be alone. He'd felt it more in the last few months than ever before.

You'll be happy again, my love, Sarah had spoken to him through a tired smile on cracked lips just hours before she'd passed on. *Promise me you'll try.*

He hadn't believed her. Couldn't.

He'd held her hand for hours, crying into the blankets that covered the lifeless body that also carried their child—couldn't be consoled and had isolated himself for weeks after they'd come to collect them. He hadn't shared that last burden with anyone, and it still pained him to think about what he'd lost.

Many women over the years had caught his attention, but none with whom he'd desired to pursue anything more than friendship.

Until now.

He figured he could include more information about his

requests in a letter, but if he wanted the handcrafted items from his brothers to arrive before Christmas, he needed to get the basic information over to them now.

"That'll be thirty-two cents, Mr. Redbourne."

Raine tossed the man four bits.

He collected the mail bag from the floor and walked outside into the fresh, crisp mountain air. One whiff told him that a storm was brewing, but when he glanced up into the bright blue sky there was nary a cloud. He hoped the weather would hold a few more days at least. He wasn't too keen on experiencing a full Montana winter and wanted to hold it off for as long as possible.

With that thought in mind, he decided that maybe he would buy thicker winter underwear to help get him through.

The streets of Thistleberry bustled with commotion as farmers, quilters, ranchers and more lined the boardwalk with their wares, produce, and livestock. What had been merely the bones of wooden frames yesterday had turned into fully ornamented booths and pens full of animals. The pavilion had been completed and now boasted an elevated platform accented with tables full of produce and other goods all around.

He admired how the layout of the town had allowed for such a thing, still leaving plenty of room for wagons to get by on either side. When his eyes fell on several crates turned upside down to display different types of cheese, wool-lined hats and gloves, and brightly colored skeins of yarn, he searched for any sign of Mary Jane.

Tessa popped up from behind the table and placed several blocks of linen-wrapped butter and small mason jars filled with lotions and ointments, likely produced harvesting the oils from their wool in calculated places among the crates.

"Hello, Raine. It's nice to see you."

"Tessa." He nodded.

"I heard that you might be staying around for a while. I was a little surprised you would take a position this far north. If memory serves, you aren't much of a fan of the cold."

"That's true."

"Sheriff, huh? Can't say that part surprises me, though. You Redbourne men did always have a strong sense of responsibility when it comes to what's right and wrong." She placed her hands on her hips and smiled.

A few moments of awkward silence passed.

"It looks like you're settling in yourself," he said. She'd seen the error of her ways and had asked his forgiveness. Who was he not to at least try to let it go?

"Mrs. Deardon and M.J. have been good to me. I didn't deserve it, I know, but they took a chance on me, and I don't want to let them down."

What could he say to that? He hoped she was being sincere and wanted to believe that she spoke the truth.

She chuckled.

"M.J.'s just over at the judges table dropping off her pies." She motioned toward the boardwalk in front of the mercantile where a beautifully decorated table housed dozens of different types and styles of pie.

He nodded his gratitude and started for the mercantile.

"Hey," Tessa called after him.

He looked back over his shoulder, then turned to face her.

"I never got the chance to say thank you for pulling us out of that pit the other night." Her hand self-consciously moved to the back of her neck. "I know you probably had reservations when you found out it was me, but…" she folded her arms at her waist, "thank you."

"I'm glad you're all right." He managed a smile and a nod before turning back to the judges' booth.

Fruit pies and cobblers, pumpkin and pecan, even creamed pies were all a part of the festivities and each of them were labeled on the table with a number for the judges. Too bad he hadn't been here long enough to have volunteered for that job.

He laughed to himself.

At the end of the table sat a large box with an open slot in the top with a stack of small paper squares and a few scattered pencils next to it. The sign in front had his name written in large bold letters with the words 'Yay or Nay' directly below it.

Hank had assured him that the vote was merely a formality. Most of the jobs Raine had considered in the past had been hired positions by a mayor or superior officer in the town. Since his uncle was the mayor in Thistleberry and had offered him the job several times over the course of the last few months, he'd been surprised at the need for such formality.

When Raine caught sight of Mary Jane speaking to the owner of the mercantile, his breath nearly caught in his chest. Her cream-colored blouse, adorned with a soft lace pattern, opened slightly at the neck and the tan skirt she wore hugged in all the right places.

Watch it, Redbourne.

A light breeze brushed the curls she wore away from her face and she looked up and met his gaze. Her cheeks stained a beautiful pink, and she bit her lip, then smiled. She finished her conversation and joined him.

"Just how many jobs can one Redbourne man take on at one time?" she asked, pointing at the mail bag he carried. "Sheriff, Rancher, *and* Mail Courier?"

Why hadn't he dropped the bag in the livery with the wagon? He would rectify that right now.

"Walk with me?" he asked.

Mary Jane nodded and stepped in alongside him.

"I had a wonderful time last night," she said, tucking a tendril behind her ear as she turned to look at him.

"I think that is supposed to be my line."

"Okay…"

She waited expectantly as they continued to walk.

He chuckled.

"I had a wonderful time last night," he repeated her words exactly. "I almost had a slice of that pie for breakfast, but thought I'd save my appetite for the festivities, then take the time to enjoy it when I get home tonight. Andrew tells me that the food generally served at this thing is well worth the wait."

As they curved around back of the pavilion, he was surprised to see how many men and women stood over their cast-iron baking kettles. Some sat on foldable wooden stools, others on the ground, but all presumably cooking up their stews, cobblers, beans, and chili to be served for supper before the dance. It was hard to believe that Thistleberry crammed all the activities into a single day.

When they reached the livery, Raine slipped inside to exchange one of the bushels in the back of his buckboard that he'd filled with freshly picked apples for the mail satchel.

"Ooof," a man grunted.

Sounded like trouble.

Raine peered around the corner from where his wagon had been stowed to see two brutes, whose backs were to him, and Harvey, the young owner of the livery. The man's eye looked bruised and swollen, and the corner of his mouth was bleeding.

"See, the boss don't like fellas who renege on their end of the deal." The largest of the two men landed another punch in the gut to the man.

"Is there a problem here, fellas?" Raine said, standing up tall and taking a step toward them. He set down his bushel.

"This ain't none of your concern," the shorter heavy said as he turned to glance back at him. The man's eyes widened to the size of silver dollars when he caught Raine's stare and without taking his gaze from him, he tapped the other man's arm with the back of his hand. "Mundy," he said, barely moving his lips as if he couldn't be heard.

"What is it?"

Mundy?

Why did he know that name?

As the man jerked his head a couple of times in his direction, the large brute finally turned around, recognition sparking a twitch in his eye. The knuckles on his right hand were bloodied, but he wore a leather wrap around his left hand, which appeared to be missing a couple of fingers.

"I think it is my concern," Raine said, narrowing his eyes at the men and taking another step in their direction, his hand now resting on the grip of his holstered revolver. "See, I've been charged with keeping the peace around here, and I aim to do just that."

The larger man took a step back next to Harvey, pulled the livery owner up by the shoulders of his shirt so he was standing up tall, then straightened the man's clothes and dusted him off.

"There's no trouble here, uh…"

"Sheriff," Raine filled in for him, then turned to the man who looked the worse for wear. "Is that true?" he asked, catching the liveryman's eyes.

Harvey looked up at Mundy, then back at him, then dipped his head.

"They were just leaving, Mr. Redbourne," he said, his jaw flexing. "Weren't you, boys?" He reached up and wiped the blood at the corner of his mouth with his thumb, then hobbled over to the worktable in the corner.

"Of coursin' we was," Mundy said. "Always good to catch up with old friends, just as long as they don't overstay their welcome."

As he passed, he bent down, retrieved a pair of apples from the bushel and tossed one to his friend. Then, standing up to his full height—still an inch or two shorter than Raine—he bit into the fruit and looked up until his eyes fixed on his.

"Sheriff." He chomped down on the bits of apple in his mouth as they headed out.

Once they'd left the livery, Raine relaxed his hand away from his gun and stretched his fingers.

"Who were those men, Harvey?"

While the vote hadn't been finalized yet, he was the closest thing Thistleberry had to a lawman right now—except the marshal.

Before he could answer, Mary Jane rushed inside through the big open door, her eyes searching from side to side until they found him. Relief washed over her near color-drained face, but her quick, short breaths told him she struggled for air.

He was at her side in a moment.

"What is it?" he asked, reaching out and tilting her face upward.

She sucked in gulps of air.

"M.J.," he coaxed, trying to keep the urgency he felt from his voice. "I need you to take a slow, deep breath for me, can you do that?" He demonstrated with a long intake of air, then blew out through his mouth.

She shook her head. "We have to find Sarah Jane."

"We will. Tell me what's wrong so I can help."

She pushed his hands away from her and frantically ran back outside, brought up short as three children ran past them, nearly knocking her to the ground, rolling hoops with their rounded stick paddles.

"Sorry, Miss Bennett," one of the young boys called back as he ran.

Raine caught up to her in seconds, following her eyes to a section of boardwalk across the street to the small open space between Mrs. Doherty's bakery and an empty building with a sign in the window that said 'Lyla's Café, Coming Soon' where several children huddled around each other, crouched down, and quiet.

Something had caught their interest. He recognized the little boots sticking out onto the dirt and realized that Sarah Jane was among them and must be lying on her belly.

Cheers erupted and the little girl jumped to her feet.

Mary Jane's eyes focused and moved through the crowd.

He followed her gaze and spotted the two scruffy men from the livery.

"You know those men?" he asked, not taking his gaze from

where they mounted two chestnuts in front of the saloon.

She didn't respond, but as they passed the gin mill on the south end of town and headed out, Mary Jane breathed out a relieved laugh, one arm wrapped around her waist and the other raised to her face. Her gaze returned to her daughter. Her fingers rubbed over her mouth and chin, and she closed her eyes with a nod and a deep breath.

Something had spooked her, and Raine had a sneaking suspicion that it had something to do with Mundy and his cohort. It was too much of a coincidence that she'd panicked just moments after they'd exited the livery stables.

Mary Jane cleared her throat, then turned to look at him, the previous fear and worry completely erased from her features.

"I'm sorry, did you say something?"

Before he could ask the question again, she clapped her hands together in front of her and turned to face him.

"We have a lot of things to do today, Mr. Redbourne," she said, moving her hands to her hips. "So, what do you say we get started with getting those apples where they need to go?"

His eyes narrowed.

Either she was fooling herself into thinking nothing had just happened, or she was just plain mad.

Maybe both.

CHAPTER SEVENTEEN

"Would you like to tell me what happened back there?"

Mary Jane knew that Raine deserved an answer, but she wasn't sure she was ready to give him one. They were still getting to know each other and while she felt she could trust him, only time would tell if her trust had been misplaced.

She looked over and saw Lyla Driscoll handing out samples of her Gooseberry Sweet Bread to people as they passed by her table.

"I heard that the woman over there is considering opening a café right here in Thistleberry." She'd seen the sign in the window next to the bakery.

"M.J.?" Raine asked in a low, even tone.

"And see that man over there in the bowler hat standing next to Andrew on the boardwalk? That's Mr. Dunbar. He owns the bank and the deeds to several of the properties in and around town. I don't know why he didn't call the bank a saving and loan. That would make much more sense, don't you think? He's—"

"M.J.?" he tried again.

"There are just so many people for you to get to know here

that I hate to waste another moment of your time." She turned toward the booth they had set up for the goods available from Happenstance. "I probably should be getting back to the booth to check in on Tessa. I mean, I know that Astrid and Casey are there to help with the table, but…"

Raine reached out and caught her by the hand.

"Mary Jane."

Tears verged on her lashes, but did not spill. Her smile faltered and she turned serious for a moment, meeting him squarely in the eyes.

"I know you don't understand what just happened. I barely understand it myself, but this is not the day or the place I wish to engage in that unpleasant conversation."

"I've seen that look before, M.J. You were scared."

"Yes." She cleared her throat. "I don't take kindly to brutes and thugs who claim to uphold the law all while breaking it."

"Are they," he leaned closer to her, "lawmen?"

She forced a smile that would convince him to leave it alone for now. "I hope not. All I will say for now, my daughter is safe, I have a booth to run, and as long as that Mundy fellow stays away from town, we will all be the better for it."."

"So, you do know him? Mundy?"

It was her turn to narrow her eyes at him.

"Do you?"

"He was having words with Harvey, and I intervened. First time I ever laid eyes on the man."

"And, hopefully, it will be the last. For any of us." She dropped her hands. "Mr. Redbourne," they had passed that formality what felt like ages ago, but she needed him to understand, "I will tell you everything you want to know, but for now, we have work to do."

"Here you are," Andrew said as he jumped down from the boardwalk and joined them on the street. "I've been looking all over for the two of you." He glanced between her and Raine. "Is everything all right?"

"Yes, Andrew," Mary Jane assured him with a hand on his arm. "We were just picking up the apples Mr. Redbourne brought to give to Mrs. Rhoades, who is brewing up her cider for tonight. Will you help?"

"Well, I'll be," Andrew said with a grin, "M.J. Bennett asking for my help. Are you feeling all right, ma'am?" he joked.

"I could get them myself, if you'd rather," she picked up the hem of her dress and took a step toward the open livery stable door.

"That's quite all right. I think *Mr. Redbourne* and I can manage." He stepped in front of her, then tugged on Raine's coat sleeve.

Before he turned to go with his cousin, Raine looked down at her, concern laced through his brows. "Are you sure you're all right?"

She shrugged and smiled. "I hear the new sheriff in town is really good at his job."

"That he is," he replied, none too humbly.

"So, yes, I am all right."

He nodded, then ran to catch up with Andrew.

Within a few moments, both men emerged from the livery, each heaving a large bushel of apples in his arms.

"Where is this Mrs. Rhoades?" Raine asked.

Mary Jane directed them to the side of the pavilion where the woman stood over a huge stock pot braced above a newly created fire pit. No fire had been lit beneath it yet, but Mrs. Rhoades was already busy quartering apples and tossing them inside.

"Well, we've got enough men," Andrew said after setting his bushel down next to several others, "and ladies," he clarified, bringing a smile to M.J.'s lips, "to make up five four-person teams. Since we are not raising the barn from scratch, I would imagine that we'll be done with plenty of time to spare. Well, maybe not the painting part, but it should be as sturdy as they come when we're finished with it."

"What time are we heading over?" Raine asked, glancing down at some portable timekeeping contraption on his wrist.

"My brothers' wives and Aunt Mara will be expecting us for lunch around noon. We'll get to work shortly after that. Daniel and Kieran are on their way out there right now with the rest of the lumber. I still need to stop in to chat with Mr. Gibbons about the new hinges and bolt latches for the doors," he pointed at the blacksmith shop. "Then, we all want to be back with plenty of time for hot cider, pie, dinner, and dancing."

"And what time is it now?" she asked.

"Just past eleven," Raine provided.

It would take a good twenty minutes to get out to the old barn, so they had a few minutes before they needed to get going.

With Evaline staying in the fields in constant contact with the sheep since the bear had been cheeky enough to come down the mountain looking for its winter foraging in her flock and Lissa still laid up and limited in what she could do, Mary Jane figured if she left Tessa and Astrid in town to run the booth and look after Sarah Jane, that would still leave her with Judith and Casey to help out at the new barn.

"I'm surprised at how many people have turned out to this thing," Raine said as they walked from booth to booth. "Just how many people are there in Thistleberry?" he asked.

"One hundred and thirty-two, including Dusty Sorensen's new baby." Hank appeared from behind the railing on the new pavilion steps.

"It seems there are a lot more people here than that," Raine observed.

"Wait until tonight. Mr. Beverly over at the hotel informs me he has a full house. So far, I've seen visitors from Hendale, Murphy, and Middleton."

"What's bringing them all around? Don't they have their own festivals?"

"They do." He nodded firmly. "A lot of the ranchers in the territory are both curious and furious that we have allowed a sheep herding operation to get started up here."

"But we—" Mary Jane started.

Hank held up his hand.

"They are worried that we are opening the doors for more sheep ranchers to come and that their flocks will make the land unsuitable for cattle. I'm hoping they haven't come to stir up any trouble, but Raine, you may want to keep a lookout for anyone looking to cause a fuss."

Raine shot Mary Jane a look—a brow raised, but he said nothing.

The Deardons ran one of the largest cattle ranches in all the Montana territory, so she believed his word would carry weight with the others.

"This isn't something that is going away, M.J." Hank warned. "But I am assured they are just here to learn more about how cattle and sheep ranches can work together."

A chill stirred the air.

Mary Jane looked up into the sky, but it appeared as beautiful as ever a day was. She rubbed her arms, grateful she'd thought to bring her coat as well as her shawl into town today and made a mental note to grab it before they headed out to the barn.

Raine had obviously noticed her chill as he took off his own coat and wrapped it around her shoulders.

"Thank you for your concern, both of you. I assure you, Mayor Deardon, I will be on my best behavior today. And Sheriff Redbourne, your coat is much appreciated."

"All right, I'll meet you kids out there," Hank said with a wave as he hustled over to catch Mrs. Smith at the judge's table.

Mary Jane glanced around, noting as Raine had seen, that there were an unusual amount of people attending during the early hours of the day before many of the festivities were even scheduled to begin. It was normal for near the whole town to come out for supper and to stay for the music and dancing, but to have so many of their farmers and other ranchers there to sell off the last of their crops before winter set in was marvelous.

It was also nice to see that Mrs. Smith, instead of begrudging them sales, was offering to help the farmers set up their displays and to use some of the children's slates from the school to make price lists and other signs.

"Have you seen anything of interest?" she asked Raine as they walked through the center of town.

"The first day I arrived," he said with a smile.

Heat rose in her cheeks, but she was pleased at his inference.

"Thistleberry has certainly grown a lot since I was here last. I think my granddad and my uncles were just about the only people for a hundred miles."

"With the mill just coming to town in the last few years, we've had an influx of residents—some families, but mostly men looking for work. It didn't take long before Mr. Fawcett had to start turning people away."

"And where did they go, these people?"

"Moved on mostly to the next settlement and the next, looking for another opportunity, I guess. Some tried to find jobs in town, others hired on with the Deardons, but there are still some that travel around these parts like vagabonds, setting up camps near the river."

Raine shivered. "Just the thought of living that close to the water in a Montana winter makes me cold."

"Would you like your coat back?"

"No. No, I'm fine." He stuck his hands in his front pockets. "We probably should go get the horses or we'll be late. I can't imagine that Aunt Mara would look too kindly on that."

They laughed.

"Need a ride?" Andrew pulled up alongside them in a wagon overflowing with mountains of unbaled hay strapped down with a rope ladder down the center.

With Hank on the seat next to his son, the only option was to ride atop the hay.

Before she knew it, Raine had jumped up onto the back of the wagon bed and held out his hands for her. With only a moment's reluctance, she slipped her hands into his and he pulled her up next to him with ease. He wrapped his hands around her waist and lifted her up the rest of the way to perch on the hay before climbing up alongside her.

The wagon jostled as Andrew pulled forward, throwing Mary Jane slightly off balance, but Raine caught her and pulled her close to him with a laugh. As they rode out of town, a young couple Mary Jane had never seen before walked along the wayside, an infant child cuddled tightly in the man's arms. Their faces, streaked and stained, looked tired and worn. The woman wore what looked like sack cloth tied with rope around her feet and yet she smiled up at them as they passed.

"Who are they?" Raine asked.

"I don't know. They must be new in town."

The wagon came to a stop.

"Howdy, strangers," Hank called out to the weary couple. "Don't know as you're interested or not, but we are headed out to fix up an old barn and wondered if you might come along and help. The Mrs. put together some roast beef, fresh-baked bread, and potato salad for anyone willing."

Mary Jane's heart warmed inside her chest.

"I imagine we are about to find out," she said with a smile.

She loved how Hank had approached it in a way that would save the man's pride.

"I'm as good with a hammer as any," the man replied. "Name's Jethro and this is my wife, Alice. And the little one here, he's Asher."

The wagon tousled, but Mary Jane couldn't see what was happening.

Andrew climbed up next to her.

"Figured they would be more comfortable on the bench seat," he said with a smile.

They rode quietly for the remainder of the trip. When they

reached the old barn, it seemed that all the Deardons had congregated there along with some of the ranchers from neighboring farms. Most of them she recognized, but there were several with whom she'd never been acquainted.

Hank introduced Alice to Lucy and Alex. Her boss put her arm around the young woman and led her over to the table where the food had been laid out. Alex strode over to where her husband stood and leaned over to whisper something to him. In moments, she was on horseback and headed toward home. Mary Jane had no doubts that the young woman and her child were in good hands.

She slid down the hay until her feet touched the sides of the wagon.

"May I help you down from there, m'lady?" Andrew asked, bending over at the waist in a proper bow.

While he was bent down, Raine didn't waste any time and held his arms open for her.

She jumped.

"Too late, my dear cousin. Too late," he said, one arm still around her and the other patting Andrew on the shoulder.

Sam handed Jethro a saw and pointed over to a group of men working on the doors that would be raised up to cover the loft. When he looked over at Mary Jane, he raised a hand in greeting.

"I think we have everything ready to go, M.J. The ladies are chomping at the bit to get these men fed, but I think we can get a good hour's worth of work in before we take a break. What do you think?"

"When you Deardons do something, you certainly do it big. I imagine Lucy is thrilled with the turnout."

"She is," Lucy said, walking up behind them with Casey and Judith. "Lucas and Garrett have been out here since sunup, writing up a list of everything that needs to be done with each section of the barn. They said it has better bones than we could have asked for."

"We've been blessed that the weather has held out long enough. Evaline will be thrilled she won't have to spend another night out in that freezing wagon." Judith shuddered. "I don't know how she does it."

"Oh, don't go feeling bad for Evaline. She likes being out there all alone with the sheep," Casey said. "And have you seen that thing she sleeps in? She's made it up quite cozy with her books and her curtains and her tea kettle."

Mary Jane looked at Sam, realizing she never actually answered his question.

"I think you're right. The faster we get working on this thing, the faster we'll all be able to get back and enjoy Mrs. Rhoades' hot apple cider."

"Amen," one of the men shouted, followed by several more.

She bent down to the toolbox at the base of the lumber pile, took out a hammer, and handed it to Raine.

"I've seen your work with one of these. What do you say you build a pent roof off the side of the barn?"

He snatched the hammer away from her with a sly grin.

"Challenge accepted."

CHAPTER EIGHTEEN

Raine could not get the little vagrant family out of his head. He'd learned from Hank that Jethro had been living among the Sioux people for a time, but after the atrocities that both preceded and followed the horrendous Battle of Little Bighorn, he'd left his new friends behind and had been unable to find steady work. With only a trunk full of utensils and the clothes on their backs, they had landed in Thistleberry with their last hope before winter.

From his position on the roof, he could see his little farm, only slightly obscured by the large apple and walnut trees that shaded the house. His Shropshire Down sheep dotted the pasture, but from this distance it was impossible to distinguish the ewes from the lambs. The ram was corralled on the opposite side of the house out of view.

It fascinated him that while the baby lamb that had endeared itself to him looked chocolatey brown with a dark face, legs, and ears, the older sheep, though still having dark faces, legs, and ears wore a thick white coat.

How had Mrs. Isaacson done it all?

He thought of the aging woman trying to take care of all her animals and felt how hard it must have been for her to leave them behind. He was sure that the sheep had gotten out of hand, growing more than she could have handled on her own as there had been no one else to look after or watch over them.

Hank had told him he didn't think there were any more than a dozen, but there had been significantly more last he counted. It was a wonder that the lot of them had not ended up on the butcher's block. If he was going to stay in that house, he would need to make sure he had someone to care for the place while he was seeing to his responsibilities in town.

That's it!

An idea sparked inside of him, and suddenly he found himself working faster, anxious to finish replacing the large section of roof that had caved in, likely at some point in the last few months as the breaks still appeared fairly new.

A light swirl of wind picked up.

"Blamed cold," he muttered under his breath.

Part of him was grateful not to have the bulky coat to inhibit his movements while up on the roof, but a bigger part of him could imagine the warm wool lining insulating him from the cold. His fingers were growing stiff.

Done.

He pounded the last nail into the wood and turned to sit, knees up and arms resting on them. From this vantage point, he could also see the town to the south and Whisper Ridge to the east. A light mist rolled in across the landscape and he tilted his head to the sky. The bright blue had now faded to a muted grey, and a few clouds now appeared overhead.

With his hands now clutched together, he brought them up to his mouth and blew warm air into them. It was growing colder by the minute. With the hammer tucked into the back of his britches, he climbed down the side of the barn.

Raine stood back and admired the respite section he'd created to the side of the barn with the pent roof as well as the repairs he'd made on the main roof.

"You look like you may be growing ice crystals off the end

of your nose." Lucas had four wooden planks strung across his shoulder and was headed for the interior of the barn. "Where's your coat?"

The sound of Mary Jane's laugh pulled his gaze toward her as she and one of the other women helped Andrew lift the door.

"Ah," Lucas breathed. "What we'll do for our women."

Before Raine could object that Mary Jane wasn't his yet, Lucas was out of sight. He made his way over to where the women were handing out platefuls of food. He rubbed his hands together, and with the sight of three different steaming pots, he hoped for something to warm his hands and belly.

"We've got coffee, chicory, or hot lemonade?" Aunt Mara asked with a smile, holding a tin ladle in her woolen gloved hands.

It had been a long while since he'd had a nice hot lemonade and he had to stop himself from licking his lips.

"I'm betting if you are anything like your daddy, you're going to go for the lemonade with just a splash of chicory," she said as she removed the lid on the pot closest to her.

"Yes, ma'am," he said. "That sounds quite inviting. Thank you."

"How are your folks?" she asked, pouring a tin of coffee and handing it over to the gentleman standing next to him, bundled up in a scarf and woolen cap beneath his hat.

"And just where do I get one of those?" he asked, pointing at the man's neck.

"Mr. MacPherson here bought it from Happenstance last winter."

"Well, I have a feeling I'm going to have to invest in the ranch just to keep warm up here."

Mr. MacPherson patted him on the shoulder.

"Might want to start with a coat, son," he said as he walked away.

Brilliant idea.

Raine leaned up against the wagon next to Aunt Mara.

"He's right, you know." She grabbed a blanket from behind her and shook it out to place around his shoulders.

"Thank you."

The initial chill from the blanket settled into a radiating warmth and he hugged it around him, careful not to spill his drink.

"Mama is good. She's thrilled to have one more of her son's married off, and Dad couldn't be happier to finally have a granddaughter." He took a sip of the lemonade, and it left a warm trail from his throat to his belly. He hunched his shoulders a bit, holding the cup close to him. "Leave it to the only daughter to have the only granddaughter," he said with a chuckle.

"And how are you, being so far away from home?"

"I haven't decided yet. Will's been in England now for a long time—though he's considering a move back. Tag's in Texas. And Cole's in Colorado. I just never really thought of anywhere other than Kansas as home."

"It must be hard on Leah having so many of her children far away. I feel very fortunate that my boys have stuck right around me. Not every mother gets that."

"Why do you think Levi went to work for the railroad?" Raine laughed. "He understands the importance of keeping family connected and felt that he could help make that happen for all the mamas out there missing their children."

He caught another glimpse of Mary Jane as she held up the final barn door so Andrew could finish securing the hinges he'd picked up this morning at the blacksmith shop. A few moments later, she took a step back to assess their work. From this angle, it looked straight. She must have thought so as well because she nodded.

She didn't move. Raine guessed that she was taking in the sight. It had to be quite satisfying to have the building come together so quickly with so many hands here to help.

"They say it won't be long before the railroad makes its way through Helena. That would make your trip back to Kansas significantly shorter."

"Yes," he said, still not taking his eyes from Mary Jane. "Yes, it would."

"She's a catch that one," Aunt Mara said. "Stubborn as all get out and determined, but a good soul. It doesn't surprise me one bit that a Redbourne man is who can see it."

"She is something all right." He finished off his lemonade and handed the tin cup back to his aunt.

"Isn't it beautiful?" Lucy asked, joining him at the wagon. "With a little more work on the inside, it will be just perfect to provide shelter for the sheep during the winter months."

"You've done well for yourself, Lucy," he said, turning to focus on his cousin's wife. "Happenstance is quite incredible. What you do for those women is highly admirable."

"Thank you."

The Deardons had set up a ring of logs around a newly created fire pit. Raine spotted Jethro and his wife sitting near the fire, eating and feeding their baby. He was grateful that Hank had stopped the wagon. It is something he, his dad, or any of his brothers would have done as well. He'd watched today as the man tirelessly worked to help with any task asked of him. He did not stop until the work was done and that impressed Raine.

"Will you excuse me a moment, ladies?" He pushed away from the side of the wagon, the blanket still wrapped around him, and walked over to where the young couple was seated.

He noted immediately that Alice's feet were covered with boots and both she and her husband wore scarves around their necks.

I have got to get me one of those.

"Excuse me," he said, tapping the man on the shoulder, "might I have a word?"

Jethro handed the remaining portion of his roast beef sandwich to Alice, leaned over and kissed the woman and baby, then stood to follow him.

"Sorry to take you away from your family, but I wondered if you might be looking for work."

The man's eyes lit up.

"Yes, sir."

"I'd like to hire someone to look after a small herd of sheep—say thirty-eight to be exact. I don't really know your situation, but something is telling me that I need to offer you the job, so I'm offering—if you're interested."

"*If* I'm interested? Yes. Yes, I'm interested."

Raine remembered the apartment built into the back of the barn and suddenly they made sense. The barn was used for the sheep during the winter and the rooms were for the shepherd.

"I can offer you and your family a warm place to stay at the farm along with a fair day's wages."

"Mr…I'm sorry, I don't even know your name."

"It's Raine." He extended his hand and Jethro took it with vigor.

"I don't know what to say."

"Say you'll start today."

"You are an answer to prayer, Mr…Raine. I can start right now if you need me."

"How about we ride out of here in a few minutes to collect your things, then we can take them back to the house and get you settled before we head into town to enjoy the rest of the festival?"

"Alice!" Jethro called loudly, rapidly waving his arm for his wife to join them.

She immediately hurried over to stand next to her husband.

"This man just offered me a job. Looking after his sheep."

Her eyes widened and a huge smile crossed her face.

They laughed and he hugged her close.

"How did you know?" Alice asked, holding Asher tightly against her chest.

"Know what?"

"That Jethro is…" she glanced over at her husband, her

brows scrunched together, then back at him, "a…shepherd. You didn't know?"

Raine laughed too, shaking his head.

"Really?"

"Yes, I grew up on a small farm in the Wood River Valley in Idaho. We raised sheep along with goats and pigs and chickens."

"Well, you will fit right in at home. Although, there's only one pig, Fred, and Gertrude the dairy cow."

"God is good," Alice said, reaching out for his hand and squeezing. "Thank you."

He was embarrassed to think about how long it had been since he'd stepped foot in church, but it warmed him to think that just maybe God had used him to help these people. And him.

"It's my pleasure, ma'am. I should be the one thanking you."

"I should also be thanking you for helping out today," Mary Jane said, stepping up from behind him.

Something leapt inside Raine's chest at the sound of her voice.

"It was Jethro and Alice, right? Every helping hand was needed today to get this barn ready before winter really sets in, so thank you for being here. Because of the help we received today, we'll have a shelter to protect our sheep against the impending weather."

"I actually find that the sheep love the cold. We used to have to coax the flock into the barn in the wintertime. I found that using a little grain usually does the trick. It's important to keep them dry." Jethro smiled and held out his hand. "You must be Mrs. Raine."

"Redbourne," Raine corrected. "I mean *my* name is Raine Redbourne. This is M.J. Bennett. She is the foreman at our neighboring ranch. This barn," he pointed to the structure they had just finished repairing, "belongs to Happenstance Ranch."

Raine liked the color that flooded Mary Jane's cheeks.

"So, the two of you aren't…?" Alice started, but didn't finish her thought. Didn't need to.

At the mention of his last name, Jethro grew quiet. He stared at Raine for a moment, an odd expression crossing his face, his brows scrunched, and his eyes narrowed as if trying to reconcile some point of confusion.

"Jethro," Mary Jane asked, skipping the woman's question all together, "how do you know so much about sheep?"

"Grew up with them," the man managed, finally diverting his gaze away from Raine and onto Mary Jane.

"I've hired Jethro to shepherd my sheep." Technically, they weren't his sheep, but they were his responsibility. He tried to gauge the man's reaction, but whatever had bothered him, seemed to have passed.

"That is wonderful news," Mary Jane said, stepping over next to Alice and putting her arm around the woman. "Will you be staying in the barn apartment there?"

How did she know there was a living space in the barn?

"You must have known Mrs. Isaacson pretty well," Raine said.

"I helped her out on occasion. The property really was too big for her to handle on her own."

It didn't surprise Raine at all that Mary Jane would go out of her way to help an aging neighbor. He watched how her face lit up as she talked about it.

"I couldn't help but notice the enormous fields of cattle on the way," Jethro said. "How do the ranchers up here like having two sheep ranches in the area?"

"I don't know that I'd call the farm a sheep ranch exactly," Raine said.

"Those were Deardon cattle," Mary Jane answered. "Their niece, Lucy, owns the Happenstance. They've made it work."

"Hank told me today that some of the ranchers from the surrounding towns aren't being as understanding," Raine said.

"He expects trouble before too long."

"Why would they care?" Mary Jane asked.

Raine had grown up around cattle ranchers his whole life and knew all too well the attitudes they had about sheep. He thought for a moment on how he could put it delicately.

"Most believe sheep to be…meadow maggots," he'd heard the term often, "overgrazing the land and polluting the water."

Mary Jane narrowed her eyes.

"What does that mean, exactly?"

"Cattle ranchers believe that the sheep make the grazing land unsuitable for their cattle," Jethro shrugged. "They think the flock's hooves cut up the grasses on the range and leave the ground with a scent that is unpleasant to their herds. Up until about twelve years ago, my family lived in peace with the other farmers in the area, but a group of cowboys from Texas moved into the area with their vast herds of cattle and within a couple of years all that changed."

"Changed how?"

"Let's just say the cattlemen and the sheepherders did not get along."

"Honestly," Raine said, "I think it's their livelihood and they feel like sheep get in the way of their profits. If they have to share the range or their water rights with other livestock, their returns are diminished."

Mary Jane turned to look at him. "You come from a ranching family. Is that how you feel too? Do you think that sheep are…are meadow maggots?"

"My family, the Redbournes that is, we're horse ranchers. It's different. And the cattle ranchers in the family are all right here. Last I saw, they have gone out of their way to make sure that Happenstance has a chance of surviving."

"You didn't answer my question."

"I don't know anything about sheep. Why do you think I hired Jethro to help out?"

Mary Jane's hackles were up and that would get him

nowhere.

"If I thought they were maggots, M.J., would I have let one of them sleep on my bed last night?"

Mary Jane opened her mouth to say something in return, then seemingly thought better of it. Then, after a minute, she spurted out a laugh, then another.

"The lamb? I would have loved to have seen that." Her eyes grew wide, and her cheeks again flooded with color. "I mean, it's funny to think about a man your size cuddling with a little lamb."

There was the smile he'd hoped to see.

"Well, I wouldn't say cuddle exactly." Though that is exactly what it had amounted to in the end.

"When will I get to meet my flock?" Jethro asked.

Raine loved that he'd only hired the man a few minutes ago and he already had taken responsibility for the sheep.

"I'll get Andrew to take us over there right now. I can show you the apartment and we'll head out to pick up the rest of your things on the way to the festival."

Jethro nodded. He placed an arm around his wife and squeezed.

"Mr. Redbourne, Miss Bennett. I can't thank you enough for what you and your family have done for us today." He looked down at Alice's feet, which were now covered with a sturdy pair of fine boots and squeezed her again.

"Glad to have you on board," Raine said with a firm shake of his hand.

"Did you get some food and hot chicory?" Mary Jane asked.

"Yes, thank you."

Raine turned to go find Andrew.

The hay from the wagon they had rode in on had all been unloaded just beneath the pent roof he'd built, and he didn't think anyone would mind if he borrowed one of their wagons for an hour or two this afternoon. After all, Aunt Mara and Lucy had each brought a wagon from Whisper Ridge, and Alex and

Daphne, along with most of the men had ridden their horses.

"It was very kind of you to offer Jethro a job," Mary Jane said, struggling to keep up with his stride.

"Kind had nothing to do with it. I needed someone to watch over the sheep and the farm while I'm seeing to my duties in town and the opportunity presented itself." It had seemed a logical decision, but if it helped a struggling family at the same time, all the better.

"How is the lamb?"

Raine smiled.

"I turned her out with the other sheep this morning. She seemed quite anxious to find her mama and feed." Before she could say anything else, he added, "Already fixed the hole in the fence where I suspect she got through."

"Did you really let her sleep next to you last night?"

"She didn't give me much of a choice. Who would have guessed that something so little could jump up onto a man's bed?"

Mary Jane giggled.

"Thank you," she said, stopping where she stood.

It took him a moment to realize she was no longer walking alongside him, and he stopped to face her.

"For what?"

"For being different."

He wasn't sure whether or not to take that as a compliment.

"I'm serious. You are unlike any man I've ever met."

Again, he was unsure what she was trying to say.

"You haven't met my brothers." Well, except for Rafe, and with the mood he'd been in, the resemblance may have been difficult to see.

"M.J.," Lucy called and hurried to her side.

"Excuse me, ladies," he said with a quick raise of his hat.

While they were busy with chatter, Raine turned back with a chuckle to find Andrew. He spotted his cousin over by the food wagon speaking with his mother. They had just finished unloading the last of three hay wagons into a two-story sized stack to the side of the barn in front of the pent roof.

A quick memory of the twins jumping off the roof of the barn at Redbourne Ranch into the haystack brought a smile to his face. It was odd to think of them now as being married with children of their own.

"It's a good thing you're doing, Raine," Aunt Mara told him. "And I'm sure you are relieved that you'll have help out at the farm. When my husband told me he'd turned the place over to you, I knew you'd need some extra help—especially when you were in town. It was like Mr. Miller and his family were dropped right into your lap."

That was exactly how Raine felt.

The responsibilities of a sheriff did not cease because of festivals or Sundays. While he technically had not yet been voted in, he wanted to make sure everything was in place to take over the position, and that included his responsibilities on the farm. He could easily get the morning chores done, but caring for the sheep was a whole other matter and he was more than happy to share that responsibility with Jethro.

He still could not believe his good fortune that the man already had experience working with the animals and he offered up a silent prayer of gratitude.

When they reached the farm, Raine took Jethro and Alice into the barn and showed them all the repairs and improvements he'd made over the last couple of days, including the upgrades he'd made to the two-roomed apartment, now complete with a wood-burning potbellied stove and several new lanterns for better lighting.

"It's not much, but I've already ordered a new mattress for the bed—it should be finished and ready for pickup by the end of next week. I bought some curtains there," he pointed to the small table he'd repaired the previous day, "but I haven't had a chance to hang them."

"This is more than we could have hoped for," Alice said,

beaming as she ran her fingers over the curtain material.

"I'm sure there are some extra linens and blankets in the house. Or we can just pick some up in town this afternoon."

"This is truly generous of you, Mr. Redbourne."

"Please," he told the man, "call me Raine."

"I'm ready for you to put me to work, Raine. Where are the sheep?"

Since the buildings at the farm were fairly close together, it did not take much time to introduce Jethro to Gertrude, the chickens, the Clydesdales, the mare, and Fred. When they reached the pasture where the sheep were grazing, Jethro spotted the quarter filled bushel basket of apples he'd left at the base of the gate to finish tomorrow afternoon.

"May I?" he asked, pointing down at them.

"Take whatever you'd like," Raine said.

Other than the roast beef and bread Aunt Mara had fed them, he had no idea when they'd eaten last. Raine wanted to make sure to get the couple back into town in time for supper.

The new hire stuffed a few apples into his pockets, then climbed over the fence and walked out to be amongst the sheep.

Rudy and Bo growled, both running at the new shepherd.

"Steady," he issued the command to slow down. "Wait."

He moved to be in the center of a small group of sheep that had clustered together to graze and waited. While the dogs stayed and watched, they laid down in the grass next to him as if sensing he was their boss. After a few minutes, Jethro extended one of his hands with an apple in his palm and waited again.

Baaa. Baaa.

Raine looked down. His little friend from last night stood just on the other side of the gate and scratched at the wood with her hoof.

"Well, hello, little one," he said, climbing the fence and reaching down to scratch behind her ears.

She raised her head to meet him.

"It's getting a little cold out here, don't you think?" He stood up straight and looked back over at Jethro.

To his amazement, two of the ewes had become curious enough and felt safe enough to approach him. The dogs still lay silent in the grass.

The lamb batted at his leg, yearning for more attention. He laughed.

"If you want to survive out here, girl, you're not going to be able to sleep in the house anymore I'm afraid." He bent down and gathered her up into his arms.

Now, Jethro was surrounded by another couple of ewes and the apple was gone from his hand. He was petting one of them. Raine stood there amazed at what he was seeing.

He glanced down at his wristwatch. It was well after four o'clock and he imagined supper would likely start around five or five thirty, but he did not want to disturb the man while he worked. As if sensing it was time to go, Jethro turned around, both hands still extended as he slowly walked toward him, grazing his hands over as many sheep as stood near him. Touching them. Making contact with them.

"You said you wanted to go back to the festival, did you not?" he asked, scrunching his forehead as he glanced at the lamb in Raine's arms. "I thought you said you didn't know anything about sheep."

"I don't."

"Well, not every lamb is trusting enough to let someone hold her—especially, if they haven't been around a lot of people."

"I think this one is just a little different. She escaped over into the Happenstance fields. They found her and brought her back yesterday. She's wanted my attention ever since."

"Would you like me to take her?" he asked.

Raine looked down at the little lamb resting peacefully in his arms. If Hannah could see him right now, his little sister would be awed and amazed that he'd been persuaded to hold a baby sheep, of all animals.

"It's fine," he said, setting the little one back on the ground. "That's her mama over there." At least he hoped it was. He pointed to the ewe just a few feet away from them. He'd watched the lamb this morning when he put her back into the pasture, hungry, to see where she would go but they all looked pretty much the same to him at this point.

"You don't really know, do you?" Jethro asked knowingly.

"Nope."

The caretaker nodded with a chuckle.

Raine shrugged, good-humoredly.

"We should go."

"Yep."

After collecting Alice and the baby from the barn, along with a few supplies Raine thought they might need, they headed toward town.

"May I ask why you haven't just gone back to Idaho to work your family's farm?" Raine asked as they rode.

"When you said your name was Redbourne, I have to admit I didn't know what to think. Ranchers and sheep don't generally mix well." He chuckled to himself.

"Sounds like you have some experience with that."

Jethro didn't say anything for a good half mile or so, and Raine sensed it was difficult to talk about.

"After my father died in a conflict with one of the cattlemen back home, my mother was worried the harassment wouldn't end and couldn't bear the thought of raising us six children on her own under such harsh conditions. I was only nine at the time, too young to take over the farm, so she sold the flock and the land to a small Basque family, and we moved back East to live with my aunt."

As they approached the river, Jethro pointed to a small inlet across the bridge where a rough canvas had been pitched like a tent.

"Whoa." Raine pulled to a stop next to a humble fire pit

with a hanging iron pot and tea kettle.

"I guess city living didn't agree with me." Jethro jumped down from the wagon and held out a hand for his wife.

"Alice, why don't you stay here. I'll help break camp," Raine said, wrapping the leather straps around the rein hitch and climbing down before she could insist otherwise.

Relief washed over the woman's face. "That would be most appreciated, Mr. Redbourne."

"It's my pleasure, ma'am." He raised his hat.

Raine glanced over the small encampment.

Straw poked out from beneath a large quilt that had been spread and smoothed on the ground as a bed next to a makeshift crib that had been crafted from a broken whiskey barrel and old newspapers. A single trunk sat in the back of a small handcart and a sturdy-looking crate appeared to serve as their table, adorned in the center with a little ceramic vase sporting a collection of twigs and multi-colored leaves.

He couldn't believe he had not seen them before on his trips back and forth from town and determined to make more of a concerted effort to find those who might need food and shelter, especially in the coming months.

After Jethro took the canvas down from one of his makeshift poles, Raine joined him on the opposite side and together they folded the large cast of material.

"Let's put the cart into the back of the wagon first, then we can cover it with the canvas and tie it down along with the rest of your things." He dropped the tailboard.

Jethro nodded and pulled the cart around to the rear of the wagon.

"I'm sorry about your dad."

Even with the oversized travelling case inside, they were able to lift it into the back with ease and Raine closed the wooded gate.

"It was a long time ago. I just wish the ranchers could all be like you."

"How's that?" Raine picked up the heavily worn quilt from the makeshift bed and folded it.

"It's just nice to see a rancher with an open mind, I guess."

He'd never really thought about it before, but he had been blessed to grow up in a home where unkindness was never tolerated. To anyone. Ever.

Once they had collected their meager belongings, crate, and cooking utensils, they tossed the canvas over the top of the wagon bed and secured it with the rope Raine had brought along.

When they pulled into town, rows of improvised tables and crude chairs lined the street in front of the mercantile. The savory scent of stews, biscuits, and meat cooking on the fire mingled with the heady aroma of fruit cobblers and sweet rolls.

The livery teemed with wagons and horses from the hordes of people now gathered near the food. It looked like Harvey was directing newcomers over to the barn attached to the feed store for overflow. Raine searched the crowd for any sign of Mary Jane, but with no success.

Alex, Mara, and Daphne reached them before they could park.

"Let me see that cutie," Aunt Alex said as she reached her arms up to take the baby from Alice as she got down from the wagon seat. Then, they whisked off in the general direction of the booths at the center of town.

"Women and babies," Raine said with a quick shake of his head and a laugh.

"I can take care of the wagon, Mr. Redbourne." Jethro held out his hands for the reins. The man had more color in his face than when they'd first met several hours ago and appeared bolstered in spirit.

Raine reached into his pocket and pulled out a small, folded stack of one-dollar notes and handed them to Jethro along with the reins. The man looked up at him.

"What's this?" he asked, staring at the notes in disbelief.

"Think of it as a signing bonus. We'll discuss a proper wage once we get back to the ranch, but for now, that should help you get a few things you and that beautiful wife of yours might need to hold you over until payday—which for now will be every Monday. Is that acceptable?"

Jethro's jaw flexed and he swallowed hard.

He nodded.

"Mr. Redbourne. Mr. Redbourne." Little Sarah Jane ran up to him, grabbed his hand, and dragged him toward the booths. "I thought you were going to miss it," she said, stopping just a few feet from the pie judging table.

"The judges have made their decisions," Hank called from the podium at the top of the stairs on the pavilion.

Mary Jane and three other women stood next to him. She'd pulled her hair up on the sides, but the length of it still draped over her shoulders and the moment she caught his stare, a beautiful blush creeped onto her face, and she smiled.

A slender woman in a rose-pink dress and spectacles slipped up the stairs and handed Uncle Hank a piece of paper.

"Okay, folks," Hank said, his voice booming and boisterous as he unfolded the note, "it looks like this year's winner for overall appearance is…" he paused, gazing out among the crowd, obviously in attempt to create anticipation, "Mrs. Doherty with her Peach Cobbler Crisp."

Everyone clapped, including M.J. Then, she raised her hands in front of her and shrugged.

"What? How can that be?" Sarah Jane exclaimed, turning to look up at him. "My mama makes the best pie in the whole territory," she mimicked something he'd heard Lucy say before.

Raine raised a brow at her, and she looked down, shoulders slumped.

While amusing as it was, sore losers were never in good company.

"Sorry," she said, her voice lowering. "Good job, Mrs. Doherty." It was the most unenthusiastic congratulations he'd ever heard.

He laughed. Couldn't help himself. And he picked up the little girl and set her on his shoulder.

As everyone congratulated the older woman, Hank raised both hands in the air.

"And that's not all, folks," he boomed, "this year, the judges have decided to implement a new award for the best overall taste. And that award goes to…"

"Come on, Hank," a man called from the crowd.

"M.J. Bennett."

Sarah Jane squealed and clapped loudly next to his ear, then she leaned down and whispered.

"Told you."

"I've been informed," Hank continued, "that each of these winners provided an additional pie and with just six slices each, they will sell fast. Of course, there are plenty more varieties available that won't disappoint," he assured everyone. "Each slice has been carefully boxed up for those who wish to wait until after their supper to enjoy the treat."

Raine wrapped his arm around Sarah Jane's legs and strode quickly over to the cash box where they were selling the pie. He was first in line.

"I'll take all six slices of Miss Bennett's apple pie, please."

Groans erupted from the crowd rapidly forming behind him.

Mary Jane shot him a questioning glance. He did have an entire pie still waiting for him on the railing of his porch after all, but he had a plan.

The woman at the cash box shook her head, grumbling something about being greedy, but Raine just smiled as he paid her. She slid his purchases down the table, so she could attend to the next person in line.

He set Sarah Jane down on the ground and whispered into her ear. She nodded heartily, a huge smile spread across her face, then picked up the first boxed slice and walked it over to the milliner's shop where an older woman sat in a rocking chair, her cane resting next to her.

The woman's eyes lit up.

"Bless you, child," she exclaimed. "I just love your mama's apple pies, but with my hips the way they are, I just can't get around as well as I used to and would never have been able to get in line soon enough to get a slice. Thank you!" She raised the box to her nose and breathed deeply.

"You're welcome," Sarah Jane said before returning for the next slice.

This time, she took it to a little boy standing at the back of the line who leaned heavily on a raggedy pair of old crutches.

"For me?" he asked with disbelief.

Sarah Jane nodded.

The boy looked up at his mother, who had a tear in her eye.

"Thank you, Sarah Jane. Billy thought he was too slow to get some of your mother's pie."

The little girl leaned over and placed a kiss on the side of Billy's face. His face turned beet red and he raised a hand to wipe it off.

"What'd ya have to go and do that for?" he complained.

Raine laughed out loud.

Little Sarah Jane came back for more, and each time, she found someone to give it to who was unlikely to have been able to get it for themselves.

"You really are something, Mr. Redbourne," Mary Jane said over his shoulder as she came up behind him.

"It wasn't me," he said. "I just told her to give the slices to anyone she thought needed a smile today. That's all Sarah Jane."

By the time the little girl was finished, a woman with two young children on her hip and a third at her feet, a man leaning up against the railing column in front of the mercantile wearing dark glasses, and Alice all had slices of Mary Jane's pie. There was only one left. Sarah Jane scanned the town, and holding the small box in her hands, she made her way toward them with a satisfied smile on her face and held it out for her mother.

"What's this?" Mary Jane asked.

"I think this last piece should be for Miss Evvy. She never gets to have any fun."

Raine's heart melted at the thoughtfulness of the little girl.

"That is very kind of you, my love. I am sure she will be very pleased." M.J. said, beaming down at her daughter. She walked over to the Happenstance booth and placed the slice into one of the crates.

Folks started lining up with tin plates and cups in hand behind the various baking kettles. His stomach grumbled. The only thing he'd put in his belly today had been a cup of hot lemonade and it now protested embarrassingly loudly.

Surprised that the weather held, he pulled his jacket around him a little tighter, though it did seem significantly warmer today than it had all through the last week. Still, he was grateful to have worn several layers today, and had remembered to bring along his thick winter coat which he'd stuffed into a compartment in the back of the wagon—never again wanting to be caught unaware.

He scanned the streets for any sign of Jethro and his wife.

When he finally located them, he smiled as they were already sitting down at one of the tables with a modest amount of food in front of them. Behind them, he noted a man on the boardwalk, leaning against the corner of the bank building, whose hat rode low, obscuring a good portion of his face. A gun sat at his hip, and a long piece of straw protruded from his large moustache-topped mouth. He'd never seen the man before, but he'd not been in Thistleberry long enough to know everyone.

"Are you going to get something to eat?" Mary Jane asked.

He turned to find her holding out a tin plate and a cup for him.

"I figured you may not have known to bring one along."

He smiled at her thoughtfulness.

Like mother like daughter.

"M.J., do you know that..." he turned back to the bank, "man?" He spun around, but the stranger was nowhere to be seen.

"What man?" she asked, following his gaze.

It had been a long few days, and Raine was sure he was starting to see trouble where there wasn't any. Especially after his run-in this morning with Mundy at the livery.

"Never mind." He shook his head and smiled. He wanted to focus on more pleasant things, but couldn't help the odd feeling in his gut that something was amiss.

The meal reminded Raine of home and he wondered what they would do now that Lottie was gone. His mother could cook, but had always left that responsibility in the hands of the Spanish woman who'd become like family over the years.

Uncle Hank got back up to the top of the pavilion steps.

"Hopefully, all you fine folks of Thistleberry have had your fill of some of the best food I've had in a long while."

"Better not let your wife hear that, Mayor," someone called out from the crowd.

"His wife agrees," Aunt Mara yelled back. "Any meal I don't have to cook is best in my book."

Laughter followed.

"Well, as you know, Thistleberry has been without a sheriff since Rutledge over there left us for his new job as a territory Marshal." Hank looked down at the table closest to him and nodded.

Marshal Tyler took off his hat and raised it in the air. Raine hadn't seen him come back into town, though the man with the moustache from the bank sat next to him and Raine realized he must be one of the marshal's deputies. The knowledge should have put him at ease, but he found himself watching them even closer.

"After a near unanimous yay vote, please join me in welcoming our new sheriff, Raine Redbourne, to Thistleberry."

After several pats on the back and cheers from the crowd,

he stood, raised his hat, and nodded, then reclaimed his seat. He was neither accustomed to, nor did he desire any of the pomp that was being thrown his direction.

He didn't remember Uncle Hank as being quite so animated while he was growing up, but he could see why the people had chosen him as mayor. He had their trust, a working knowledge of ranch life, and the means to make a difference.

Music soon filled the street. Raine glanced up at the pavilion where several musicians with their banjos, guitars, a bass fiddle, and harmonica all plucked at and played their instruments with vigor, adding a spark of energy to the air.

Collectively, the tables were cleared and taken down as men grabbed their gals and the main road filled with couples dancing. Lanterns had been strung between the shops and the pavilion and down several yards of the boardwalk on either side of the street. It appeared that a lamplighter somewhere had been busy as they all now contained a soft glow that illuminated the street below.

He turned to ask Mary Jane to dance, but the marshal beat him to it.

"Miss Bennett, you are a sight to behold this evening. May I have the pleasure?" His tone was cool, but dripped with syrup.

She looked over at Raine, then back at the marshal.

What are you waiting for, Redbourne?

"Sorry, Rut," Andrew called, grabbing Mary Jane's hand and pulling her out into the middle of the street, "but she promised the first dance to me."

The marshal's jaw clenched, his smile faltered, and his nostrils flared as he strode to the opposite side of the pavilion to sulk. Raine guessed the man was used to getting exactly what he wanted.

"Mr. Redbourne," Sarah Jane called, tugging on the side of his pant leg, "will you dance with me?"

He'd never had a sweeter invitation.

"Why, it would be my pleasure, Miss Bennett," he said,

holding out his hand for her.

He picked her up and set her feet down on his boots and together they hopped around in the dirt to the lively tune of the music. He loved the sound of her little giggle as he scooped her up for a spin, then set her back down on his feet.

After a few laps around the pavilion, his Uncle Sam tapped on his shoulder.

"May I cut in?" he said, transferring Sarah Jane's feet to his own without missing a step.

With a chuckle, Raine headed to the side, but his Aunt Alex stepped in front of him, her arms open. Without any hesitation, he clasped her hands in his, and they continued the dance, revolving around the building at the town's center, careful to avoid any remaining coals from the food pits.

Next, Uncle Sam swept his wife into his arms, and her place was taken by Meg, his cousin Daniel's wife. He searched the other dancing couples for the little girl and found her cheerfully set on his cousin Philip's feet.

Each time they completed a full resolution around the pavilion, a new partner awaited him, until finally, his cousin Garret swung Mary Jane into his arms just in time for the spirited music to end and a slow melody to begin.

"And, here I was, afraid you didn't want to dance with a lawman," Raine teased.

"Only if that lawman," she said, looking up and meeting his eyes, "is you."

Be still my heart.

He really should marry this woman.

The thought shocked him.

What would Sarah say?

With Mary Jane's hand clutched in his, he twisted it in to rest on his chest and pulled her closer with the other. Despite himself, he looked down at her lips, so full and inviting, and reminded himself to breathe as he slowly bent his head down toward her.

CHAPTER NINETEEN

Enveloped in the warmth of the lawman's embrace, Mary Jane closed her eyes, anticipating the simple touch of his lips to hers. Heaven help her, she'd not realized how much she'd wanted him to kiss her until that moment.

She waited.

Wet, thick snowflakes landed on her face and encumbered her lashes. She blinked her eyes open, acutely aware of how close she was to Raine. The snow itself appeared to be dancing across the evening sky. It was beautiful. She hadn't noticed the sudden drop in temperature, but now, a crisp breeze swirled in the space between them.

"Mr. Redbourne," Jethro called, making it to their side in moments. He placed a hand on Raine's arm. "I beg your pardon, ma'am. I hate to intrude, but we have to go. Now."

"What's wrong?" Hank asked, stopping near them and leaning over, his wife still in his arms.

The shepherd turned to look at her. "Please, Miss Bennett, you have to believe me. We must hurry. You should move your flock into that new barn of yours tonight."

"What are you talking about?" she asked, unwilling to leave

the comfort of Raine's arms just yet. "It's only a few little snowflakes."

His urgency seemed disproportionate to the amount of snow that was falling.

Raine stared down at her, his jaw flexed, his eyes piercing.

"No. Trust me," Jethro said, pleading in his voice, "I have seen this type of storm before. It seems harmless in the beginning, but within minutes it can turn deadly. If we do not get back to our flocks and get them indoors as quickly as possible, they will be frozen by morning." He was genuinely concerned.

The spell was broken.

Surprised by the sudden vacancy she felt the moment Raine finally let her go, she pulled her shawl tighter around her. Mary Jane had lived in Montana long enough to know how quickly the weather could shift. While she had never experienced such a drastic change from one hour to the next, she supposed anything was possible and it would be better to err on the side of caution.

Sarah Jane.

"Where is my daughter?"

"I'm right here, Mama," the little girl said with a giggle as Seth spun her around and placed her in Mary Jane's arms.

The music stopped and the mood of the jubilant crowd turned serious.

"I need everyone to gather your things quickly. There's a storm coming in and it looks like it's not going to be pretty," Raine shouted directions.

"It's pretty sad that you are all going to let a Kansan scare you into thinking that you need to rush home to beat a few little Montana flurries." Marshal Tyler scoffed.

"And we ain't going to listen to no sheepherders either," a man Mary Jane recognized as a cattle rancher from Middleton called out.

"Please," Hank said, "I've lived in Montana long enough to

know that the unexpected sits around every corner where the weather is concerned." He glared at the marshal. "Wouldn't you all rather make sure your herds are safe tonight than to wake up in the morning and have lost them because of your pride? Or Rut Tyler's?"

"The mayor's got a point," Mr. MacPherson said, garnering several affirmations from Thistleberry ranchers.

"Maybe we'll just stop the sheepherders from protecting their maggots, and we'll all have less to worry about come morning."

Another man took a step toward Jethro, and Raine pulled his gun.

How did they know the man was a sheepherder? He'd only been working at the farm for a few hours.

"Come on, fellas," Raine said, "I don't want to be the bad guy here, but it is my job to make sure that everyone—cattlemen and sheep ranchers alike—are protected."

"Come on, Giff," a man said to the one threatening Jethro, "just how much damage can a ranch run by nothing but womenfolk do? They won't last through the winter. Let's get on home."

Mary Jane breathed out a sigh of relief. Why did men always have to be so aggressive?

"I'd suggest you boys stay in town for the night," Hank interjected. "Don't you already have reservations over at the Thistledown?"

"Yes, but what about my livestock?"

"You have a good foreman?"

"The best in a thousand miles," the man boasted.

"Then, trust the man to do his job," Hank told him. "You try getting back to Middleton tonight, Humville, and you just might be what's frozen by morning."

The cattleman harrumphed, but backed away, storming toward the hotel with three of his friends behind him.

"If any of you would like to send a telegram back home,

I'm sure Mr. Tulley would be happy to help."

They all waved him away as they turned toward the hotel.

Astrid, Tessa, and Judith all came to Mary Jane's side.

"What do you want us to do, boss?" Astrid asked.

"We need to warn Evaline and get those sheep down to that far south pasture. Best to get any wagons home before this snow really starts to stick to the ground."

"Yes, ma'am."

The women headed for the livery.

Raine turned to Jethro.

"You should do the same," he said. "Get the wagon, and get you and your wife back to the farm. I've got my mare here and will join you as soon as I can."

"Thank you," the shepherd said.

"For what?"

"Trusting me."

"Go!" Raine urged.

Once Jethro disappeared, he faced Mary Jane.

"Do you still have my coat?" he asked.

"Yes."

"Good. Put it on. That shawl looks pretty but it won't do anything to stave off the cold. And you, young lady," he said to Sarah Jane, "where are your mittens?"

"I left them over by Miss Hawthorne. I couldn't throw the bean bags very well with them on."

Mary Jane picked up her daughter.

"Well, how about you go with your mama and Miss Hawthorne and the others, and make sure they get home safely. Can you do that for me?"

Sarah Jane thought about it for a moment.

"That's a pretty big responsibility," she said.

Mary Jane laughed and kissed her daughter's face.

"But I can do it."

"There's no time to waste, M.J. You and Sarah Jane need to get home. I'll stick around here long enough to make sure all these people get out safely," he told her, motioning to all the vendors who busily cleaned up their booths and were heading for the livery stables and feed store.

Why did she have to fall for a lawman?

"What about you?"

"I'll be fine," he said.

She didn't want to leave. She wanted to stay close to him, to make sure he would be all right, but she looked at her little girl and knew he was right.

"Be safe," she said, relenting to their fate.

He nodded, then took a step toward her and leaned down close for her to hear.

"And just so we're clear," he said firmly with a look that turned her insides to jelly. He bent down, so his lips were mere inches from her ear. "That kiss…*is* going to happen."

Mary Jane sucked in a breath, the flurries in her stomach blowing wildly about, and she bit her lip at the thought.

"See you soon, Mr. Redbourne." Sarah Jane squirmed out of her arms and went to Raine.

He hugged her close to him.

"Yes, you will."

Mary Jane said a silent prayer that he was right.

"Come on, love," she said, taking the little girl back from him.

He smiled.

With one last, meaningful look, she turned for the livery to find the others.

By the time the last wagon pulled out of Thistleberry, Raine was exhausted. It had been a long day and he still needed to get home and see what help Jethro needed.

Poor Fred.

Maybe he should take a few more blankets out to cover the

pig tonight. Or maybe he could move him into one of the empty stalls in the stable. As he headed to the livery, a light flickered in the window of the sheriff's office and Raine froze.

The snow now covered the ground like a thick, white blanket, and it didn't show any signs of letting up. He wished he'd had the wherewithal to get his winter coat from the back of Andrew's wagon instead of being stuck with this flimsy old jacket, but he pulled the collar up around his neck, drew his gun, and gingerly made his way over to his new office.

The boardwalk creaked under his feet.

Blast it all.

He sidled up against the wall of the building and waited a good couple of minutes before leaning forward to peek inside the window.

Marshal Tyler opened drawers and cupboards, obviously looking for something.

Raine stepped to the front door and pushed it open, his gun drawn and pointed at the man.

"Can I help you find something, marshal?"

Tyler's gun was also drawn.

"A man could get himself shot sneaking up on someone like that, Redbourne." He returned his gun to its holster.

Raine did not.

"Something you wanna say, Sheriff?" the marshal asked, pulling out the chair and setting his lantern and hat on the desk. He sat down, leaned back in the chair, and raised his feet up next to the light.

"I'm going to ask you again," Raine said coolly, "can I help you find something?" He moved further into the room, aware that having his back exposed to an open doorway was just plain asking for trouble. He closed the door with his booted foot and took the chair opposite Tyler.

"You know, I was just looking for this old file of a case I had here. The Cochran Gang. Ever heard of them?" He took his feet down from the desk and leaned forward. "Well, of course you have, seeing as you're courtin' Lionel Cochran's widow and all."

Raine's mind raced.

"I thought you said her husband was the sheriff here."

"Was. Then, he went and got himself killed when he married the wrong girl."

"What is that supposed to mean?" He slowly lowered his weapon.

"Ah, the lady foreman hasn't told you."

"Told me what?"

"She's the one that killed him."

Raine narrowed his eyes at the man. Mary Jane was strong and highly skilled, but he doubted her capable of murder.

The marshal chortled.

"That's what I thought."

If what Tyler said was true, there had to be a good explanation.

"You said he was part of a gang. If he was the leader, and he's dead, why would you be looking for your old file?"

"Seems like some of his old pals are up to their old tricks again and are headed back to Thistleberry."

"What makes you so sure?"

"Let's just say I spoke to an old friend of his. Maybe you know him—Moses Rigby?"

"I've met him," Raine said, remembering the man who'd held him at gunpoint the night Malcolm was taken into custody. "I thought Moses was in jail."

"Let's just say he offered information that got him out. At least for now."

"What's so special about Thistleberry that they'd risk getting caught coming back here?"

The mine.

"I was hoping you'd be able to tell me. I know you've only been in town a short while, but you seem to be cozied up to all the right people."

"The Deardons are family."

"On your mother's side, I know. But I was referring to Mrs. Cochran."

"Who? Oh, you mean, M.J. What exactly makes you think that she has anything to do with whatever they've got planned?"

"She's as good a place to start as any." The marshal pushed himself away from the desk, replaced his hat and picked up the lantern. "I would watch your back, Redbourne. She already killed one sheriff, I would hate to see you be the next."

Raine stood.

"I'm in room four over at the Thistledown. Let me know if you find anything." He swung the door open wide, the bitter chill sweeping into the room with its vicious bite, then stepped out into the growing storm.

Tyler had given him a lot to consider, and he sat back down on the wooden chair, unsure his legs would support him at the moment. Snippets from the night in the mine came back to him with infuriating vagueness.

He'd been in so much pain that night that much of what had happened after he and Mary Jane had fallen through the support beams was still mostly a blur.

What about the payday, boss? the man had said. But what payday?

The hour was late and Raine needed to get home. He locked the office up with the key Hank had given him when the vote returned a yay response, but he made a note to contact a locksmith as soon as possible to have the locks redone.

The normal fifteen-minute ride turned into nearly an hour as Raine trudged through the growing drifts of snow that had rapidly accumulated with the increasingly heavy winds.

"Come on, girl," he said as he pulled into the stables. "Let's get you warm, brushed, and fed."

"Can I help?" Jethro appeared in the entrance and turned to close the door against the still raging storm.

Raine shivered like he'd never shivered before. He was

drenched from head to foot, and he longed for some of Lottie's steaming lentil stew and a hot bath.

"All the sheep are resting comfortably in the barn. You were wise to repair the barn when you did. It is quite well insulated against the weather."

That was a relief.

"And the lamb?" Raine asked, wondering about his little friend.

"Well, as you know there are fourteen lambs in our flock, but last I saw her, your lamb was safe, sleeping peacefully on the hay at Alice's feet."

"She's lucky the lamb is not nudging herself into a spot on your bed."

Everything hurt—especially when he laughed.

"I hope you don't mind, but I told my wife to go into your house to get a fire started and put some soup on to boil."

"Mind? A fire and a cup of steaming soup sounds a little like heaven about now." Raine grabbed a spare blanket from the hook near the hidden room and worked to dry the mare off while Jethro fed and watered her.

The Clydesdale's were calmly resting as if the storm hadn't bothered them a bit.

"And Fred?"

"Ah, the pig. Well, I think he's about as stubborn as a mule, but we finally got him into that shelter you made for him. He should be nice and cozy tonight."

It was funny how in just a short time, he had grown to care about the animals on this little farm.

"And the—"

"The chickens are hiding in their coop," Jethro said, anticipating the question. "I think they will actually sleep warmer tonight than we will."

"Do you have enough blankets?" Raine asked. He'd made sure earlier in the day that there was plenty of wood for the potbelly stove in the kitchen area of the apartment, but had not considered blankets.

"Your cousin, Lucy, made sure that we had several woolen blankets from her ranch."

Raine's head felt like it weighed as much as a bushel of apples.

"Honestly, without your generosity, my little family would be out there tonight in the cold. We likely would not have survived until morning. I only hope that I can return the blessi— Whoa, there."

All strength suddenly fled and Raine dropped to the floor.

"You are burning up. Let's get you into the house." Jethro bent down to try to pick him up.

The idea that someone the size of Jethro could pick up and carry someone his size made him laugh, followed by a round of thick, heavy coughs. The shepherd draped Raine's arm around his shoulders, willing him to his feet, and slowly they made their way up the porch stairs and into the house.

They made it as far as the couch in the living room in front of the fire before everything went black.

November

"When will this weather relent?" It had been snowing on and off for nearly ten days straight and Mary Jane was done with it. She peeked out the front room curtains and sighed at the sight of more snow falling.

At least it was no longer accompanied by heavy winds and freezing temperatures, but it still accumulated thickly across the ground. Most days, the women congregated in the main house, crocheting and talking.

"Mama, look what I made." Sarah Jane said, joining her this morning in front of the large fireplace. A long, single strand of crocheted stiches draped around the little girl's shoulders. "I'm going to make Mr. Redbourne a scarf to keep him warm."

"What a beautiful color of blue you chose. I think he is going to love it."

Sarah Jane beamed at her mother.

"Can I show you something?" Mary Jane asked, reaching down into the basket beside her chair.

She dug through several skeins of yarn to find what she'd been looking for—a thin, wooden slab, open in the middle, with a dozen metal pegs on either side and a handful of hooks of different sizes and materials.

"Come here, love," she said, moving over to the couch and patting the cushion beside her.

Sarah Jane crawled up next to her, and M.J. proceeded to show the little girl how to wrap the yarn and secure each loop with her tiny fingers on the makeshift loom to make a simple patterned scarf.

"That doesn't look much like a scarf," her daughter said with a scrunched nose.

Mary Jane looked up as Astrid walked into the house and shivered, immediately moving to the hearth and placing her hands in front of the fireplace.

"You really should teach the girl how to crochet without a crutch, M.J. It will serve her well."

Mary Jane knew it was true, but had found that she enjoyed using the little loom the Deardons had given to her last Christmas and believed it would be an easy introduction to the craft for her daughter.

"Don't worry, Miss Astrid, it just looks like a big bunch of snarls in the yarn anyway." Her lips pouted slightly, and her brows crumpled together.

Mary Jane laughed. "Just keep going, love," she said with a quick squeeze.

"Any word from Whisper Ridge?" she asked. "Or the Isaacson farm?"

"Not yet." Astrid turned to warm her backside. "I'm sure

everyone is fine, M.J."

"At least Evaline is not out there all alone."

With some combined effort, they'd been able to get the flock out to the new barn before the thickness of the snow had settled on the ground. Mary Jane was grateful that they had all listened to the nomadic man Raine had hired and shuddered to think what could have happened had she dismissed him.

The thought of the lawman brought flutters to her stomach. The storm had made it nearly impossible for any communications to get through and she'd not heard whether or not Raine had made it home safely—though she still prayed for it every day. She refused to believe anything else.

Casey and Evaline had volunteered to stay with the flock down at the new barn until the storm passed, but that was more than a week ago.

"Luckily, Sam agreed to build that little addition to the barn where they can rest—though I cannot imagine what it's like being cooped up in a barn, even one that size, with near a hundred ewes," Mary Jane said, cringing at the thought. "Maybe the little shepherd's wagon will provide some needed solitude from the noise."

"And the smell," Astrid added.

"Yes, the smell!" Mary Jane's nose crinkled, and she shuddered. "How are the rams doing?"

"To tell you the truth, I think they like being in the stable with the horses. They get all the feed they want and fresh hay to lie on every day."

"Thank you for finishing up the afternoon chores, Astrid."

The door opened again.

Tessa and Judith came inside, brushing the snow off their coats, and hanging their hats on the hooks near the window. Since the individual bunk rooms did not currently have fireplaces, all four of the women had been sleeping in the main house to stay warm.

They all settled in with their warm woolen blankets, balls of yarn, and crochet hooks.

"If this is what it's like to be big, I just want to stay small forever," Sarah Jane announced after a while.

Mary Jane laughed. "Why is that, love?"

"It's bor-ing."

Knock. Knock.

Mary Jane looked at each of the women sitting around the cozy little room. They all shrugged.

Maybe it's Raine.

The thought pushed her to her feet, and she jumped up to answer the door.

"Howdy, neighbor." Hank stood on the other side of the door holding a large wooden crate that appeared to be filled with all sorts of foodstuffs.

Not Raine.

But she was still glad to see someone from Whisper Ridge.

"Please come in."

"'Fraid we can't stay long. Just wanted to check in and make sure everyone over here is all right, bring you a few food items…" he held up his arms.

"And some firewood," Andrew said from behind his father.

The older Deardon walked into the kitchen and set the crate down onto the counter while the younger of them filled the near empty log rack near the hearth with freshly cut wood. The woody scent of soft pine mingled surprisingly well with the indulgent aroma of fresh baked bread and creamy chicken stew.

"That is very generous of you," Mary Jane said. "The bread loaves just came out of the oven, can I get you a fresh buttered slice?"

"It smells right heavenly. Thank you."

Mary Jane grabbed the small plates from the cupboard and quickly slathered two thick bread slices with the butter Tessa had just finished churning last night.

"Sam and Philip have gone down to the Isaacson place to check in on Raine and the Millers," Hank called from the front room. "Just thought you might want to know."

"Who are the Millers?" Mary Jane asked, trying to sound unconcerned, but to remember anyone in town with that surname.

"Jethro and Alice," Astrid said.

"And little baby Asher," Judith piped in.

"Ah, the Millers," she repeated sheepishly as she walked back into the main living area and handed both Hank and Andrew their plates of bread. "Do you know about anyone else in town? Did everyone make it home all right?"

Andrew smiled at the younger woman, bringing instant color to her cheeks.

"It took us three days to dig our way into the sleigh barn, and this is our first visit outside of Whisper Ridge," Andrew said. "We're just headed up to the MacPherson's next."

"The telegraph line is down and there's no way to communicate with town or anyone else for that matter other than to take the sleigh around and check in on folks."

"Can I come?" Sarah Jane asked, looking up from her loom with raised brows.

"Not this time, little one," Hank said. "Who else will keep your mama company."

"Miss Tessa, Miss Astrid, Miss Judith, the horses, the—"

Hank laughed out loud.

"I think she misses the boys," Mary Jane said quietly. "Especially Sebastian."

"I can hear you," Sarah Jane said.

"Hopefully, this weather will clear up soon and we'll be able to get around more freely."

"From your lips to God's ears," the little girl said without looking up, her brows furrowed in concentration.

Mary Jane covered her mouth with a little chuckle. She hadn't realized just how much she used that phrase until she heard it coming out of the mouth of her four-year-old daughter.

With another chuckle, Hank stepped forward and handed

her his plate.

"Thank you, ma'am," Andrew said, also handing her his plate. "That was a might delightful."

"Thank you for checking in. We are all certainly ready for the sun to come out."

"We'll be back in a day or two to check in." Hank headed outside and toward the sleigh with a wave.

"It's nice to see you are all doing well," Andrew said, his eyes flitting over to Judith before stepping out the door into the cold late afternoon air to join his father.

"Thank you for coming. And for the food and wood," Judith squeaked out the words in a rush as if not wanting to lose her nerve. With one last wave at the departing men, she closed the door before any more snow could blow inside and placed her back against it, her hand at her chest, and her lip caught in her teeth.

The girl was obviously sweet on Andrew and, by the looks of things, the youngest of Hank Deardon's boys returned the sentiment.

Thoughts of the lawman shrouded her senses with a mixture of worry, hope, and longing, and she hoped that Sam and Seth would find that all was well at the Isaacson farm.

"Mama, it's working," Sarah Jane exclaimed with delight as she jumped from her place on the couch and held up the loom with several finished rows.

"You are a natural, love. You'll have it finished in no time."

Mary Jane reverted to the thought that had kept her warm at night.

That kiss…is going to happen.

CHAPTER TWENTY

"I thought I might find you out here," Jethro said as he walked into the stables.

"Here," Raine said, "can you just help me for a moment?" He pointed to the opposite side of the wheelless wagon bed. "I'd like to see if we can lift it enough to fit these runners underneath it."

Jethro looked skeptical, but moved to where he'd been directed.

Raine placed the runner up next to the wood, hoping to help gain some leverage as they lifted.

"You are as stubborn as they come," the flockmaster said. He squatted down to find a place where he could get a good grip.

"I just have a job to do. You should understand that more than most. You took ownership over this flock the moment I hired you."

"But I hadn't been out in the cold and snow for an hour on horseback."

With a raised brow, Raine looked over at him. The man had been sleeping under a piece of canvas and on some old straw on the cold ground for who knew how long.

"All right, but I didn't collapse."

"Neither did I," Raine protested. "I was just too tired to keep standing." He stood to the side of the runner with his back to the wagon bed and his fingers beneath the wood. "All right, lift."

As much as they strained, it was just too heavy.

"Hello," a deep male voice called from outside the stable.

He dusted off his hands, and he and Jethro went out to greet them.

Seth and Sam had pulled up in their sleigh, the latter with a large wooden crate in his arms.

"Ma thought you might need some foodstuffs," Seth said, then stepped forward with an extended hand to Jethro. "We didn't get to officially meet at Lucy's barn raising, but I am Raine's favorite cousin," he said with a teasing grin. "Seth Deardon."

"I think you are the fourth one to tell me that," the shepherd replied with an easy smile. "Jethro Miller."

Raine raised his hands in the air. "I have a lot of favorite cousins."

He could see how well the new addition to the farm would fit in around here, and with his family, and was grateful the opportunity to hire him had presented itself. They were helping each other through a very transitional time.

"I am so glad to see the two of you. We need a little help in the stables."

Uncle Sam set the wooden crate on top of the worktable as Raine turned and headed back for the wagon project without waiting for a response.

"What on earth are you trying to do in here? With that?" Seth asked. "Are those runners?"

They looked old, Raine knew, but they seemed sturdy enough to accomplish what he desired.

"You've found Hal's old project I see," Uncle Sam said

knowingly.

"I'm trying to attach the runners to this wagon bed and restore it," Raine told them. "I think it could come in really useful one of these days."

"One of these days?" Jethro scoffed. "Earlier, he was talking about trying to take it into town tonight."

"Well, I think it's a little late for that don't you think?" Sam said. "Just what do you need from us?"

"I think with the four of us, we'll be able to get the bed up and onto the runners."

It took more than half an hour, but they were finally able to secure the sleigh runners to the undercarriage of the wagon.

"You've definitely got your work cut out for you," Seth said, standing back a bit to look over the old wagon turned makeshift sleigh.

"Maybe, but she has a lot of potential."

"We'll see," his cousin added skeptically.

"Can I invite you up to the house?" Raine asked. "There are still a few biscuits that may still be warm."

"Nah, it's all right," Sam said, "we should probably be getting on home before this new snow decides to freeze to the ground and we won't be able to get any traction. You're the first visit we've been able to make, but it's good to see that you are all right and are surviving these crazy storms."

It had been snowing so much, Raine felt like it had just been one big storm.

"Tomorrow, weather permitting, we'll attempt to get out to the Sorensen's place and to see how some of the others fared." The older man picked up the wooden crate that overflowed with dry goods, fruit jerky, meat jerky, and a few potatoes, then handed it to him.

It was heavier than Raine had anticipated it to be.

"Are they expecting to feed an army?"

"I told her it was probably unnecessary, but Ma included a sack of flour and several of her biscuit cookies to go with Aunt

Alex's peach preserves and pickled beets." Seth shook his head.

"There are seven more crates almost just like this at home," Uncle Sam said as he headed out of the stable. "The womenfolk have been putting them all together for days now—I think partly to keep themselves busy and not think about being snowed in. Lucy's been telling us for years to build up our food stores for just an occasion like this, and we have quite the stockpile. Even after all that." He climbed up into the front seat of the sleigh and unwrapped the reins from the hitch.

"How are the ladies up at the Happenstance?" Raine asked nonchalantly.

"Only two sleighs are working right now. While we came down here, Dad and Andrew were headed over to see the women before reaching out to the MacPhersons," Seth told him. "They've already had a hard go of it this year. That was a rough night. We estimate we lost a little over a hundred head in all. I just hope that M.J., Evaline, and the others were able to get their sheep down to the barn in time. It's not that far from here. Too bad you can't climb up that enormous walnut outside and take a look," he said with a knowing grin.

"Now, don't be giving the kid any ideas, Seth," Uncle Sam said. "We just got the sheriff. We don't want him to die in the first weeks on the job."

Raine wasn't amused and he raised a brow, but when his cousin broke out into a belly laugh, he couldn't help the smile that formed and the chuckle that followed.

"Seriously, there may be a lot of folks who'll be needing some help to get through the winter," his cousin said, and he nodded his understanding.

"How'd you do? Lose any of your animals?" Sam asked.

"We were lucky. It was a good thing I hired Jethro here when I did. He's a champ. He was able to get everything buckled down, all the animals inside, before the brunt of it hit. And his wife had a fire and hot stew waiting for me when I got home." He shot his foreman a look that told him not to say anything about his…tired legs.

"Which reminds me, I've got a wagon in my barn that doesn't belong to me. Andrew let me use it to take the Millers into town and they brought it back here the first night of the storm after the festival. I'll try to get it back over to you as soon as the weather clears a bit."

"Don't worry about it at least until spring, son. Montana winters aren't like Kansas. It'll be at least April before you see any real grass again. Wagons'll be useless to us for the next couple of months."

"Mrs. Isaacson," Seth said, leaning on the worktable, "had several barrels full of feed in her fruit cellar. It should last you until you can get out to the feed store."

"Well, I'm glad to hear that everyone here is doing well, that you survived the storm, and I am sure that Mary Jane will be too." Uncle Sam clapped him on the shoulder, sending a stabbing pain through his chest.

He bit back the groan that threatened. As if his body hadn't been through enough with the fall a few weeks back, the last little encounter with freezing snow had just about done him in. Not that he wanted to admit that to anyone.

"So, you don't know if everyone got home safely then?" Raine asked.

"Won't know until tonight about the Happenstance, but we'll try to bring word about M.J. and her daughter tomorrow when we head down again." Sam winked.

"And about the others, please. And thank you," Raine nodded. "I'm hoping most folks got home before it really started coming down—or before the freeze that followed. Have you heard anything from town?"

Seth shook his head. "Telegraph's down. Might be some time before we can get it fixed."

The cattlemen who had come to the festival from Middleton had Raine a little worried, and he wondered if they'd headed back home trying to beat the storm or if they had decided to follow Hank's advice and stay at the hotel. He really didn't like the idea of discovering dead ranchers anywhere near his town.

His town.

The concept surprised him. The first time Uncle Hank had invited him up to Thistleberry to be the new sheriff, he'd laughed at the mere idea of visiting somewhere so cold during the winter months, let alone living there, yet the mantel of responsibility had hit him hard the moment he'd agreed to take on the job.

While he wouldn't be able to get this sleigh up and running in the next few days, he could get around town on the mare, and when he needed to pick up some of the smaller foodstuffs or other items, he could use the cutter that had been locked up in the corner of the barn. He imagined that if he needed more supplies to help him be more prepared for another storm like this, he could employ the help of any one of his cousins' sleighs.

"All right, boys," Uncle Sam said, "Alex and Mara shoved as many extras as they could into this crate, hoping you would have plenty to eat, but I'm glad to hear that Mrs. Miller was able to find enough in Mrs. Isaacson's cupboards to make up some stew." He turned to Jethro. "Thanks to you, and your wife, for looking out for this kid," he said with a pat to the man's arm as he motioned over to Raine. "He's good people."

Jethro nodded. "Well, I'm mighty grateful for the job. And the boss." He nudged Raine in the arm—who folded his lips inward fighting another grown. His whole body still ached.

"How does it feel?" Seth asked.

Raine stared at him, wondering how he knew about the pain.

What could he say?

"To be sheriff in this little old town?"

Ah.

Raine smiled, relieved for the added clarity to the question. For a moment he'd wondered where his façade had faltered.

"It feels like there's already a lot to be done. You'd think I'd just have to worry about misconduct and wrongdoing, but the general safety of the town usually falls on the shoulders of the sheriff. I hadn't really counted on weather being the criminal. It's kind of hard to lock up the snow and wind."

They all laughed.

"We'll be around again tomorrow. Maybe you can come with us, as the safety of the *entire* town does lie on your shoulders *alone*."

He knew his uncle was teasing, but it was a good reminder that he didn't have to do everything by himself. As much as he hated to admit it, he was a little lonely without any of his brothers around—which hadn't happened in a very long time.

"What time?"

"We'll be here around eleven."

"I'll be ready at ten."

As he watched the men ride back toward Whisper Ridge, another chill washed over him. He carried the crate into the house where Alice was cleaning up the kitchen. The baby was sleeping peacefully in a cradle in front of the fire and the little lamb was on the makeshift bed he'd made for her what seemed like ages ago.

"I hope you don't mind," Alice said. "I found the cradle in the closet at the end of the hall, and it was easier to clean up after supper with Asher sleeping where I didn't have to worry about him."

"Not at all. You should have it," he said without thinking. Technically, the cradle was not his to give, but he figured they could use it until Mrs. Isaacson returned. "I mean, you are welcome to use it for as long as you need. I obviously hadn't counted on having a baby living out in the barn apartment. I hadn't really planned on anyone actually, but I'm so glad you're all here."

He set the crate down on the table in the kitchen.

"My uncle and cousin stopped by with some extra

foodstuffs," he said, noticing her interest. "Please help yourself to whatever you need."

"I was just thinking some nice griddle cakes and peach jam would be a nice breakfast in the morning."

Another epiphany struck.

He didn't know why he hadn't thought of it before, but he needed someone to cook and keep up on housework and indoor chores as well.

"Alice," he asked, leaning up against the counter with his arms folded and his feet crossed in front of him, "would you be interested in earning some extra money by taking over the responsibilities of cooking and cleaning here—maybe doing a few other chores inside the house?"

She looked at her husband, who shrugged and nodded, then back at Raine.

"You would like to offer me a job? Here?" she asked incredulously.

"Yes, ma'am. I don't really cook, and I'd be mighty appreciative if you could take care of the household tasks while I'm seeing to my other responsibilities."

He thought of Lottie. She'd started out as a housekeeper and a cook for the Redbourne family so many years ago, but over time had become so much more. She'd needed them almost as much as they'd needed her. As he waited for her answer, he hoped that maybe he could offer the Millers the same type of mutually beneficial arrangement that could grow into a different kind of family.

When Mrs. Isaacson returned, he may have to figure out another way, but for now, it seemed the perfect solution.

"I would like that very much," Alice said, a wonderous smile lighting her young face.

"It's settled then." Raine pushed himself away from the counter, grabbed a handful of dried apples from the bowl in the center of the table, and headed for the door. He turned back to say something to Jethro, but paused as he watched the man take his place next to Alice at the counter and pull her into a tight squeeze before bending down and kissing her smack dab on the mouth, both of them nearly shaking with excitement.

They were happy and the thought of it warmed Raine's heart. He'd just talk to the shepherd tomorrow.

He plucked his coat from the rack near the door and slipped it on, grateful Jethro had found it in the wagon before he'd closed it up in the barn. For now, he would head on out to the stables.

With the weather the way it had been, he was sure that the horses were getting a little restless as they had not been out to run in the pasture for way too long. The air was too cold to allow them out tonight, but he knew they needed some attention, and he suspected they could all use a good brushing.

Between the new job, new neighbors—particularly a certain foreman and her daughter—taking care of the farm, wanting to get to know the people of Thistleberry, and missing home, he had a lot to think about and thought that being out somewhere familiar with horses may be just the ticket to help him clear his mind.

What he really needed was a good, hot bath.

He'd seen a round washbasin in one of the rooms in the house, but yearned for a good soak. He needed to order one for the house, but maybe he could stop by the bathhouse for a long bath and a trim once he was finally able to get back into town.

Raine was grateful to see that Jethro had already fed and watered the horses. He admired how well kept the stable looked. The small platform next to the stalls was stacked with haybales, the floors had been swept, and the hinge on one of the stall gates had been fixed. The man was undoubtedly a hard worker. It surprised him that he'd not found another job before now.

Once the sheep were back out and grazing in the fields, he wondered if the shepherd would have time to do these kinds of things or if he would need to hire another hand to help out with these types of chores while he was in town seeing to his sheriff duties.

That kind of thinking was best left for another day.

Without wasting any more time, he offered the Clydesdales a couple of the apple pieces he'd taken from the kitchen, then picked up a brush from the wall and proceeded to groom them, talking softly, and rubbing their muscles. He guessed they were getting a little antsy with all the snow falling outside as they were the perfect team for the sleigh.

"I think I'll call you Clyde and Dale." He chuckled out loud at the clever names.

The light stomping and soft neighs from the next stall told him that the mare was anticipating their time together.

"How are you doing, girl?" he asked as he walked over to the mare's stall.

It had been so simple to name the other horses, so why was it such a struggle to find the right name for her? He held out a couple of the dried apple slices, and she readily snatched them out of his hand.

"How did I get so lucky?" he asked quietly.

He rubbed along her side, chuckling when she nuzzled her face up against him. With a hardy scratch at the withers, he gently moved down her body. He worked his fingers through the knots in her tail and removed several stray pieces of straw that had burrowed their way in there, then he picked up his soft dandy brush, stroking over the dock several times before moving to the rest of her.

Meow.

Raine perked up at a sound that mimicked the wind, but wasn't quite right. He paused and listened, but when he didn't hear it again after a few seconds, he kept working.

Meow.

"Tell me I'm not going crazy," he said to the mare. "Do you have a friend in here with you?" He hung the brush back on its hook and moved gingerly around the edges of the stall, careful to avoid the mare's hind legs. One kick and he'd be laid up for weeks.

Meow.

There it was again.

They had plenty of barn cats at Redbourne Ranch and Cole even had a few at the Gnarled Oak, but this sounded like a much younger cat. A baby. He closed up the mare's stall and walked the length of the stable, checking out each of the four empty stalls and even walking back around into the sleigh room—as he'd come to call it.

Nothing.

Meow.

This time is sounded a little different.

"Where are you?" He stopped in front of the platform of hay and noticed a gap between a couple of the bales. When he moved one aside, he was greeted by a mama cat with five brand new kittens feeding. Their eyes were still closed, and he guessed them to be no more than a couple days old.

He laughed out loud.

The mother did not run away, so he figured she must be accustomed to having people around her.

"Well, Redbourne," he said aloud, "with this many animals already on the farm, what's six more?"

CHAPTER TWENTY-ONE

Mary Jane breathed in the crisp November air. They'd finally had a break in the storms and she and Lissa had taken the horses down to the barn to check on the flock and those watching over them. They would also be fairly close to the Isaacson farm, and she hoped she might catch a glimpse of the sheriff who lived there.

Once she'd learned that Raine had made it back safely the first night of the big storm, she'd rested a little easier and had been better able to focus on the abundance of things that she'd put off while the weather was good.

"It's a good thing we hadn't used this pasture for grazing at all this year," Evaline told her, pointing at some of the clusters of foliage that peeked through the heavy layers of snow. "The grasses are plenty long, which makes the ewes much more willing to dig through the snow for their food. It's nice to see them content and strong. They appear to be enjoying the colder weather, now that it's not freezing anymore."

Now that all the Happenstance bands had come together in one flock, only two of the llamas were needed to help guard them. Carl raised his head as if sensing she was thinking about him. He'd been brought down here to the barn to stay with the ewes and lambs while Buckley had been kept up at the ranch with the rams. Sam and Garrett had stopped by to collect Wick and Stetson to take back to Whisper Ridge to help with the cattle.

"The Pyrenees seem to be fitting right in," Lissa said as they watched the dogs running circles around the flock, keeping them from straying too far.

"It's a good thing that we finished the barn when we did," Casey said, pulling up on her horse behind them. "It was a little cramped there for a few days, but we didn't lose a single head to the weather."

"Apparently, not all ranchers were as lucky," Mary Jane informed them. "The Blakelys lost a few calves, as did the Deardons. The MacPherson's bull is struggling, and the doc said he doesn't know if it'll make it. I guess it's pretty much the same all over town. Very few came out of this storm unscathed."

Lucy was in the perfect position to learn about all the goings on around town as the Deardons had made a point over the last couple of weeks to get down and visit the people in Thistleberry and the surrounding ranches. She'd then come visit Happenstance and share whatever she'd learned.

"I think it'll be best to continue gathering and bringing the flock inside as the temperatures continue to deep freeze everything overnight, but at least they can get out during the day and experience some fresh air—"

"Or we can," Casey added with a laugh.

Mary Jane couldn't imagine the smell that must come from having near a hundred head of sheep indoors next to where they slept.

She glanced over at the farm.

"He's not there," Evaline said knowingly.

Mary Jane realized she'd been staring at the neighboring pasture and the sheep with their little black faces peering out from their thick woolen coats, scanning the area and the

Isaacson's yard looking for any sign of Raine.

"He left pretty early this morning."

"Who? The sheriff?" she tried playing it off, but knew she wasn't fooling anyone. "I imagine he's got a lot to do in town."

"I imagine so. We could probably use some more apples to use as treats for the sheep. Maybe you could head down to the mercantile and pick up a bag of dried slices from Mrs. Smith."

She knew Evaline was taunting her, but she debated on doing it all the same. Winter months tended to be a little slower at the ranch, but the women had been using the time to catch up on weaving, crocheting, and making labels for many of their products.

"It'll keep. For now, let us give you a hand cleaning out the barn." Mary Jane dismounted and walked the horse through the crunchy snow over to the large black cottonwood tree.

It was good to see that the lambs were growing nicely. They frolicked happily, chasing each other and jumping around in the snow.

She picked up a shovel that leaned against the barn.

"How do you sleep in here?" Lissa asked, coming up from behind her as they walked in through the open doors.

The four women here had been at Happenstance the longest. Generally, there wasn't a huge need to clean up after the sheep because they spent their time out in the pastures, but mucking out a barn was the least of their worries if it meant keeping the flock safe.

Casey took a clothes pin from her pant pocket and clipped it over her nose.

They all giggled.

While Lissa and Casey worked at the far end of the barn with one large wheelbarrow, Evaline and Mary Jane stayed toward the front with the other, and they worked their way together. They would have to stockpile the manure for spreading later on. Despite not having the manpower or equipment, the blankets of snow on the ground would prevent an effective fertilizing.

She took a moment to admire the work that had been done on both the interior and exterior of the barn. Inside, two long pens on either side of the room had each been outfitted with long feeding and watering troughs that could now hold up to a hundred sheep. When lambing season came, and they near doubled their numbers, they would still have plenty of room next winter to accommodate the new additions.

With Lucy wanting to add another four or five hundred head to their numbers, they would certainly need to work on relocating and rebuilding the north barn.

"It's a good thing what Sheriff Redbourne did," Evaline said as she shoved her fork into the straw, shook it, then loaded the muck into the wheelbarrow.

"What's that?"

"His new shepherd, Jethro there, has been out with those Shropshire Downs all morning. Seems real dedicated. It's hard to believe that if the sheriff hadn't offered him that job, we'd all be in quite a mess right now. He and his family likely would have died in that storm. Did you know they were living under a canvas tarpaulin next to the river?"

It had taken a great deal of trust for Raine to hire the man, and she admired his willingness to give him a chance. It was funny, there had been a time just over a month ago when she had dreamed of purchasing the farm from Mrs. Isaacson. Circumstances had changed and now she couldn't imagine the place without the Kansas lawman living there.

"You've been all the way out here. How could you possibly know all that?" Mary Jane asked.

"When we first let the flock outside, some of them were very curious about the sheep on the other side of the fence. Jethro was out with their herd, and we got to talking. He's got quite a story."

Mary Jane sniffed.

"Is something burning?"

Carl screamed.

Evaline threw down her pitchfork, strode to the front of the barn where she'd stored her shotgun, and they all ran outside to see what had bothered the protective llama.

Thick, heavy grey clouds of smoke rose from the north into the otherwise blue sky. The richly pungent smell of pine burning in a fire had already reached them from the distance. With a quick scan of the pasture, they ruled out any sign of a predator approaching from the tree line.

Happenstance.

"We'll have to talk about it later, Ev," Mary Jane called back over her shoulder as she ran to the tree where she'd left her horse.

This was the first time Carl had ever warned them against something that didn't pose an immediate threat to the sheep, but she was grateful.

"Thank you, Carl," she called out to the llama as she rode past him and on toward the ranch.

A sinking feeling loomed over her. Happenstance was her home. Luckily, she'd dropped Sarah Jane off at Whisper Hollow to play with Sam's grandsons for the first time since it had snowed. She urged the horse as fast as she dared in the snow. As she approached the ranch, she realized that the fire was coming from beyond the homestead and her heart sank. Other than what was left of the north barn, the only building out there was…

Hers.

Lionel Cochran's.

Mary Jane hadn't been back to the little cabin since the night her husband died. The memories were just too painful, and she had no desire to revisit them. She'd taken everything she could carry, including dragging out the small dowry trousseau chest her mother had given her when she'd left home, and hadn't looked back.

Tessa, Judith, and Astrid all came running from the main house at the sight of her.

"What is it?" Judith asked, alarmed. "The mountain isn't on fire, is it?" The sheer panic in the young woman's voice struck Mary Jane with the need for clarity, for reason and calm.

"It's not trees, it's—"

"Malcolm's cabin," Tessa finished, locking eyes with M.J. and nodding.

Mary Jane narrowed her eyes, her brows furrowed together. She hadn't realized that their neighbor, Mr. Longhurst, had been using the Cochran's cabin as his own before he'd blown up the mine. She suddenly had a new kind of empathy for Tessa Hawthorne as she was all too aware of the emotional weight hanging over the small structure.

At the sight of several riders approaching on horseback, Astrid ran for the stables. Sam and his four boys along with two of Hank's sons rode up alongside her. Ryder, Sam's youngest drove the sleigh, two large barrels accompanying him in the backseat. She guessed them to be filled with water.

"We'll do what we can, M.J., but if that's what we think it is, it doesn't look good," Sam said with a shake of his head.

A big part of her wanted to tell him to just let it burn to the ground, but something inside reminded her that the little cabin had held hope for her once.

"I'm coming," she said. "And Tessa too." She looked back at the woman who had only come to them a month ago, desperately needing help. "Can she go with you?" she asked Ryder.

He immediately jumped down from the sleigh and held out his hand.

Tessa reached around the door and grabbed her coat, then joined him on the seat. She nodded at M.J.

"Thank you," she mouthed before Ryder slapped the reins and they were off.

"Let's go," Astrid said with a raised brow. "You didn't think

I would miss out on all the fun, did you?

"What can I do to help?" Judith asked to Mary Jane's surprise.

The timid girl had been reluctant to fill her new role up until now, but there she stood, chin up and ready when called upon.

"We'll need you to be here in case more help comes through. Seth will have ridden into town to collect the sheriff. Let them know we're headed out to the Cochran cabin."

Judith nodded.

It only took a quarter of an hour to get out to the place. From the soot-stained streaks on their faces, it appeared as if Mr. MacPherson and his son had arrived before the rest of them and had been trying to extinguish the blaze, but to no avail. The majority of the small building had already been consumed in flames, and all they could do was stand back and watch.

"This wasn't an accident," Mary Jane overheard Philip whisper to his father.

She slid down from her horse and walked over to face him.

"Who would have done this?" she asked, knowing it had been impolite to eavesdrop, but she didn't care if they knew she'd heard them. "Lionel's been gone nearly five years now. And, even if Longhurst was staying there, he's been taken back to Kansas to face trial. What could have possibly been gained by destroying an unused cabin out here in the middle of nowhere?"

It did not escape her that they were only a few hundred yards from the entrance to the mine.

"I don't know, M.J., but the outhouse was knocked over, and it looked as if the floorboards in the main room had been ripped up and the place ransacked before the fire took over. Who do *you* think could have done it?"

"Mundy," she said under her breath, the idea making her a little sick.

"What was that?" Sam asked.

"Mundy, Lionel's stage robbing friend and one of his cronies. I saw them in town the day of the festival coming out of the livery. Raine said the imbecile had roughed up Harvey a little before he could intervene." She turned to look at Sam, fighting to keep the panic from her voice. "Why is he back here?"

Mundy, Moses Rigby, and Cletus, the dead man from the mine, had all been in the cabin when Lionel died. The only reason she was still alive was because she hadn't been afraid to use her departed husband's loaded pistol.

"What could he possibly want here in Thistleberry after all these years? If he'd wanted revenge," she said with a chill running down her spine, "he could have taken that a long time ago."

Sarah Jane.

She pushed the thought from her mind. She knew there was no way Mundy could possibly know about her little girl, but she wanted to hold her daughter in her arms all the same.

Mary Jane looked up just as Raine pulled alongside her on his mare.

"I'm sorry it took so long." He swung down from his horse and was at her side in an instant. "What's happened here?"

She just wanted to collapse against him, to be in his arms, and have him tell her that everything would be all right.

"Arson," Philip told him.

"Was anybody hurt?"

Sam shook his head.

"The cabin's been empty since Longhurst was taken into custody."

"This is where Malcolm was staying?" Raine paused for a moment to consider the information. "Do you think this may have had something to do with the mine explosion?" he asked.

"We don't know. The cabin actually belonged to Lionel Cochran. I guess, technically, it belongs to M.J."

She closed her eyes, afraid of what she might see in his.

Disappointment. Disdain. Mistrust.

"Lionel's been gone now coming up on five years. We

didn't know it at the time," Sam said, "but Cochran and his boys were wanted men. Mundy ended up serving three years when he got caught by the Territory Marshal at the time. I figure he's only been out a few months. I don't know what would have drawn him back here unless there was something important he'd left behind."

"Any ideas what that might be?" Raine asked.

One by one they all shook their heads when he looked at them.

"M.J.?"

She shook her head too, still unable to meet his eyes.

She'd scarcely known the man five minutes before they'd been married, and they'd been married all of one day when he died. She barely knew any of this town's goings on at that time, and had it not been for Lucy Deardon taking her under her wing and giving her a roof over her head and a way to earn a living, she didn't know where she'd be.

"Mary Jane," Raine repeated, tucking a finger beneath her chin and lifting her face toward him. "Are you all right?"

His question surprised her, and she found the courage to look at him. When all she saw in his eyes was genuine concern for her, she rushed into his arms, burying her face in his shoulder.

"Whoa there, little lady," he said, wrapping her tightly in his arms. "We'll figure it out."

Ryder cleared his throat.

"Sheriff, you might want to come and see this."

Raine pulled back and bent down to look at her once again. "I'm sorry about the house. Let's find out who did it, all right?"

He didn't understand. How could he?

She didn't care about the cabin. Remarkably, the thick logs of the small home, though charred, seemed better able to withstand the flames. The roof had been completely consumed as had the doors, likely within minutes, but the corners of the structure had not crumbled to ash.

As she glanced at the cabin, she noted the stone fireplace that had remained mostly intact and her eyes were drawn immediately to the hearth floor. At least the blood stains would be replaced with soot and ash.

Remnants of the scorched rug that had likely saved her life, added tiny specks of color to the otherwise broken and blackened floor. The land may technically belong to her, but she had no desire to benefit from her husband's ill-gotten gains.

Behind the fireplace was a set of horse tracks leading away from the cabin toward the mine.

"Can't be much older than an hour or two at most," Ryder said as he crouched down into the snow.

"Sam," Raine said, turning to his uncle, "why don't you, the MacPhersons, Kieran, and Lindon stay here and make sure that fire gets out completely. Then, see if you can find anything in the rubble that will be useful. I'll take Seth, Daniel, and Philip with me. Ryder, will you kindly escort the ladies back home, then head into town and tell Marshal Tyler what's happened and ask him to meet us at the mine?"

"You don't seriously expect me to just turn around and go home, do you?" Mary Jane asked. "Astrid and I can hold our own."

"So, I've heard," Raine said, one brow raised.

What was that supposed to mean?

Astrid pulled her rifle from the side of her horse and handed M.J. a revolver.

"We're coming with you."

Tracks led right up to the mine, then dispersed in circles and in several different directions. Whomever they were following, knew how to cover up their tracks. One set led to the river, another behind the MacPherson property, and yet another up into the mountains.

"Something's off," Raine said. He dismounted and took a minute to look around. He scanned the trees on the mountainside, those on the opposite side of the river, and the ridgeline backing the MacPherson and Deardon properties.

Nothing.

He squinted at the mine's opening, noting the snow had not been disturbed—at least within the last day or two. The last time he'd been here, it had been dark, and he'd been in too much pain to take in his surroundings, and he was sure there was something that he'd missed.

"You think they're trying to separate us?" Daniel asked.

"It looks that way, but I'm not sure yet to what end. For now, let's stick together."

Daniel and Seth dismounted and walked over to inspect the mine's entrance. It had been boarded up and sloppily written signs read, 'Keep Out' and 'Danger Explosives'.

"What do you want to do?" Seth asked.

"Let's rip it down. I have a gut feeling that we'll find more information inside that mine than we will at the end of wherever those tracks will lead us tonight." He looked up into the sky and then down at his wristwatch.

Two-thirty.

They still had plenty of time before dark to inspect the room at the front of the mine. If there was anything of note, it would be there.

Once the boards had been torn off the entrance, Daniel stepped inside and returned with three torches.

"I'll keep watch," Philip said, still mounted on his horse, his rifle slung across his lap.

Raine glanced over at Mary Jane and Astrid, wishing they had just gone back with Ryder. She'd become more of a distraction than he wanted to admit. He knew M.J. wanted to be independent and to constantly demonstrate her competence, but there was no need. He'd seen it in her the moment they'd met. He was afraid that having her along would compromise his instincts and decrease his reaction time for anything that didn't involve protecting her.

The women slid down off their horses. Mary Jane headed down to the mine while Astrid stood outside next to Philip and his horse.

"I'll stay out here with Mr. Deardon," Astrid said with a nod at her boss.

Grateful he'd thought to bring it, he unhooked his lantern from the back of his saddle bags, and pulled out his tinderbox. With a quick flame, the lantern filled with light. He took a moment to light the torches Daniel had found, then stepped past everyone to light the way as he entered the mine.

He was still surprised that the ground immediately overhead had remained intact, but figured it was because the majority of the shafts and corridors had not been shored up properly as the miners dug farther and farther beneath the ground.

Rubble lined the walls and floor. The railroad ties still appeared to be unbroken, but several of the tunnels had been blocked off by piles of rock and debris while others had been illuminated where the ground had caved in, and sunshine broke through.

"Looks like someone's been here," Seth said, noting the brush marks on the ground where someone had used a broom to sweep the dirt.

They scoured the room for several minutes, but there didn't appear to be anything of note.

"What's this?" Daniel asked, handing Raine an iron bar with two wing bolts protruding from either end. "A part of a vice maybe or a clamp?"

It was hard to make out in the limited light, but whatever it had been, it was now broken beyond recognition.

"I'll keep looking," his cousin said.

Raine scoured the bases of the wall, looking for anything that didn't fit, but everything appeared to be as one would expect after being blown up. The ground rumbled above, and several streams of stone and dirt sprinkled down on top of them.

That can't be good.

"We need to get out of here," Raine said. "I'd hate for the ceiling to cave in and fill this entire chamber."

"I found a cogwheel of some sort," Seth said, pulling at a large, toothed wheel from the wall behind him. "It's stuck."

"Leave it," Raine told him. "We'll come back for it if we can."

Daniel rushed out of the mine, his arms folded above his head as more debris continued to fall.

"I've almost got it," Seth said with determination. Streams of dirt cascaded over him and tried to shake it from his hair and face.

More dirt and rock broke free from above.

It was coming faster now, accompanied by the sound of protesting beams.

"Let's go!" Raine shouted.

Where is Mary Jane?

He held up the lantern, but couldn't see where she had gone.

The wooden supports lining the edges and framing the passageways groaned and creaked. Without any more warning, one of the beams at the far end of the large open room gave way on one side and fell at an angle, bringing a wall of earth down with it.

"Got it!" Seth said and sprang for the entrance.

"Mary Jane Bennett!" Raine called in his most authoritative voice, "We need to get out of this mine right now. Where are you?"

A splash of color appeared beneath the open corner of the fallen beam. M.J. lay on the ground, wiggling through from the other side.

He ran across the distance as fast as his feet could take him.

With surprising alacrity, he grabbed ahold of her arms at the shoulder and pulled her across the floor and to her feet.

As the whole of the room began to cave, Raine grabbed her hand and they sprinted together toward the entrance to the mine.

There wasn't time. They weren't going to make it.

Raine reached his arm around her backside and with all the force he could muster, scooped her up, thrusting her forward as far as he could.

CRASH!

He slammed face first into the hardened snow.

Pain ripped at the tender flesh of his cheek, but he spun around onto his back and sat up, his arms around his knees.

The ground just a few feet away from where he sat collapsed over the mine entrance and into the earth with an enormous cloud of dust and ice crystals. He bent his head and closed his eyes, willing his racing heart and rapid breathing to calm.

Thank you, Lord.

He got to his feet, picked up his hat, and turned on Mary Jane, wanting to shake some sense into the woman.

She stood, brushing the snow from the front of her shirt and trousers. When she looked up at him with a sheepish smile and a shrug, he wanted to scream. She was safe, but all he could think about was how he could have lost another woman he loved.

The realization hit him like a slap in the face, and he took a deep breath.

He loved her, blast it all.

"I found something," she said, offering him a small, damaged leather carrying case.

With another deep breath, he snatched the case from her hands, not daring yet to speak as fear and worry and frustration still churned inside of him. He unbuckled the straps and lifted the top to find a mess of banknotes. He flipped through them, noting they were of various colors and sizes. Some with smeared ink and others with printing only on one side.

"Counterfeit?"

He closed his eyes, praying for strength. When he opened them again, he focused intently on Mary Jane, unsmiling. "I don't know whether to kiss you or turn you over my knee and paddle your backside." His voice grew very quiet. "Don't you ever do that to me again."

It took everything inside of him not to pull her into his arms and hold on. He opted to shake his head with a frustrated groan, wipe the dirt off his face, and mount his horse while she stared after him.

She was safe.

CHAPTER TWENTY-TWO

"What do you mean you want me to come to Whisper Ridge for the Deardon Thanksgiving Day tournament and family feast? Isn't that just for family?" Mary Jane looked at Lucy, believing whole-heartedly that the woman had completely lost her mind this time. She picked up the woman's lunch plate from the table and took it to the kitchen to be washed.

"Well, strictly speaking, I guess that's true, but I thought that maybe since Raine is going to be there, you might consider being my guest," she called from the living room table.

"What does Raine Redbourne being there have anything to do with me or the fact that Thanksgiving is about spending time with family? I'm not family." M.J. dried her hands on a towel hanging over the sink, then returned to the living room.

"Yet." Lucy's smile spread clear across her face, "Who knows, you may be part of the family one day?" She raised her brows and scrunched her shoulders innocently. "You've already known him longer than I knew Lucas when we got married."

"Oh, no. I've had about enough of that man for the time being." She wagged a finger and shook her head.

His comment at the mine still stung. Regardless of whether

or not she'd deserved it—which she decidedly did—she had not appreciated being on the wrong end of his ire. She did have to admit, much to her chagrin, that she could not stop thinking about him carrying out the idea of kissing her though.

"Seth told me about your little spat at the mine," Lucy placed a hand over hers. "Don't you think it was kind of sweet that he was so concerned about you?"

"I just don't know why he had to get so upset. I'm fine."

Raine had barely spoken a single word to her on the way home. When they'd reached Happenstance, he'd simply raised his hat, acknowledging their parting, and then ridden away. Every time she'd ridden down to the south barn, she'd tried to get a glimpse of him, but it was always the same, he'd already gone into town for the day. He seemed to be leaving earlier and getting home later than before.

"Oh, honey." Lucy paused a moment, her lashes downcast, and her smile softening to one with a hint of sadness. "Raine closed off his heart a long time ago when his wife died. In eleven years, I have not seen him smile the way he does when he looks at you. That sweet and fun-loving man has lost more than you know. Give him some time to open up to you. Then, maybe you'll understand just how deeply his affections can run."

"He was married before?"

Lucy nodded.

"What happened to her?"

"I think that is a story best left for Raine to tell. When he's ready."

"Patience isn't exactly my strong suit."

"Mine either."

"I'll try," she promised.

It surprised her that someone like Raine with his easy smile and generally gentle demeanor could be weighted down with grief.

"Now, about Thanksgiving," Lucy said.

"You just don't give up, do you?"

"Do you want me to?"

"No. Do I get to participate in the tournament?"

"Do you want to?"

"No," she said with a giggle. "I imagine that Sarah Jane will be thrilled to spend more time with her Deardon friends. She told me the other day that she thinks Sebastian is in love with her."

The women both laughed.

"The men in our family certainly have good taste." She winked at Mary Jane. "At least it won't be like my first Deardon Thanksgiving. Lucas's granddad, God rest his soul, offered me up as a prize to the unmarried man who won the tournament."

"No!" Mary Jane said in disbelief.

Lucy nodded. "We lost Liam that Thanksgiving."

"Oh, I'm sorry. That must have been difficult."

"It was. It's funny, I'd only known him a good six weeks, but we were kindred spirits he and I, and I loved him." She looked down at her hands, smiling. "It was only a year later that plans for Happenstance began. It took me several years, but I think we've done a pretty good job with it, don't you?"

By the time Lucy left, Mary Jane's head was swimming with every detail and activity that went into planning and carrying out a Deardon Thanksgiving. Archery targets, leg wrestling, a caber toss—something to do with how far the men could throw a really big log, a stick pull, a horse race…

She was sure there was more she wasn't remembering, but it seemed like their family affair was even bigger than the town festival. The meal preparation alone would take days.

You may be part of the family one day.

She couldn't get Lucy's words out of her head.

It shouldn't have surprised her that Raine had been married before, but it hadn't occurred to her he'd lost someone. She thought about his wife. Had she been tall or short? Had she had blond hair or brown like her? Had she been sweet or spirited?

"Mama!" The door burst open, and Sarah Jane rushed

inside. “Look what I made.” She handed Mary Jane a collage of colored paper and dried leaves in the shape of a turkey.

“Why, it is the most beautiful turkey I have ever seen!” Mary Jane exclaimed. “Where do you think we should keep it?”

Sarah Jane marched over to the fireplace and pointed at the mantle.

“Luckily,” Alex said, closing the door behind her, removing her coat, and hanging it on the hook near the entry. “Meg had collected and pressed quite a few fall-colored leaves before the snow hit. This little one is an aspiring artist if I ever saw one.” She came in and sat down on the couch in front of the fire.

“Is that so?” Mary Jane stood and joined her daughter in front of the hearth. “You know,” she said, “I think you’re right. If we put it there, everyone who comes for a visit will be able to enjoy it.” She set the turkey up on the mantle next to the only pictures she had of her family back home—her parents, two sisters, and a brother.

She had been nineteen in that photograph with hopes of a very different future than the one she’d had. Her siblings were all grown now with families of their own, but sometimes she longed for those simpler days when she hadn’t a care in the world.

She ran a finger across her mother’s face. The woman’s intentions had always been in the right place, but when Mary Jane had been twenty-three and still unmarried, Meredith Bennett, had encouraged her to find a man through an agency. That had been nearly five years ago, and she’d scarce heard a word from her family ever since.

Thank you, Mother.

Without that encouragement, she wouldn’t have her beautiful little girl.

Her daughter ran into her bedroom.

Alex patted the seat on the couch next to her.

“We passed Lucy on the way over. She said you will be joining us this year for Thanksgiving.”

"I hope that's all right." Mary Jane placed another piece of wood on the fire, picked up her hooks and yarn from the basket to the side of her chair, and joined Alex on the couch.

"Of course, my dear. The more the merrier. It's hard to believe just how much our family has grown since coming to Thistleberry—and I'm not just referring to those from the Deardon line. You and little Sarah Jane have become like family to us."

"I appreciate you letting her come stay with you and the other children while I am working. I don't know what we would have done without you."

"It's wonderful to have a little girl among all those boys. Still can't decide if it's a blessing or a curse."

"What?"

"Having only boys. In a place like this, there just aren't a lot of young women to come by and I worry about my grandsons being able to find wives. Or Ryder for that matter—though I think he's a little sweet on Tessa truth be told. Of course, Daniel's oldest is barely thirteen, so we have a while yet before any of them come of marrying age. A lot can change in just a few years."

Sarah Jane returned with her loom in hand. She crawled up onto the chair and held it out for Alex to see. She'd added nearly three feet to the length of it and was ecstatic about the idea of giving it to Raine.

"How are you?" Alex asked.

"We're doing well. The snowy weather gave us plenty of time to catch up with our spinning, weaving, and preparing labels for our cheeses as well as our wares."

"That's not what I mean," she said knowingly. "You haven't been back up to that cabin in nearly five years, and now it's gone. Are you all right?"

Mary Jane thought long and hard about how to respond.

"I think watching it burn was cathartic for me. It took me years to understand and accept that Lionel's death was not my fault, but seeing the place, remembering the sounds, the smells, the feelings from that night made me realize that I would not be who I am right now without having gone through it. I would not have her."

They both looked over at the little girl who was engrossed in her task.

"You are exactly where you are supposed to be, my dear. And we love who you have become."

They sat there a moment, pondering.

"Well, I still have seven more pies to bake, several archery targets to cover, and I may even make some of my juneberry bread." Alex stood up and headed over to the door. "Oooo, maybe you could bring some of your aged cheeses. Don't tell my husband, but I much prefer your cheese to ours—especially, the ones with the little crystals in them." She placed a finger over her lips.

Mary Jane laughed.

"I think that can be arranged."

Alex walked over and kissed Sarah Jane on the top of her head. "You are a natural," she said, earning her a pleased smile from the little one.

"Thank you, Aunt Alex, for helping me make a turkey today." She set her loom down in her lap and looked up at the woman. "I had a lovely time."

"Me too," Alex responded with a giggle. "Now, you be good for your mama, all right?"

"All right."

The Deardons were a good family.

With a glance up at the mantle at the photograph next to Sarah Jane's turkey, Mary Jane realized that Thanksgiving *was* a time for family, and it was high time that she contacted hers. With a giddy little flutter bubbling to the surface, she strode into the bedroom and retrieved an old stationary set from the top of her trousseau.

Nearly an hour had passed as Mary Jane added her signature

to the letter she'd finished writing to her parents. Surprised that the ink well from the box had still been wet enough to use, she set it aside and looked over her message. It was to her satisfaction.

She glanced over at Sarah Jane, who'd fallen asleep against the back of the chair, her little loom still clutched in her fingers and lamented that she hadn't had the foresight to schedule an appointment with the town photographer, Mr. Smith, whose wife ran the General Store. It would be nice for her parents to have a photograph of their granddaughter. Maybe she could send it as a gift to them for Christmas.

With a deep breath, she carefully folded her correspondence and placed it in a matching envelope.

"S.J., love?" She glanced back over at the girl who still slept peacefully.

Feeling only a moment of guilt at the idea of waking the child, she crept over to the chair and sat down on the floor next to the chair. She slid the loom out from Sarah Jane's hands and set it on top of her yarn basket.

"Sarah Jane," she called quietly.

"Boo!" the child yelled with a happy little giggle, her eyes open and shining bright, a huge smile lighting her face.

"Oh, you," Mary Jane said, getting to her feet and bending down to tickle her sides.

The laughter was contagious.

"I scared you, didn't I, Mama?" the little girl asked as M.J, swept her up into her arms.

"No, you startled me. There is a difference."

"What is the difference?"

"Well, to be scared means that you are afraid of something or someone. To be startled means that you were surprised suddenly by something unexpected."

Her daughter nodded.

"Will Mr. Redbourne be startled when we give him my scarf?"

Mary Jane laughed again and squeezed her daughter tighter. "Something like that."

"Mama, I can't breathe."

She loosened her hold, but did not let go. As Mary Jane looked around the homestead, she couldn't help but feel gratitude for all they had been given over the last few years. A job, a warm place to stay, food to eat, friends…she glanced back over at the mantle…and family.

"How would you like to go for a little ride into town?"

"Can we stop in the mercantile and buy some lemon drops?"

"Yes."

"Can we buy some licorice whips too?"

She thought about it for a moment. "Yes."

"And what about some of Mrs. Smith's walnut fudge?"

"I think this little girl will have a bellyache and no room for her supper with all those sweets, so maybe just the lemon drops and licorice whips for now."

It didn't take long for Mary Jane to hitch the new single-bench cutter that Lucas had brought up to the ranch. With the letter for her parents in her skirt pocket and her daughter by her side, they made the short trip into town.

As they pulled into the livery, she spotted Raine walking into the sheriff's office and her heart made a little flutter. They hadn't spoken since the encounter at the mine, and suddenly, she found herself nervous at the thought of seeing him again. Grateful she'd donned a skirt and blouse to come into town, she reached for her long, thick braid and pulled it forward to the side of her neck and face.

"Thank you, Harvey." As she climbed out of the small sleigh, she handed the liveryman the reins, then picked her daughter up off the seat by the waist and set her on the ground, keeping one hand clasped around hers.

"Shall we stop at the post office first?"

Mary Jane was surprised at the number of people who were

in town. She guessed that many of them had felt cooped up over the last few weeks and just wanted to stretch their legs and get some fresh air. As they crossed the street, Mrs. Smith rushed out of the mercantile to greet them.

"M.J., we have completely sold out of the blankets you brought in last month and I am in desperate need for more. Please tell me you have more."

"Good afternoon, Mrs. Smith. I am glad to see you well. Of course, we have more blankets. I would be happy to bring them by come Monday afternoon. Would that be acceptable?"

"Yes, yes. I must say that when Lucy Deardon first told us of her plans to start a ranch run by women, we all thought she was a little mad, but I'll be the first to admit, that little sheep ranch of yours has become quite an icon in this town."

"I'm sure Mrs. Deardon will be pleased to hear that."

"Yes, well, who knew what to expect from this mail-order business?"

"Isn't it wonderful to see women who are doing something about their misfortune instead of relying solely on the charity of others to make their way? I hope everyone else in this town will be as welcoming to any newcomers as you are, Mrs. Smith."

The mercantile owner brushed awkwardly at the apron on her dress.

"So, I should expect you and those blankets on Monday?"

"Yes, ma'am." Mary Jane nodded. She took a step toward the post office, then turned back. "Oh, Mrs. Smith, I wonder if your husband is still in the business of taking photographs."

"Why, yes, he is. When should I tell him you'll call?"

"I should like to get them done in time for Christmas. Would you say Monday afternoon would leave plenty of time for that?"

"Of course, dear." Mrs. Smith leaned in a little closer and spoke in a whisper. "He's had nary a customer in weeks because of this weather. He will welcome the business."

"Monday it is, then. I promised Sarah Jane some lemon

drops and licorice whips, so we'll stop by after I drop this at the post office."

"A letter to your…" The woman bobbed her head, waiting for Mary Jane to fill in the rest.

"Parents." She held up the post. "It's a letter to my parents. In Iowa." As if it was any of her business.

"That's lovely, dear. Just lovely." Mrs. Smith did an awkward sort of bow before turning back to her store.

As she stood in front of the postmaster, suddenly, the idea of sending the letter was terrifying. What if they didn't want to hear from her? What if they never wrote her back?

You are being silly, Mary Jane Bennett. Give the man the letter and be done with it.

Sarah Jane squeezed her hand, which gave her just the courage she needed, and she placed the missive on the counter.

"That'll just be three cents, ma'am," the man said.

With that behind her, they stepped back out onto the boardwalk.

"There she is," a man yelled from across the street before marching toward her over the compacted snow with three others she recognized as ranchers from Middleton. The same men who'd come out to the Fall Harvest Festival last month and were trying to stir up trouble.

"You M.J. Bennett?" the first man with a large, rounded belly asked rather abruptly.

"That's me," she responded matter-of-factly. "What can I do for you, gentlemen?"

Sarah Jane stepped behind her, clinging to her skirt.

"You the foreman of that devil of a ranch? We hear yer bringin' in four-hundred more head of sheep. Where exactly do you expect them to graze, 'cause I tell ya, you won't be using any of my land."

These men were obviously heated by the news of the ranches intended growth.

"I work for Lucy Deardon as foreman at the Happenstance,

yes," she said, standing as tall as she could on the boardwalk, "and I would kindly ask you to lower your voices and talk to me like gentlemen. You are scaring the girl."

"No, they are not," Sarah Jane said, stepping out from behind the men. "I am not scared of you. You bullies. You just startled me is all," she said, narrowing her eyes at the men. "Didn't your mamas ever teach you that it's not nice to yell at a lady?"

Mary Jane's eyes opened wide.

The men were taken aback by Sarah Jane's brazen words.

"If you want to talk to my mama, you should do it with kindness and respect." She nodded her head deeply, adding emphasis to her words.

Who was this courageous little girl and when had she become so grown up?

"I'm sorry, gentlemen, but she's right. I'm happy to discuss any issues and ideas for solutions, but only if they are presented with at least the same level of maturity that my four-year-old daughter can display."

"There a problem over here?" Raine's voice sent a trail of gooseflesh down Mary Jane's body as he walked up behind her.

She could feel the warmth of his body radiating from him.

"Mr. Redbourne," Sarah Jane squealed, her scrunched face lighting up with a smile as she ran over to him and jumped up into his arms.

"Hey, darlin'."

"Are you the sheriff now?"

"I am," he affirmed. He turned to the men in the street. "Is there something going on I should know about?" He shifted the girl into his left arm and looked at Mary Jane, then back to the men.

"No, sir," the man with the belly said. "We just wanted to make sure that no more sheep get brought into the territory and wanted to have a..." he looked at Sarah Jane, "...polite conversation with Miss Bennett here about her ranch."

"What does it matter to you if the Happenstance increases the size of their herd?"

A taller man in a ten-gallon hat and wielding a large wiry white moustache stepped forward. "Before you know it, those stinkin' varmints will ruin our grazing lands."

"Last I heard, Montana was an open range territory. As far as the law goes, if you don't want livestock to graze on your lands, you'll have to put up your fences to keep them out. Besides, aren't you gentlemen from Middleton? Why are you taking such an interest in the sheep ranches in Thistleberry?"

"See, Verl, ranch*es* he says. As in more than one. It's starting already. If you allow one, more will come, and soon they'll be everywhere. My cattle won't feed off the land where sheep have grazed. They don't like the stink of them anymore than we do."

"Have your cattle grazed on land where sheep have been?" Raine asked with interest.

The men stared at him, blank looks on their faces.

"Come on, Humville, they're obviously not going to listen to reason."

"Oh, I'll listen," Mary Jane said, "when there's reason to be heard. What is it you would like us to do? Right now, our sheep are only grazing on private land."

"That'll change with growing numbers, rest assured."

"Then, why can't we share the range? The Deardon's cattle and the sheep from Happenstance share many of the same fields now and there haven't been any problems. Why would you think that would change?"

"Of course, you, the sheep rancher, would say something like that," the man called Humville said.

"You are welcome to take it up with the mayor. Hank is both a successful cattle rancher and a sheep supporter."

Without a response, the men turned away from them and strode down the boardwalk back toward the hotel.

"You all right?" Raine asked Mary Jane.

"Fine, thank you. Come on, Sarah Jane. If you still want to

stop by the General Store for lemon drops, we should be going."

"Goodbye," the girl said as Raine set her down. She slipped her hand into Mary Jane's, then looked up at him. "How come we don't see you no more? I miss Fred."

"Anymore," Mary Jane corrected. "How come we don't see you *anymore*?"

"Anymore?" Sarah Jane repeated without missing a beat.

Raine laughed.

"I tell you what," he said as he bent down so his face was even with hers, "you can stop by and see Fred anytime you want—as long as it's okay with your mama. Jethro and Alice are always there."

"But you're not?"

"No, I'm not. I have a job to do here in town."

"You're the sheriff."

"That's right."

"So, does that mean you can't be our friend anymore?"

"Of course, not. I'll be your friend for as long as you want."

"Forever?"

"If that's what you want."

"All right. It's a deal," she said, holding out her hand to shake on it. "Forever."

He glanced down at the little girl's hand. "Forever," he agreed with a shake, then stood up.

His jaw flexed as he met Mary Jane's eyes.

"Look, M.J., about the way I acted the other day at the mine…"

"You were right," she blurted.

He narrowed his eyes at her, pulling back a bit with obvious surprise.

"You told us to stay in the main cavern and I didn't listen. If you hadn't pulled me out of there when you did, it could have ended very differently. I'm sorry."

It took a moment before he found his voice.

"Aw, kiss and be friends already," Sarah Jane said, taking

her mother's hand and putting it in Raine's.

Heat flushed through Mary Jane's face and down her neck, but she didn't let go.

Neither did he.

"Can I escort you ladies somewhere?" he asked.

"Um, yes. Thank you. I'm supposed to pick up one of Edna's Peach Cobbler Crisps over at the bakery for Thanksgiving, then Sarah Jane made me promise to take her over to the General Store for some sweets while we're in town. You are welcome to join us."

"Mrs. Smith brought a sample of her newest batch of walnut fudge over to the office, and I must say, I think it might be the best I have ever had."

The awkwardness of the past few days seemed to melt away as they walked over to Doherty's bakery. It didn't take long for Edna to box up one of her crisps.

"Are you spending Thanksgiving with the Deardons too, Sheriff?" the bakery owner asked.

"Yes, ma'am. Can't wait to try some of your famous crisp."

Edna beamed.

As they started for the General Store, Raine took the boxed crisp from her and put it in the crook of his arm, then slipped his hand back over hers as if it was the most natural thing in the world. She tucked one side of her bottom lip behind her teeth, then smiled.

"Oh, Sheriff," Cornelia Wilson called from the open door of the building where Lyla was preparing to open her new café. "Would you mind? I'm afraid that neither of us is tall enough to get that box down from that shelf."

Her voice grated on Mary Jane's nerves.

"I'd be obliged, miss."

He let go of her hand to step inside the café, his warmth being replaced by cool crisp November air, and she rubbed her fingers together in its absence.

"Oh, no, Sheriff, I think I can get it." Lyla stood on her

tiptoes on a chair, reaching for the box, when the chair wobbled, and she lost her footing and fell backward.

Raine caught her in one arm before she could hit the ground.

Whew. The crisp appeared unscathed as did the woman.

"Mama," Sarah Jane whispered, tugging on her hand and pulling her down to hear. "Miss Wilson did that on purpose. She kicked the chair legs and made her friend fall."

"That's not how we treat a friend, is it?"

Her daughter shook her head.

Mary Jane straightened and stared at Cornelia. When she caught the girl's eye, she raised a knowing brow.

"We were so lucky you were here, Sheriff," the young woman cooed, her smile never faltering.

Lyla's face was flushed with color, her breathing labored as Raine set her down on her feet. He braced his arm against her back until she regained her balance.

There were plenty of unwed men in this town for the likes of Cornelia Wilson to dig her hooks into, but Mary Jane felt sorry for the lot of them. Whomever married the spoiled imp would certainly have his hands full.

Raine was at least twelve years her senior, and had already expressed his non-interest in pussyfooting around. Cornelia was a scheming child trying to play a woman's game.

"Here, Miss Driscoll, maybe you should sit down." Raine placed the chair she'd been standing on behind her.

"Oh, I'm fine. I don't have time for this kind of nonsense." The café owner waved it off, placing her hands on her hips. "It was a good thing you were standing there, Sheriff. I don't know what happened. It's definitely time to invest in one of those step ladders Mrs. Smith keeps touting over at the General Store."

"Next time, Lyla," Mary Jane said, leaning over to her ear, "you may want to invest in a friend who isn't trying to kill you."

The smile fell from Cornelia's face, and she glared at her.

Mary Jane stood up straight, meeting the young woman's

scowl with a refined smile and a genteel nod. Then, she turned to the other woman. "Congratulations on the café, Lyla. You're a wonderful cook. Let us know when you're open?"

"Oh, I will, M.J. Thank you."

Mary Jane walked past Cornelia with nary a glance.

"Here you are, Miss Driscoll. Ladies," Raine said.

While Mary Jane couldn't see, she imagined him getting the box from the top shelf, handing it to the café owner, and raising his hat at the women like a gentleman.

He ran to catch up with her as she and Sarah Jane crossed the street, but stuck his free hand in his pocket as he walked this time.

She tried not to let her disappointment show.

The mercantile doors were open while Mr. Smith helped one of their patrons load their sleigh with some supplies.

She turned. "And here we are. At the mercantile."

"Yeah. So, I, uh," he rubbed the side of his neck with a breathy chuckle, "am just waiting for the marshal to finish with his shave and then we'll be taking some of those fake notes you found over to have Mr. Dunbar take a look—see if anyone's tried to pass something like them off through his bank. He might even have some of the bills in his vault right now and not even know it."

She was glad that even though she'd caused the man an ample amount of grief, that her efforts had paid off and she'd been able to find something of value to his investigation.

"Do you think it was Mundy?" she asked. The thought sent shivers down her spine.

"I've been asking around town, but it seems like no one has seen hide nor hair of him or any of his brutes since the festival, so it's hard to say."

The front door to the mercantile swung open wide and Mr. Smith and Mr. Sorensen both came out, their arms full as they descended the steps to put things in the wagon that waited there.

Mary Jane turned back to Raine. "So, when did you and

Rutledge Tyler become so chummy?"

"Are you serious?" Raine said, holding the door for Mr. Smith as he returned. "I don't trust that man any farther than I can throw him, but the best way for me to keep my eye on him is to keep him close."

"Is somebody talking about me?" Marshal Tyler stepped up onto the boardwalk in front of the store, raised his hat and with a slight bow, offered a wide toothy smile.

"Mama?" Sarah Jane looked up at her questioningly, bouncing up and down, obviously anxious to see what delicious treats Mrs. Smith's candy counter might offer her today.

"Go ahead, love." She let go of the child's hand and the little girl ran happily into the store.

As Mary Jane looked up at the marshal, she had to admit that with his beard trimmed up and with him donned in fresh, clean clothes, he was actually quite handsome, and if she didn't know any better, she would say he appeared gentlemanly.

For a lawman.

Then, she glanced over at Raine who still held the door for the men loading the wagon, and noted how his denims conformed nicely to his strong legs and slender torso.

There was no comparison.

The two men were similar in both height and stature, but Raine had proven to be more than just his handsome face and broad shoulders. He was kind and playful, generous, and mature. He checked all the boxes.

That realization startled her a bit. She hadn't looked over her list in the month since the sheriff had come to town. Hadn't really even thought about it. Until now.

"It was real lucky you found that case, Miss Bennett," the marshal said, scrubbing his newly trimmed face with his fingers. "The sheriff here told me that while following a lead to the mine, you'd gone off, out of the main chamber, and just happened upon it."

"That's right."

"How did you know where to look?"

She didn't like where his question was leading her.

"I didn't. I was just…" she trailed her words and eyed the man closely. "Are you trying to accuse me of something, Marshal Tyler?"

"No," he said, shaking his head with his hand raised slightly in front of him. He glanced over at Raine.

"Don't look at me," the sheriff said. "Just ask her what you want to know."

"All right."

M.J. glanced about her. It had taken years for the people in this town to give her a fair shake after her husband had died. Some thought she'd murdered him. Some believed that she was a part of the gang that had robbed the stage carrying military payrolls. Well, she hadn't done any of those things and she was growing tired of having to prove herself over and again.

"Did you know your husband was a counterfeiter?"

"I knew the man in person for less than twenty-four hours. That is not something most men would want to advertise."

"You didn't answer the question."

"No. I did not know that Lionel was a counterfeiter."

"Did you kill your husband, Miss Bennett?" he pressed.

She looked at him, dumbfounded that anyone could still believe that. She glanced at Raine.

"Do you think I killed my husband?"

"I'm sure there is a perfectly good explanation for whatever happened that night."

"Not good enough," she said, turning away from him and taking two steps toward the marshal, her head cocked back to look up at him. "Lionel Cochran lied to me."

Both lawmen towered over her.

She glanced around, looking for something she could use to stand on. Her eyes fixed on an empty crate in front of the mercantile window. She flipped it over, slid it between the two men, and stepped up onto the new platform, facing Marshal

Tyler, nodding with satisfaction when she nearly met him eye to eye.

"Yes, he lied," she continued. "The man had written to me for months, telling me about this town and touting all the wonderful things about Montana. Then, he paid for a ticket on a steamboat—which was not an easy trip, mind you—and brought me up here to this untamed, freezing cold land with a promise of a good life and love. What I got instead was a living nightmare and a stash full of broken dreams."

"M.J.—" Raine called her name, but she didn't want to hear it. Not if he was going to believe anything Rutledge Tyler had to say.

He allowed the store doors to close and took a step toward her.

"Oh, I'm not finished." She held up a hand.

He stopped.

Mary Jane's nails dug into her hands as they balled into fists at her sides. "When I discovered that my husband for all of one day—the sheriff and supposed good guy—was in fact the leader of the gang that had robbed the stagecoach I'd come in on, he couldn't have that." She flailed her arms up in the air.

Townspeople had started to gather, slowing their pace and staring, but she no longer cared.

"No! He picked up his pistol, but didn't want to get blood on the floor, so he aimed to take me outside and shoot me like a sick dog."

Some of the women on the street gasped.

"If it hadn't been for a thick woven rug on the floor in front of that fireplace and his clumsy feet, I wouldn't be here. He fell, Marshal, and hit his head on the hearth. And died. Right there in front of me. Mundy, Moses Rigby, and Cletus were all there to witness it, but because I was a woman and a stranger in town, you, Mr. Deputy-at-the-Time, decided to take the word of known criminals over mine."

It felt good to finally be able to release the frustration she'd carried around for years.

"That true?" Raine looked at the marshal, who narrowed his eyes and cocked a shoulder, but did not say a word.

Raine shook his head, then held out a hand to help her down from her soapbox. "Feel better?" he asked.

"Much." She fought the urge to ignore him completely and step down on her own, but she reminded herself that she was too old to behave so childishly. With a deep breath, she slipped her hand into his and he squeezed as she hopped down.

"A simple no would have sufficed," the marshal said.

Raine elbowed him in the gut and Mary Jane had to bite her lip to stop from smiling.

"Oof," Tyler grunted. "I, uh, apologize, ma'am, to have offended you so."

The mercantile doors swung open again, but this time, it was a little girl peeking her head outside.

"Come on, Mama," Sarah Jane called, motioning for her to follow with a single finger. "There's lots of fudge." The little girl's tongue traced her lips, and she reached out and grabbed Mary Jane's hand.

"Don't you both have a bank to visit?" she asked as her daughter pulled her into the store.

"Yes, ma'am."

Raine winked at Sarah Jane before heading down the steps and into the street.

Why was it so hard to stay mad at the man?

"All right, fudge."

CHAPTER TWENTY-THREE

"Sheriff Redbourne, I regret that we haven't had the pleasure." A balding man with thick mutton chops and a fancy cravat practically ran to the door to greet them, both hands extended. "I'm Alvis Dunbar, the bank's proprietor. I've been expecting you." He grabbed Raine's hand with both of his and shook it.

"You have?" Raine asked.

"Why, yes, of course. Any man in my business knows the holdings of the Redbournes to be," he leaned forward, "shall we say, significant?" he whispered, then cleared his throat and righted himself with a knowing smile and a nod.

Heat warmed Raine's neck. He was accustomed to people knowing he came from money, but it wasn't something he generally talked about. Especially, with strangers. He ran a finger along the inside collar of his shirt, then pulled the counterfeit bills from his pocket.

"I imagine you will want to get an account set up immediately." He waved for a tall, slender young man with a high-buttoned collar and u-neck vest to come over to them.

Rutledge nudged him and motioned to the far corner of the small room. An older man leaned up against the wall, his faded brown slouch hat pulled low on his head, his booted feet crossed in front of him.

"Actually, I wondered if you had ever seen anything like this before." Raine handed him one of the bank notes that had only been printed on one side.

Mr. Dunbar looked up at him, his eyes wide.

"What's this?" The bank owner looked down at the bill in his hand and pulled a monocle from his vest pocket and held it up. He quickly tucked the glass back to where he's retrieved it and dropped his hand.

"Can I help you, sir?" the young clerk asked.

The bank owner brushed him away.

"Nevermind, I'll take care of the sheriff myself."

As soon as the teller was back behind the barred countertop, Mr. Dunbar leaned forward again, his face the color of beets, his body tense.

"What are you playing at, Sheriff? This is not legal tender. It's," he looked around to make sure no one was listening and spat through his teeth, "a spurious note. Counterfeit."

"I know." Raine said, calmly reaching down to take the bill from his hand.

He tugged, but it was tightly wadded now in the bank owner's fist. When it came loose, he held it in his palm and turned it over.

"Where did you get that? Ohhhhh." Mr. Dunbar reached into his pocket, pulled out a handkerchief, and wiped a small bead of sweat that had formed just above his lip. "You can't bring something like that in here. This is an honest establishment. Do you have any idea what would happen if the townspeople thought for one moment that there might be fake notes in my vault?"

"So, you haven't seen any of these," Raine tried to remember the word he'd used, "spurious bank notes pass through here?"

"Certainly not." Dunbar was simply indignant.

The man who'd leaned against the wall made his way with

a slight limp to the front of the bank and walked outside.

"I'll follow," the marshal said in a low tone, excusing himself.

"Maybe your clerk there has seen them?" Raine moved to talk to the man, but the bank owner stopped him.

"You will not sully my good name, sir. I suggest that you leave."

"Or what? You'll call the sheriff?" Raine wasn't trying to be difficult, and he understood the predicament the man would be in, but he needed answers.

All of the patrons had left the bank. Only the clerk, the owner, and Raine remained.

"You know a man goes by the name Mundy?" Raine asked.

"Mr. Mundy has come in a few times to sell gold nuggets he found out on his claim."

"And do you happen to know where that claim is located?"

Mr. Dunbar shrugged. "I never thought to ask, but his gold was good, I assure you."

"Oh, I have no doubt about the authenticity of it, just the origin."

This was getting nowhere.

Raine held up a finger, then reached into his coat pocket where he'd tucked the metal pieces Daniel and Seth had found up at the mine.

"What about these?" He held them out for Mr. Dunbar to inspect. "Do you know what they might belong to?"

The man dabbed at his face again, then looked down at his hand.

"This looks like a gear or cog or something." He pointed to the teethed wheel. "This, well, it could be a part of anything really, now couldn't it? Why? Do you think they have something to do with that?" He motioned to the front pocket in Raine's coat where he had placed the fake note.

The marshal stepped back inside with a shake of his head.

"What you got there, Redbourne?"

Raine held them up.

"I'm not sure. We found them in the main chamber of the mine before it caved in. Thought Mr. Dunbar might be able to tell us what they are, but he doesn't know anything." He returned them to his side pocket. "You know," he said as the thought occurred to him, "my sister-in-law helped the Secret Service bring down a master engraver in Illinois last year. I'll bet she can tell us what we need to know."

"Please," the bank owner said, his confidence all but gone, "if I see anything suspicious come through here, you'll be the first to know, but please don't even breathe that word out there. You'll ruin me."

"Have a little faith, Mr. Dunbar," Raine said with a tap on his arm. "I get the feeling that the people around here can be quite forgiving."

The man blew out a grieved sigh, his hands in the air, and marched into the back office.

"I guess you won't be opening a bank account then?" the marshal asked.

Raine chuckled as they left the bank.

"Your sister-in-law—she really in the Secret Service?"

"Nah, she just helps out occasionally. She used to be a Pinkerton, but that's a hard life with little ones. I do think she might have some insight though. I'll send a wire over tonight and ask about this Mundy fella. We'll see what she has to say."

Mundy

"Something has to be done about the sheriff."

Click.

Click.

Click.

"Put the guns down, boys. Somebody could get killed out

here."

"Sorry, boss." Mundy slipped his pistol back into its holster. "Just can't be too careful."

The others followed suit, most sipping on their hot coffee and hunkering down in their bedrolls for the night.

The man who'd taken over when Leo died crouched down next to the fire and put his hands out to warm himself.

"Heard about your handiwork up at Cochran's cabin. You find it?"

"Nope. It wasn't there. We went through everything—even ripped up the floorboards—before we set fire to the place. That should take care of it." Mundy had rather enjoyed watching Leo's old hut burn to the ground, but it still hadn't eased the itch to squeeze the life out of the little tart who shot him.

His hand always ached worse during the winter months, and hiding out in a blasted cave didn't help any. The walls were damp and the air cold, but it had protected them against the bitter freeze the nights brought. He rubbed over the stubs where his fingers used to be, then put them up by the dwindling flames to get warm.

Blamed female. She deserves what she's got coming to her.

"I certainly hope, for your sake, that the payday was not hidden inside."

He hadn't thought of that.

"I get the feelin' you didn't come all the way up here just to chew the fat."

"No, Mundy," the man said with a hint of exasperation in his voice as he stood up, "I did not come up here to simply 'chew the fat' as you say, but to talk a little business." He threw a bag, jingling with gold coins, down on the ground in front of him. It opened at the top, spilling some of its shiny contents.

"We're listening." Nigel, the oldest of the small group, propped up onto one arm and spit in the dirt next to his bedroll.

Mundy sat down, leaned forward, and rested his arms on his knees, holding his last fill of drink for the night.

"Thought we could lay low until spring when we could start moving product out again with the stage, but now that Redbourne's here and aiming to expose our little operation, he needs to be dealt with."

"What did you have in mind?" Mundy asked.

"Accidents happen up here in the harsh winters of Montana. I'm sure we can think of something that won't draw any unwanted attention from his family."

"Unscrew the bolts on his cutter?"

"Bigger."

"Hypothermia."

"Better. How?"

"If only there was a way to get him out of town and no way to get back. Hmmm," Mundy said, trying to think of how to separate the man from his horse in the middle of nowhere in a storm.

Can't really create a storm, he scoffed at the thought.

"I'll leave you boys to think on it for a bit. Mundy, can I talk with you outside?"

"Sure thing, boss." He got to his feet and tossed the last of his drink into the fire before heading out into the cold. With a shiver, he pulled his worn coat higher up around his ears and folded his arms.

"Seems Redbourne knows your name, Mundy, and he knows you're working with counterfeit notes. That's bad for business."

"It won't matter once the sheriff's out of the way."

"True, being a sheriff is a dangerous occupation. Just ask ol' Lionel when you see him."

"What?" Mundy scrunched his brows.

With a firm shove, the boss pushed him off the side of the cliff.

Mundy grasped at the air, trying to grab a hold of anything that could stop his fall.

"The Lord is my Shep—"

CHAPTER TWENTY-FOUR

"Thanks be unto God for his unspeakable gifts," the preacher quoted the second book of Corinthians as Mary Jane and her daughter walked into the small sixteen-pew chapel and quietly closed the doors behind them. She immediately spotted Raine sitting at the back on the opposite side of the church next to Jethro and his little family.

His manner of dress was a far cry from how she was accustomed to seeing him. He no longer wore fitted denims, a button-down shirt, and his Stetson, but a dark gray suit with a frock coat, neutral gray-brown vest, and hyacinth-red cravat. He looked dashing with his well-groomed short, boxed beard and kempt hair that was usually hidden by his hat.

She'd never seen him in a suit before and guessed he only wore it on special occasions. He sat up straight, focused solely on the preacher and his words.

Mary Jane scanned the chapel. The other hands from Happenstance had all made it in before the meeting had begun and sat clustered together on a full bench in front of several members of Hank's family, including Andrew, who couldn't take his eyes off Judith. The only open bench was the one directly in front of Raine. She closed her eyes and shook her head.

God certainly had a sense of humor.

With Sarah Jane's hand in hers, she slid into the pew.

"Can I sit with Sheriff Redbourne, Mama?" the little girl asked.

"Not today, love." She patted the seat next to her, but noticed her daughter wave at the man behind her before sitting down.

The Thanksgiving sermon had been the same for the last three years and she suspected it would be no different this year, but still, she had a hard time focusing on his words with Raine taking up the space in her thoughts.

She wondered how he was adjusting to life in Thistleberry. She knew from experience just how drastic of a change it could be from the comforts and conveniences of the eastern part of the country.

"It has come to my attention that there are several families who lost livestock, whose homes were damaged, and whose food supplies were ruined in this last storm, so I implore you that as you contemplate your gratitude to our merciful God, that you reach out with a generosity of spirit and means to those who have been less fortunate than you. Be His hands in this time of need."

The preacher's words touched her. Mary Jane began thinking of the things she could do over the next few weeks to help ease the burdens of her neighbors and friends, and she wondered if she could incorporate the sheriff into any of those plans.

"Amen."

And just like that, the service was over.

The townsfolk stirred as they rose from their seats and began to converse one with another.

Sarah Jane spun around on the pew to face Raine.

"Are you going to Whisper Ridge for Thanksgiving?" she

asked, resting her chin on her arms that folded over the back of the bench.

Jethro and his little family stood.

"Mr. Redbourne," Alice said with a smile and a wink at Mary Jane, "We'll have plenty of chicken pot-pie this afternoon in case you were thinking of inviting any guests."

"Subtle, Al. Real subtle," Jethro said, scooping his son from his wife's arms.

Raine laughed.

"Apparently," he leaned forward, speaking to Mary Jane, "my new Lottie is making an abundance of food this afternoon, if you and this little angel would like to join us for an early supper," he said, rising to his feet and tapping Sarah Jane on the tip of her nose.

It had been nearly a month since she and her daughter had visited Fred at the Isaacson farm.

"Lottie?" she asked, unfamiliar with the term as she stood up and turned to look at him.

"It's a long story. Mrs. Miller has been gracious enough to accept a position of keeping house and cooking for me."

"Congratulations, Mrs. Miller."

"Please, call me Allie." The young woman seemed far wiser than her nineteen or twenty years would have provided. "It really is sad to watch Mr. Raine eat all alone in that big old house."

Raine raised a brow.

"You and Jethro eat with me almost every day," he protested.

She smiled conspiratorially with a slight shrug of her shoulders.

"Well," Mary Jane said, playing along, "we can't have him eating all alone, now can we? Yes, we accept. I look forward to visiting with you more, Allie. Chicken pot-pie is one of my favorites." She glanced over at Raine, who chuckled at their banter. Apparently, he had not been too perturbed by Friday's little outburst with the marshal.

Allie took her son back from her husband and escaped out of the pew. "See you soon," she called back as she disappeared out of the church.

Sarah Jane slipped her hand into hers as they moved out into the aisle, then looked up at Raine.

"You never answered my question," she said.

Raine dropped down onto his haunches. "Yes, S.J.—can I call you that?" he asked.

She nodded.

"I will most certainly be going to Whisper Ridge for Thanksgiving. I'm hoping that you and your mama will be there too."

"We are. Mrs. Deardon invited us."

"I heard. Did you know that the Deardons are my family? Cousins. The whole lot of them."

Her eyes opened wide. "You are so lucky," she breathed out with awe. "I wish I had cousins. Especially, if they were like Hayden and Sebastian." She thought for a moment, bringing a crooked finger up to her chin. "Can you marry your cousins?"

Mary Jane laughed out loud.

"It was so good to see you come in today, Miss Bennett," the preacher said as he approached, then looked down at Sarah Jane. "And you too, Miss Bennett."

"Thank you for your sermon, Mr. Greene. It was inspiring like always." Mary Jane smiled, placing both of her hands on her daughter's shoulders.

"It's good to see Thistleberry growing again." He turned to Raine. "What you did for the Millers, son, that was right kind of you."

"Nah, it's just good business. I needed folks who could help take care of the farm while I'm seeing to my duties as sheriff in town. Jethro and Alice are more than I could have asked for."

"The Lord certainly brings the people we need into our lives when we least expect it."

"Yes, sir."

Mr. Greene nodded. "Well, the Mrs. is holding supper for me," he clapped his hands together, "so I best be on my way. Roast beef and potatoes. It's true that when the Lord closes a door, somewhere he opens a window. This storm's window was an abundance of fresh meat."

"Yes, sir."

Mary Jane thought about those poor ranchers who had lost livestock in the freeze and wondered how many of their animals had gone to spoil. The Deardons and family had spent several days helping other ranchers dress their lost stock for the butcher and the tanner, drag unusable carcasses out to open fields for the buzzards and other scavengers to clean, and patch holes in roofs and other structures where the wind or weight from the snow and ice had broken through.

The townspeople had all pulled together to support their neighbors. The icebox at Happenstance was overflowing with fresh cuts and the rafters of their smoke house were currently filled with drying salted meat.

"Well, I also should be going," Mary Jane said, running through the list of things she needed to do in her head. "I have a few things to drop off at the Sorensen's place and then a quick visit over to Old Mrs. Weller's. Lucy told me she's just taken in her three recently orphaned grandchildren, and we want to make sure they have some warm underthings and plenty of blankets, meat, and firewood."

"Mind if I tag along?" Raine asked. "I haven't had the pleasure of meeting Mrs. Weller yet, and I promised Mrs. Sorensen I would check in on them this week to see how they are coming along with mending their coop."

She thought about saying something witty or protesting, but the reality of it was, she welcomed the idea.

"You know, I would really like that. I think we both would, isn't that right, love?" She squeezed Sarah Jane's shoulders.

"None of the people Mama visits have children for me to

play with." She leaned over to Raine with her hand cupped around her mouth. "Maybe if you come along, I won't be so bored."

He scooped her daughter up into his arms and carried her to the back of the church where he collected his coat before they headed outside.

"So," Raine started as he climbed onto the sleigh bench beside Mary Jane, "Have you ever been to Thanksgiving with the Deardons before?" he asked.

"No."

"It's been a long time for me. But I am looking forward to it."

"Me too."

Why was she only offering him one and two-word answers?

"I hear that the tournament can be quite competitive," she blurted. "Lucy said your granddad even offered her up as a prize years ago."

"It's true. He just knew she was the right person for Lucas is all. I don't think he would have let any of the others marry her—no matter who had won." He chuckled. "I think it's real nice that you and Sarah Jane will be there."

"Yes, I am looking forward to it very much."

Both families lived on farms on the south side of town. She visited the Sorensen family on a consistent basis when the weather permitted, but it had been a while since she'd been out to check on them and she looked forward to seeing Dusty.

She'd never actually been out to the widow's home as she usually ran into the woman in town either at the General Store or at church, but it had been too long since she'd seen her and hoped that their visit might bring some joy to the otherwise bitter November day.

Lucy had brought over a two-seated sleigh this morning and together they had filled the back bench with some of their warmest blankets, a few different sized pairs of winter underwear, and various crates filled with cheese, jerky, potatoes, and a single loaf of bread.

"How is it possible to have the sun shining so brightly in the sky and it be so cold?" He shivered, pulling his coat more tightly around him.

Mary Jane laughed to herself. While they were living currently at freezing temperatures or below, if he thought this day was cold, he was in for a rude awakening come January.

She looked down at her daughter who was all bundled up with her woolen coat, scarf, hat, and gloves. The tip of her little nose and her cheeks were rosy, but she seemed otherwise happy and comfortable.

The Sorensens lived just a little over a mile to the south of town, so that would be their first stop.

"Sheriff," the young Sorensen boy called when they pulled up in front of their house, "I did what you told me. Would you like to see?"

"If you'll excuse me while I go inspect his handywork."

Sarah Jane saw two young goats playing in the snow near the fence across the way. She looked up at Mary Jane with wide eyes and raised brows, her hands clapped together, her fingers resting under her chin. Her lips moved as if mumbling something akin to pleading permission to go and see them.

Mary Jane nodded.

"Do not climb up on that fence, little girl, do you understand me?" She called after her daughter, remembering the experience with Raine's pig.

"I won't."

"And I shored it up with a crossbeam here and it worked, just like you said it would." The young boy returned with Raine from the side of the house where the chicken coop was located.

"We can't thank you enough for all your help around here, Sheriff," Dusty Sorensen called out to him. She glanced between Raine and Mary Jane then over at her eldest daughter, Sue, who stood staring out the window from inside the house.

"It was my pleasure, ma'am."

Mr. Sorensen joined his wife on the porch.

"Your idea to supplement the income I make from the mill has already helped us to catch up on our account with the Smith's," he said with his hand extended. "And we even have a nice big bird to cook up for Thanksgiving supper. Thank you."

Raine shook the man's hand. "You do good work. And I ought to know. I come from a family of craftsmen of one sort or another. My brother Taggert would be particularly impressed."

Mrs. Sorensen pulled Mary Jane aside and whispered quietly.

"You know, I had my sights set on the sheriff for my Sue, but after seeing the two of you together, I must say, I think you're a lovely pair."

"Oh, I think you've mistaken…we are not a…not yet, we're not…"

She didn't know what she was trying to say. That she hoped they would officially start courting? That she liked him, and he liked her? But what did that mean exactly?

"Thank you, Mrs. Sorensen. Raine is a good man and I'm glad you can see that."

"You're a good woman too, Mary Jane Bennett. Don't you let anyone tell you any different."

The Sorensen's were still new in town. She may feel differently after speaking with some of the women there. She reached into the back of the sleigh, pulled out one of the crates and handed it to the woman. Her eyes lit up with delight.

"I see you, Miss Bennett, sharing the gifts that God has given you with the people here in Thistleberry—even when they don't. I learned a long time ago that what other people think of you is not nearly as important as what you think of yourself—what God thinks of you."

"Maybe you should be giving the sermons on Sunday." She laughed. "Oh, don't tell Mr. Greene I said that. His sermons are lovely."

"You deserve someone who will cherish you. I see the way that man looks at you. He *sees* you too." The older woman placed an arm around her and squeezed.

"You still think they'll be done in time for Christmas?" Raine asked the older man, raising his cupped hands to his mouth and blowing into them.

Poor thing.

"Yes, sir. I expect I'll have them finished round this time next week."

"I'll be by to pick them up at your say so."

"Thanks again, Sheriff." Mrs. Sorensen winked at her and nodded. "And Mary Jane, thank you for the foodstuffs. Please be sure to pass along our gratitude to Mrs. Deardon."

"I will."

"If you folks need anything, you know where to find me," Raine said, his shoulders scrunched to the cold.

As they walked back to the sleigh, Mary Jane slipped on the ice layered over the impacted snow on the walkway between the house and the drive. Raine reached out to catch her, but it was too late. His booted feet lost their traction, and he slipped backward, unwittingly pulling her down on top of him.

"Owww," Raine said with a light chuckle, groaning from the impact of the fall. He tried to sit up, but slumped back down. "Are you all right?" he asked, staring at the sky, his arms enveloped around her.

Mary Jane's hands rested on his chest as she looked down at his beautiful cold-ridden face, then dropped her head onto his shoulder and started to laugh—quietly at first, then she raised her head again, the sound growing into a hearty belly laugh.

Raine laid his head against the ground, his arms still around her.

Giggles erupted from the house.

And Raine's body started to shake from laughter.

Mary Jane pushed herself off of him and turned over onto her rump. She had to face it, there was no ladylike way to stand up from here without help.

Raine got to his feet, brushed the snow from his person, and held out a hand to help her up. She eyed it warily, knowing where she'd ended up the last time he'd tried to help her.

It hadn't been so bad.

Then, another smile broke across her face and she slipped both hands into his.

"Are you sure you have your footing?" she asked.

"I'm sure. Trust me."

"Okay."

He pulled her up, a little harder than she had anticipated, and he caught her up against him.

"I've got you."

She pulled away enough to look up at him and cursed herself when her gaze fell to his mouth. A breath caught in her chest and heat rushed into her cheeks.

"Thank you," she said, taking a step away from him.

She cleared her throat and glanced up at Mrs. Sorensen whose lips pursed in a knowing smile.

"Sarah Jane," she called, looking for her daughter.

Two white and brown goats frolicked, jumping around in the snow. When one of them nuzzled up against her little face, she wrapped her arms around its neck with a giggle.

"It's time to go, sweet girl."

"Mama, watch." Sarah Jane knelt down in the snow and the smaller of the two goats jumped up onto her back, eliciting another giggle from her daughter.

They reminded her of Mrs. Isaacson's goats, though these seemed a little bigger. When she'd asked the old widow how hers stayed so small, she'd simply said it was so they could keep her company, but Mary Jane still had no idea what that meant.

"Tell them goodbye, love. We still have another stop to make before we head in for supper."

"Goodbye," Sarah Jane said, kissing the goats' faces. "Maybe I'll come back and play again next week," she told them before running back to stand next to Mary Jane.

"They are so cute, Mama."

"She's a natural with them," Mrs. Sorensen said.

"She loves animals and it's that way between her and most of them—even the ones who aren't always as tolerant of her avid affection," Mary Jane told the woman as she climbed up onto the sleigh bench.

"Even with old Fred," Raine said, "out at my place."

"That old pig Mrs. Isaacson keeps around?"

"One and the same."

Sarah Jane climbed up onto her mother's lap.

"Have a wonderful Thanksgiving!" Raine said. He sat down next to them and raised a hand to wave. Mary Jane and her daughter waved too as they pulled back out onto the path headed south.

The Weller home sat at the farthest edge of town on the border that separated Thistleberry and Murphy. As they pulled up toward the house, it appeared void of activity. There were no chickens in the coop or pigs in the pen, and there were no tracks in the snow leaving the property. The only indication that someone lived there was the freshly chopped wood piled to the side of the front door.

"Are you sure someone lives here?" Raine asked, wrapping the reins around the hitch on the side of the sleigh.

"I've never actually been out here." Mary Jane lifted her hands with a shrug. "All I know is that her grandchildren just came to live with her. Lucy wanted me to bring a whole load of blankets, winter underwear, hats, and a few other things to help her and the children stay warm in this weather and to help them feel welcome. My understanding is that they arrived just before the big storm."

As Raine took a step toward the house, a long, steel black barrel edged out through the window next to the door.

"That's far enough."

A gun cocked.

The voice was too young to be much older than twelve or thirteen.

"Hello," Raine called out. "We don't mean any harm, we're just looking for the Weller farm. Is this the right place?"

"Who's askin'?

"Name's Redbourne. I'm sheriff here in Thistleberry."

"How do we know yer tellin' the truth?"

"Why would I lie? Take a look around, and pardon me for sayin' so, but it doesn't look like you've much to loot. No livestock, no wagon that I can see, and—"

The door burst open and two children, the oldest no more than eight, ran out of the house and threw their arms around Raine. The older of the two, a boy of maybe ten, hugged him at the waist while the little girl, appearing to be just about Sarah Jane's age, four, maybe five, clung to his leg.

"No!" A young man appeared in the doorway, his shotgun still in his arm and held close, but now pointed at the ground. "Georgia May, Clovis, come back here. He's a perfect stranger."

They didn't move.

Mary Jane set her daughter down onto the seat next to her. "You stay right here in the sleigh, love. I'll be right back."

"Who are they, Mama?"

"They are Mrs. Weller's grandchildren." Mary Jane kissed the top of her daughter's head and slipped out of the sleigh, and next to Raine.

"What's with the warm greeting?" Raine asked. "You know it's not wise to point a gun at a lawman, don't you?"

"Please don't hurt our brother," the boy said, looking up at him. "He's just doin' what he thinks he has to do to protect us."

"Protect you from what? From whom?"

Mary Jane crouched down to look at the little girl.

"Hello," she said, reaching out to touch her wispy and matted braids. "I am Miss Bennett. What's your name?"

The girl continued to stare at her, but did not speak.

"Where is your grandmother?" Raine asked. "Can we speak

with her?"

"You can try. She won't exactly talk to us."

"Clovis, stop tellin' the man our business."

"Clovis," Raine addressed the younger boy directly, a hand on his back. "Where *exactly* is your grandmother?"

He looked up at Raine, then pointed over at a tree-topped slope just east of where they stood. Mrs. Weller sat on a bench overlooking the valley in the shade of the old tree.

Mary Jane breathed a sigh of relief.

"Well, why didn't you just say so?" Raine asked.

"I'll go talk to her," Mary Jane said.

The little girl shook her head.

The young man at the door threw his hands up. "I wouldn't do that if I were you."

She squeezed the young girl's shoulder, lifted up her skirt, and trudged through unbroken snow up the slight hill toward the woman.

She couldn't imagine being the widow's age and having to take on three young children. The adjustment had to be difficult, but the loneliness the woman must have felt when her husband had passed on would have been a challenge of its own. Maybe having grandchildren around would help her not feel so lonely anymore.

"Mrs. Weller, you should probably come in out of the cold," she said as she approached the top of the gentle hill. "You'll catch your death out here." Mary Jane paused a moment to catch her breath. She looked out over the countryside and noticed the marker peeking through the snow just a few feet from the bench.

She must be visiting with her late husband.

"Mrs. Weller?" she called again. "It's Mary Jane. Bennett. From Happenstance."

No reaction.

She placed a hand on the woman's shoulder. It was like touching stone. Cold—even through her gloves—and hard.

Panic filled Mary Jane's chest, and she apprehensively walked around to the front of the bench, and gasped.

Mrs. Wellers eyes were closed, a soft smile on her face, and she appeared frozen solid with ice encrusting her lashes. She looked perfectly preserved. It was a wonder scavengers hadn't gotten to her.

Mary Jane dropped her head, saying a quick prayer for the dead and for the children she was supposed to be caring for. With heavy heart, she slowly made her way back down the hill, careful not to take another spill. As she descended, she looked up long enough to catch sight of a mound of small animal corpses that had been piled into the crease of a modest ravine a good distance from the back of the house.

They must have all died in the unexpected storms, and the children…

She couldn't finish the thought.

"How did you get all the way out here?" Raine was asking the young orphans when Mary Jane reached them. He sat on a snow-cleared stump with the two younger children now sitting on his lap. Their clothes were old and worn, their faces dirty and sunken. And now, she knew why.

"Did Grandma talk to you?" the young man who still stood at the door scoffed.

She ignored him.

"Sheriff, may I speak with you for a moment please?" Mary Jane asked.

"Clovis, Georgia May," Raine said to the children he held, "will you excuse me for a moment? The lady would like a word."

"I guess it's all right," Clovis said, jumping down from his lap.

Raine picked up the little girl and set her down next to the boy.

"Come here, love," Mary Jane said, picking up her daughter from the front seat of the sleigh. "Do you see that little girl?"

Sarah Jane nodded.

"I think she needs a friend right now. Do you think you can try to be her friend?"

Without answering, she skipped over to where the little girl and boy stood.

"Hello! Are you new here?" Sarah Jane had no qualms about talking to anyone.

The little girl nodded.

"What's your name? I'm Sarah Jane Bennett." She held out her little hand. "It's a pleasure to meet you."

The little girl slowly reached out for Sarah Jane's hand. "Georgia May Wallace."

Progress!

Raine met Mary Jane over at the sleigh.

"These children cannot be left alone out here. Not tonight. Not for one more minute."

"What did Mrs. Weller say?"

"She didn't have much to say." How could she put this? "The woman has been sitting up on that bench for days, if not weeks."

Raine narrowed his eyes at her. One brow raised.

"Are you telling me that she is—"

"Frozen solid." Mary Jane nodded. "Yes, I am."

He swallowed hard, but did a good job at keeping the shock from his face. He glanced over at the children.

"The chickens and other small animals have been dragged to a gully behind the property."

"Uncle Hank or someone must have noticed that she's been missing."

"With all the folks needing help after the storm, it appears that she slipped through the cracks."

"So, what do you want to do?" he asked. "We obviously can't leave them out here all on their own."

"There's an orphanage over in Murphy. We could try reaching out to them." Even as the words came out of her mouth, she knew sending these children away would not be in their best interest.

"For now, we'll take them back to my place," Raine said to her surprise. "They look like they could use a good meal."

"And a bath," Mary Jane added.

"Clovis, Georgia May, come on now. You're coming home with me tonight." Raine motioned with a wave.

"Really?" The children came running along with Sarah Jane.

Mary Jane removed three blankets from the pile and pushed the others to the side to make room for the children in the back seat. The food crate still sat on the floor with the bag of other winter wear, but there was nowhere else to put that, so they would have to rest their feet on top of it.

"What about Ridley?" Clovis asked once he was situated on the bench.

"So, that's his name," Raine said, throwing one of the blankets over the top of them. "Well, I'll go get Ridley." He stepped away from the sleigh, but the young man turned back for the house and shut the door behind him.

"Go away," she heard Ridley scream. "I don't need you. I don't need anyone."

Those same words could have easily come out of her mouth just months before, but she'd since seen that having people in her life who cared about her, protected her, did not make her weak. In fact, it made her stronger. Hopefully, the young man would be able to learn the same.

Raine looked back at her, his eyes locking momentarily with hers before he attempted to push the door open.

"He probably put a chair up against the knob. We do that when we're scared," Clovis told her.

"Are you hungry?" Mary Jane asked.

"Ah, a little," Clovis said, but his eyes betrayed him.

CRASH!

The children jumped.

Raine had kicked in the door, then disappeared inside.

"It's all right," she said with a smile. "Are you hungry,

Georgia May?" she asked again, specifically to the little girl.

Georgia May looked up at the boy, then back at her, but didn't speak.

Mary Jane reached down into the crate and pulled out the loaf of bread she'd just baked this morning.

The children's eyes grew wide.

After several minutes, Raine and Ridley emerged from the cabin, the sheriff's hand on the young man's shoulder. When they reached the sleigh, Ridley stepped up to join the others.

Raine cleared his throat.

"I'm sorry I held a gun on you, ma'am."

Raine raised a brow.

"And for talking to you disrespectfully."

"Thank you, Ridley," she said, working to keep the smile from her face.

Raine nodded.

"Are we going to leave Grandma here?" Little Georgia May spoke to her for the first time.

"Not for long, sweetheart," the sheriff told her.

They stopped in town long enough for Raine to collect his mare from the livery.

When they reached the bend in the road that would take them to the Isaacson farm, Raine pulled up alongside the sleigh.

"I'll join you shortly. Just need a quick word with Hank."

Mary Jane saw something glint from the trees near the pond at the back of the Isaacson farm. She strained to see if someone lurked in the distance. Ever since seeing Mundy at the town festival, she had been a little jumpy.

It was nothing.

"M.J.?" Raine followed her gaze. "Did you see something?"

She shook her head. "I think I'm starting to see things everywhere I look. I'm sure it's nothing. Be safe, and we'll see you at supper."

Allie would certainly be surprised when she brought an additional three mouths to feed, but she had a feeling the young woman would be more than happy to feed the hungry children.

"How did the animals survive?" Ridley asked as they pulled up to the house, the chickens clucking wildly, and the dogs barking.

Fred stood at the front of his pen, happily eating the scraps of food and grains that the Millers had set out for him, and the sheep roamed the pasture freely.

"Sheriff Redbourne hired Jethro," she pointed to the man standing out in the middle of the field, "who knows all about ranching and how to take care of animals in all sorts of weather."

"I wish we'd had a Jethro before our chickens froze," Clovis said with a disheartened sigh.

"Well, today we are going to focus on the things we can do something about," Mary Jane said, turning around in her seat, her arms folded on the back rest. "Like filling those empty bellies." She gently poked at Georgia May's tummy and the girl giggled.

Hallelujah!

"Good afternoon, Miss Bennett," Jethro said, coming in from the pasture to help her with the sleigh. "I see we have some additional guests today."

"Yes, I hope that's all right."

"Of course. It's funny, my wife had a feeling she needed to prepare a little extra today. She'll be glad to find out why."

As expected, Allie was thrilled to have the children also join them for Sunday supper. The warm, buttery aroma of chicken pot-pie baking in the oven greeted them as they walked into the house.

"Miss Bennett," Georgia May said, tugging on the side of her skirt. "I don't feel so well."

"What's wrong, sweetheart?" she bent down to talk to the little girl.

"My tummy hurts."

Mary Jane's heart wrenched. Who knew how long these children had gone without having anything to eat? The wonderful smells coming from the kitchen certainly had her own stomach growling in anticipation.

"I'll bet that once we get some food in your belly, you'll be feeling a whole lot better. Should we give that a try?"

Georgia May nodded.

"The wash basin is just through there." She pointed to the large, galvanized tub just off the kitchen. "I expect all of you to wash your hands and faces before joining us at the table."

"Yes, ma'am." The children's voices harmonized and echoed one another.

"You too," Mary Jane told her daughter with a wink.

The little girl obediently followed the other children into the kitchen.

"And the sheriff?" Allie asked, switching baby Asher from one hip to the other.

"He'll be along shortly. Had business to discuss with the Deardons."

"Understood. It seems like your visits resulted in a turn of unexpected events."

"You have no idea." Mary Jane recounted briefly what had transpired before the children returned.

"Supper will be served in just a few more minutes, everyone," Allie announced as the children filed into the dining room.

"I know," Mary Jane said, "what do you say we play a game of Lookabout while we wait?"

Ridley slumped down into an armed chair next to the fireplace.

"What object will we use, Mama?" Sarah Jane asked.

"Why not this?" Allie held out a cowbell that was missing its clapper. She shook it with a giggle, but no sound came out.

"What good is a bell if it doesn't even ring?" Ridley asked.

"I think it is rather good for playing a round of Lookabout, don't you?"

Georgia May looked at the bell, then up at Mary Jane. "Miss

Bennett, what is Lookabout?" she asked quietly.

"Well, it is a game where one person hides an object and the rest of us have to look about to see if we can find it. The last person to find the object then has to hide it for the next round. Who would like to go first?"

"I will," Clovis volunteered.

"Okay, everyone, let's go into the other room while Clovis hides the bell. You too, Ridley."

"Do I have to?"

Mary Jane couldn't imagine what it was like to be in these children's shoes, but she did know a thing or two about grief. And she knew that sometimes a little distraction is what was needed to get through the day.

"No, I suppose not. I'm sure Jethro could find something for you to do out in the yard."

Ridley got to his feet and took a step toward the front door.

"But…" Mary Jane added, "I'd like it if you decided to stay in here and play with us."

"Me too," Clovis chimed in.

"And me," Sarah Jane said.

Georgia May walked up to her brother. "Please play with us, Ridley." She slipped her hand into his and pulled him along.

They all gathered into the room just off the entry and huddled together as they waited.

"I'm ready," Clovis called from the living area.

"Okay, children, now, as soon as you spot the bell, don't tell anyone where you saw it. Just sit down somewhere. The last person to find it, will then have a go at hiding it."

They moved into the living area, each looking both high and low for the broken bell.

After near a quarter of an hour, Georgia May jumped up onto the couch next to Mary Jane.

"I found it," she whispered loudly.

It was hard to believe that she was the same little girl who had barely spoken a word to them just an hour ago.

Sarah Jane was the only one who hadn't yet spotted the bell.

"Clovis, would you like to show S.J. where you hid the object?"

He jumped up from his place on the piano bench and walked over to the wooden bookcase in the corner of the room. He'd used it as a bookend for several old leather-bound volumes of various colors.

"Dinner is ready," Allie called from the kitchen.

Jethro must have come in through the back door because he was already washed up and sitting at the long rectangular table as the children ran to find their seats. Their focus quickly honing in on the large steaming dish brimming with a buttery flaky crust. With their arms in their laps, they all stared at the center of the table with wide eyes and protruding tongues.

The front door opened and Raine stepped inside the house. "It smells wonderful in here, Alice." He took off his coat and threw it over the back of the couch. "You little ones didn't eat it all without me, did you?"

"No, sir."

Raine rubbed his hands together and hurried toward the last empty chair at the table, the one next to M.J. Before he sat, he leaned down behind her, his breath warming the sides of her face and the familiar butterflies in her stomach started to dance. She remained faced forward, afraid what might happen if she turned to face him.

"Lucy is making up a room for them for the night at Whisper Ridge. Hank and Sam are taking care of everything else." He kissed her cheek, then slipped into his chair, and picked up his fork. "Let's eat."

CHAPTER TWENTY-FIVE

Thanksgiving Day

They'd buried Mrs. Weller on the hill next to her husband. It had taken three men several hours to chip away at the frozen ground until they'd dug a hole big enough to hold her. The preacher had said a few words as the children stood stoically between Lucy and Lucas.

Ridley, Clovis, and Georgia May had moved into Whisper Ridge for the time being and Raine was glad they would have people around them for the holidays who could bring a little joy into their lives. Ridley especially had made quick friends with Seth's boys and was looking forward to today almost as much as he was.

He'd arisen even earlier than usual this morning, unable to sleep. Thoughts of Sarah and their baby had plagued his dreams throughout the night, piling guilt and casting doubt on his growing feelings for Mary Jane and her daughter. The familiar pangs of regret seeped in and as much as he tried to push them aside, they grew stronger.

He hoped that his exertion in throwing around a caber,

using his skills with a bow to bullseye a target, and racing with the mare over his family's land would help him to dispel the new wave of awful gloom that had settled in his belly. The despair had hung over him like a persistent dark cloud for years—until he'd met Mary Jane.

Now, Raine looked forward to Thanksgiving at Whisper Ridge more than he wanted to admit. He pulled on his boots and headed out into the kitchen. While there was bound to be an abundance of food over at his family's place today, he thought he could do a little something this morning to show the Millers in a small way how grateful he was for them by making breakfast. Lottie had taught him a thing or two about cooking and he thought he'd put that knowledge to work.

By the time the sun peeked out over the mountains, biscuits were in the oven, bacon sizzled in a large cast iron pan alongside a hearty portion of sliced potatoes, and fresh-cooked eggs were already laid out on the table.

"What is this?" Alice asked as she walked into the house with baby Asher on her hip. "It smells wonderful. You told me you don't cook," she said in mock accusation.

"I said I don't, not that I couldn't." He winked.

"I guess that's true. But isn't this what you are paying me for?"

"It's a day of thanks and giving, so I am expressing my thanks to you by giving you some breakfast." He smiled as he scooped bacon out of the pan and onto a large serving plate he'd found in the cupboards next to the stove.

"You work fast," Jethro said as he joined them. He bent down and kissed his wife on top of her head, then sat down next to her."

"Apparently," Alice said, "Raine knows how to cook."

Jethro eyed the eggs in the center of the table with a raised brow. "Are we sure they're edible?"

"You're funny," Raine said, his words all but dripping with sarcasm.

It didn't take long before the morning food was gone.

"I wouldn't have believed it if I hadn't seen you in the kitchen cooking myself," Jethro said, sitting back in his chair and patting his belly. "You're a might fine cook."

Raine bent slightly at the waist in a quick bow. "I'm glad you approve."

"I'll get the dishes," Alice said, standing up with Asher still in her arms and knocking into the cabinet behind the table.

Sarah's picture fell to the floor and the glass cracked.

"Oh, Raine, I am so sorry." She handed the baby to her husband and bent down to pick it up. "She is beautiful," she said, brushing off the frame. "Who is she?"

"It's all right," he said, holding out his hand. He looked down at the photograph. It wasn't damaged, and neither was the frame—just the glass, and he figured he could find a place in town that could get him a new fitted piece. "She was my wife." He rubbed over her face, remembering the last Thanksgiving they'd spent together. "Lost her eleven years ago next month."

"How did she…?"

"You know, I'm unclear on many of the details. All I know is that she fell through the ice on a pond near our home in Stone Creek and I wasn't there." He stopped. Didn't want to think about his failures.

"Surely, you don't blame yourself for it."

He returned the picture to the cabinet, ignoring the question he knew was impossible for him to answer. How could it not have been his fault? He should have been home.

"Stone Creek, Kansas?" Jethro asked.

"Yeah." Raine nodded. "How did you know?"

"I have family there."

Raine didn't recall any Millers in Stone Creek, which was strange for a town that size. "Who were your kin?"

"The Wendells," Jethro said in between bites. "Leta and Grisham. Their oldest son, Parnell, is my age."

"The mill owner?"

"That's the one."

"I know them well. The mill property sits just on the south edge of Redbourne Ranch."

The Wendells had almost lost their only son right around the same time as Sarah died.

"How is Mr. Wendell these days?" he asked, knowing the pain that came with this time of year.

"I wish I could say. I regret that I've lost touch with him over the years, ever since...well, it's been a long while." An odd expression crossed his face as he glanced at Raine, his eyes narrowing.

"Last I heard, Mr. Wendell was selling the mill and heading back East to be with family."

Jethro looked up at the grandfather clock.

Raine's eyes followed.

Eight o'clock.

"Don't you have a tournament to get to?" Jethro asked.

"Yes, sir, I do," he said, pushing back his chair. "Are you sure the three of you wouldn't like to join us?" Raine knew that Lucy and the others would be more than happy to have them.

"Thank you for the invitation, but this is where we belong today."

"I thought you might say that." Raine headed to the front door and picked his hat from the rack on the wall. "So, there is a fresh bird, plucked and cleaned, and waiting for you in the icebox. Happy Thanksgiving." He pulled the door closed behind him with a grin on his face.

The mare pranced about excitedly as he walked out into the stable.

"Come on, girl! We're going to go have some fun."

There was a lot to think about today. He looked forward to spending some leisurely time with Mary Jane and her daughter as well as the rest of his family, but his excitement for the festivities was clouded over with his memory of the last Thanksgiving he'd had with Sarah—when she'd told him he was going to be a father.

Guilt nagged at him as he strained to recall every detail of that day only to find images of Mary Jane and little Sarah Jane as they'd baked pies for the Fall Harvest Festival pushing their way into his memory and overshadowing the pain.

He rode unhurried and relaxed on the snow packed path to Whisper Ridge, appreciating the few moments to himself in the quiet of the morning in the beauty of nature with a warm coat to protect him from the chill.

It didn't last long as the sound of a rider quickly approached.

"Sheriff!"

Raine turned to find Mr. Gibbons' son, waving wildly as he approached.

"The bank," he sucked in air in an attempt to catch his breath. "I was helping my pa with the chores at his shop this morning and saw men with guns pushing Mr. Dunbar into the bank. I think they aim to rob it."

The timing of robbery was too coincidental to ignore. Hank had said they rarely had any troubles in Thistleberry, but Raine had found just the opposite to be true since he'd been here.

So much for a relaxing Thanksgiving with family and friends.

It wouldn't be the first Thanksgiving he'd missed, nor, he suspected, the last.

With a moment of regret, he turned the mare around and urged her toward town, following the Gibbons boy. He would have to send his regrets and explain later. There was just no time now.

Luckily, he'd made a habit of donning his gun belt each morning, and he reached down his leg for confirmation his revolver still sat holstered there. He glanced down to where the butt of his rifle peeked out from the scabbard he'd secured just beneath his knee space on his saddle. While he hadn't anticipated needing the guns today, he'd been caught unaware once before as a deputy in Stone Creek and never wanted to repeat the experience.

Young Mr. Gibbons stopped at the edge of town, to the north side of the livery.

From this vantage point, Raine had a clear view of the bank.

"What do you want me to do?" the boy asked.

The center of town was quiet except for the man who'd just secured a large canvas bag to the back of his saddle and mounted his horse at the corner of the empty building next to the bank. Two more mounts waited near him. Raine swung his leg wide and dismounted.

"Stay here," he said to the boy, "and watch my horse." He crouched down a little and hustled across the street and around back of Mrs. Doherty's bakery and Lyla's Café, hoping to catch the thieves where they'd least expect it.

Just as he reached the corner of the building next to the bank, he braced himself up against the back wall to stay out of sight, his gun drawn. He wasn't about to rush in without having an idea of what he was facing. Especially with no one to watch his back.

"Come on, Nigel, the marshal's coming." The man already seated on his horse in front of the bank called out.

Thunk.

Groan.

Crash.

The sounds all came from inside the building.

Raine started out from his position, but pulled back when an older man, with graying hair and a faded brown slouch hat, burst out through the open door into the bank. He ran with a slight limp to his gait as he headed toward his associates with a small chest cradled under his arm. It was the same man he and Tyler had spotted the other day.

"That'll be far enough!" Raine yelled, his gun cocked and aimed as he stepped out from behind the building.

CRACK!

A gunshot whizzed by his ear, close enough that its wake

brushed his cheek, then splintered the trim on the back corner of the building wall. He ducked, returning fire as he took cover behind the bank.

After several hoots, hollers, and gunshots, the faint whinny of horses told Raine that they were getting away and he couldn't let that happen. Still hunching low, he rounded the corner of the bank and stepped up onto the boardwalk, sticking his head into the open door for a quick look. It didn't appear any more outlaws were inside the building.

Mr. Dunbar leaned up against the counter, holding a handkerchief to the side of his head, a trail of blood streaking down his face, and Raine rushed inside to help.

"Go!" the banker demanded. "I'll be fine. They got it all. Every last dime."

It was too convenient, too clean.

Why would the brutes wait until the holiday to rob the bank? There would be no guarantee that the banker would be around, and it didn't seem that the group had had the equipment necessary to blow up the vault. Raine's gut screamed at him that something was amiss, but he'd have to figure it out when he got back…with the town's money. He ran across the street to collect the mare from the Gibbons kid.

"They headed out toward the Sorensen place," the boy told Raine, pointing toward the church.

Reaching up to grab hold on the saddle, he pulled himself up, squeezed his knees, and nudged his mount to a quick gallop. It still amazed him that the mare was so in tune with what he needed. Almost like she knew before he did. When he reached the church house, he spotted Rutledge coming up on him from behind on horseback and within moments was on his heels.

Raine slowed a little to weigh the marshal's intentions. When the man didn't slow down, but met his pace, he relaxed a little.

"I heard gunfire," Tyler said, his unbuttoned coat flailing wildly behind him. "Thought I'd join in on the fun."

"Bank was robbed," Raine yelled loud enough to be heard. "Three of them from what I could tell." He wished he could explain further, but the thieves already had a several minute advantage and were out of sight.

Marshal Tyler nodded. "I'm with you."

Another fresh snowfall overnight allowed them to follow the deep horse tracks of the men they were pursuing. At once, they took a sharp turn into a wooded glen—a shortcut leading up to the mountain pass. If they made it through the pass, there would be too many places for them to double-back and hide, which would make him and the marshal easy pickings on the road. With another squeeze, he pushed the mare even faster.

The methodical rhythm of motion as he galloped through deep blankets of fresh snow seemed to slow everything down around him. The deafening silence honed his focus into a crisp point as the tail end of a horse came into view just ahead.

"Up there," Rutledge yelled, motioning with an abrupt jerk of his extended arm toward the top of the first ridge. He pulled back on his reins, shifted directions, and headed up the mountainside after a man who appeared to be on foot.

Raine focused on the men still riding directly ahead of him. He crossed the long bridge leading into the pass, and as they rode further up the mountain, those he followed cut new trails up higher onto the mountainside where the trees grew thicker and where the slopes rose higher into the sky. He leaned down, rubbed the side of the mare's neck, and folded his hands even tighter around his reins, pushing forward, feeling at one with the movements of the mare beneath him. "Come on, girl. We've got them."

BOOM!

The mare reared.

Unprepared for the swift action, Raine gripped the reins in his hands, the full force of his body yanking against his arms as he struggled fiercely to regain his footing in the stirrups while the mare fought to keep her traction on the uneven ground.

Unable to maintain his grip, he slammed backward into the firm crusted cushion of several weeks of accumulated snow.

The deep rumbling sounds of thunder shattered the silence of the clear morning—unusual for this time of year.

His lungs depleted, his heart racing, the wind had been knocked right out of him and he fought to breathe. At last, he swallowed several gulps of air. With furious determination, he pushed himself to his feet, searching the tree line for any sign of the mare.

She was gone.

There was also no sign of the bank robbers.

He'd failed.

He brushed himself off, defeated, picked up his hat that had fallen just a few feet from him, and slapped it against the side of his leg before putting it back onto his head—which still rumbled like thunder in his ears.

He tapped the side of his head with his hand to clear it, but to no avail.

The sound just grew louder.

And louder.

He turned around to face a wall of white and trees now towering over him. Enormous cracks had appeared in the snowbanks at the top of the ridge, breaking into huge slabs and boulders as it now rushed down the sloped mountainside toward him. His eyes grew wide.

RUN! was his only thought.

He'd heard stories of avalanches before, but had never experienced one, and cursed himself for not recognizing the signs earlier.

After just a few steps, his feet were overrun with the flowing river of snow, and he lost his footing. Still unwilling to yield to the whitewashed rapids, he flailed about in an attempt to stay on top of the slide of powder, rocks, and debris that bumped, scratched, and bit into his flesh as it ripped through his clothing from below and around him. He reached out to a tree branch in his path, and was able to grab ahold, effectively halting his decent. The sting of the rough bark cut into his hands.

The branch broke.

He again was swept up into the current, hurled several more yards before coming to a stop, his hat covering his face, his bare skin exposed on his arms, neck, and chest. He drew in a deep breath as the rush of snow continued to pile on top of him, growing heavier by the second.

In moments, the thundering stopped, and all was still.

He couldn't move.

It had been a trap to lure him out here.

Alone.

No one knew where to find him. Except Tyler, who was dead for all he knew. The man had been close to that explosion.

The direness of his situation impaled him.

He was stuck.

There was no way out.

Breathe.

While the air was growing thin, he could still take a breath.

Don't panic.

This was not the end of his story.

He would not die here.

Think, Redbourne, think.

How could he get himself free? He closed his eyes and offered a silent prayer.

Lord, please.

A soft nicker reached his ears.

It was the mare.

That was fast.

Gratitude filled him.

"Thank you," were the only words he could manage to speak aloud.

Come on girl, I'm here. Come find me.

Not that there was a lot a horse could do in this situation, but it was something. She offered comfort while he was alone.

A spark of hope ignited in his heart.

The mare snorted. She was much closer now. Her loud purr told Raine she'd found him.

Minutes passed.

Raine could not think what else to do. The air around his face was growing thin and stale. The pains from being thrown around, battered, and broken began to manifest and his eyelids grew heavy.

Dogs barked in the distance.

A voice called out in the darkness.

Sarah?

Jethro Miller

Jethro looked around the small two-room apartment that sat at the edge of the barn big enough to house a hundred or more heads of sheep comfortably. Gratitude filled his mind and heart as he thought of what could have been just a few short weeks ago had he and his little family been left out under their canvas tent during the first Montana freeze of the season.

Now, they had secured employment—both for he and his wife—that would provide the necessities needed to build a life.

Several of the smaller lambs and their mamas still preferred to stay close to the comforts and warmth the barn provided, and he made sure they had plenty of food and water before heading back up to the main homestead.

As he approached the house, the delicious aroma of roasting turkey wafted beneath his nose. He jumped up the front stairs and into the living area where he could watch his beautiful wife standing in the kitchen beating a bowl full of mashed potatoes. He walked up behind her, slipped his arms beneath hers and around her waist, then brushed her hair aside to place a light kiss on her neck.

"Will you set the table, honey? Supper should be about ready."

Coo.

Jethro stood up, his ears perked at the sound.

"He's awake." With one last squeeze, he left Alice to peer over the edge of the cradle to see his son, whose eyes were bright and wide. He scooped Asher up and nuzzled his face into his child's little belly, eliciting a giggle from the babe.

He moved to the cabinet behind the table with the baby in his arms, and reached up to the top shelf to collect two plates. His eyes were drawn to the photo of the woman Raine had said was his wife. He picked up the frame, the cracked glass extending from one corner to the other. As he looked down into her face, he recognized her.

He'd shaken off the feeling before, but now, his breathing grew faster, his heart sinking in his chest.

It *was* her.

"Al," he called, unable to avoid the crack in his voice. "This is her."

Alice looked over her shoulder, then turned to face him.

He dropped into the chair, tucking Asher even closer to his body.

"Raine said her name was Sarah."

"No," he looked up at her and held out the photograph, "this is the woman who saved my life. It's her." He'd never learned her name or knew what had become of her.

She was Raine's wife.

The truth of it struck him like a jolt.

He didn't talk much about his time in Stone Creek with Uncle Grisham and his family. It was too painful. Shortly after moving back East to live with their mother's sister, she had decided she could no longer care for her six children and had carted them off to various family members. The Wendells had taken him in for a few days, but the arrangement hadn't lasted long.

The grandfather clock chimed one.

"The turkey will be ready. Give me a moment while I pull it out of the oven."

Jethro returned the frame to its place on the cabinet, retrieved the dishes, and proceeded to set the table, but he'd grown contemplative. Raine had told them that his wife died falling through the ice, but that is exactly what she had saved him from.

He and his cousin Parnell had been playing on the water wheel. They'd believed that the pond by the side of the house was frozen through completely, but as they ran out onto the ice, it started to crack and before they knew it, they were sinking into the freezing water. He still wasn't sure how or why she had even been out in the woods that day, but she'd known exactly what to do.

This woman had seen them, but instead of running for help, she'd picked up a large branch that had broken off one of the trees and made her way out to them on the ice. After she'd pulled both Parnell and him from the hole in the icy pond, she'd told them to lie on their bellies and spread out their arms to distribute their weight, then crawl as best they could to the edge.

They'd done as instructed. By the time they reached the edge, he turned back to thank her, but she was no longer there.

Had she died saving him? The thought haunted him.

Alice set the small turkey on a ceramic divot in the center of the table. It was likely the most plentiful meal they'd had in all their two years of being married. When the rest of the food was all laid out, he took his wife by the hand, bowed his head, and offered a heartfelt prayer of gratitude and thanksgiving for both the generosity of the man who'd taken them in and provided an opportunity to earn their keep, and for the woman who may have sacrificed her life for his.

How could he tell Raine?

Or ever make it up to him?

Ethan Redbourne

"How did I ever let you talk me into this, Ethan Redbourne?" Grace asked as she huddled closely with their two small boys, pulling the buffalo hide tighter around them. "It'll be educational for the boys, you said. It'll be an adventure, you said."

Ethan hardly blamed his generally sweet wife for her current temperament seeing as how they'd been travelling with their children for the better half of three weeks with several unexpected delays. This last leg on a stagecoach in the snow hadn't been enjoyable for any of them.

"Ah, come on, sis," Jack Nolan said, "it hasn't been that bad."

Ethan was grateful he was not on the receiving end of the stare his beautiful wife shot at her brother.

As they pulled into the small town of Thistleberry, he was surprised to see that the streets were mostly vacant. He opened the door and exited the stage in front of the Thistledown hotel and restaurant. Most of the tables in the eating establishment appeared to be filled with patrons, so the town wasn't completely void of life.

Jack climbed out of the coach and stretched his legs. Ethan reached up for each of his sons and set them on the boardwalk next to their uncle, then raised a hand to help Grace down from the box.

She stood up tall, stretching her neck and arms.

"I'm hungry, Mama," little Oliver said, snuggling up next to her.

"Me too," Luke chimed in. "How long before we get to Uncle Raine's?"

One of the stage drivers climbed up on top of the coach and handed down three large trunks to Jack. The other driver moved to the back where a substantial, elongated crate and several smaller bags had been strapped to the baggage boot. Ethan held one end and together he and the driver carried the crate with the smaller cases on top to the boardwalk where they set it down amongst their other things.

He slipped each of the men a little extra money for their efforts in making sure the cargo, and the passengers, had all arrived undamaged.

"Boys, why don't you take your mother inside the restaurant and order something wonderful to eat while I go rent us a sleigh?"

They both nodded excitedly.

"Thank you for loving me, my dear," he said, stepping forward, clasping his wife's hands in his. He bent down and placed a light kiss on her lips. "We're here."

"Jack?" Grace said, not taking her eyes from Ethan's.

"I know. I know. Watch our things." He mimicked what he thought she sounded like as he sat down on the largest trunk and leaned against the boardwalk post, then pulled his hat down over his face.

Grace's lips curved up into a smile. "I'll order for you. Is there anything in particular you would like to eat?"

"I'll take the biggest steak they've got, some hot potatoes and gravy, and—"

His sister kicked Jack's extended foot.

"What? You weren't talking to me?" He smiled, then raised his hat with a wink.

"Look around," Ethan said, stepping down from the boardwalk. "See what everybody else is having. I'll have that," he called back to her as he crossed the street to the livery with an anxious spring in his step.

Knock. Knock.

He opened the door and stepped inside, looking for the liveryman.

"Can I help you?" A young man stood up from behind a

desk in his office, wiping the corners of his mouth."

"Is Thistleberry always this quiet?" Ethan asked.

"Nah, but this isn't just any ordinary day, is it?"

Ethan's brows furrowed.

"Thanksgiving Day," the liveryman said with a light scoff.

Ethan looked heavenward with a sigh. How could he not have realized?

"Today?" Ethan took off his hat and shoved his fingers through his hair. "Today is Thanksgiving Day?"

"Yep."

No wonder the restaurant had been full, but the rest of the town quiet. Folks were home enjoying the day with family—which was exactly where he should be.

"You got a sleigh I can rent?"

"Yep."

Ethan handed the man five dollars.

"Can you have it out in front of the hotel in less than half an hour?"

His eyes brightened. "Yes, sir. Mr.?"

"Redbourne."

A smile touched the man's face. "Of course."

Ethan put on his hat, strode out the door, and over to the hotel restaurant.

As he reached for the door, he caught a glimpse of his little family sitting at a table in the far corner of the room and smiled. It was hard to believe that he and Grace had already been together nearly seven years.

"You're a lucky man, Redbourne," Jack said, pushing off the trunks and coming to his feet. He placed a hand on Ethan's shoulder. "My sister is quite a catch."

"That she is, little brother."

Ding-a-ling.

The little bell over the door rang as he opened it. His belly grumbled at the smell of warm gravy and buttery rolls.

The food was better that Ethan could have expected. He

placed his silverware on top of his plate and picked up his freshly filled cup of hot apple cider.

"It's been hours and nobody's seen hide nor hair of the sheriff."

Ethan's ears perked up to the conversation behind him, his gut tightening. He turned in his seat.

"I beg your pardon, gentlemen, did you say that the sheriff is missing?"

"Yes, sir. Bank was robbed this morning. Roughed up Mr. Dunbar over there." He pointed to a man in a dark green suit and a yellow tie with a little bump on the side of his head. "Sheriff took off after them this morning with Rut Tyler—he's a territory Marshal now, you know. I reckon it's been three or four hours by now with no sign of hide nor hair of either of them."

"And no one's gone looking for him?" Ethan pushed his seat backward.

"Wouldn't know where to start," another man said. "Besides, four hours isn't much cause for alarm, is it?"

Ethan placed several coins on the table next to his plate and bent down.

"Sweetheart," he said to his wife in as calm and quiet a voice as he could muster, his jaw firm, his breath forced, "we need to go."

She looked up at him, searching his face, then nodded.

Oliver had fallen asleep against her. Ethan reached down and scooped the toddler up into his arms and held out his hand for Luke.

"What is it?" Jack asked quietly as they made their way to the door.

"Raine's in trouble."

"You know him, mister?" one of the men from the back table called after them. "The sheriff that is?"

"He's my brother."

CHAPTER TWENTY-SIX

"Maybe he's not coming." Mary Jane had awoken early this morning to help get all the daylight chores finished and still give her plenty of time to dress for her day with the Deardons. And Raine.

All Sarah Jane had been able to talk about from the moment she'd gotten up was how much she wanted to spend the day with the sheriff and eat a lot of fancy food.

"He really should have been here long before now." Lucy looked up at the big clock sitting at the far end of the kitchen. "I don't know what's keeping him. Maybe I'll send Lucas over to the Isaacson place to check on him."

It was not like Raine to be late, let alone miss half of his family festivities.

Sarah Jane poked her head into the kitchen.

"Is he here yet?"

"No, love."

She dropped her head and walked over to lean up against Mary Jane. "Is he coming?"

"I hope so." What else could she say?

The horserace this morning had been quite intense. It was

interesting to her that none of them had been allowed to use their own horse, but instead, several horses from some of the surrounding ranches—mostly the MacPherson place, Happenstance, and the Johnsons from across the river had been brought in to assist with the event.

When they'd started chasing around a wild turkey, Mary Jane had come inside to find Lucy, who was busy putting together some activities for the children.

Georgia May's little face appeared in one of the small rectangular bottom windows.

Mary Jane nudged her daughter, who looked up. An instant smile lit her features.

"You'll tell me as soon as he gets here?" the little girl asked before leaving.

"Yes, love."

Satisfied with the answer, Sarah Jane ran to the door, swung it open, then glanced back with a smile, and closed the door behind her.

"How has it been having the Wallace kids here?" Mary Jane asked.

Clovis appeared to fit right in with some of the younger boys, and Georgia May got along well with Sarah Jane, but she wondered if Ridley had come around yet.

"I was a little nervous at first, but we are really starting to see them open up. I can't imagine what they've gone through, and we're just trying to be patient and take it slow."

The front door slammed open.

"Lucy, where's Hank?"

"Ethan? What in the world? What's wrong?" Lucy said, dropping the scrapped paper she held and rushed to him.

"Raine's in trouble. Where's Hank?"

Lucy wiped her hands on her apron and ran for the back door. "Come on."

Mary Jane followed.

She grabbed the thick iron striker and rang the triangle

dinner bell until all commotion in the yard stopped and men and women alike gathered at her feet.

"The bank was robbed this morning," Ethan said, stepping out in front of Lucy.

Mary Jane watched as several of them turned to each other in an awed whisper.

"Raine went after the culprits just after eight o'clock this morning with someone named Tyler and neither one of them has returned."

"Pardon me." A beautiful blond woman holding a toddler in her arms smiled softly as she quickly moved past her across the back porch and over to where Alex and Mara listened intently.

The two Deardon women each put an arm around the woman and squeezed her close. Another man she'd never seen before walked around from the side of the house, a young boy riding on his shoulders. When they joined Alex and the others, he lifted the youngster down.

"I know it's Thanksgiving," Ethan said, "and you're in the midst of the traditional tournament—which I was so looking forward to by the way—but I need your help." His voice carrying a powerful plea. "My brother needs your help."

Ah, brothers.

"You heard him, boys," Hank called from the crowd, making his way toward them. "A man needs our help. He's family."

Men and women scattered in every direction.

The moment the eldest Deardon reached Ethan, he pulled him into a fierce hug.

He pulled away from his nephew. "I have a lot of questions for you, son, but they'll keep for now."

Mary Jane found Lucy.

"Can Sarah Jane stay here with you?"

"M.J., you aren't seriously considering going with them?"

"It's Raine, Luce."

The woman nodded.

"Be careful."

"Of course." She hugged her friend.

After a moment of looking, she spotted her daughter sitting on the porch swing beneath the kitchen window with Georgia May, their little legs dangling as they talked.

At the sight of her, Sarah Jane jumped off the swing and into Mary Jane's arms.

"Is Sheriff Redbourne going to be all right, Mama?" she asked, a fat tear welling up in her eye. M.J. placed one arm around the girl.

"We will do everything we can to bring him home safely, but Mama has to go, okay?"

"All right."

"Will you be a good girl for Mrs. Lucy and Aunt Alex?" Mary Jane looked up at a frightened Georgia May and extended her other arm in an invitation. The little girl climbed down from the swing and rushed into her embrace. She held both girls tightly for a few moments, tears brimming her own eyes, then, with a squeeze, she let them go and stood up.

Unsure of exactly when it had happened, Mary Jane had fallen for the man—heart and soul. If he was out there hurt or stranded, she'd never be able to forgive herself if she didn't at least try to help.

As she rushed out to the cutter she'd come in on, she raised the seat and pulled out a canvas bag containing a change of clothes she kept packed for occasions such as this.

She darted into the house, changed out of her skirt and blouse for a pair of denims and a button-down, pulled her hair back with a tie, and headed out to the stables as she buttoned up her coat.

The stables at Whisper Ridge housed several horses that were familiar to Mary Jane. After pulling a work saddle off its stand, she swung it up onto the young grey mare with the black mane.

"M.J., I hope you're not thinking what I think you're thinking," Andrew said from the stall next to hers.

"I'm coming."

"Dad's not going to like that."

"I can ride as well as any of you."

"I don't think it's the riding part that he'll be worried about."

Mary Jane didn't care. She finished saddling the mare and mounted, riding out into the yard with the rest of them that had gathered around the front gate.

Hank caught her eye and rode up alongside, facing her.

"I'm coming, Hank. Don't try to talk me out of it."

"I appreciate what you do and how well you do it, M.J.," he said, "but we have no idea what we are up against. Don't you think it would be best if you stayed here with Lucy and the others?"

She looked him straight in the eye.

"You know me better than that, Hank. I wasn't asking permission."

"In that case, glad to have you along."

One eye opened, then the other. Raine looked about a cozy cabin. The firelight from the small stone hearth warmed the air and the heady scent of freshly cut pinewood filled the space.

The soft leather hide covering him was smooth against his tender skin. He tried to sit up, but his head throbbed at the effort.

The cabin door opened.

Raine instinctively reached for his gun, biting back a curse when he came up short.

"He's awoken." An older man with a thick, full beard, buckskin britches, and fringed frock stepped inside, a sizable wolf-like dog at his side. He removed his fur hat and vest-like animal cloak and set them down on the chair next to the fireplace. Around his neck, he wore a pelt-covered medicine pouch and a bowie encased in a leather sheath as well as a rifle slung across his back.

Snowshoes and various sized traps adorned the walls. Meat dried in the rafters. Skins stretched on willow frames sat in the corners. A rusted lantern stood on a leveled tree stump, and a small square end table near the window held several mismatched dishes, cups, and candles.

"Here, sip some of this. It will help you regain your strength." The man crouched down in front of the hearth, stirring and scooping liquid from a large black kettle, then held the back of Raine's head and brought a ladle to his lips.

Surprisingly, the warm, flavorful and woodsy liquid tasted good, and it warmed him from the inside.

"Thank you," he scratched out, "um…Mr…"

"Most folks just call me Ridge." He returned the ladle to the kettle over the fire.

Raine laid back against the soft head cushion.

"What happened, Ridge?" He remembered chasing a group of bank robbers, then being trapped in the snow.

"The mountains are dangerous country in the wintertime out here. When your friends set off a charge at the peak, it caused an avalanche."

They're not my friends. He wasn't sure he'd spoken the words aloud. *They're outlaws.*

"I don't quite know how you did it, but you managed to stay mostly on top of the flow. You are lucky you're still breathin'."

"I'm guessing that's thanks to you." Raine found his voice. He turned his head to the side, fighting the wave of tiredness threatening to overtake him.

"And that mare of yours. I've never seen a horse before that didn't run when spooked," the mountain man said. "I'm guessing she simply got out of the way and then returned to find you. She's something special all right. If it wasn't for her, I wouldn't have known you were buried under a foot or so of snow and debris."

"Buried?"

"Yeah. She dipped her head and pointed her ears just over the area where you'd gone under. When I finally found you, you were pretty banged up, but alive. She was your deliverance I'd say." The man folded down the pelt covering Raine's body and attended to several wounds on his arms, chest, and shoulders. He unwrapped the bandages from his forearm and hands to reapply some sort of salve before wrapping them back up.

Deliverance.

That was it, the name of the mare.

By the pain in his legs when he moved, he guessed he'd also sustained several contusions there, but to his relief he didn't think he'd suffered any broken bones.

"How'd you get me here?"

"I've got a sled and a team of dogs. It wasn't that hard once I got you all dug out."

He tried to sit up again. "Where are my clothes?" he asked, still trying to clear his head.

"Don't you go worrying yourself about that. Your things are hanging there over the fire to dry." The man pointed up to the rafters just above the hearth.

Raine was surprised he hadn't noticed them before.

"But I wouldn't go getting' no ideas. You're not going anywhere for a bit." The man pushed against his chest, easily getting him to lie back down.

"My family will be worried. I've got to let them know I'm all right. And I've still got thieves to catch."

"And you will, but for now, you'll rest." Ridge raised a brow, daring Raine to defy him.

With the warmth of the cabin and the pleasing aromas swirling about him, he found it increasingly difficult to keep his eyes open. They fluttered. Then closed.

Dogs barked outside.

The cabin door opened and closed again.

He'd never been more comfortable. His whole body felt relaxed, and his mind calm as he drifted between being awake and asleep.

Soft fingers stroked his forehead, brushing his hair to one side, then trailing down his face evoking a sense of peace. Of tranquility.

"Hello, my love," a voice called out to him.

He squeezed his eyes tighter, then tried to open them, but they wouldn't comply.

"You're such a good man."

Sarah?

"Hi, Daddy."

Choked with a wellspring of emotion, tears formed in his eyes, and he thrust them open.

A little girl.

His beautiful Sarah, adorned in a soft green dress, sat on the chair next to the bed, and the most angelic little girl with blond pigtails and a dimpled smile stood by his side.

How was this even possible?

He reached out and took the little girl by her face, his fingers gently squishing her cheeks.

A daughter.

He pulled her close to his bosom and started to cry.

"We don't have a lot of time," Sarah said, getting to her feet. She placed a hand on his cheek, and he covered it with his own. "You must know it wasn't your fault, my love."

He took her hand from his face and kissed her palm.

"We're all right, Daddy. It's nice here," the little girl said as she pulled back in his arms.

"It's time for you to find love again, sweetheart," Sarah said. "Mary Jane Bennett is a good woman. I'd like to think we would have been friends in another life."

He shook his head.

"I don't know if I can let you go."

"You don't have to. There is plenty of room in that big heart of yours for all of us. You need her. You need Sarah Jane. That little girl has so much love to give."

He looked back and forth between Sarah and his little girl.

"A daughter," he said aloud, looking down into her bright smiling face. "She's beautiful."

"Almarinda," Sarah said.

Raine had never heard the name before.

"Surrendered soul."

Fitting.

Sarah reached out to take their daughter's hand.

"We have to go," she said in a whisper, then leaned down and placed a kiss on his forehead, then his lips. "I'll love you forever, Raine Redbourne."

"Not yet. Just one moment more, please." He stared into their faces, tracing every detail for his memory. "I love you."

"You love her too, silly," Sarah said with a smile, "and it's high time that you show her."

The door opened and the mountain man stepped back inside.

They were gone, but instead of the emptiness he expected to return, hope burned in his chest in its place.

"I need to get home," he told the burly mountain man, throwing the pelt off of him and yanking his now-dry clothes down from the rafters. He'd suddenly gained a boost of energy, his head was clear, and he felt strong enough to ride.

"I thought you might say that."

"I don't know what you put in that broth, but it works magic."

"It's not like drinking chocolate, but it got the job done."

"You like hot chocolate?"

"It's an indulgence a man doesn't get often in my line of work, but I've been known to down a cup or two."

Raine laughed. "My brother lives in England where there

are several master chocolatiers, and every year he sends me a new cache of cocoa powder for my birthday. It can definitely heal what ails you." After he donned his denims, he reached up for his button-down only to find that it had been all but shredded in his ordeal.

"That tattered thing won't do you no good up here. This should suffice." Ridge threw him a long-sleeved buckskin shirt with corded laces across the chest.

His brother Rafe had a few shirts like this his Pawnee friends had given him while he lived among them, and Raine had secretly always wanted one. He pulled it over his head, appreciating the warmth it would provide and the softness against his skin.

"How does it look?"

"It'll do."

"I'm sorry I don't have anything to trade you for it up here, but I'm happy to compensate you once I get home."

Home. He liked the sound of that.

"Nah," Ridge said gruffly, "a man can only have so many things or clothes to wear. It was just taking up space as it was. It's yours."

Raine sat down and pulled on his socks and boots.

"All the same, I'm indebted to you for what you've done for me. Can I invite you back for Thanksgiving supper?" He looked up, his elbows resting on his knees.

The man shook his head. "I don't do so well with a bunch of strangers around. Besides, I've got a rendezvous with Destiny."

"Destiny, huh?" Raine chuckled as he got to his feet.

"Yeah, Destiny. She's that bear keeps coming around your place. Can't have her interfering with things anymore, now can we?"

"Well, know you will always have a warm meal waiting for you in my home." He jutted out his hand to the mountain man.

They shook.

"Now, if you can direct me to my horse."

Ridge opened the door and pointed to a makeshift corral where Deliverance and an old mule were eating what looked like fresh hay from a small feeding trough.

With his hat in hand, Raine stepped outside and stretched in the waning sun. Though his body hurt most everywhere, it felt good to be out in the fresh air.

He was surprised to see there on the side of the cabin a handful of huge gray and white dogs lying around and playing in the snow.

"I've never seen dogs quite like yours before," he said, pointing to the beautiful blue-eyed creatures with fluffy tails.

"Siberian Huskies," Ridge said, leaning up against the door frame, his feet crossed, and his arms folded across his chest. "They're friends from the northern country."

"They're magnificent."

"Don't let Ol' Rex there hear you. His ego is big enough already." The mountain man laughed loudly.

Raine took a step toward the huskies, still a little unsettled at how much they looked like wolves. "Thank you!" he called out loudly.

The husky closest to him howled. Then another joined.

He chuckled.

As he approached the mare, he wished he had an apple or some other treat to give her.

"You did good, girl," he said, stretching out his hand to scratch her neck. He leaned up against her face and wrapped his arm around her from underneath. "Ridge tells me you saved my life. I appreciate that."

She nudged his hand with her nose, looking for something good to eat.

"Redbourne," Ridge called.

Raine looked up and the man tossed him an apple.

How?

So many things in the last few hours verged on the

inexplicable.

Don't question, just believe, he thought he heard a voice carry on the wind.

So, rather than question, he just held the treat in his hand for the mare to discover and smiled.

I believe.

"I finally have a name for you, girl. Deliverance. Do you like that?" he asked with another scratch to her jaw. "But it doesn't exactly roll off the tongue, does it? I think I'll just call you Livvy or Liv for short. What do you think?"

She nickered her approval.

It took him a little longer than he would have hoped to get her saddled and ready to ride. His body ached with every turn, but it would be too dark to travel soon, and he needed to be on his way.

Ridge gave him directions that should see him home without any further mishaps.

Raine tugged at the brim of his hat with a nod at the man who'd saved his life.

"Until next time."

"Look over there," Sam yelled. "It looks like boots sticking out of the snow."

Mary Jane's heart began to race. If Raine had been hurt out here without anywhere to take shelter over the last several hours, she had to prepare herself. He could be…dead.

She swallowed hard.

"M.J., maybe you should wait here," Andrew said, riding up alongside her.

"It's not him," she said with confidence. "It hasn't snowed at all today."

A body lay half covered in snow at the bottom of a cliff. Whomever it was had been out here a lot longer than a couple of hours.

Ethan rode to the front and was the first off his horse. Sam and Garrett also dismounted to get a closer look.

"It's Mundy," Sam called back.

She closed her eyes and exhaled a sigh of relief. Even though she'd known it couldn't possibly have been Raine, the confirmation was appreciated.

"Seems he fell." Sam looked up. "He's been dead a few days at least. Looks a lot like Mrs. Weller did when we went and picked her up, except for the limb that impaled his gut."

Seth and Daniel rode the small trail that led up the side of the mountain. After a few minutes, Hank's oldest peered over the ledge and called down to them.

"They were here."

Ethan climbed back up onto his mount. "There's more than a dozen of us," he said, turning his horse back toward the tracks that cut through a copse of large, dense trees. "We'll cover more ground if we split up."

"I'm with you," Mary Jane said, fully prepared to defend her reasons.

"Glad to have you along."

Andrew, Philip, who drove one of the two-seated sleighs they'd brought with them, Lindon, and Hank also joined their group.

"We'll head up toward Mulberry Pass," Hank yelled out to his brother. "You and the boys head out toward Last Chance Gulch. We'll meet back here in one hour."

One hour? That didn't give them much time.

"Well, what are we waiting for?" Mary Jane asked, pulling her horse around and heading for the tracks.

As they neared the pass, a horse approached, its rider slumped over in the saddle.

Ethan reached for his gun.

"Can't be too careful," he said, urging his pony forward.

"You all right there, son?" Hank called out.

The man tried to lift his head, but the motion caused him to lose his balance and he fell sideways off his horse.

"It's Marshal Tyler." Mary Jane dismounted and rushed to the man's side, crouching down next to him. Blood oozed from his shoulder and a large piece of jagged rock had embedded into his thigh.

Lindon was by her side in an instant.

"That the same marshal who rode after the bank robbers with Raine?" Ethan asked.

"That's the one," Hank said.

"I can't do anything for him here," Lindon said. Hank's second oldest was the only one of them with any medical experience as he was training to be a veterinarian. "He's lost a lot of blood. We need to get him over to Doc's or he won't make it to sundown."

Doc had moved to Thistleberry full time last year and was living at a small farm just south of town near the Sorensens with an office in the back.

"I'll need help getting him into the sleigh," Lindon called up to Philip.

"Wait," Mary Jane said. Leaning down closer toward him, she tapped his face.

He opened his eyes for a brief moment.

"Marshal, where's Raine?" she asked, desperate to know the answer.

"Av...Avvval…" he coughed, shaking his head. "It was a…" he tried clearing his throat, "trap." It came out barely a whisper.

His eyes rolled into the back of his head and his lids closed.

Lindon placed his ear down near the marshal's mouth.

"He's still breathing. For now."

Philip had secured a wooden boat-like toboggan to the back of the sleigh, then, grabbing one of the sturdy saddle blankets from the back seat, he laid it out on the ground next to the man. Two nods later and they had lifted him onto the covering. Ethan and Andrew also jumped down from their mounts to help, and each of the men picked up a corner, transporting him over to the long, walled sled. They stuffed blankets around him and tied his horse to the back.

Mary Jane climbed back up onto her mount.

"Good luck," Philip said, starting back for the glen with Lindon riding alongside the sleigh.

They'd only been travelling a good ten minutes or so when Hank pulled to a stop.

"Avalanche," he said knowingly, pointing to the dappled ground just ahead. "That's what Rut was trying to say. Those cowards intentionally caused an avalanche."

Mary Jane's heart sunk. She scanned the immediate landscape looking for any indication that Raine had made it through alive. Nothing.

"Raine!" Ethan cupped his hands around his mouth and yelled out for his brother.

Just a few feet beyond a broken tree, Mary Jane spotted tracks in the snow accompanied by two relatively straight-lined grooves. Someone had been here since the snow had flooded the pass.

"Over there," she said, riding as quickly as she could through the deep snow in the direction the tracks led. Her horse strained against the deep powder, but once they cleared the avalanche overflow, the terrain became much easier to manage.

She had to believe these tracks would lead to Raine.

Ethan, Hank, and Andrew didn't fall far behind.

"Raine!" she called out this time.

"Raine!" the men all echoed behind her.

In the distance, a rider came into view.

She pushed faster.

She could see the mare clearly now.

It was him.

He's alive.

Her heart flipped and swelled in her chest.

She couldn't wait.

"Whoa. Whoa." The moment her mount stopped, she swung her leg over the saddle and jumped to the ground, running toward him as quickly as she could across the snow laden ground.

The instant his eyes met hers, he pulled the mare to a stop. His hands were bandaged, his denims torn just above the knee, but he was the most beautiful sight she had ever seen. He dismounted slowly, but didn't move from his place at the side of his mount until Mary Jane was mere feet away from him.

Then, in a flash, he closed the distance between them, sinking his hands into the hair on both sides of her neck as he pulled her mouth up to his.

His lips claimed hers with an eagerness she'd never experienced. She clutched the material at his sides in her fingers and pulled him closer, welcoming him, matching his fervor as she released all of her worry and fear, replacing it with yearning and hope in this one life-changing kiss.

Raine slid his arms beneath hers, tucking his head into the crook of her neck, and clenched her tightly against him, lifting her and spinning her around. When he finally relaxed his grip around her, allowing her feet to touch the ground once again, he pulled away enough to look down into her eyes, then planted another light kiss on her lips.

"Well, I certainly wasn't expecting that," Ethan said with a chuckle.

Raine glanced up.

"Ethan?"

She smiled and nodded.

He bent over and kissed her cheek before releasing her, then rushed into his brother's open arms. They held onto each other for a good while before pulling apart.

"What on earth are you doing all the way up here? In Montana? Don't you know it's freezing up here?"

"What do you say we get you back to Whisper Ridge and

we can answer all of your questions? And get a few of our own."

"Glad you're all right, Raine," Andrew said, leaning down from his mount and patting his cousin on the shoulder.

"It's good to see you in one piece, Sheriff," Hank said with a nod. "But I've got just one question before we go."

"What's that?"

"Rut Tyler said you were caught in an avalanche those bank robbing thieves set. How in the world did you walk away?"

"Tyler's alive?"

"Barely, but yes. Lindon and Philip are looking after him. Took him to see Doc."

"Any word on those bank robbers?" he asked. "The marshal was right. When we pulled into the pass, they were waiting for us. Tyler climbed the hill after one of them, but they blasted some dynamite. Honestly, I'd never seen an avalanche before and had no idea what I was in for."

Hank stared at Raine, still expecting an answer.

"Well, I didn't. Walk away, I mean." Raine held up his bandaged hands, then raised his buckskinned shirt just enough to reveal several bruises trailing his hip and side.

Mary Jane's cheeks heated as she watched.

"A mountain man named Ridge found me buried more than a foot deep in the snow not far from here and took me back to his cabin. After a few hours of rest, some bandages, and some hot woodsy-flavored broth to warm my belly, I feel almost as good as new."

"No one has lived up here in ages," Hank said, his brows furrowed together. "The only cabin I know around these parts has sat empty going on fifteen years now—since the year Dad died."

"I'll take you there if you'd like," Raine said with a shrug. "I only left maybe five or six minutes ago. Besides, I'd like you all to meet him—maybe trade him something for this shirt he gave me."

A light breeze swept by, blowing a light layer of snow across the ground, all but erasing the tracks they'd made.

"As a matter of fact, I would. I haven't been to there in ages."

They all got back onto their horses, and Raine led the way back to the cabin.

When they crested the ridge, a small one-room cabin came into view. It's graying wall planks, dilapidated from non-use, sat in stark contrast against the snow drifts that had blown up against them. The windows and door were boarded up, and the only tracks leading up to the place were those of nothing bigger than a small deer.

Raine dismounted, staring at the undisturbed scene with knit brows and narrowed eyes.

"Ridge!" he called out, but nothing came back—not even an echo. "But there was a corral over here." He tromped to one side of the cabin. "And the dogs, they were lying around over here." He walked over to the other side. "I don't understand. He dug me out of the snow, bandaged my wounds, gave me this shirt."

"Hey, big brother, I think we need to get you home and have the doctor look over you too. Maybe you hit your head harder than you think."

"Don't question, just believe," he mumbled under his breath, but loud enough that Mary Jane could hear him. He smiled. Then started to laugh.

He looked up at her, one brow raised and a mischievous smile on his lips.

Heat flushed her cheeks as she remembered the intoxicating feel of his mouth claiming hers, and she raised a hand to casually cover her mouth.

"What?" she asked, when he didn't look away, but instead, held out his hand.

She dismounted.

He clasped her hands in his.

"M.J., I told you once before that I don't like to beat around the bush. I mean that now more than ever. Over the last few weeks, I have learned what it's like to love again—something I believed would never happen. But I can't help myself. I have fallen in love with you, Mary Jane Bennett, and I don't ever want to wonder when I'll be able to see you again. I want to spend time with you every single day that I live. I don't want to have to worry about curfews or propriety or parting from you when the day is over. Let's build a life together—you and me and Sarah Jane. Marry me. Before Christmas."

Mary Jane's breath caught in her chest. She stared into his eyes, unsure whether or not he'd indeed been knocked a little too hard in the head or if this was real. His kiss had certainly felt real. A thousand questions ran through her head, but the only one that mattered right now was could she imagine a world without him in it?

No.

She let go of his hands and slid hers up his chest and around his neck.

"Out of all the men in the world I could have fallen in love with, it had to be a lawman." She laughed with a shake of her head. "Yes, Sheriff Redbourne, I will marry you."

CHAPTER TWENTY-SEVEN

Mid-December

Overnight, the town of Thistleberry had been transformed into a Christmas wonderland. Shop owners had decorated their storefronts with evergreen boughs, pinecones, and boxwood branches. The pavilion in the town square was draped in pine garlands accented with big red bows. And Mrs. Doherty's bakery displayed new Christmas confections in the window nearly every day.

Without the immediate resources of the bank, many of the townspeople were trying to make do with a lot less this holiday season, but Raine appreciated the generosity, kinship, and small acts of kindness he'd witnessed between neighbors over the last couple of weeks.

"Sheriff," the postmaster held an envelope, waving his arm as he crossed the street at a trot, "this post came in for you today. It's postmarked Arizona."

Mrs. Isaacson.

"Thank you, Mr. Tulley," he said, taking the letter from the man. "Was there anything else for me?" He'd been hoping for a letter from Iowa, but guessed it was still too soon to be expecting a response.

The cuts in Raine's hands had mostly healed and the majority of his bruises had faded to a dull yellowish color. He still walked with a slight limp that was getting better each day, but otherwise, Doc had given him a clean bill of health. He was grateful his encounter with the avalanche hadn't been any worse.

"I don't suppose you will be seeing Mrs. Deardon at all this afternoon? Mrs. Lucy Deardon," he clarified with a raised finger before Raine could ask.

"I could make a trip out to Whisper Ridge. What do you need, Mr. Tulley?"

The postmaster handed him a telegram, then darted back across the street and down toward Mrs. Doherty's bakery.

He glanced town at the message.

> *Sterling Wallace seeking his grandchildren STOP Reimbursement for expenditures forthcoming STOP Visiting Thistleberry in three days' time STOP*

Lucy and Lucas were going to be heartbroken. They had already started making the arrangements to be able to adopt Ridley, Clovis, and Georgia May. He wondered why the grandfather had waited until now to be a part of the children's lives.

When he arrived back to his office, he sat down behind his desk and opened his own letter. Mary Jane had her heart set on living at the farm, but if Mrs. Isaacson was ready to come home, there wasn't much he would be able to do.

He slipped the short note from the envelope and quickly scanned the contents.

"Yes!" he said, jumping up from his seat, but there was no one around to celebrate the moment with him, so he sat back down, reveling quietly in his excitement.

The formal letter had offered to sell him the entire property, including all tools, wares, vehicles, and livestock at a reasonable asking price. She'd given him just three weeks to decide and said the contract could be finalized by signing the enclosed proposal agreement and delivering it to her lawyer in Murphy.

He couldn't wait to see the look on Mary Jane's face when he told her the farm was theirs. He would see to sending Mrs. Isaacson the funds through telegraphic transfer as soon as the agreement was in her lawyer's hands.

Raine glanced down at his wristwatch. He'd promised Sarah Jane that they would go out and cut down a tree today to take inside the house and decorate for Christmas. He looked forward to picking up the Bennett girls for a quick trip up the side of the mountain behind the farm.

It dawned on him that after the purchase was finalized, he couldn't very well keep calling it the Isaacson farm.

He smiled. He'd finally found the place where he belonged—and not just because they needed him here, but because he needed them. All of them. The town, his family, Mary Jane, and her adorable little girl.

"Don't you need to be on your way? I thought you were cutting down a tree today."

He glanced up at the door where Marshal Tyler leaned against the frame.

"Doc tell you you could be up already?"

"Nope. Says I should stay in bed and rest for a few more weeks, but I am going mad without much to do." He tapped his head several times against the doorframe. "Please, give me something to do."

"Isn't that what the marshal's office is supposed to do?" Raine pushed away from his desk and stood up. "Come on, you can come help me make a little girl happy."

"Traversing across another mountainside in the snow? No. But, don't you have another bad guy we could chase?"

Since the robbery, the town had been fairly quiet. It still ate at him that the culprits had gotten away because he hadn't recognized the trap in time. He rubbed his leg, which still ached from being tossed around like a ragdoll by the snow.

"Not today." Raine tapped Rutledge on his shoulder with the envelope holding Mrs. Isaacson's letter.

"How did we not see it coming?"

Raine froze.

It was a question he had asked himself many times over the last couple of weeks.

"We missed something," he said, trying to shrug off the danger in those words.

Someone obviously wanted him dead and had gone out of their way to make it happen. The sooner he found out who and why, the safer the whole town would be.

"How far is it to Murphy?"

"Maybe five or six miles from here. Why?"

"Just something I have to do. Like you said, for now, I have an appointment with a saw, a tree, and a little girl."

"And I'll just go back to the hotel, lie down, and stare at the ceiling." The marshal pushed away from the doorframe, leaning heavily on his cane, and took a step out onto the boardwalk.

"Can you ride?"

"As sure as I can sit."

Raine raised a brow.

"I can ride."

"Be ready to go in ten minutes."

As Raine crossed the street to the hotel, he watched as Mr. Dunbar walked out of the bank, pausing long enough to lock the doors, then headed toward the livery. If he were to listen to the gossip over at Lyla's Café, the man had lost everything in the robbery and was considering leaving Thistleberry to move back to his hometown somewhere in the Midwest. Missouri maybe? Tennessee? He couldn't remember.

Guilt reared its familiar head, and he pushed the thoughts aside as he stepped into the General Store. He was grateful to find that the feminine attentions of the unmarried females in town and their mothers had greatly diminished since word of his betrothal to Mary Jane had spread.

"Ladies," he said with a lift of his hat as he held the door for a small group of women on their way out.

"Sheriff," Mrs. Smith said, "what brings you in today?"

"I'm looking for four big red bows, two front hanging carriage lanterns, a ball of parcel string, three pairs of scissors, and some violin rosin." He set the list down on the counter in front of the store's owner.

Mrs. Smith looked over the list. "I think we just may have everything you need. I'll be right back."

Within just a few minutes most everything he'd requested was piled up on the countertop. He particularly liked the style of the lanterns she brought. They were made of black metal with a barn-style latched door and windows with a two-tiered vented top. They would look right superb hanging from the new sleigh.

"Now for the rosin," Mrs. Smith said, looking up at the bookcase style shelving behind her. "I know we have some around here somewhere." She pushed the sliding ladder attached to the cabinet and moved it across the back wall until she reached a spot with a crate marked Instrument Odds and Ends. With a few steps up, she retrieved the crate, and sorted through it.

"Ah, hah, ah, hah, ah," she said in a sing-song voice. "Here it is." She pushed off the shelf, riding the ladder across the floor, and stopping in the section immediately across from him. She stepped down, setting the boxed tin of rosin on top of the bows.

Mr. Smith placed a crate on the counter and proceeded to pack up his purchases.

"Mr. and Mrs. Smith," he said as he picked up the crate they had prepared for him, "as the new sheriff here, I am trying to get to know the people and the town so I can do my job properly. Is there anything happening here in Thistleberry that concerns you or that you feel I should to be aware of?"

The couple looked at each other.

"I don't think so, Sheriff," Mrs. Smith said, "but thank you for asking. We will let you know if anything comes up."

Her husband nodded.

Raine smiled.

"Thank you again."

He'd asked a similar question at each of the businesses along the boardwalk and had received a variety of answers ranging from having cattle ranchers from surrounding towns threatening ranches like Happenstance to the increase of rough characters passing through recently.

As he'd engaged the people in conversation more over the last couple of weeks, he'd been surprised to learn that while the majority of them had not invested their income in Mr. Dunbar's bank, and therefore had not lost anything when it had been robbed, most of them were tenants on his land, living in homes he owned, or running businesses out of storefronts that he'd purchased.

Deliverance had been stabled for the day over at the livery, and as Raine looked down at the contents in his arms, he realized it would be difficult to carry it all on horseback. He worried that moving the lanterns into a bag to string over his saddlebags risked the possibility of breaking the glass.

"Harvey," he said to the young liveryman, "I'd like to rent a sleigh for the evening."

"Absolutely, Mr. Redbourne."

It wasn't long before he and Marshal Tyler rode into the drive at the farm. M.J. and Sarah Jane were already there. The little girl jumped up from where she sat on the top porch step and waited patiently for him to dismount.

"Does anyone here want to go find a Christmas tree?" he asked as he walked around to the left side of Rut's horse. He pulled the man's cane from the rifle scabbard, and stood firm for the marshal to use as a support when he dismounted.

He'd offered to allow the man to ride in the sleigh with him, but he'd been too proud and opted to ride his horse—despite the obvious discomfort.

With a great deal of effort, Tyler was able to swing his injured leg around the saddle and slide down on his hip. When he landed on the ground, his bandaged leg buckled beneath him, but Raine was able to keep him upright.

"Blast it all!" he bit out, then his eyes widened as he glanced over at little Sarah Jane. "I apologize, Miss Bennett."

"That's all right. My mama says that all the time."

Color flushed Mary Jane's cheeks as she gasped with mock offense, then laughed.

"It may be a little true," she said.

Raine smiled up at her. He appreciated that she accepted her shortcomings without excuse. And they endeared her even more to him. He gave the marshal his cane and walked alongside him until they reached the stairs where he could hold on to the railing if he needed.

As soon as Raine looked up at Sarah Jane, she jumped into his arms.

Mary Jane descended the stairs, a huge smile on her face. When she reached him, he bent down and placed a light kiss on her lips.

Sarah Jane giggled.

"Are you ready, Miss Bennett?" he asked Mary Jane.

She nodded, then glanced over at the marshal, her smile turning uneasy.

"Miss Bennett?" he asked the little girl in his arms.

"Yes, please," she said in the sweetest little voice.

"M.J.," he turned back to his betrothed. "Is everything all right?"

"Yes, of course, I um…"

"Hello."

Raine glanced up at the woman who'd just ridden into the yard.

"I sort of invited Lissa to come along. She's never had a Christmas tree before, and I thought it would be nice to—"

"The more the merrier," Raine said, attempting to block any need for explanation.

"Rut, I guess that means you're coming along."

Although the marshal had initially declined the invitation to hunt for a tree, something in his eyes when he looked at the Happenstance hired hand who'd just joined them told him he'd changed his mind.

"If I must," he said, limping over to the sleigh.

"And…" Mary Jane said with raised brows, "I may have invited Allie and Jethro to come along as well."

Raine laughed as the couple walked out of the house all bundled up with little Asher wearing a wool coat and knitted hat.

"I guess it's a good thing I opted for the two-seater." Pretty soon he would not have to rent a sleigh from the livery, but they'd have one of their own.

He picked up the crate of things he'd purchased.

"I'll just take these things inside, and we'll be on our way." He narrowed his eyes at Mary Jane, before taking the opportunity to claim another little kiss.

Before long they were in the midst of a large copse of evergreen trees ranging in sizes from taller than his house to ones barely peeking above the snow. Jethro parked the cutter only a few feet from them and everyone dispersed.

Raine reached down for Mary Jane's hand, and they followed Sarah Jane around as she appraised and inspected each candidate for the farmhouse. M.J. leaned into him and wrapped her free hand around his arm.

"This is wonderful."

He couldn't have agreed more.

Marshal Tyler was able to get down from the backseat of the sleigh with only a little assistance from Lissa, whose own leg appeared to have healed quite nicely. When he looked up, he winked at Raine.

With a chuckle, he watched as the people he'd grown to

care so much about participated in one of his favorite Christmas traditions.

Without any warning, a ball of snow hit him directly in the face.

Mary Jane's hand flew over her mouth with a chuckle.

He brushed the powder from his face to the delight of his little four-year-old attacker who now sat on Jethro's shoulders. She giggled as the shepherd lifted her up, set her on her feet, and handed her another snowball.

Raine released Mary Jane's hand and bent down to collect his own ammunition. As he was gathering the snow and packing it just enough that it would keep its shape, Sarah Jane threw the contents of her hand, hitting him in the leg. Before he could return fire, he was hit again on both the side of his neck and in the chest.

Oh, that's cold.

Marshal Tyler had thrown at him from the sleigh while Mary Jane had thrown the other from her new position next to her daughter. Within seconds, the small copse was filled with flying snowballs as if they were in the midst of a great battle. He took cover behind a pine tree a good foot taller than him. Freshly loaded with another ball, he crept around, carefully staying out of sight as he watched Mary Jane and Sarah Jane search for him.

With light footsteps, he approached from behind, thrilled he hadn't yet been detected, and with a giant roar, scooped the little girl up into one arm and pulled Mary Jane close to him with the other, eliciting light screams followed by contagious laughter. His leg smarted, but he ignored the pain. Afterall, he'd only experienced several large contusions on his legs, but the marshal had a large piece of jagged rock dug from his flesh.

He'd gotten off lucky. They both had.

"I found it," Sarah Jane said with a beaming smile.

"The Christmas tree?" Raine asked.

"Yep."

"Yes," Mary Jane corrected.

"Yes," Sarah Jane repeated. "It's right behind you." She pointed.

He turned around. The tree stood a little more than a foot taller than him with wide, sturdy branches. "It's perfect!" he told her. "Let me get the saw."

After the main tree was down, Raine noticed that Mary Jane kept looking over at a smaller tree about ten yards away from her. She tilted her head one way, then the other, and when a smile crept onto her face, he decided they needed two trees.

"I was thinking that maybe we should cut one down for Happenstance too, what do you think?"

"Really?" she asked.

He didn't wait for any further response, but proceeded to cut down the second tree. This one was much shorter than the first, it's branches more sparse, but it still held a good color and scent. Jethro and Alice had also found a small tree for the barn and the little tree Rut had selected would go well in his room—if Mr. Beverly at the Thistledown would allow it.

After the trees were all loaded and strapped, he stepped back near a large section of snow that was still undisturbed, despite their jovial fun. Mary Jane eyed him with curiosity. He raised his arms shoulder height and fell backward into the snow.

"Snow angels!" Mary Jane exclaimed. "I haven't done them since I was a child." She took Sarah Jane by the hand stood above another patch of fresh, unbroken snow next to him and followed what he had done, instructing the child what to do. They both fell backward together.

Assured that his flapping arms and spread legs had done their intended jobs, Raine stood, careful not to disturb the image, then stepped back to admire the angel impression his body had created. He waited for the girls to finish, then reached out his hands to help them to their feet. He lifted Sarah Jane up onto his shoulders.

"Now look down. What do you see?" he asked.

"They're angels," Sarah Jane responded in awe. "It's a snow angel family."

A tear brimmed in Raine's eye, and he chuckled, quickly raising a finger to wipe it away.

My family. Angel and otherwise.

CHAPTER TWENTY-EIGHT

"It's not going to open itself," Lucy said, sitting on the bed next to her.

Mary Jane stared at one of the only possessions she had brought with her from Iowa. Her cedar dowry trousseau chest. She noted with a hint of sadness how the base and trim had been scratched and scuffed when she'd pulled it out of the cabin the night Lionel died.

One of its contents was a marriage blanket that had been passed down to the eldest daughters in her family for generations. With everything that had happened the day after her wedding, the blanket still sat untouched since she'd arrived in Thistleberry. She'd had no reason to pull it out before, but now, as she dreamed of making a life with Raine, it was different.

She opened the lid. The heady aroma of the cedar wood greeted her warmly. Her journal sat on top along with her list of qualities she desired in a husband. She stared at it for a moment, then handed it to Lucy.

"What's this? Not a lawman. Tall. Wealthy. Big family." She looked up at Mary Jane. "This is your list. Honest. Loves children. Loves God. Not afraid to be affectionate. Trusts me implicitly. Cooks. You sure aren't expecting much," she teased.

"But he is all of those things, Lucy. When I made that list, I thought I was protecting myself and Sarah Jane because no man could possibly have all of those qualities. I mean, 'plays the piano'? Really? What man knows how to play the piano?"

"I'll bet he does. But he doesn't actually meet all of your requirements," Lucy said with a shake of her head.

"What's he missing?"

"He's a lawman."

Mary Jane laughed. Lucy did too.

"But he's a good one." She looked back at the open chest, finding her stationery and several of the things she'd either made or kept from when Sarah Jane was a baby. She pulled out a pair of little lavender booties that Lucy had made for her daughter.

"Awww, I remember those," the woman said, reaching out for them. "It's hard to believe she was ever that tiny."

A beautifully tatted baby dress, a cornhusk doll, and small handcrafted brush sat above a set of embroidered dishtowels, an ornately decorated sugar bowl, and a boxed set of silver wares. As she lay them all out on the bed, she smiled. She didn't have very many things from home or family, but the things she did have held special meaning for her.

She paused a moment at the dress box. When she'd arrived in Thistleberry, Mr. Cochran had taken her immediately to the preacher to be married, leaving barely enough time to breathe, let alone change into a special dress for the occasion, before taking her to the small cabin that was to be theirs.

At the time, she'd believed it to be a romantic gesture that he hadn't wanted to wait for them to begin their lives together. Now, she knew all too differently.

Mary Jane caressed the top of the box, then lifted it from the chest. When she removed the lid, she carefully folded back the flimsy paper covering and was pleased to see that the garment still looked about the same as the day she'd packed it away. The dress had been worn by her Welsh great grandmother, Catrin, on her wedding day to Gareth Cadogan.

"Look at that plunged neckline," Lucy commented, her eyes wide, and her lips curved upward as she reached in and traced the fabric with her fingers. "It's exquisite."

Fashion over the decades had changed dramatically, having been much more evocative in bygone eras than the standards set in nineteenth century Montana, but Mary Jane had always fancied the idea of being married in her grandmother's dress.

"It is wonderful, isn't it?" She stood up and held the gown up against her.

The bodice was made of simple silk with a crease down the front, a bunched neckline of the same color, and three-quarter length sleeves, but the skirt was more intricately ornamented with delicate embroidery along the edges.

"I think you should try it on."

Mary Jane didn't need convincing. These were the types of experiences she'd always dreamed of as a child in preparing for her wedding day and only wished Grandma Catrin could be here with them now.

"Neither the men nor the women of this town will be able to take their eyes off of you." Lucy waved her arm in a circular motion, her finger stirring the air, telling Mary Jane to spin around.

With slow movements and some effort, she complied.

"Look at those cascading back pleats," Lucy said. "It's like an elegant cape has been sewn onto the dress. It is simply lovely."

"I can hardly breathe," she said.

"You can't tell, but if you're uncomfortable, maybe we can have Mrs. Fawcett let it out a little and make any additional adjustments that you'd like."

The mill owner's mother had recently lost her husband and had taken to dressmaking to keep herself occupied. Her work was truly quite remarkable.

"Do you think she might be able to get it done in time?"

"Knowing her, she'd probably have it done tomorrow if you asked her to."

She breathed out a laugh. The woman actually reminded her a great deal of Grandma Catrin. Mary Jane sat down on the bed, resulting in the most dreadful of sound as the fabric at the back of the dress gave way.

After a brief inspection, Lucy laughed. "I guess the cape serves as more than for a decorative purpose. You can't even see the tear."

"Mrs. Fawcett?"

"We'll talk to her today," Lucy said with a smile.

Mary Jane quickly shrugged out of the garment and lay it carefully across the foot of the bed. There was still one thing left in her wedding chest.

With a deep breath, she reached in and pulled out the neatly folded quilt that Grandma Catrin had pieced together and quilted from a variety of colors, patterns, and styles of material to pass down to all the female heirs through her Cadogan line. It was said that the blanket had been blessed with good fortune for all those to sleep beneath it on the eve of their wedding. Lionel had not fancied such an antiquated notion and it had therefore remained inside the chest.

As she stood up to shake out the creases over the beautifully intricate patterns, a large piece of parchment paper fell onto the bed.

"What's this?" Lucy asked, picking it up and turning it over to see a man's face staring back at her from a wanted poster. "Sullivan O'Donnell. Wanted for forgery, embezzlement, larceny, and…" Her eyes grew wide. "…murder." She turned the parchment around for Mary Jane to see. "Do you recognize him?" she asked.

Mary Jane draped the quilt over the foot of the bed, sat down, and took the poster from Lucy.

"He does look a little familiar, but I can't place him." She turned the parchment over, but there were no other markings on it. "What was that doing in my trousseau?" She peered over the side of the cedar chest. A large canvas bag labeled U.S. Mail lined the bottom, but it did not belong to her. She reached in, pulled it back, and sucked in a breath.

"What's wrong? Is there a creature in there?" Lucy asked.

Hundreds, if not thousands, of stacked greenbacks laid out evenly across the bottom stared back at her.

Lucy came up next to her and looked over the side.

"M.J., there has to be ten thousand dollars or more in there. Is it real? Where did it come from?"

Mary Jane reached inside and pulled one of the bills from its stack and turned it over. No smearing, printed on both sides, it looked pretty real to her.

"It doesn't appear to be counterfeit, but I don't know enough about it to tell. The bills we found in the case at the mine didn't look anything like these. I've never seen it before and have no idea how it could have gotten into my trunk."

Lionel.

It made sense. It was the only explanation. She hadn't opened that trunk—except to get to her journal or stationery—in the near five years since that fateful night. It was his money. It had to be.

"It has to be Lionel's," she said aloud. "At least what he stole from a countless number of people."

"We should tell Raine."

Mary Jane agreed.

"Are you, Lucas, and the children still coming out to the farm this afternoon to string popcorn and cranberries and make decorations for the trees?"

Motherhood looked good on Lucy. She'd been beaming over the last couple of weeks as they'd made preparations to adopt Mrs. Weller's grandchildren.

"Yes. Clovis is very excited to see Raine again and Georgia May can't stop talking about all the things she wants to do with Sarah Jane."

"And Ridley?"

"He's been like Lucas's shadow ever since my husband showed him one of his trick-riding stunts." Lucy shook her head.

Knock. Knock.

"M.J., you here?" Casey called from the living room.

Mary Jane threw her quilt over the top of the trunk and both she and Lucy headed out to meet her.

"Oh, good, you are both here. We have just a little problem." She removed her gloves.

Since the barn had been finished and the flock moved down to the south pasture, there hadn't been any issues. Over the last two weeks Evaline and Casey had been rotating the sheep's grazing pastures, and with the growing unease of the Middleton ranchers, she worried they could be influencing those from other neighboring towns. She took a deep breath and waited for the news.

"Let's have it," Mary Jane said, preparing for the worst.

"Dutch," Casey scratched the back of her head, "may have paid a visit to the Isaacson farm's northern paddock. The sheriff's fence doesn't extend all the way up the mountainside, and it appears our over-achieving ram wandered around and made friends with one or two of the Shropshire yearling ewes." She bit the inside of her cheek, then looked up to meet her eyes.

Mary Jane breathed out a relieved chuckle.

"Jethro was able to separate him, but I thought you'd want to know the farm may have a few extra lambs later than expected."

"Did Mrs. Isaacson tup her sheep before she left?" Lucy asked.

Casey shook her head.

"I guess we'll find out this afternoon," Mary Jane said.

"What kind of lamb would a Rambouillet and a Shropshire even make?" Lucy mused.

"Is Dutch back with our flock?"

"Yes."

"Then, I'll speak with the sheriff this evening and we'll get it worked out," Mary Jane said. "Thanks for letting us know, Case." She narrowed her eyes, sensing there was something more that the hired hand wanted to say. "What else is bothering you?"

"I know Happenstance is supposed to be a temporary arrangement, but I don't know what we'll do without you, M.J." She slapped her gloves against her leg, waited a moment, then turned, brushing her face with the back of her wrist before striding out the door without another word.

"I'll be right back," Mary Jane told Lucy as she ran outside after her friend.

"Casey," she called. She hadn't really considered what would happen with her job after she and Raine were married.

The woman stopped and turned to face her. She quickly wiped away a tear that had fallen down her cheek and chuckled. "I'm sorry. I know we're supposed to be strong and all, prove to everyone that we are capable of doing a man's job, but—"

"We're not men," Mary Jane finished for her. "Wouldn't want to be. You are strong and independent. But you are also kind and gracious. We come to Happenstance because of unfortunate circumstances, but what we get out of it is so much more." Mary Jane threw her arms around Casey and hugged her close.

"I'm going to miss you."

"Not if I can help it," Mary Jane said. "In the least, we'll be neighbors, right? And we'll always be friends."

With another quick hug, Casey left Mary Jane to her thoughts.

Christmas was just a week away. When they'd spoken with Mr. Greene, he and his wife had been on their way out to Helena to visit with Mrs. Greene's sister and would be staying for a few weeks, but he'd said that he would be returning in time for his sermon on Christmas Eve and that he'd be happy to marry them that morning. Otherwise, they would have to wait for another month as he would be travelling to visit the other parishes on his circuit throughout the territory.

Christmas Eve.

While they had decided to keep the wedding a simple affair, they still had much to do to prepare.

Lucy headed back to Whisper Ridge to collect her budding little family.

It had been a couple of days since they'd picked out their trees, so everyone was anxious to get them decorated. It appeared that Mary Jane and Lissa were the last of those expected to arrive at the farm. The Deardons were bringing Sarah Jane—who'd spent the morning with the Wallace children and Hayden and Sebastian Deardon.

Mary Jane took a deep breath. She'd spent much of the morning trying to decide how to tell Raine about her cedar chest find and not have it ruin this afternoon's festivities.

"Don't you think the marshal cleans up nicely?" Lissa asked with a raised brow, catching her bottom lip in her teeth.

Rutledge Tyler could be seen through the farmhouse's large front window speaking with Lucas Deardon.

"He's an acquired taste," Mary Jane said with a chuckle. "Though the two of you seemed rather cozy when we picked out our trees."

Lissa smiled.

"He's charming."

"I wouldn't go that far, but Raine is generally a good judge of character and seems to like the man, so…" she looked at her friend. "…I approve."

Jethro came outside.

"May I take your horses, ladies?" he asked.

He'd certainly adapted to his new role with ease.

"Thank you, but wouldn't you rather be inside with your family?"

"Oh, I will be in shortly," he said. "Right after I take care of your horses."

Mary Jane laughed.

"Thank you, Jethro. You have been such a godsend for Raine."

"I like to think we work well together," he said graciously.

He was right. The two men had become quick friends.

She dismounted, grateful she'd worn her new split skirt which allowed her to ride comfortably and still look the part of a lady. When she reached the front doorstep, she noticed a ball of mistletoe hanging from the ceiling on the covered porch.

Where in the world did he find that?

She bit her lip and smiled.

The house bustled with people. Raine's brother Ethan, his wife, Grace, her brother, Jack, and his two young boys were sitting at one end of the dining table with paper and scissors while Alice, Raine—who was holding baby Asher—and Sarah Jane strung popcorn at the other end. The Wallace children and Lucy sat in the living room with string and a large bowl of cranberries, and Lucas was speaking with the marshal near the fireplace.

"They're here!" Raine called out the moment the door opened. He hopped up from his place at the table and met her at the door. "May we take your coat, ma'am?" he asked, managing with one hand.

"Asher, is Uncle Raine already teaching you how to be a gentleman?" she asked, tapping the baby on the nose.

"Uncle Raine is," he said, bending down and kissing her softly on the mouth. "Welcome."

"It smells wonderful in here," Mary Jane said, reveling in the sweet aroma of warm cookies baking.

"Alice has a tray of sugar jumbles in the oven."

Lissa waved at the marshal, and he motioned for her to join them near the fireplace where the large tree they'd cut down for the farmhouse stood waiting to be decorated.

"I thought you'd never get here. Is everything all right?"

Raine asked, holding the baby up on his shoulder. "Lucy said she left you hours ago and expected you to beat everyone here."

"Everything is fine." She smiled. "Just taking care of a few things that need to get done for the wedding." She knew she needed to talk to him about Dutch's misadventures this morning and the money she'd found, but thought it best to wait until most everyone had gone home.

"Well, come in and join the festivities."

Mary Jane sat down at the dining room table next to Grace.

"These are really wonderful," she said, picking up several of the different styles and shapes of snowflakes the people at the table had made.

"I don't think I've ever seen Raine as happy as he's been the last couple of weeks," Grace said quietly, then leaned over to her and whispered, "He really loves you, you know."

Mary Jane looked up at Raine, who was helping Sarah Jane tie off her long strand of popcorn garland. He met her gaze and winked. Her heart swelled inside her chest.

"But I'm the lucky one. I didn't believe men like him existed."

"He's a good man. Set a good example for all of his siblings."

"There are seven of them, right?" It was so nice to have someone to talk to who really knew him.

"Yes.."

"That's a lot of siblings."

"Yes." Grace chuckled. "It was just me and my brother Jack for a while after our mother passed away, so gaining a family the size of the Redbournes took some getting used to—but you will never find better people."

"Christmas cookies are out of the oven," Alice called from the kitchen. "And I've made up a batch of hot apple cider if anyone would like some."

The children all scrambled from their spots in the house and hurried to the kitchen. Even Ridley seemed to have caught some of the holiday spirit as he joined the others with a big smile on his face. And it wasn't long before the adults succumbed, leaving Mary Jane and her intended alone at the table.

"Aren't you going to make an ornament, Miss Bennett?" Raine slid down into the chair next to her.

"Yes, I was just thinking that I should do that. I see you have thought of everything," she said, indicating the variety of garnishments he'd made available for everyone to use.

She picked up a stick a little smaller than her little finger from the center of the table and two corner-cut scrap pieces of paper that had been discarded from the snowflakes.

"Will you pass me that burlap twine?"

Raine slid the thickly wrapped spool across the table in front of her.

"Okay, we'll just fold the paper like this." She shaped the corners into two separate narrow triangles. "Then we'll tie a long piece of twine to the end of the stick, put it between the two pieces of paper, then weave and wrap, weave and wrap, then wrap the string around the papers from the bottom to the top like this, and secure it at the top by tying a knot around the first—leaving plenty of room to make a loop and tie it off at the top." She cut the remaining string above the last knot. "And there you have it." She held up the tree ornament and dangled it in front of him.

"Have I told you today that you are beautiful?"

"No."

"Incredibly talented and smart?"

"No," she said, shaking her head.

"What about the fact that I love you?"

"'Fraid not."

"Well, Miss Bennett, you *are* beautiful," he said, bending his head toward her. "Talented and smart." He leaned a little closer. "And I am completely…" closer, "and utterly…" closer, "in love with you."

She closed her eyes.

His lips hovered over hers only a moment before claiming her kiss.

Mary Jane resisted the urge to pinch herself. For years she had kept a list that she would use to evaluate any man who displayed even a modicum of interest. She found excuse after excuse as to why they weren't the right fit. Too short, too stubborn, too arrogant, whatever it was, she always found herself looking for what was wrong with a man. But with Raine, it was different. Despite her pigheadedness about him being a lawman in the beginning, he'd been charming, courageous, unselfish, and kind. And her daughter adored him.

"Just a few more days, Miss Bennett, and I will call you my wife. But for now," he slipped her string-wrapped ornament from her hand, "it's time to trim the tree."

With strings of cranberries and popcorn, a variety of paper snowflakes, and a box full of colorful ribbons and bows and ornaments Raine had found in the attic, as well as her little burlap twine decoration, they soon were in the midst of decorating the tree.

Garlands went on first, followed by ribbons and bows, then each of the children assisted in layering on the snowflakes and ornaments—balls of color, pinecones with ribbon, dried orange slices, and apples with string.

When they were finished, they formed a half-circle around the tree and stared.

"What about the top?" Sarah Jane asked.

Jethro cleared his throat and stepped forward.

"This is for you," he told Raine as he handed him an ornately crafted angel topper for the tree. Small chips of wood had been adhered together to make up the cone-shaped body while thin strands of wire had been molded into a head with a halo on top and wings. Small copper bells and straw accented the neck and the angel appeared to be holding a baby Jesus.

"I don't know what to say, Jethro," Raine told him. "You made this?"

"I did."

"Thank you. It's perfect."

"I'm glad you like it."

"You have no idea how much it means to me."

"I might," Jethro said, shoving his hands into his pockets. "Do you remember how I told you that I stayed with family in Stone Creek for a short time when I was young?"

"Of course. The Wendells, right?"

"The mill owner?" Ethan asked.

Raine nodded.

"What I didn't tell you is that one December afternoon, exactly eleven years ago today, my cousin Parnell and I were playing on the frozen pond behind their house."

"Stop," Raine said, his face drained of all color.

Mary Jane went to him. She didn't understand, but he needed her in that moment, she could feel it. She slipped her hand into his and he squeezed it hard. Her other hand wrapped around his arm. Ethan moved to the other side of him and placed a hand on his shoulder.

"The ice broke," Jethro continued, "and we fell into the freezing water. An angel appeared out of nowhere and pulled us both from the ice. She gave us instructions on how to get back to the bank safely, but when I got to the edge, I turned back to say thank you and she was gone. I never saw her face again until—"

"The other day at dinner when her picture fell off my cupboard shelf."

Jethro nodded. "I'm so sorry, Raine. I had no idea. I—"

"Sarah," Raine said knowingly. "Your angel was my Sarah."

My Sarah. How could she ever compete with the memory of an angel?

Raine let go of her hand and stepped forward, pulling the man into his embrace, and cried. They both cried.

"Thank you," he whispered with two firm pats on Jethro's back, then he stood up straight and wiped the tears from his eyes. "She must have known you had great things ahead of you, my friend. That yours was a life worth saving."

"I don't know what to say."

"It's all right," Raine told him. "Sarah's death was no more your fault than it was mine. I realize that now. She died helping someone else. That's who she was, and we will both honor her memory by living our lives in a way that would make her proud."

"Thanks to you, I will have that chance, and I won't let either of you down." Jethro turned to his wife, put his arm around her shoulders and leaned down to kiss his baby.

"And neither will I," Raine said, scooping Mary Jane's hand back into his and bringing it to his lips. "God's given me a second chance at love, and I intend to make the most of it." He leaned down and gave her a light kiss right there in front of everyone.

Then, he stood up on his toes to place the wooden angel at the top of their tree.

"It's beautiful," Lucy said.

Lucas walked up behind his wife, slipped his arms around her waist, and kissed her head. "Just like you," he whispered, barely loud enough that Mary Jane could hear.

Color tinted her friend's cheeks, and she squeezed her husband's arms against her.

"Well, children," Lucy said, "this has been wonderful, but alas, it is time for us to get home." She picked up a small box containing several cranberry and popcorn garlands and handfuls of freshly cut paper snowflakes.

"We should be going too," Ethan said, putting his arm around his wife and squeezing her in close to him, then turned to Raine. "Let's talk tomorrow. I'll come by around ten."

Raine nodded. "You can help me with a project I've been working on."

"You know how I love a good Christmas project."

As everyone collected their coats and boxes of Christmas tree decorations, Mary Jane grew anxious at the inevitability that awaited her. It was time to tell Raine about the money and show him the wanted poster they'd found.

She walked to the door and stood on the porch, leaning against the column and waving to all her friends, both old and new, as they climbed into their sleighs to head home. The hour was getting late, and she knew she also needed to be getting her daughter back to Happenstance, preferably before dark.

Raine handed his cousin a slip of paper and Lucas's brows quickly furrowed, his jaw set. He handed the paper over to his wife. Lucy's hand immediately shot to her mouth. Mary Jane started forward.

"Mama, Mama," Sarah Jane called in distress. "Help!"

She closed her eyes and returned to the house to find her daughter's braided hair caught on one of the branches of the tree.

Lissa had also jumped up from her place at the table with the marshal and the Millers, but Mary Jane reached her first.

"How in heaven's name did you get tangled up in the tree? You could have brought the whole thing down on top of you."

"I'm sorry. I just wanted to smell the orange. It looked so good."

Mary Jane laughed, looking at the orange slice ornament next to her daughter's head, accented with a sprig of holly and rolled cinnamon.

"It does look good."

"S.J., why don't you come with me, and we'll make a few more snowflakes for our tree back at Happenstance?" Lissa said, holding out her hand to the girl.

As Raine started back for the house, Mary Jane met him at the door.

"May I speak with you for a moment?"

With everything he'd already been through tonight, she wasn't sure she should drop one more thing on him, but it would only be worse if she waited any longer.

"Of course."

She slipped the rolled parchment poster from her coat on the way out the door.

"First," she said, "where on earth did you find mistletoe up here?"

He laughed, following her gaze to the kissing ball that hung from the porch roof.

"I didn't." He cleared his throat. "My mother sent it up with Ethan in the hopes that I would finally find true love," he said with a dramatic flair. He stepped toward her and slid his arms around her waist. "I'm afraid it came too late. I'd already found her."

Mary Jane smiled.

"And second?" he asked with a raised brow.

"Okay, maybe you shouldn't stand quite so close to me. You're a little distracting."

He laughed again, but he let go and took a step away from her, his hands raised shoulder height, palms facing her.

"Is everything all right with Lucas and Lucy?" she asked.

Raine's smile fell.

"They will be all right. The Wallace children have a grandfather who has been looking for them. He aims to take custody of them."

"Oh, no. Lucy must be devastated."

"They are going to wait until tomorrow to tell them, but it looks like he'll be here before Christmas." He turned and sat down on the top step.

"I'm guessing there is a third."

"And a fourth," she told him, joining him on the stairs. "And a fifth. Lucy and I were looking through my trousseau and came across this." She handed him the wanted poster.

He unrolled the parchment and scanned the contents.

"Why would you have an old wanted poster in your trousseau? Did you know the man?"

"No, and that's just it. I did not put it in the chest. There is something a little familiar about him, but I can't place it. Lucy either. And that's not all." She took a deep breath. "It was sitting on top of a canvas bag from the postal service..."

"And?"

"Number four," she said with a half sort of smile, "there was at least ten thousand dollars in bills beneath it." The words came out so fast she wasn't sure she'd said them all.

Raine opened his mouth to say something, twisted his head, narrowed his eyes, and closed it again.

"Let me get this straight. You are telling me that you just happened to come across an old wanted poster and a large amount of cash this morning in your wedding chest that you knew nothing about?"

"Yes. We think it may have been Lionel's."

"Your dead husband," he said flatly.

"Yes."

Raine dropped his head. "Is it counterfeit?"

"I don't think so, but how would I know? It doesn't look anything like the bills we found in the mine."

"That *you* found in the mine." There was a slight edge to his voice that verged on accusatory.

"You are starting to sound like the marshal. Maybe I shouldn't have told you, but I thought we were mature adults." She stood up and opened the door to the house.

"Why didn't you tell me this sooner?"

"Oh, I don't know, where was I supposed to fit it in? Somewhere between making Christmas ornaments and talk of your dead wife? I didn't want to ruin the festivities. I guess it's too late for that now." She walked into the house and lifted her coat from the rack near the door. "Sarah Jane, Lissa, it's time for us to be going."

Jethro pushed his chair back and headed outside with a nod.

Mary Jane wrapped the remaining garlands around rolled pieces of paper and slipped them into one of the canvas bags from the crate of ornaments.

"M.J.?" Lissa could tell when something was wrong. It had

always been one of her gifts.

She shook her head.

"Thank you for your lovely cookies and apple cider, Allie. You truly have a talent in the kitchen." She turned to her daughter. "Do we get to take all of these snowflakes with us to decorate our tree at home?" she pointed to the ornaments that were scattered over the table.

"Yes!" Sarah Jane shouted with glee.

"All right. Well, let's get things cleaned up here, shall we, and then we can get back."

"Don't worry about this, M.J.," Allie said. "I will take care of it."

She nodded her gratitude.

By the time they finished collecting all their things and got outside, Jethro had the horses saddled and ready.

"M.J., may I speak with you?" Raine met her out in front of the stable.

Mary Jane handed her daughter over to Jethro, who set the little girl up into the saddle, then turned to look up at the man to whom she was engaged and about to be married, but at the moment, she didn't feel much like talking to him. So, she turned back to her horse.

"I may be in love with you, Raine Redbourne," she said, sticking her foot into the stirrup and swinging up behind Sarah Jane, "but that does not mean that I have to like you right now. I'm done speaking with you today, but when I am ready to have a civil conversation, I will let you know."

Lissa waved at the marshal who had just stepped out of the house, leaning heavily on his cane. "Thank you for an enjoyable afternoon, Sheriff," she said.

Raine nodded.

"M.J.?" he tried again.

"No." She nudged her horse around and started down the drive.

"Mary Jane," he called after her, but she didn't turn around to look at him.

Couldn't.

"Are you angry with Sheriff Redbourne, Mama?"

Trusts me implicitly. Uncheck.

"Yes, love."

"Are you still going to marry him?"

The question caught her by surprise. She thought for about it for a few moments before responding, then blew out a long breath resigned to the truth.

"Yes, love," she said quietly.

At least I hope so.

"Good."

CHAPTER TWENTY-NINE

Sleep had eluded Raine through the night, and he'd found himself up before the sun, out in the stable working on his project by lantern's light. The extra-long wagon bed had allowed him to add backed bench seats to either side that would accommodate a total of ten to twelve passengers along with a storage box beneath the driver's seat that could hold blankets, travelling cases, or firewood.

He'd even installed a rear retractable step that would allow the womenfolk easier access to climb aboard. With the tightening of the last bolt, the addition of the steel posts that rose above the wagon with hooks for the lanterns was complete. The only thing left to do was to stain and varnish the wood.

A low, appreciative whistle alerted him that someone had come into the hidden room in the stable.

"Jethro told me you were out here," Ethan said as he peered into the room. "I have to say, big brother, this is not at all what I was expecting to find. I'm impressed."

"You're early." Raine threw his wrench into his toolbox, drawing a loud clanking noise.

"Told you I'd be here around ten. It's ten."

Raine looked at his wristwatch.

Blast it all!

Where had the morning gone?

"I'll bet we could add an extra hook here on the curve of the shaft on either side where you could hang additional lanterns to give the horses more visibility at night."

It was a good suggestion, but right now he couldn't stop thinking about the wanted poster Mary Jane had given to him, the money still hidden in her wedding box, and the way they'd left things last night. He hadn't meant for her to find out about Sarah the way she had and could only imagine what had been running through her head. He'd wanted to talk to her, but he hadn't handled the situation very well. He knew he'd crossed a line and he wasn't even sure why. He trusted her completely, was grateful for her, loved her.

It hadn't been his intention to accuse her of anything. He knew she wasn't involved or intentionally trying to keep things from him, but for weeks he'd struggled with accepting the fact that thieves had gotten away with the town's money on his watch. And now, thousands of dollars suddenly appeared in his betrothed's wedding chest with no explanation.

He didn't much believe in coincidences, and something told him the two incidents were related, but he had no idea how.

Ethan walked around the sleigh, admiring and inspecting every aspect of it.

"You've done good work with this, Raine. I had no idea that you had an interest in restoration."

"Me either." Raine climbed up into the back of the sleigh and sat down on one of the benches.

His brother leaned against the back gate on his forearms, his hands folded together.

"Why are you here, Ethan?"

"You said you wanted help with a project."

Raine raised a brow.

"Come on," he said, pushing away from the sleigh and

walking out of the secret room.

When Raine joined him, Ethan stood next to a tall package covered with a canvas sheet.

"Is that what I think it is?"

His brother pulled the sheet away to reveal a beautifully handcrafted sled with the words 'Sarah Jane' inscribed in script lettering along the side. He'd seen so many things that Ethan had created, but it never ceased to amaze him at just how talented he was.

"It's beautiful," Raine said, reaching out to touch the varnished wood. The scrollwork in the metal was unparalleled with anything he'd seen before.

"I'm glad you like it. I have to admit, I can see how that little girl wiggled her way into your heart so quickly. She's adorable."

"She is, isn't she?" He smiled thinking about her face when she opened the sled on Christmas morning, and it warmed his heart. Then, for just a moment his thoughts turned to little Almarinda, but instead of lamenting what he had lost, he appreciated that his heart had the capacity to love another.

"We were going to have a little girl, you know," he said quietly.

"Who?"

"Sarah and I. That Thanksgiving, just two weeks before she died, she told me we were going to have a baby." It felt so good to finally get it off his chest.

"What? Raine, why didn't you ever tell anyone?"

"I didn't want to burden any of you with it."

Ethan grabbed him and hugged him.

"Big brother, we all hurt when Sarah died, but we got through it together. I'm so sorry for the pain you've had to carry all on your own for so long. That must have been really difficult. I can't imagine what you went through, but I am so glad you told me. I'm here now. What do you need?"

"Thank you. It's taken me a long time, but I know that my

little girl and my wife are all right. I just know. And I know that I love Mary Jane and Sarah Jane today even more than life itself. I need to focus on them. I need to make it right with M.J. I'm afraid I've made a muck out of things."

Ethan reached into a crate that sat at the foot of the sled. "Maybe this will help. You didn't think we would forget to bring the rest, did you?" He pulled out the large butter dish he'd requested and set it on the worktable. "And…" He pulled out not one, but two large tins labeled Cadbury's Cocoa Essence.

"Yes!" He could all but taste the delicious drink now. "You all know me too well. Thank you for all of this. It's wonderful." His thoughts suddenly turned to Ridge.

It's an indulgence a man doesn't get often in my line of work.

He determined he would find a way to get the mountain man who'd saved him a little something to indulge.

Christmas was always larger than life at Redbourne Ranch. Raine missed his family and was thrilled Ethan had come to spend the holidays with him, but there was something more he wasn't telling him.

"How are you doing?" Ethan asked. "December has always been a hard time of year for you, but you seem to be holding up all right. Happy even."

"I finally realized that Sarah wouldn't want me to wallow in self-pity for the rest of my life. I believe she guided me here to Thistleberry. To Mary Jane."

Rutledge hobbled into the stable.

"All right if I don't go into Murphy with you today?" he asked.

"Sure. Everything all right?"

"Yep."

"You want me just to drop you off in town?"

"Nah, I can ride."

Raine looked at him skeptically.

"Well, I can."

"What's in Murphy?" Ethan asked.

"The good sheriff is buying himself a farm," the marshal answered for him.

Ethan looked at Raine. "In Murphy? I'm confused."

"Mrs. Isaacson, the woman who owns this farm offered me a deal that I couldn't refuse. After I show this poster around town this morning, I'm heading over to finalize our deal with her lawyer in Murphy."

His brother clapped him on the shoulder. "Congratulations. I think you should have led with that."

"Mary Jane doesn't know. I'd like to surprise her for Christmas."

"Oh, she'll be surprised all right," Ethan said appreciatively. "And thrilled. Grace said that from their conversations, she seems to love the place."

"She still mad?" Rut asked.

"Yeah."

"What did you do?" Ethan asked, assuming it was his fault.

Of course, it was.

"I reckon since the marshal here isn't going, maybe I'll come along with you to Murphy, and you can explain along the way."

"I'd like that."

After Tyler left, Raine and Ethan took the two-seater he'd rented from Harvey out of the stables and hitched up the Clydesdales, figuring they'd appreciate being able to stretch their legs a little more than normal.

"Clyde?" Ethan asked with a smirk.

"Okay, so maybe I'm not as original as I thought." His brother had reminded him that one of their father's Clydesdales was also named Clyde.

His brother laughed. "At least the other one is Dale and not Mathilda."

Somehow, just having his brother around seemed to brighten his spirits.

Raine chuckled.

As they pulled out onto the road to town, he fought the urge to turn the sleigh around and head over to Happenstance. She'd told him she'd come when she was ready, and he intended to be patient. Besides, he reasoned, it would also give him time to get the house ready for the girls to move in and the new sleigh decorated and stocked.

Eyes forward, Redbourne.

It wasn't long before they drove over the bridge into town. Raine pulled the wanted poster from his pocket.

"I wish Cole were here to duplicate this so I could stick them up all over town, but this one will have to do for now." In the new year he would have to find someone with the ability to do complete renderings or make copies of wanted posters.

He parked the sleigh in front of the sheriff's office, and they proceeded into each of the establishments along the boardwalk to speak with proprietors, employees, and patrons alike, but no one had expressed any recognition of the man.

"I should have ridden out to Happenstance to examine the money Mary Jane found," Raine said as they approached the General Store. "In the least, I could have taken one of the bills as evidence and asked the town banker for his expertise on whether or not it was counterfeit."

A book in the window of the mercantile caught Raine's attention with its brown leather cover and gold foiled writing. He swung the door open wide.

"Have you asked Cadence about it?"

"Yes, I wired her just after we discovered the fake bills in the mine, and she responded longhand. She said she would have someone from the Secret Service come out to provide assistance, but who knows how long that might take?"

"Mrs. Smith," Raine called to the woman behind the counter, "I'd like a copy of that Dickens book," he said, pointing to the copy of A Christmas Carol he'd seen in the window.

The store owner bent down to a shelf beneath the counter and set it out for him.

"Here you are, Sheriff. Will that be all for you today?"

"I'll also take a pound of jerky and nine watermelon candy sticks."

"Have you gained a sweet tooth up here, big brother?"

"Nah. They're for the Sorensens who live just outside of town on the way to Murphy."

"Brother?" Mrs. Smith said, her interest piquing.

"Mrs. Smith, this is my little brother, Ethan Redbourne."

"Well, hello, Mr. Redbourne. Are you looking at moving up here to Thistleberry too?"

"Well, I guess that depends on how well I like the town," he said smiling.

Interesting answer.

"You won't find better folks around, and my husband and I pride ourselves on keeping up a good inventory—even in the wintertime, don't we, Harold?"

Raine glanced over to where Mr. Smith was making a display from some fancily packaged soaps.

"Yes, dear," he responded without looking up.

"Good to know," Ethan told her with a wink.

Raine rolled his eyes. All of his brothers could be charming when they wanted to be, and he wondered what Ethan wanted from the woman.

"Mrs. Smith," he said, setting the poster down on the counter facing her. "You ever heard of a man by the name Sullivan O'Donnell?"

She shook her head, her mouth turning downward with the motion. "Should I have?"

The tower of soaps Mr. Smith was building tumbled over.

"Dag nab it!" the man muttered, hurrying to pick up the wrapped bars, inspecting them for damage.

"If you could just look at the picture, ma'am," Ethan said with a lower and slower voice than usual, "it would be very helpful." He pointed at the face on the poster.

The woman looked down at the picture and squinted, tilting

her head to one side, then straight up again.

"No. Can't say as I have. Well, I guess it might look a little like..." she tilted her head again and Raine held his breath. "Nah, never mind. Don't know him."

"Who, Mrs. Smith? It's important."

"Well, I was going to say it looks a little like my Harold." She laughed awkwardly.

He glanced over at the man who'd just dropped his display and tried to picture him with facial hair. He didn't see much resemblance, but he suddenly wondered how long the Smith's had been in town.

"Thank you for your time, ma'am," Ethan said.

"Here are your things, Sheriff." She leaned forward. "And I threw in an extra candy stick for each of you," she whispered.

Raine shook his head with a good-hearted chuckle.

"What was that?" he asked as soon as they were out of earshot.

"What?"

"Well, I guess that depends on how well I like the town," he repeated Ethan's response with mock imitation. He tucked his bag in the back seat of the sleigh next to one of the tins of powdered chocolate and climbed up front.

Ethan shrugged, then stuck his candy stick in his mouth with a smile.

Disappointed that their inquiries hadn't turned up any real leads—unless he wanted to believe Mr. Smith was behind it all—Raine had an idea. He jumped back out of the sleigh, ran into the telegraph office with a quick message for Rafe.

Need information on wanted criminal Sullivan O'Donnell STOP Raine.

He paid the man, then ran back out to the sleigh.

"Rafe might know him."

"Good thought."

"Hey," Raine said, turning to his brother, "I've been meaning to ask about Lucy and Lucas. How are they holding up with the Wallace children's grandfather coming to get them?"

"As if the news they wouldn't be able to adopt them wasn't enough to handle, Uncle Gabe showed up out of the blue at Whisper Ridge yesterday. He's moving back."

"I thought Uncle Gabe hated this place."

"Just Uncle Hank. I don't know the whole story, but his presence has everyone tiptoeing around."

"Have you seen him?"

"He's staying at Whisper Ridge, so yes, I've seen him in passing. I honestly have never really known him. It was always just Henry, Jonah, Noah, and Lucas who ever came to visit. Mama thinks it will be good for him to be with family. He and Jonah haven't exactly gotten along. Maybe it will be better here. For all of them."

"Maybe. But, it must be lonely," Raine said.

"What?"

"It's hard enough being separated from family in distance but when your relationships are non-existent, well, I imagine it gets pretty lonely."

"Lucy will work on him. He'll come around sooner or later."

Both men laughed at the truth of it.

Though their visit with the Sorensens had been short, Raine had left their home with a smile on his face. They were good folks and the children had been extra excited about their candy.

As they approached the glen leading up to Mulberry Pass, he turned the sleigh to climb the mountain.

"Another detour?" his brother asked, amused.

"There's one more thing I need to do." Raine was careful to follow the pathway Ridge had instructed to avoid any potential disasters.

By the time they reached the old cabin, he was surprised to find it still boarded up and the snow untouched. There was no denying that he had experienced something miraculous and inexplicable, but he needed to show his gratitude with something more than words.

He climbed down from the two-seater and reached into the back for the tin of powdered chocolate.

If Ethan thought he was mad, he didn't say so.

Raine walked up to the cabin and set the tin down next to the door with a little tag.

"Thanks, Ridge," he said aloud the words in his note. "I hope you can indulge in a cup or two on me."

He smiled. It was the least he could do.

As they approached the town of Murphy, Ethan pulled his candy stick from his mouth.

"So, what would you say if I told you that we're looking to expand Redbourne Ranch into Montana?"

"Wait. Whoa," Raine said, stopping the sleigh in the middle of the road to look at his brother. "Are you saying that you were serious back there at the General Store? About considering a move here if you like the town? You weren't just trying to get free candy?"

"Levi said construction on the Northern Pacific is finally set to resume in the new year. While progress may only be from the western side at first, he anticipates having a working rail line through Helena within five years, barring any more unforeseen difficulties."

Raine didn't speak, just stared.

"I wasn't going to tell you until Christmas, but you know me. I'm horrible at keeping secrets."

"You best not toy around with me right now."

"As much as we love you, would I really have dragged my entire family all the way up here during the holidays if I didn't have a good reason?"

"Redbourne Ranch in Thistleberry?"

Ethan nodded.

Raine elbowed him in the arm.

"What was that for?"

"For not telling me sooner."

Redbourne Ranch in Thistleberry.

"Whoopee!"

"Mrs. Fawcett, it is just magnificent," Mary Jane breathed as she stared into the free-standing oval mirror in front of the window in Lucy's bedroom.

With the seamstress's help, she'd come up with a short list of changes to be made to Grandma Catrin's wedding dress, but never had she imagined that it would turn out quite so beautifully.

The bodice had been altered to accommodate a high neckline with soft fur lining the join of the stomacher and collar, and several layers around the hips were removed—some being used to create a small bustle appearance at the back and the rest incorporated into a beautiful, hooded cloak with white fur trim.

"You look beautiful, my dear," Mrs. Fawcett said. "And I'm pleased as punch you like it."

"M.J.," Lucy said appreciatively. "Wow!"

Mary Jane beamed under their praise.

She hadn't seen or spoken to Raine since their exchange the other night. It was no surprise that he hadn't called. She'd told him she would contact him when she was ready to talk. For days she'd continued making preparations without reaching out.

Coward.

Mostly, she'd been trying to prepare herself for him to withdraw his proposal. Then, she reminded herself that he was not the kind of man to walk away when the water got a little hot.

I want to spend time with you every day that I live, he'd said on that mountaintop. *Let's build a life together.*

She'd gone back out to the farm two days ago to talk, but he and his brother had already started for town and had been too far ahead to catch safely in the snow. She'd just sat there and watched them go, wishing she'd built up the nerve earlier to go out and see him.

Since then, her time had been spent repairing a couple of downed fences along the north pasture, securing a new wagonload of hay from the MacPhersons, and teaching Judith and Tessa how to check in on the flock to ensure the sheep had plenty of water and food so they would be able to help Evaline and Casey in the coming months.

As Mary Jane looked at her reflection, something was missing. Raine wasn't standing beside her.

She missed him.

It was time to make another trip out to the farm.

Sarah Jane burst through the already cracked open door.

"Mama, are w—" She stopped at stared up at her mother. "You look like an angel."

Mary Jane laughed, scooping her daughter up into her arms. "You *are* an angel." She rubbed her nose across her daughters.

"We are going over to the farm today, right, Mama?" the little girl asked.

Whether it was divination or pure hope, Sarah Jane had voiced Mary Jane's thoughts.

"I was just thinking that we should do just that." She set her daughter down.

Lucy looked up at the clock.

"What a great idea. Maybe we'll join you," she said, winking at Mrs. Fawcett. "After all, the children said they wanted to visit the sheriff before their grandfather arrives. It would be the perfect opportunity for them to say goodbye."

Mary Jane looked at her friend, who was trying to put on a brave front, and put her arm around her with a squeeze.

Lucy leaned into her, their heads touching. "I think Ridley just wants to help Jethro with the sheep, if truth be told. Clovis has determined that he will be sheriff one day, and little Georgia May simply wants to go wherever Sarah Jane goes."

The women laughed.

"All right, help me out of this thing," Mary Jane said, waving at the back of the dress.

Before long, they were on the road to the Isaacson farm. Mary Jane looked behind them, surprised to see a train of sleighs and horses following them. It appeared that all of Sam's and Hank's families would be joining them as well.

She got the feeling that something was going on that she hadn't been privy to.

"What are you up to, Lucy Deardon?" she asked.

"Whatever do you mean?" her friend replied innocently.

Mary Jane nodded, her eyes squinted, but she did not press.

When they pulled up into the drive, a large wagon-converted sleigh, decorated in pine bough garlands, ribbons, and wreaths blocked the way. Large black carriage lanterns adorned posts on each side of the driver's bench and smaller lamps dangled from the shafts on either side of the huge Clydesdales that were hitched and ready for a drive.

Raine sat in the driver's seat, his light-colored hat rode low on his head, casting a shadow over his face, and the collar of his blue wool coat raised up to his ears. He smiled as he climbed down from the vehicle and made his way toward them.

"Miss Bennett," he said, holding his hand up to her. "May I have a word?"

Mary Jane looked at Lucy, then slipped her hand into his and allowed him to help her down from their two-seater. He didn't let go.

"Hi, Sheriff," Sarah Jane said, waving.

"Hello, darlin'," Raine said with a wink at her daughter.

Her hand still in his, he pulled her to the base of the porch where they could still be seen by everyone, but they were out of immediate earshot. He looked down at her, the smoky blue of his eyes brightened against the navy tones of his coat.

"I'm sorry. It's my fault. Please forgive me. I crossed a line without realizing it until it was too late."

"We've known each other a whole of two months, *Sheriff*," she emphasized, reminding herself why they were in this situation in the first place. "I should have expected that you would do your job—you're good at it—even if that meant asking about things that could be potentially questionable. To be clear, however, I knew nothing of Lionel's criminal dealings, nor have I now or ever been a part of a counterfeiting scheme."

"I know."

"I found that case in the mine by pure accident."

"I know."

"I had no idea there was money in the bottom of my—"

Raine stopped her this time with a kiss that still promised forever, and she gladly surrendered to him.

"I love you, Mary Jane Bennett," he said, meeting and holding her gaze.

She smiled. "And I love you, Sheriff Raine…what is your middle name anyway?" she asked.

He threw his head back and laughed loudly.

"Jameson," he said, still chuckling.

"Well, R.J., looks like you'll fit right in."

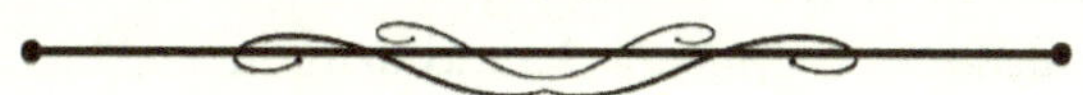

Sarah Jane Bennett

It had been too long since Sarah Jane had seen Sheriff Redbourne, and she had been very excited that they were finally going to visit the farm. She loved visiting all the animals there—especially Fred. When Luke had told her his uncle had something special planned for everyone later in the evening, she'd been so happy.

Georgia May, Luke, Sarah Jane, and Sebastian Deardon—the boy she was sure was in love with her—had all crowded into the backseat of Mrs. Deardon's sleigh. Now, as they waited for the sheriff to talk to her mama, she looked down to see a little gray and white striped kitten peek its head out from the corner of the stable doors.

It's a kitty.

She had never seen kitties around the farm before and she just wanted to hold it.

Sarah Jane nudged Luke with her elbow and pointed down at the furry animal that had now been joined by two more.

"I didn't know Uncle Raine had kittens. Do you want to go see them?" her new friend asked as he jumped down from the bench and held his hand up to help her.

It was a little farther down than she liked. She looked at the runners, then decided it would be better if she climbed down on her own.

"Where you going?" Georgia May asked.

"You stay here with Seb," she whispered. "We'll be right back." Once her feet were firm on the runner, she jumped down the rest of the way and they ran over to where she'd spotted the kittens a minute ago, but they were gone.

"Where did they go?" she asked Luke.

He shrugged.

"Listen," he said a second later.

A small, squeaky mewing sound came from the far edge of the stable. She looked under the worktable and around the walls, but could not see any kittens.

Livvy, the sheriff's horse, nickered at them as they searched under the gate and around the open doors.

"There's one," Luke said, pointing to the large stack of haybales at the edge of the stable.

One of the kittens toppled over another as they played with each other in the hay on the ground. Both children ran over to them. Luke kneeled next to the hole in one of the bales where the kitties had come from.

Sarah Jane sat down, leaning up against the base, her legs extended. When one of the kitties jumped onto her lap, she squealed with delight.

"Oh, they're so cute," she said with a giggle as the little one in her lap rooted its head, and suckled the tips of her fingers. "You're fluffy," she said, lifting it up to look at its face. It looked different than all the others because it didn't have any gray on it, but was all white and really light brown.

"Sarah Jane!" her mama called from outside.

"I guess I have to go," she told the little kitten, not wanting to put it down. She looked over at Luke, who smiled as he opened his large coat pocket and tucked the grey and white striped one he held inside before running out of the stable.

"Do you want to go for a ride?" she asked her new little friend.

Her pockets were too small to carry the kitten, so she slipped it inside her coat at the neck and held her hands across her belly to support it. Its little head poked out from above her collar, its fur tickling her skin.

"If you want to come," she said quietly, "you're going to have to hide," and she pulled her collar a little higher.

The kitty squirmed until it found a nice little cozy place in the crook of her arm.

"Okay, be real quiet now," she instructed the animal before walking out of the stable.

"Where did you get off to?" her mama said with a smile.

"I'm right here," she said innocently as she stepped outside.

"Yes, you are."

"Hey, darlin'," the sheriff said, coming up behind her mama. "Do you want to go for a ride in the new sleigh?" he asked. "We're going to sing songs and stop by Miss Lyla's Café for some hot apple cider in town."

Sarah Jane nodded.

"Look at this," he said, pulling down a small step hooked to the back of the sleigh that was just her size.

She stepped up, careful not to move her arms. She stared at the back of the sleigh, trying to figure out how to climb up without losing her hold on the kitty. Some of the children were already in the back and had moved to the front of the bench seats. Georgia May, Sebastian, and Clovis gathered around Luke—whose hand was still tucked inside his pocket—giggling.

"Here, let me help you there, little lady," the sheriff said, picking her up by the waist and setting her down at the back.

She didn't move.

Mew.

Sarah Jane tucked her arm a little tighter, careful not to squish the kitten. She tilted her head as she turned to face him and smiled.

"What was that, darlin'?" the sheriff asked with tall eyebrows.

"Sheriff," she started, "when you and mama get married, will I be your little girl?" she asked.

"Yes, ma'am," he said with a wink.

"What will I call you then?"

"Well, that depends," he said, leaning against the side of the sleigh. "What would you like to call me?"

Sarah Jane thought about it for a moment, then looked up at him with as big a smile as she could.

"Daddy."

CHAPTER THIRTY

Daddy.

Raine's heart melted at the word.

Before he could pull her into his arms and squeeze her tight, she ran to join the other children at the front of the sleigh.

"Are you all right?" Mary Jane asked, walking up behind him and linking her arm with his.

He dabbed his eye with the back of his gloved hand.

"Wind just blew something into my eye is all." He bent down for a quick kiss.

He'd missed doing that over the last few days and was relieved to have their first quarrel behind them—if he could even call it a quarrel. Gratitude filled his heart and mind for the good Lord seeing fit to bring Mary Jane and her daughter into his life.

"Those front lamps were a good touch," Ethan said, clapping him on the back.

"Of course, you would think so." It really had been a good idea to include them, and he hoped they would offer plenty of light in the darker evening hours.

His brother climbed up into the back of the sleigh with his

wife, brother-in-law, and Oliver, the two-year-old toddler. Mrs. Fawcett, the mill owner's mother, along with Lucy and Lucas, also got in.

"I'm told this is where I'm supposed to be."

Raine turned to see his uncle Gabe ready to climb up behind Lucas.

"It's been a long time, sir. I'm glad you could join us." Raine held out his hand in greeting.

"Well, that makes one of us." Gabe ignored his proffered hand, grabbed onto the side of the wagon, and lifted himself up with a grunt.

Definitely the Scrooge in the family.

Raine brushed his hand on his denims.

That's going to be interesting, he thought, knowing the difficulties Lucas and his brothers had had with their father over the years.

Full, he closed the back of the sleigh and tucked the little step back up beneath the bed.

"Will you sit up front with me, m'lady?" He regretted his use of words the moment they left his mouth, but felt the need to bow to her with an extended hand.

"Why of course, kind sir," she responded with a curtsey and a laugh, indulging his clumsy attempt at being a knightly sort.

All of his Deardon aunts, uncles, and cousins, along with their families, had agreed to be a part of this night and with their own sleighs, made a train behind the Christmas beast he had created to hold more than a dozen comfortably.

He'd made arrangements at Lyla's Café to have hot wassail and gooseberry cream scones waiting for the caroling crowd when they finished singing to as many of the townsfolks as they could reach in one evening.

"God rest ye merry gentlemen, let nothing you dismay…"

Raine smiled to hear the voices of his family as they came together with several different harmonies. One of the things he had missed the most this season was singing with his family back home. Having Ethan, Grace, and the kids especially, meant more to him than he could have imagined.

They stopped at each of the houses and farms along the road and circled around Thistleberry to hit the homes on the outskirts of town.

"Dashing through the snow, in a..."

"...two-horse wagon-turned sleigh," he sang, altering the lyrics with gusto, arousing a laugh from all those who heard him.

By the time they pulled up in front of Lyla's Café, night had started its decent over them. The sun would disappear within minutes. Luckily, he'd given his cousins enough notice that they all had gathered and attached their own lanterns and torches to aid their ability to see in the darker hours of the evening.

The streets were still occupied with several townspeople and shop owners, though many of the businesses had already closed for the day, including the General Store.

"Love and joy come to you, and to you your wassail too..."

Lyla Driscoll emerged from her café to greet the carolers.

"Please, please come in and warm yourselves a moment."

Raine dropped the back of the sleigh bed and pulled out the step, helping each of his passengers down. When it was Uncle Gabe's turn, he took a step back, giving the man plenty of room to get off the sleigh on his own. When he reached the bottom, he turned to Raine and held out his hand and cleared his throat.

"It's good to be with family," he said.

A true testament to the power of music, he thought.

As Mrs. Fawcett attempted to climb down on her own, her foot missed the step and she fell forward into Uncle Gabe's unsuspecting arms.

"Oh, goodness me. Forgive an old woman her inelegant footing," she said, looking up at Gabe as he helped right her on the ground in front of him.

"Ma'am," he said with a raise of his hat before turning on his heel and heading into the café.

"Thank you," she called after him.

Raine laughed.

The children still gathered at the front of the sleigh, giggling about something.

"I guess none of you would like to try Miss Lyla's new creamed scone recipe," he called out, hoping to entice them out of the sleigh.

"I do," several of them echoed at the same time as they rushed toward him.

"And, just what are you doing, Miss Sarah Jane that has all of these children enthralled and willing to be last in line for goodies?"

She didn't answer him, just jumped into his arms.

"Thank you for a wonderful time," she said, placing a light kiss on his cheek before squirming down and running into the café behind her friends and soon-to-be cousins.

He reached up and touched his face.

"She loves you too, you know," Mary Jane said, capturing his arm in hers.

"The feeling is mutual."

"Caroling for Christmas?" Mr. Smith asked as he stepped out of the now crowded café. "The Mrs. saw you coming and didn't want to miss out on one of Lyla's new scones." He held a small paper bag up. As he headed back across the street toward the General Store, he stopped to admire the new sleigh. "It looks right smart. Is it yours?"

"Thank you, sir." Raine nodded. "It's a tradition in my family to sing for the neighbors at Christmastime."

"Sheriff," Miss Driscoll said, scurrying out of the café, carefully balancing two cups of her wassail—one for him and one for Mary Jane. "Two men came into town just a half hour or so ago looking for you."

"Who were they? Did you get their names?"

"I don't know, but they rode in alongside the stage—which was very late today, and by the way they carried themselves and asked questions, I would guess that they are either U.S. Marshals or Pinkertons."

Cadence's Secret Service friends.

"This used to be such a quiet town," Mr. Smith said, raising a brow and shaking his head as he turned around and hurried back to the General Store, still grumbling about something under his breath.

"Mr. Tulley over at the post office," Miss Driscoll continued, "sent the men over to the Thistledown to speak with Marshal Tyler."

When Raine looked down the boardwalk toward the hotel, he spotted Mr. Dunbar attempting to lift two decent sized trunks into his arms from several that sat in front of the stage depot.

"How long ago was that?" he asked without looking up at the woman. "And what on earth is Mr. Dunbar doing?" He asked without waiting for a response.

There was something definitely off about the banker, but he couldn't quite put his finger on it. Everything about him seemed to add up, but his gut told him there was more to the story.

"Tsk. Tsk. Tsk." Cornelia Wilson joined them out on the street. "It's a real shame about that man," she said. "As you know, Sheriff, he lost everything in that robbery a few weeks back. But he hasn't been able to secure enough funding to recoup his costs or repay those in town who lost their investments. He feels just horrible and believes his only choice is to leave Thistleberry."

Well, he certainly wasn't going anywhere tonight, so why was his luggage out on the boardwalk?

"It looks more like he's moving in than out," Raine said, watching the man struggle to haul the trunks he carried into the bank.

"Yes, well, poor thing was supposed to leave on the stage earlier today, so he had everything down here on the boardwalk ready to load when they arrived," Miss Driscoll said. "As I already told you, the stage was delayed, and the drivers informed him they wouldn't be leaving until morning. They even took their horses and wagon over to Harvey at the livery before checking in at the Thistledown."

When the banker returned to the boardwalk to collect more of his luggage, Raine squeezed Mary Jane's arm, then let go. "Please excuse me a moment, ladies," he said before running over to the man to help with his things.

"Looks like you could use some help," he said, stacking one of the smaller travelling cases on top of a large trunk and heaving them up into his arms.

"Please, Sheriff, don't let me pull you away from your festivities. I can get them." He reached out to take them.

"Nonsense," Raine said, walking past him to the closed bank door. "With an extra set of hands, it will just take a moment. Then, you are welcome to join us over at the café for wassail and scones."

"I appreciate the offer," Mr. Dunbar said, following him, "but I don't feel much like socializing these days. You understand." The man nodded with a half-shrug as he put down his smaller load long enough to reopen the door into the darkness of the bank.

Gaslights had become a new feature on the streets of Thistleberry just within the last month and the glow from those lanterns extended a few feet into the open door of the building illuminating the outlines of what appeared to be a total of five large trunks and three smaller travelling cases, including those in his arms, already on the inside. Three more still sat out on the boardwalk. Raine had never seen anyone travel with so many pieces of luggage—especially a man.

"I didn't see the need to carry my things all the way back upstairs when I'll just be bringing them down again tomorrow morning. Please, just set those down next to the others."

"Look, Dunbar," Raine said, taking a step inside the bank, "I know you are probably tired of rehashing that day, but I never told you how sorry I am that I couldn't apprehend the culprits." He squatted down with the trunks in his arms and set them near the door.

"You risked your life going after those criminals," Mr. Dunbar said, sliding a few of the heavier cases to one side. "Couldn't have expected more from anyone."

"I appreciate you saying that." Raine stepped back outside, then realized he could just hand the banker the remaining cases from his position on the boardwalk.

"I still can't believe that you made it out of that avalanche alive," Mr. Dunbar said.

"I had help." Thoughts of Ridge crossed his mind as he picked up another travelling case from the boardwalk to hand over to the banker. He wondered if the mountain man had found the gift he'd left for him.

"Yes, well, who would have ever guessed a trapper would be there to save your life?" As the banker reached for the last case, Raine let it go before the man had a good handle on it and the case dropped with a thud to the ground.

"Sorry."

"No harm done." Dunbar picked it up, checking the trunk for damage.

One of the latches had flipped open and when the banker tried to lock it back in place, it would not stay closed. "I understand that you will be sticking around Thistleberry," he said, trying again to push the latch down, but it still would not seal. "And marrying the Bennett woman."

"Here, I can fix that for you," Raine said, reaching out to take the case from the man.

"No," Mr. Dunbar spat, turning away from him with the luggage piece. "Haven't you already done quite enough?" He blew out a frustrated breath.

Raine took a step backward, surprised by the sudden transformation in the man's tone.

The banker closed his eyes and a smile returned to his face.

"It's been a long day. I apologize, Sheriff. What I mean to say is, it is an old case, probably not even worth fixing." He set it down between his feet.

"All right, well, yes, I am staying in Thistleberry and am getting married. And, speaking of Miss Bennett, I've kept the lady waiting long enough and should probably be getting back, but, um, where did you say you are headed? I'm sure I could ask Miss Wilson, but I would rather my information come straight from the source—especially if we are ever able to recover the bank's money and I need to get in touch."

"Cornelia does tend to be a gossipmonger, but you will find that living in a small town, everyone knows your business—sometimes before you do."

He'd certainly seen that.

"My sister lives in San Francisco," Mr. Dunbar said. "Her husband runs a small accounting firm there. It's not much, but it will suffice until I can get back on my feet. Is there anything else, Sheriff?"

"Nothing else for now. Are you sure you won't join us?"

"Harold offered to buy me a drink over at the hotel. With the day I've had, I think a good scotch will suit me more than some sweet breads and cider."

"Good luck to you, Mr. Dunbar." Raine held out his hand, surprised by the banker's firm grip.

"And to you, Redbourne."

Up on the house, no delay, no pause, Clatter the steed of Santa Claus.

The singing had started again without him, and he hustled past the land office and back up to the café.

"O! O! O! Who wouldn't go?" He joined in the chorus. "O! O! O! Who wouldn't go? O, up on the housetop. Click! Click! Click! Down through the chimney with good St. Nick!"

"You are a good man, Raine Redbourne." Mary Jane slipped her arm in his and laid her head against his shoulder. "It was very kind of you to help Mr. Dunbar."

When the banker stepped back out onto the boardwalk, he

turned and locked the building. A few minutes later, Mr. Smith crossed the street and joined him. Dunbar looked over and caught Raine's eye.

"Look, Mama," Sarah Jane said. "It's the man on your paper."

He looked down to see the child pointing at the two men now strolling down the boardwalk toward the hotel.

"What paper, love?" Mary Jane asked, then her eyes grew wide, and she turned to face him. "She means the wanted poster, Raine. She must have seen it sitting on my dresser the morning of the tree-trimming party. Is it possible that…?" her voice trailed, leaving the remainder of her question unspoken.

He tapped his pocket, cursing the fact that he'd left the parchment on the kitchen table at home. Even after he and Ethan had tried using scratch paper to create facial hair, alternate hairstyles and hats, they hadn't recognized Sullivan O'Donnell as anyone from town. However, they were also the newest residents with the least amount of exposure.

With squinted eyes he tried to envision if either Mr. Dunbar or Mr. Smith could have been the man from the wanted poster. With no luck, he realized there may be only one way to know the truth for sure.

Down at the end of the street, two strangers stepped out of the Thistledown and started up the boardwalk toward them. One wore a western bowtie and fedora while the other was adorned in a long, wool, button-down coat that extended to his knees. He guessed them to be the Secret Servicemen Cadence had sent.

"M.J., I need you to get everyone into the café and off the street, but try not to alarm anyone."

Raine checked his holstered revolver, resting his hand around the grip, then stepped up onto the boardwalk, slowly walking toward the men. He took a deep breath in and released it.

"Sully O'Donnell!" he called out.

Dunbar and Smith slowed their pace to a saunter, but did not stop.

He waited, then took another few steps toward them.

"Sullivan O'Donnell," Mary Jane called from the base of the short staircase on the pavilion in the center of the new Town Square. She glanced at him and nodded, her rifle in her hand.

The men slowed down even more, but when the agents were about upon them, they casually turned around and started back up the boardwalk toward him, this time at a decent clip.

What were they playing at? Were both of them involved?

There was no sign that either of them had a weapon, but Raine pulled his gun and held it at his side as a precaution. If either of those men was indeed Sullivan O'Donnell, anything could happen.

Ethan appeared just behind the agents on the boardwalk, then whispered something as he stepped out in front of them.

"Sullivan O'Donnell," he called out.

Dunbar and Smith both stopped, looked at each other, then bolted toward him.

The men at the end of the boardwalk must have recognized their sudden retreat as pursuit worthy, as they picked up their pace to run after them.

Raine stopped.

"Stop, Dunbar!" he yelled, choosing between the two.

"Sheriff," the banker said, slowing down as they reached him, his hands raised in the air. "If the invitation is still open, I think I'll have that cider now."

Without warning, the banker shoved an unsuspecting Mr. Smith into Raine, effectively knocking them both off their feet in a tangled mess on the ground, and started for the livery. Glancing back over his shoulder, he changed midstride, jumping up onto the front bench seat of the new sleigh and slapped the reins.

The Clydesdales jerked forward, and Dunbar pushed the sleigh toward the bridge at the north end of town.

"Raine!" Mary Jane called out.

He looked up to see her already mounted on someone's horse. She threw him down the reins to another. His uncles and cousins scrambled back into their vehicles and onto their horses.

"Sarah Jane is in the back of that sleigh!" she yelled out for everyone to hear, the urgency in her voice unmistakable. "Do not shoot."

His heart dropped, and a renewed determination filled his belly.

He swung up into the saddle, leaned forward, and squeezed his calves with a little pressure at his heels and the horse set to a gallop after Dunbar and the expropriated sleigh. Mary Jane rode barely a head behind him as they both raced to save their daughter.

If the man made it across the bridge and onto the open ice of the pond, it would be all but impossible to catch him.

CRACK!

Raine ducked.

The shot had come from somewhere behind him. He glanced to the side and caught sight of the two servicemen coming up behind him on horseback. They'd obviously not heard or not cared that Sarah Jane was on board.

CRACK!

He veered slightly to the left, close enough he could yell at the agent.

"STOP!" he screamed as loud as he could to be heard over the incessant roar of horse's hooves. "Stop shooting! There's a little girl in that sleigh."

The man put his gun away, so, without waiting, Raine pulled ahead, continuing his pursuit.

As he reached the bridge, he watched Dunbar push the Clydesdales out onto the pond.

His heart nearly stopped.

Frozen pond.

Sarah Jane.

Grateful for Hank, who'd listened to his advice about securing a lantern around his mount's neck, he pulled his uncle's horse to a stop, searching frantically for another way around—a trail with enough traction on the ground that he wouldn't risk injuring the horse or giving up the chase.

Quitting was not an option.

"Raine," Mary Jane pleaded, "he's getting away. What do we do?" The dim light from her lantern mixed with the brightening glow from the moon allowed him to see the worry and dread hardening her beautiful features.

The secret servicemen did not stop, but pushed past them to continue their chase. One of their mounts pulled to a stop just seconds before hitting the pond, sending its rider overhead and sliding across the ice. The other horse did not have the same sense, but three strides out onto the frozen pond and his front hooves slid out from under him, and he went down onto his left shoulder, crushing the rider's leg—the agent screaming out with pain in the process.

Raine winced.

The horse slid another several feet as he tried to push himself up onto his knees, grappling for some traction against the ice.

"We have to do…something."

He reached out for her hand and squeezed. "We will."

For months he had been living in Thistleberry and in that time he had yet to visit the pond. Now, he cursed himself that he was not more familiar with the terrain. He gingerly padded his way up the east side of the water, slowly moving forward along the snow-covered bank on his mount.

With squinted eyes, he strained to focus on the fleeing sleigh. While the Clydesdales' mass and weight often helped them navigate the snow and icy conditions, they were no match for the slick sheet of ice.

"Daddy!" a little voice called out, wrenching his gut into a little ball. "Mama!"

"Sarah Jane," he called back, swallowing the panic that tainted the sound of his own voice. "We're here. Your mama and I. And we're coming."

Raine watched in horror as Dunbar lost control of the sleigh and the giant draft horses went down as if in a synchronized movement, the waxing momentum throwing them into a spin of lantern lights reflecting off the shiny surface of the frozen water.

CRASH!

Wood splintered.

Metal clanked.

Horses squealed.

Then, silence.

"NO!"

I can't do this again. Please don't make me do this again.

"Sarah Jane," he forced himself to remain calm, "can you hear me, honey?"

Silence again greeted him.

Raine dismounted. He unclipped the lantern from the front of his horse and with a deep breath, stepped out onto the ice. Testing every step in front of him, he put one foot in front of the other until he finally reached the sleigh bed.

There was no sign of Dunbar anywhere. He must have been thrown in the crash.

"Sarah Jane," he called the little girl's name again.

He dropped the back gate on the sleigh. It was empty. He held up his lantern, searching for any indication of where she might be.

Nothing.

The sound of creaking wood shattered the silence and Raine drew his gun.

"Daddy?"

His heart leapt inside his chest, and he shined his light back into the sleigh bed where the little girl held up the lid on the blanket storage he'd built beneath the driver's seat. He quickly re-holstered the revolver, set the lantern down, and jumped up onto the back of the sleigh, pulled the child from the box, and wrapped his arms around her, squeezing her close to him.

"You're safe, little lady. I'm right here."

Mew. Mew. Mew.

"What in the…" He pulled back to find that Sarah Jane had a baby kitten tucked in her coat. "Where did that come from?"

"Marshmallow got scared, so we hid in there." She pointed down at the box.

Raine breathed a laugh and pulled her into another tight hug, careful not to squish the kitty. "Marshmallow was very smart," he said. "What do you say we call it a night?"

"Where's Mama?"

"I'm here, love."

He whipped his head backward at the sound of her voice.

She held up her lantern.

Relief washed over him as the warm glow from the lamp's light illuminated her face.

"Where did…? How?" Raine moved to the back gate, reaching down as Mary Jane heaved herself up into the back of the sleigh, and helped her to her feet.

She wrapped an arm around her daughter and sunk against Raine. He pulled her close, kissing the top of her head, and closing his eyes, offering a silent prayer of gratitude that they were all together and they were safe.

Mew.

Mary Jane's voice cracked with emotion as she chuckled at the sight of a tiny cream-colored kitty in her daughter's coat.

"Of course, my daughter would have an animal tucked somewhere in her clothes right now." She shook her head.

Raine laughed too.

"How in the world did you get out here?" he asked.

"I remembered Lucy telling me the plank bridge across the length of the pond had been completed at the end of August. It took me a few minutes to find the starting point, but I took a chance. I knew I would have to take it slow, but figured it would be safer than trying to cross directly."

Crackle.

A fracture sounded in the ice.

"That can't be good," Raine said. "We need to get off this pond. Now!"

He held his lantern high and was able to ascertain that the front driver's side corner of the sleigh had crashed into the bank, the pole miraculously extended up onto solid ground.

Somehow, the tongue, pole, evener, and covered connecting chains had come loose from the rest of the sleigh, and the shaft boards on either side appeared to have been snapped in two, but Clyde and Dale were still harnessed together with their collars and neckyoke intact. While their ears tilted forward and their tails swished occasionally, they appeared otherwise calm and uninjured as they stood below a large tree with a few broken branches on the bank near the head of the sleigh.

"I don't trust this ice. I'll have to jump in order to pull you to safety."

"Then, we'll jump too," Mary Jane said with confidence.

Raine nodded.

If he could reach the bank without traversing the ice, he should be able to get the horses reattached at least to the pole, so they could pull the sleigh up onto the bank and off the growing instability of the pond.

He lifted Sarah Jane up onto the front seat of the sleigh and offered a hand of support for her mother to climb up behind her.

Using the bench seat-back as a support, he climbed up onto the side of the wagon bed railing. He eyed his targeted landing area, and made a leap of faith, shoving off hard enough that he was able to set down with both feet on solid ground, his lantern still intact and glowing. He set it down in the snow, walked as close to the edge of the bank as he deemed safe, and held his arms out for Sarah Jane to jump.

It amazed him at the trust the little girl had. She didn't appear scared in the least.

Mary Jane stood behind her, giving her a little boost as she jumped.

Crackle.

The ice was becoming more unstable.

He brushed off several layers of snow from the remnants of a large hollow log and set the little girl down before returning for her mother. He needed to get Mary Jane off the sleigh before it broke through the ice and sunk into the freezing cold water of the pond.

He again walked as close to the edge as he dared and held out his arms.

"Now," he said, "let's go get you—"

"Raine, look out!" she screamed.

Dunbar slammed into him from the side with the momentum of his full weight, thrusting him hard to the cold, snow-packed ground. Pain shot through his shoulder as it took the full brunt of the hit, and his chest tightened as he gasped for air.

He tucked one arm close to his body, protecting his side and torso from several continuous blows the criminal banker dealt as best as he could.

Dunbar stood up, yanking on the front of Raine's coat and landed another punch to his jaw.

The taste of iron seeped onto his tongue as he still struggled to suck air into his lungs. He hadn't been blindsided in a long time and didn't much care for the feeling.

"You couldn't leave well enough alone, could you, Redbourne?" Dunbar spat. "You couldn't have just let me go. No one would have been the wiser."

Raine scrambled to get to his feet. He shook his head in an attempt to clear the fog that impeded his ability to think straight.

"You ruined everything," the banker continued. "Should

have gone back to Kansas with that bounty hunter brother of yours."

Another blow to his gut sent him sprawling back several feet. He reached for his gun, but it wasn't there.

"Are you looking for this?" Dunbar said with a sly grin, holding Raine's revolver up next to his face.

Raine dropped his head back into the snow.

Get up, Redbourne.

His body would not comply.

Every fight is won in your mind before you even throw the first punch.

In a split-second's time, everyone and everything important to him flooded his mind. At last, air filled his lungs with much needed relief. He exhaled completely, then breathed in again.

"You leave him alone, you no-good, dirty, rotten snake."

Sarah Jane.

"Sarah Jane, no!" Mary Jane called from the sleigh.

Why hadn't she jumped onto the shoreline?

Raine sat up and pushed himself forward onto his hands and knees, noting the still-lit lantern that only sat a few feet from his position.

"O'Donnell!" he called out to the brute.

Dunbar's raucous laughter turned Raine's stomach.

"A little girl, Redbourne? Coming to your rescue?"

Sarah Jane squealed.

Dunbar's hand gripped the child's arm.

The half-moon now gave off more light than Raine would have expected.

"Let go of me!" the child demanded.

Pure spunk. Just like her mama.

"If you do as she says right now, Sully—can I call you that? Sully?" Raine drove himself to his feet, wrapping his hand around the lantern's handle. "You might just live to see the sunrise."

The crook's eyes narrowed, and all humor left his face.

With a heavy step toward them, Raine grunted as he tossed

the lantern high overhead.

Dunbar's gaze followed, raising his chin into the air.

Raine charged, head down, catching the man unaware. At the moment of impact, he wrapped his arms around the man's legs and lifted, effectively hauling him away from the girl and knocking him to the ground.

The gun discharged, but was knocked from the brute's hands.

Raine rolled away, quickly getting back on his feet, making sure he stood between the girl and their attacker.

O'Donnell was surprisingly spry and agile. He'd played his part as nervous banker well. But now, he was again on his feet, his movements slow and deliberate. He bent down and picked his dark bowler hat up from off the snow and returned it to his head.

"Why won't you just die?" he said, spitting sideways into the snow.

"Too much to live for." Raine bent slightly at the knees, his feet wide, his hands raised in fists at his shoulders.

Another cracking sound from the ice told him it would not withstand the weight of the sleigh much longer.

"M.J., I'm going to need you to climb down from there, sweetheart."

"I am trying. I'm caught."

From his position, he could not see what was stopping her, though he noticed that as the Clydesdales had shied away from their confrontation, they had moved into a position that may allow him to reconnect the pole and pull the sleigh from the ice without much effort.

As O'Donnell lunged at him, he sidestepped, using the man's forward motion against him, gripping his coat and pivoting enough to send him flying back toward the pond and away from Sarah Jane.

The brute recovered too quickly, yanking off his coat and throwing his hat on the ground.

Raine needed to end this quickly, as it was growing increasingly difficult to see.

Pleased the man's nerves were showing wear—quick shallow breaths, big, exaggerated movements, and a low growl rumbling in his gut—he pushed.

"Can't be too smart, Sully. You're caught," he taunted.

"Arrrrrrrrrgggg!" O'Donnell rushed toward him, but Raine was prepared.

One punch and the man fell backward into the snow, knocked out cold.

He didn't waste any time. He stepped over the unconscious brute and raced to the front of the sleigh where Mary Jane was caught.

"What's wrong?" he asked.

"My blasted boot is caught, and I can't get my foot out." She held up her lantern and pointed down at the spot where her booted foot had slipped between one of the wood planks on the footboard below the driver's seat and one of the metal bars supporting it, seeming to pinch tighter the more she struggled.

He held onto the edge of the footboard and leaned forward, stretching to reach the place where her boot had fallen through, but it was just too far out of his grasp. He tried again, but just couldn't get to it. He needed to get closer, but was afraid that if he climbed down onto the ice to be in a better position and gain leverage, his weight would be the final straw.

"It's going to be all right," he reassured her.

It has to be.

He hurried over to where the Clydesdales stood, grateful they'd already instinctively lined themselves up to be reconnected with the sleigh. He took ahold of one of the loose tugs and backed them up enough that he could re-join the pole with the neckyoke, then ran his hands along the leather straps down the length of the horse, searching for the reins.

Please, Lord, let this work.

"See you in purgatory, Redbourne."

Raine whipped around to see O'Donnell, arm raised above him, knife in hand.

CRACK!

The hair to the side of Raine's face blew backward as a bullet whizzed past him, finding its target with a sickening thud.

The man fell lifeless to the ground.

The horses' high-pitched squeals warned Raine to jump back in the moment they bolted forward, their bell strings jingling as they dragged the sleigh up onto the solid ground. They ran into the darkness, taking Mary Jane with them.

He ran after the sleigh, but it was moving too fast for him to catch.

"Whoa. Whoa."

The sound of Mary Jane's voice attempting to calm the horses set him at ease and he dropped backward into the snow, indifferent toward the cold.

Where had that shot come from?

"Are you all right, Sheriff Redbourne?" Sarah Jane asked with a giggle as she piled on top of him.

"What happened to Daddy?" he asked, a little disappointed.

"I was practicing before."

"Well, I liked it," he said, wrapping his arms around her.

"Me too." She laid her head down on his shoulder and the kitten peeked its fluffy little head out from the collar of her coat.

Mew. Mew Mew.

"Yeah, I think Marshmallow is getting hungry." The little girl's tummy grumbled.

"I don't think he's the only one," Raine said with a smile as he playfully tickled the child's sides, prompting a contagious giggle.

"Well, isn't it just like a sheriff to be lying down on the job."

Raine stared up at Rut, never so pleased to see a man in his life. He sat up, set Sarah Jane on her feet, and got to his own.

"Nice shot," he said, holding a hand up to his friend.

"Good thing I got here when I did," the marshal said. "All

joking aside, I'm glad to see you in one piece."

"That's thanks to you."

"And we caught the bad guy. Thanks to *you*."

"Um, a little help, please," Mary Jane called from the driver's seat of the sleigh.

Words he'd never thought he'd hear coming from the mouth of the foreman at the Happenstance Ranch.

"Coming."

CHAPTER THIRTY-ONE

Christmas Eve – Wedding Day

"Oh, Lucy, it's breathtaking." Mary Jane stepped into the formal dining room.

Her eyes feasted on the special touches they'd added to the room for the wedding. Evergreen garland boughs wound with white sheer ribbon and red bows draped across the large wooden beams at the ceiling. Several small tables with chairs sat at the back of the room and were adorned with freshly pressed red tablecloths. In the center of each was a small black lantern topped with pine branches, cinnamon sticks, and what looked like sprigs of winterberries.

"I can't believe you did all this for me."

"Don't be silly," Lucy said. "We did it for Raine too." She giggled. "Besides, it really warms up the house and makes it feel, I don't know, cozier somehow. I may have to decorate like this every Christmas."

"I wouldn't complain," Lucas said, joining them with a kiss to Mary Jane's cheek and on the lips for his wife. "Have you told her yet?" he asked, popping a candied walnut into his mouth.

He was even happier than usual.

"Are you getting into the wedding food, Lucas Deardon?" Lucy said, snatching one of the treats from his hand and popping it into her mouth with a grin. "Oh, that's good."

"Tell me what?"

Lucas stood behind Lucy and slid his arms around her, leaning down onto her shoulder with his chin, and rubbing her belly.

"Let's just say I may need to borrow those booties from your wedding chest come this time next year," she whispered.

"Really?" It was almost too much to hope for.

Lucy's head bobbed with excitement.

Mary Jane squealed, then thrust her arms around them both.

"When?" she asked, finally allowing them a moment to breathe.

Fifteen years was a long time to wait for children, but they had made the best of their situation. Her heart nearly burst with excitement, and she trailed her hands down Lucy's arms and squeezed.

"Sometime toward the end of spring."

"It's all still so unreal. You are having a baby, and I am marrying Raine Redbourne," she said as if convincing herself it was true. "Today. In less than an hour." She looked at Lucy, then down at the trousers she wore. "Maybe I should change."

Lucy nodded again.

"All right, husband," she told Lucas, "now, shoo."

He laughed, bent down and kissed her temple, then left to work on whatever he was doing for the wedding this morning.

"Come on. I have something else I want to show you," Lucy said, grabbing her by the hand and dragging her through the house to her bedroom.

When they walked into the room, her grandmother's altered wedding dress hung in front of the window like an angel looking down on them, and she had to fight the tears that threatened to spill down her cheeks.

Lucy held out a beautiful arrangement of soft cypress boughs, pinecones, woody stems with little white blooms on them, cinnamon sticks, and several winterberry picks all woven together with ribbon into a wedding bouquet.

"Wherever did you find them?" she asked, reaching out to touch the small red berries.

"Allie overheard me lamenting the fact that nothing with any color ever blooms in a Montana winter, and she told me of a place down by the Thistleberry bridge where winterberry bushes are growing alongside the stream. I went yesterday and picked them myself. Aren't they beautiful?"

"Knock. Knock," Lucas said as he walked into the room with a small canvas mail bag. "I hate to intrude again, M.J., but Mr. Tulley from the post office apologizes as it appears that several letters and telegrams that were supposed to have been delivered to the farm ages ago, got misplaced. He said he just came across them this morning before coming over."

"Shouldn't you be giving this to Raine?" Mary Jane asked.

"I would," Lucas cleared his throat, "but the groom is not exactly here yet," he said with an apologetic shrug, heading back out of the room.

Mary Jane looked up at the exquisite antique clock on top of their dresser.

Half past the hour.

"Where *exactly* is our dear cousin?" Lucy asked.

"He'll be here," Lucas called back as he slipped out the door.

Lucy picked up the canvas bag, walked over to the bed, and dumped the contents out on top of the covers.

"What are you doing?" Mary Jane asked with a giggle.

"I'm just curious to see what kind of mail our dear cousin Mr. Redbourne receives."

She picked through a few letters, then her brows lifted, and she handed Mary Jane a thin package that had been tied up with parcel string, addressed to her.

"It's from Kansas," she said.

"Raine's family?" Mary Jane held the package, running her fingers over the words.

Ms. Mary Jane Bennett.

Mountain Ridge Ranch.

Thistleberry, Montana

"Where is *Mountain* Ridge Ranch?" she asked, sitting down on the edge of the bed.

Lucy glanced at the package and shrugged. "I've never heard of it."

Unable to stand the anticipation a moment longer, Mary Jane pulled the string down around the sides and off the mail. She carefully lifted the edges and pulled out a small, thin box with a letter inscribed on parchment sitting on top.

"Dear, Miss Bennett," she started reading aloud. "I wish I could be doing this in person, but I suppose our meeting will have to wait until the new year. Welcome to our family. I'm afraid our son…" she glanced down to the end of the letter. "It's from his mother." She held it up against her chest and took a deep breath before opening the letter again. "I'm afraid our son has only written us briefly about your courtship, but I know if you have been able to open up his heart again, you must be very special."

Tears formed in her eyes, and, this time, she let them flow freely down her face.

"I'm told we have a new granddaughter as well, and I look forward to meeting the both of you very soon. I wore these pins on my wedding day, as has my daughter and each of my daughters-in-law, and I would be pleased if you would consider wearing them on your special day."

She tucked the letter behind the box and lifted the lid to reveal three simple hair pins each adorned in white silk wildflowers and pale greyish green leaves.

"Ahhh," Lucy exclaimed, peeking over her shoulder, "Aunt

Leah has always had such good taste. They are beautiful, M.J."

Something borrowed.

A pin, smaller in size with tiny white pearls sewn into the center, sat apart from the others.

For Sarah Jane.

She pulled the letter out again to continue reading.

"You will also find something for our newest little granddaughter to wear as she joins the Redbourne clan. We hope you know how anxious we are to visit. Please know that you and your daughter are loved already. With affection, Leah Redbourne." Mary Jane set the letter down on the bed and looked again at the beautiful hair pins.

"There is also a letter here addressed to Raine, from Iowa."

Mary Jane snapped the case shut.

"Let me see that."

Lucy handed her the letter. Something floated around inside of it.

"It's my father's handwriting." Her heart sped up and she ran her fingers over the distinct penmanship he'd taken great care to learn.

"Open it," Lucy encouraged.

"I can't," she said, shaking her head. "It was not meant for me." She set it back down on the bed.

"There are a few others here, but nothing else that appears of particular interest. Except for the fact that so many of them are addressed to that Mountain Ridge Ranch." Lucy shrugged. "Oh, wait, here's a telegram from Rafe." Lucy read over it. "It's just old information about O'Donnell," she said, tossing it aside.

"Will you help me with these?" Mary Jane asked, opening the box with the pins.

Lucy glanced at the clock.

"M.J., the wedding is supposed to start in a quarter of an hour. We need to get you into your dress and do your hair."

As she brushed over the material of the gown with her hand, smoothing out any imagined wrinkles, her thoughts turned to her grandmother Catrin. With her hair upswept, braided, and swirled on the top of her head, she even looked a little like the woman.

She smiled.

Something old.

"I wish you were here, Grandma," she whispered as she glanced into the mirror. "He's the one. He's my true love."

"Are you ready?" Lucy asked.

"More than ever."

As they walked out into the hallway, she sucked in a breath at the sight of Raine standing at the foot of the stairs. His black button-down vest and puff tie were complimented by his dark gray waistcoat. The moment he looked up and locked eyes with her, his whole expression brightened with an appreciative smile.

Lucy hugged her close. "I'll see you inside." As she passed Raine on the way into the dining room, she handed him one of the letters from the bag.

He looked down and didn't waste a moment opening it.

Mary Jane walked toward him, curious as to what could have pulled his attention from her so quickly.

He chuckled, slipping something from the envelope.

When she reached him, he held up the letter.

"It's from your father. He has given us his blessing to be married."

Her heart filled with five years' worth of emotion, and she turned away from him, not wanting to show the tears that again welled in her eyes.

Raine walked up behind her, reached his arms out in front of her, a beautiful sapphire necklace dangling from his fingers. He slipped it around her neck and fastened the clasp. She reached up and caressed the stone.

"It's my mother's," she said through a tearful chuckle.

Something blue.

"And you're wearing my mother's pins. How?"

She spun around to face him, her hand resting on his chest.

"I am so happy right now, Sheriff. You make me so happy." She looked down.

"But?"

"I know you loved Sarah very much and she—"

Raine put a finger over her lips.

"Sarah was my past and a part of her will always be with me, but you, Mary Jane Bennett, are my future. I love you. And I love your daughter. Our daughter."

She closed her eyes, smiled, and nodded.

"You," he said, kissing the tip of her nose, "are my everything. Now, what do you say we get married?"

"Absolutely."

"Mama. Mama." Sarah Jane ran down the stairs. Her long, beautiful hair hung down in ringlets to her waist and the pale ochre of her lace dress was ornamented in a small collection of silk flowers.

Mary Jane bent her knees until she was nearly eye level with her daughter.

"You are the most beautiful little girl who ever lived," she said, leaning forward until their foreheads touched, and closed her eyes.

"I love you, Mama."

"I love you, baby," she said, pulling her daughter in for a tight hug.

"Mama, you're squishing me.

"Of course, I am," Mary Jane said with a laugh. "You know what? Grandma Redbourne sent you something special to wear today just like me." She opened her hand to reveal the small pin with the pearl-centered wildflower.

"That's for me?"

"Yes, ma'am." Mary Jane slipped the pin into her hair.

"I think I'm going to like having a grandmother."

"Sarah Jane," Lucy called quietly from the back of the dining room and motioned for the little girl to follow.

The corridor filled with music.

She glanced up at Raine. Where was the beautiful piano music coming from?

"Ethan," he said as if that answered everything.

It did.

Raine jutted out his crooked arm for her to take. "This is your last opportunity to back out," he said, facing forward.

"Not a chance."

Snowflakes floated lazily to the ground as they traversed the road back to the farm. Mary Jane pulled the wool blanket tighter around them as Sarah Jane snuggled up next to her on the sleigh bench, asleep after a full day of wedding and holiday festivities including Mr. Greene's Christmas Eve sermon.

As they pulled into the drive, Jethro stood outside of the stable waiting to take care of the horses and sleigh. He and his family had been at Whisper Ridge for the wedding, but had not followed everyone into town.

When Raine pulled the rig to a stop, he rushed around to the other side, and held out his arms for their daughter.

"Stay," he said to Mary Jane, one eyebrow raised. Then, he carried the little girl up the stairs and into the house.

"Welcome home, Mrs. Redbourne," Jethro said with a smile.

She knew that one day, the name would be like second nature to her, but for now, she loved hearing it.

She was now Mary Jane Redbourne.

"Could you just say it one more time, Jethro?" she asked.

He chuckled. nodding his understanding.

"Anything for you, *Mrs. Redbourne.* I trust you've had a good day."

Mary Jane laughed too.

"Yes. And thank you so much for coming this morning. It meant a lot to me to have you and Allie and baby Asher there. I know it meant a lot to Raine as well."

Their conversation felt a little forced and Mary Jane believed it to be her nerves. She looked up at the house, scarcely believing it would be her home—at least until Mrs. Isaacson returned. How odd it would be not running the day-to-day operations at Happenstance. Casey had been a good choice for her replacement.

"We appreciated the invitation. Whisper Ridge is a beautiful place."

"Yes, it is. And Jethro, please, for the future, you can just call me M.J."

"How does it feel marrying into such a large family? It must be nice to have so many people who care about you."

"It is. But Jethro, you don't have to be born a Deardon or a Redbourne or even marry one to be a part of their family. You just have to be loved by them. And you, my friend, are loved. You are a part of their family. Our family."

Raine took the porch stairs three at a time as he returned to collect her from the sleigh.

"Mrs. Redbourne," he said reaching up for her.

Mary Jane placed her hands on her husband's shoulders, and he lifted her to the ground. With a wink and a smile, he whisked her up into his arms and strode across the yard.

"Goodnight, Jethro," she said as they headed for the house. "Merry Christmas."

"Goodnight, Mrs. Redbourne. Merry Christmas."

When they reached the door, he tapped it open with the toe of his boot.

"Welcome to Mountain Ridge Ranch, Mrs. Redbourne," he said as he carried her across the threshold, then captured her lips with his the moment they were inside the house.

"Hello, wife," he said quietly, setting her gently down on the floor.

"Hello, husband."

Raine helped her remove her cloak and hung it from a high

reaching peg behind the door. It appeared as if it had been made specifically for the cloak as the long hem did not reach the floor. A fire was burning in the hearth and the house smelled of warm chocolate and cinnamon.

"What do you mean, Mountain Ridge Ranch?" she asked.

"I bought the place from Mrs. Isaacson, and it is officially ours."

She rushed back into his arms, kissing him.

"Ours?" she asked in disbelief. "Ours." She was sure her smile reached from ear to ear.

"M.J.," Allie said, emerging from the kitchen, "you looked absolutely beautiful this morning and are still glowing. A true vision."

"Thank you."

"Raine," she turned to look at him, "the hot chocolate is sitting on the stove along with a few servings of Christmas bread. If there is nothing else for the night, I think I will take my own little one home and get him snuggled up in bed." She looked down at the small child sleeping in the cradle near the fireplace.

"That's everything for tonight, Alice. Thank you!"

The young woman picked up her baby and headed out the side door into the yard.

"All of your things have been moved into the bedroom. I thought we might enjoy a nice cup of cocoa essence before retiring for the evening. If you'd like to change out of your wedding dress, I've laid out something for you that might be a little more comfortable."

She bit her lip.

Mary Jane wasn't sure what she had expected. Everything was very different this time around. Raine continued to amaze her, and she realized more and more just how much she adored him.

He leaned over and gave her a light kiss.

"Go," he encouraged as he reached up and loosened the

puff tie at his neck.

When she walked into the bedroom, she found her travelling trunks sitting untouched beneath the wardrobe and her wedding chest sitting at the foot of the bed with a beautiful pale green, long, woolen nightshift draped across it with a pair of wool-lined slippers at the foot. She caressed the material through her fingers, impressed by her husband's good taste.

After she'd changed, she opened her wedding chest.

Raine had taken the money she'd found at the bottom and had seen to it that the military payroll had been returned, but as there had been no way to know to whom the other funds belonged, it was being used to help needy families in Thistleberry get back on their feet.

It had been such a relief to learn that Mr. Smith had not been a part of Sullivan O'Donnell's schemes and that all the money the bank robbers had stolen had been counterfeit while the real funds had been stashed into several large trunks the now former banker had intended to sneak out of town.

Mary Jane pushed all thoughts aside of the unpleasant events that had transpired. She pulled out the beautifully quilted marriage blanket that had been passed down to her from generations past. She shook it out and spread it neatly over the top of the already made bed and smiled, biting her lip.

Soft music filled the house. The resonant sound of a beautifully tuned violin danced through the air like the Pied Piper's tune, beckoning her outside. The lyrics to the familiar Christmas carol swept through her mind, and she began to hum.

What Child is this, who laid to rest…

After a few moments of searching, she finally found the box she'd been looking for, and pulled out three beautifully crocheted Christmas stockings along with a few small packages and treats she had for Raine, Sarah Jane, and the Millers.

She slipped her robe over her new nightshift and hurried out into the living room where she hung the stockings over the fireplace and set the wrapped gifts beneath the tree, before following the sweet melody out onto the front porch.

Two new rocking chairs sat out with the others, and she sat down in the one closest to the door and watched Raine at the far end of the porch as he played the instrument like a master. He'd changed into a pair of smokey blue long johns and denim trousers with navy suspenders. She couldn't help but admire his manly physique as his body swayed with movement as the piece seemed to take on a life of its own, and she found herself feeling the swelling emotion of the music, not just hearing the notes.

After a few minutes of reveling in his talent, Mary Jane stood up and walked over to where he stood, slipping her arms around his waist and kissing the back of his shoulder.

"While shepherds watch are keeping," she spoke the lyrics softly—fully aware of the irony in those words.

As the music came to a close, Raine slowly dropped his arms, then turned to face her.

"I have something for you, Mrs. Redbourne," he said with a smile.

When they passed under the mistletoe, he set down his violin and pulled her close to him, gently cradling her face in his hands as he bent down slowly, tilting her chin upward. He slipped his arms beneath hers and around her body, then lifted her up to meet his kiss.

"I will never get tired of doing that," he said with a grin. "Come on," he said, picking up his violin and taking her hand to pull her back into the house.

He set her down in the overstuffed chair in front of the fireplace.

"Mary Jane, did you make these?" he asked, noticing the stockings hanging from the mantle.

She nodded.

"They are beautiful. Thank you. Now, wait there."

Pleased he had noticed them, she was even happier that he liked them.

A few moments later, he emerged from the kitchen carrying

two mugs full of rich, steaming liquid. He handed her a mug and sat down on the floor in front of her, resting an arm over her legs.

They spent the rest of the evening talking, sipping hot cocoa, and kissing. They laughed, and cried, and shared their hopes for the future they would have together. But she especially loved the kissing.

As the fire in the hearth crackled down, Raine retrieved the poker to spread out the few remaining glowing embers, then reached into the bucket to the side of the hearth and sprinkled a handful of baking soda over the top of the nearly extinguished fire.

He bent down and scooped her up from the chair and kissed her well.

"Are you ready for bed, my wife?" he asked quietly, his voice low and throaty.

"I thought you'd never ask."

"It's Christmas!" Sarah Jane squealed as she ran into their bedroom. "It's Christmas! Santa came!"

Raine opened his eyes, smiling down at the woman whose chestnut hair sprawled across his arms and pillow as she slept soundly. He put his finger up to his lips, threw the covers off of him, then gently slid his arm out from under his wife. He picked up his new daughter and whisked her out into the living room.

"Should we make some breakfast?" he asked with a smile.

"Can we open one of the gifts under the tree first?"

When he looked over at the tree, there were a few more gifts than he remembered putting there last night and wondered if Mary Jane had awoken in the night to place them there.

"We should probably wait for your mother to open any of the gifts, but what do you say you help me cook up some puffed pancakes or popovers?"

"What are those?"

"What are…oh, we are going to have some fun, little lady."

While the food was cooking, Raine decided to read the letters Mr. Tulley had neglected to deliver over the last few weeks.

The first was from his mother. News from home was good. Brenna had finally had her baby. It was another boy—Joshua. Abby and Tayla were both expecting, and Lily had become engaged to Harrison Davis—the fake preacher who had falsely married Cole and his wife the first time around.

Will had decided to move stateside with his little family, and Levi had accepted a position with the Northern Pacific as the Director of Forward Progress to help assure that the railroad would get to Helena and eventually be completed across the northern portion of the country. And Hannah and Eli would be moving to Montana in the spring to help build the new branch of Redbourne Ranch.

By the time breakfast was ready, Mary Jane appeared in the doorway.

"Why did you let me sleep so long?"

"Because, Mama, we have a surprise for you." She held up a plate of freshly baked popovers. "You should try them. They are delicious."

When they'd finished eating, Sarah Jane stared at Raine until he acknowledged her.

"Yes, Sarah Jane, is there something I can help you with?"

"Now, can we open the gifts under the tree?"

"Yes, Sarah Jane, now we can open the gifts under the tree."

"Gifts?" Mary Jane leaned over and asked. "As in more than one? Don't tell me you are going to spoil this child already."

"Of course, I am." He leaned down and kissed the tip of her chilled nose. "I'll be right back."

He retrieved the small picnic basket he'd hidden beneath his coat near the door and walked out with it to the stables, where he quickly walked over to the haystack to collect little

Marshmallow from the comforts of his snuggling siblings and gently wrapped a little red ribbon around his neck. He set the kitten in the basket with a thick folded blanket, closed the top, and took it into the house, careful not to let Sarah Jane see him as he placed the basket beneath the Christmas tree.

He moved to sit on the couch next to his wife and wrapped his arm around her shoulders, then they watched as Sarah Jane began to open the remainder of her presents.

The kitten's little head poked out from the top of the picnic basket, pushing up on the flaps until it was wide enough for him to crawl through. Then, he happily walked and jumped over the gifts, curiously exploring around the tree until the little girl finally noticed him.

"Marshmallow!" Sarah Jane snatched him up into her arms and snuggled him close. "Does this mean he gets to stay in the house?"

Mary Jane looked at him.

He hadn't even thought about asking her if it would be all right.

"Yes, love," his wife said with a smile, leaning into him. "He can stay in the house."

Baa. Baa. Baa.

Raine looked at the door to where his favorite little lamb bleated, wanting to come in.

How in the world had she gotten out of the barn?

Jethro.

The man knew how much he'd grown to care about the lamb.

He looked over at Mary Jane, a questioning smile on his face.

"She can come in for now too, but if she messes on the floor, you are cleaning it up."

He jumped up and went over to the door. The lamb happily came inside and immediately curled up next to Sarah Jane in front of the fireplace. Pretty soon, she would be too big for that, so he wanted to enjoy every minute now. And, he realized, that wasn't just true about the lamb.

"Look," Sarah Jane said, pointing to the mantle. "There's something in your stockings too,"

Raine glanced up at the fireplace and sure enough, there was something bulky poking through the stockings Mary Jane had hung for them. He reached over to unhook them, then handed Mary Jane's to her and waited.

She reached into her stocking and pulled out a tiny pair of baby moccasins. She glanced over at Raine, who held his hands up.

"Don't look at me," he said, shaking his head. "It wasn't me. Lucy maybe?"

He reached into his stocking. There was a note.

> *Thank you for the Cadbury Cocoa Essence. It hit just the spot. Here's a little indulgence for you. After all, there's nothing quite like a good hot bath.*
>
> *Ridge.*

Raine looked over at Mary Jane. She'd had no idea what he had done. Only Ethan knew and there was no way his brother would leave his little family on Christmas morning to be a part of some elaborate scheme. He smiled to himself.

You're welcome, Ridge.

When he reached to the bottom of his stocking, he pulled out a chunky bar of crisp scented soap, and laughed.

"I have something special for you, Daddy," Sarah Jane said.

He would never get tired of hearing that.

The little girl handed him a package that had been wrapped in newspaper and string. Not feeling delicate, he ripped the newsprint open to reveal a beautiful dark blue woolen scarf that would match his coat.

"I made it myself," she said, puffing her chest out proudly.

Mary Jane nodded.

"How did you get to be so talented at such a young age?" he asked, immediately draping it from his neck.

"Just lucky, I suppose," Sarah Jane said with a shrug.

"Humble too," Mary Jane said with a smile and a wink. She handed him a small box. "And I made you the matching winter hat."

"Really?" He leaned over and kissed his wife. "Well, you have no idea how long I have wanted one of these," he said holding up the ends of the scarf. "I think from the day of the Fall Harvest Festival when I saw them at the Happenstance booth. And it means so much more to me now that I know you both made them special, just for me. Thank you."

"Now, maybe you won't be so cold all the time."

He laughed out loud.

"From your lips—"

"To God's ears," both Mary Jane and Sarah Jane said together.

"Well, my darling," Raine said with a smile, "I have something for you as well. Maybe two somethings."

He reached behind a photo of his parents on the mantle and retrieved a small velvet box, then handed it to Mary Jane.

"What is this?"

"I know it's late, but…"

She popped open the box, her hand rushing to her mouth.

"Oh, Raine, it is beautiful."

He took the simple round-cut ruby center stone ring from the green velvet case and placed it on Mary Jane's finger.

"It belonged to Grandma Sophia—my mother's mother."

"Thank you," she said, then kissed him.

I think there is still one more that you haven't seen yet, Miss Sarah Jane," Raine said, pointing to the large burlap sheet-covered gift standing up next to the fireplace.

"What…is that?" she asked, her eyes wide, Marshmallow draped over her arm. "It's enormous."

Raine walked over to the hearth and slowly raised the sheet

from the gift Ethan had made for her.

"Ahhhhhhhhhh," she gasped. "It's a sled! Can we go outside and play with it?"

"Yes, we will take it with us when we go visit the Deardons this afternoon and you can play with Hayden and Sebastian," Raine told her.

"And Clovis and Georgia May?" she asked.

The children's grandfather had been delayed, so he would not be coming to collect them until the end of the week.

"Yes, Sarah Jane, and Clovis and Georgia May too," Mary Jane said with a smile.

"When are we going over to the Deardons?" the little girl asked.

"For supper."

"Mama, don't forget to give him the other thing," Sarah Jane whispered loudly.

"There is another thing?" Raine asked with interest.

Mary Jane stood up and picked up a small thin box and handed it to him.

"What could this possibly be?" As he pulled back the sheets of thin paper, two of the most beautiful women he'd ever seen stared back at him. It was a photograph of both of his girls taken just before the wedding yesterday.

"When did you have time to do this?" he asked.

"Did you know that Grace is an aspiring photographer? She took care of everything and was able to get it developed rather quickly. I have this one for you, and I have a few that I can send to our parents."

"I'm sure they will appreciate that. What a wonderful gift. I know just where we'll hang it."

When all the presents had been opened, Raine stepped over to pick up the beautiful leather-bound book he'd purchased from Mrs. Smith at the General Store.

"All right, well, I thought we could start a new Redbourne Christmas tradition."

"A Christmas Carol?" Mary Jane asked. "How did you know it is one of my favorites?"

Marshmallow jumped down from Sarah Jane's arms and the little girl chased him into the washroom.

"Mama, Daddy, come quick!" she called.

Raine hopped up and hurried to the washroom. To his surprise, a large copper clawfoot bathtub stood smack dab in the center of the room. A small notecard sat on the rim. It was signed ~R.

A loud guffaw escaped him.

There's nothing a good night's sleep and a hot bath won't cure.

Mary Jane picked up her daughter and headed back for the living room. As they sat down on the couch she looked around the house.

"You are one very lucky little girl this morning, aren't you, love?"

"Yes."

"We both are."

"Did you get everything you wanted for Christmas, Sarah Jane?"

"Almost."

"What else did you want?"

She thought about it for a moment, then looked at both of them.

"A baby brother."

"Well, I think that is something we can work on, don't you, Mrs. Redbourne?"

"I do, Mr. Redbourne."

"How did I get such beautiful girls in my life?"

"Just lucky I guess."

If you enjoyed Raine and Mary Jane's story, please take a few moments to return to the book's product page and leave a review now. They are very appreciated, and every one helps draw more readers to books they might also like.

Just scroll down to the stars and immediately below the "Review this product" section, click on the gray box that reads, "Write a customer review."

Thank you in advance!

To sign up to receive Kelli Ann Morgan's new release alerts and newsletter, visit www.kelliannmorgan.com.

DEARDON FAMILY TREE

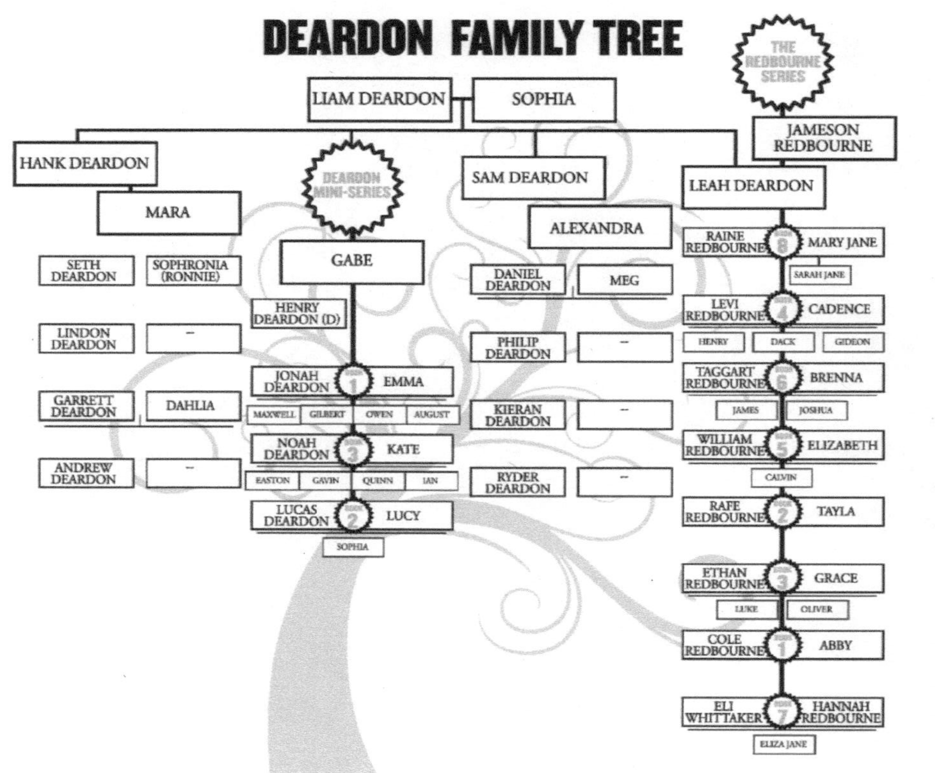

ABOUT THE AUTHOR

KELLI ANN MORGAN is the international bestselling author of the beloved Redbourne Series, Deardon Mini-Series, and the Silver Springs Series. She writes inspirational romances with handsome, chivalrous men, strong, intelligent women, and a host of other characters that will feel like family. Her novels are highly romantic, full of action, and always leave you with a happily-ever-after. She lives in northern Utah near the beautiful mountains where she writes, runs her graphic design business, and enjoys many creative and artistic hobbies.

If you would like to receive new release alerts from Kelli Ann, please visit her website at http://www.kelliannmorgan.com where you can sign up for her newsletter.

FACEBOOK:
https://www.facebook.com/KelliAnnMorganAuthor

E-MAIL:
kelliann@kelliannmorgan.com

NEWSLETTER SIGN UP:
https://bit.ly/3pKJplE

www.ingramcontent.com/pod-product-compliance
Lightning Source LLC
LaVergne TN
LVHW041054080826
845145LV00007B/1566

* 9 7 8 1 9 3 9 0 4 9 6 0 5 *